I0522975

"The golden ellipse contains dark energy that existed before us, and it will be around long after we are gone."

Rachel Haig awakens with a start, facing a cream-colored wall. Shivering beneath the full-blast AC vent inside a veranda stateroom aboard the Mediterranean Star, she curls into a fetal repose and shifts onto her left side. With a silent sigh, the 24-year-old lifts her toned right arm and tugs a flaxen mess of hair from her face, acknowledging slumber time is over. Twisting into an over-the-shoulder glance toward her new husband, she sees him sleeping like a baby, cocooned in all the bedding. Meanwhile, she lays twisted into a pretzel, wearing a thin smiley-face t-shirt and underwear to shield her goose-bumped skin from the refrigerated air.

This is her new life. From now on, controlling the covers will be a constant struggle, but she loves Owen. And despite his current cozy repose, she knows he loves her, too. Rubbing the sleep from her eyes, the weight of their current predicament floods her mind. Did she possess the mental fortitude to see their strange new journey to a successful resolution? Her long-lost ancestor's confidence exceeded what she had in herself by leaps and bounds. It's just the fate of the world.

No pressure.

by John Hopkins

THE POWERS THAT BE trilogy

The Golden Ellipse

The Lost Ship

The Blue Spark

THE POWERS THAT BE short stories

Operation Bigfoot

Firing Henry

Dog vs. Alien

Thundercorp No. 5

The Special

Big Shots Club

Doc's Brain

LOST CACTUS comic strip anthologies

Lost Cactus - The First Treasury

Lost Cactus - The Second Treasury

LOST CACTUS ARCHIVES short stories

Middle of Nowhere

The Pixel Pusher

Emmitt's Encounter

Warehouse of Secrets

The Gremlin

LOST CACTUS ARCHIVES graphic novels

Volume 1:
The Wormhole Particle Project (future release)

Volume 2:
Tank and Gremlin (future release)

Volume 3:
Fox Gambit (future release)

Volume 4:
Zint and Daphne (future release)

**THE POWERS
THAT BE**

BOOK ONE

JOHN HOPKINS

The Golden Ellipse

Copyright © 2021 John Hopkins. All rights reserved, including the right to reproduce, distribute, or transmit in any form or by any means.

NO AI TRAINING: Without in any way limiting the author's [and publisher's] exclusive rights under copyright, any use of this publication to "train" generative artificial intelligence (AI) technologies to generate text is expressly prohibited. The author reserves all rights to license uses of this work for generative AI training and development of machine learning language models.

The Golden Ellipse is a work of fiction. Names, characters, places, organizations, and events portrayed in this novel are the product of the author's imagination or are used fictitiously. Any resemblance to actual events, locales, or persons, living or dead, is coincidental.

This book or any portion thereof may not be reproduced or used in any manner whatsoever without the express written permission of the publisher, except in the case of reprints in the context of reviews. Please do not participate in or encourage piracy of copyrighted materials in violation of the author's rights. Purchase only authorized editions.

LOST CACTUS is a registered trademark owned by John Hopkins and is registered with the USPTO.

a subsidiary of Hopart LLC

Publication Date: November 2021

Trade Paperback ISBN: 978-0-9965067-7-9

Hardcover ISBN: 979-8-9862338-1-9

eISBN: 978-0-9965067-8-6

Library of Congress Control Number: 2021916816

johnhopkinsauthor.com

Cover illustration and interior page design by Hopart LLC.

Dedicated in memory of Shirley Hopkins.

Preface

I have a confession to make. The roots of my science fiction series begin at the pen-and-ink-blotched nascency of my original aspiration: creating the next *Calvin and Hobbes*. Before scoffing with righteous indignation, understand that I hail from a family of artists. The pie-in-the-sky idea of joining the hallowed ranks of Watterson and Schultz, et al., wasn't far-fetched to a modestly-talented art school student back before the internet turned the world on its head.

Inspired by my favorite book and author, Michael Crichton's seminal novel, *Jurassic Park,* I hunched over a drawing board and developed a lab-grown dinosaur and bee comic strip duo. However, real-life distractions relegated my hammy, gag-filled strips to a dog-eared folder tucked inside a flat-file. Fast-forward a couple decades to an older, not wiser, version of myself stumbling upon this same folder. While sifting through reams of inked vellum strips, xeroxes, and pencil-sketched character studies unseen for years, the spark to create a comic strip rekindled with gusto. Or, I lost my mind. It depends on who you ask. Following a year of honing my original strip using online resources and digital tech—nonexistent during my initial foray—*Lost*

Cactus came alive in 3-panel comics. Lost Cactus is the eponymous code name of a top-secret base tucked behind a barbed-wire perimeter in the southwestern hinterlands. Sound familiar? It should. In addition to the original bee and dinosaur, I added mutants, zombies, and aliens co-mingling on the ultra-secret base managed by white-coated scientists clashing with quasi-military and bureaucratic foils. Envision *M*A*S*H* meets the *X-Files,* and you get the idea.

Cognizant of the remote chance of success, I mailed submissions to syndicates hither and yon. After too many rejection letters—and an interested party's suggestion to lose the alien—I realized wedging my creation into a shrinking comics section of a vanishing newspaper industry was a nonstarter. Instead, I coalesced my strips into self-published anthologies. This is the point where I broadened the creative scope of the Lost Cactus shared universe via short stories and humorous essays. While my early fiction writing is indeed cringe-worthy, it is those strange tales that introduced a host of memorable characters and sci-fi plots foundational to The Powers That Be trilogy and beyond.

* * *

Researching the sometimes controversial topics and principles underlying my sci-fi novels has expanded my armchair knowledge to a deeper, albeit limited, grasp of a host of subjects—Omega Point, artificial intelligence, transhumanism, the Fermi Paradox, and the Fibonacci Rule, to name-drop just a few. Furthermore, the artful inclusion of historical people, places, and events inside this book and its sequels lends invaluable credence to the out-of-this-world storylines.

A final thought: Humanity's place in the universe is an astonishing mystery to behold. Embrace your inner skeptic by rejecting settled science and daring to imagine: *What if …*

See you in the funny papers.

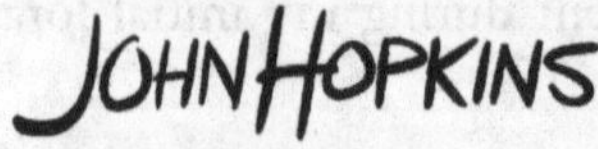

Characters

90,000 BC

Light Specters	Universally-revered energy beings, the proverbial lights in the sky, aka foo fighters
Dark Specters	Splintered Light Specters consumed with a virulent hatred of the human race
The Beacon	Proto-pyramid lighthouse bursting a forbidding message into the cosmos to avoid Planet Earth
The Golden Ellipse	The beacon's enigmatic source of infinite power from before time
The Machine	The beacon's autonomous defensive shield

2550 BC

Khufu	Second Pharaoh of Egypt's Fourth Dynasty, builder of the Great Pyramid of Giza

The Black Cat	Light Specter's emissary dispatched to oversee Khufu's pyramid construction
The Gork	Amiable seven-foot reptilian engineer from an otherwise violent, marauding race
The Surveyors	Squat and furry aliens skilled in mathematics and astronomy
The Designers	Nordic race of alien telepaths renowned for their elegant design aesthetic
The Miners	Ill-tempered race of expert excavators, distant Gray cousins

1799 AD

| **Napoleon Bonaparte** | French emperor and self-proclaimed conqueror of Egypt |
| **Armand Dreyfus** | Senior archeologist in the French Expeditionary Force in Egypt, Napoleon's pyramid guide |

1944 AD

Captain Neil Alexander	Pilot in 57th Fighter Group, 64th Squadron Black Scorpions, and Rachel's grandfather, twice removed
Lieutenant Harry Stark	Neil's mercurial wingman, flaming-red crew cut, sparkplug build, and bare-knuckle Bronx orphanage past
Colonel William Drake	Chain-smoking commander of 57th Fighter Group
Carol Alexander	Neil's wife, Rachel's grandmother, twice removed
Major General Thompson	British intelligence officer
Black Suits	OSS investigators

Anna	French resistance fighter
Hans Gruber	Nazi spy stationed in Cairo
Hodges	US Army quartermaster
Girl in the pink dress	Harry Stark's netherworld muse

2043 AD

Professor Tarek Hamed	Archeologist obsessed with controversial pyramid theory
Cartwright	Hamed's rotund Cairo Museum colleague
Yasmine Sardouk	Cairo Museum research assistant
Jean-Claude	Ill-fated Provence backpacking enthusiast

2044 – Present Time

Rachel Haig	24-year-old heiress reconciling her past, married life, and the fate of the world
Owen Haig	27-year-old financier, extreme sportsman, and Rachel's resourceful new spouse
Louie	Kobayashi C-Class robot chauffeur
Niyo	Gray freelance operative employed by the PTB
IOSC	International Outer Space Consortium
The Powers That Be (PTB)	Clandestine organization shepherding humankind toward a transformational omega point
Artemus Pennywell	The Powers That Be CEO
Andrew	Kobayashi C-Class robot, Pennywell's right-hand man, valet, and fixer
Flynn	PTB field agent assigned to Rachel and Owen

Ping	Gray alien advisor, Pennywell's lifelong friend, and mentor
The Advisors	Coalition of pro-human aliens in collaboration with the PTB
Nina	Fashion-forward administrator with a manicured finger on the PTB pulse, aka Chanel
Chrysalis Air	PTB shell company
Astrid	Chrysalis Air pilot
Nicole	Chrysalis Air pilot
Greta Thornberry	PTB statistician, aka Plain Jane
Roy Kendall	PTB psychologist, aka Doubletake
Dr. Richard King	Eccentric PTB research scientist, aka Doc
Mr. Kobayashi	Reclusive robotics pioneer
Julius Hart	Aeronautics wunderkind
Francois	Unscrupulous robot technician employed by Louie's French cab company
Ahmed	Tunisian car rental salesman and purveyor of antique vehicles
Hassan	OASIS Hotel bellman
Reverend Earl Warren	Texas-based pastor on bucket list Egypt vacation
Mabel Warren	Earl's outspoken wife
Cassandra	Giza Pyramid Complex tour guide
Captain Mohammed Faisel	Burnt-out Egyptian Army officer assigned to guard duty on the Giza Plateau

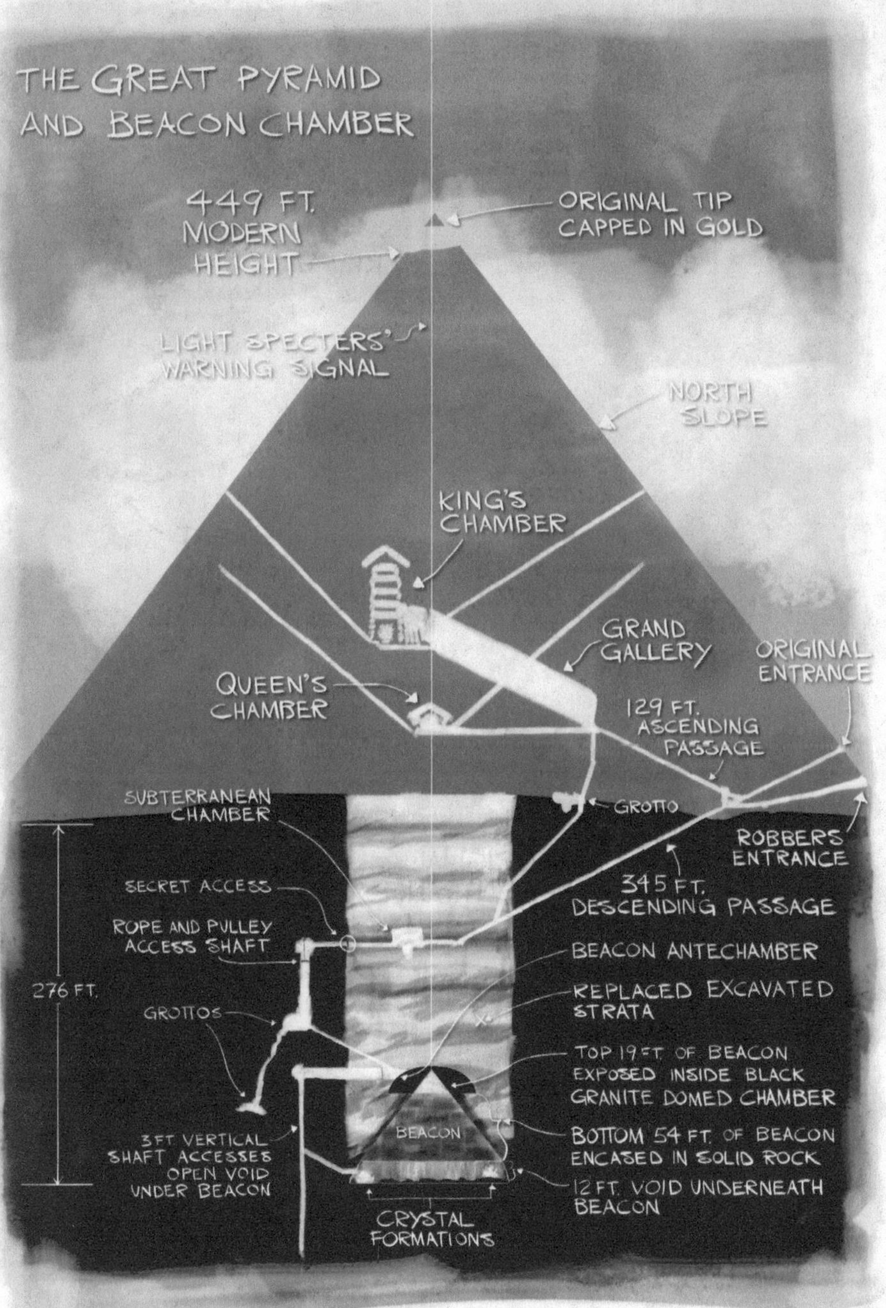
THE GREAT PYRAMID AND BEACON CHAMBER
449 FT. MODERN HEIGHT
ORIGINAL TIP CAPPED IN GOLD
LIGHT SPECTERS' WARNING SIGNAL
NORTH SLOPE
KING'S CHAMBER
GRAND GALLERY
ORIGINAL ENTRANCE
QUEEN'S CHAMBER
129 FT. ASCENDING PASSAGE
SUBTERRANEAN CHAMBER
GROTTO
ROBBERS ENTRANCE
SECRET ACCESS
345 FT. DESCENDING PASSAGE
ROPE AND PULLEY ACCESS SHAFT
BEACON ANTECHAMBER
REPLACED EXCAVATED STRATA
276 FT.
GROTTOS
TOP 19 FT. OF BEACON EXPOSED INSIDE BLACK GRANITE DOMED CHAMBER
3 FT. VERTICAL SHAFT ACCESSES OPEN VOID UNDER BEACON
BEACON
BOTTOM 54 FT. OF BEACON ENCASED IN SOLID ROCK
12 FT. VOID UNDERNEATH BEACON
CRYSTAL FORMATIONS

THE GIZA PYRAMIDS
MODERN ROAD
PARKING LOT
ROBBERS ENTRANCE
WESTERN CEMETERY
EASTERN CEMETERY
KHUFU
MODERN ROAD
KHAFRE
GREAT SPHINX
MENKAURE
N
W E
S
ORIGINAL ENTRANCE
BASTET
WOODEN COFFIN
(CONTAINING MUMMIFIED KITTY REMAINS)
ROBBERS ENTRANCE
(CIRCA 820 AD)

International Outer Space Consortium (IOSC) Passenger Ship

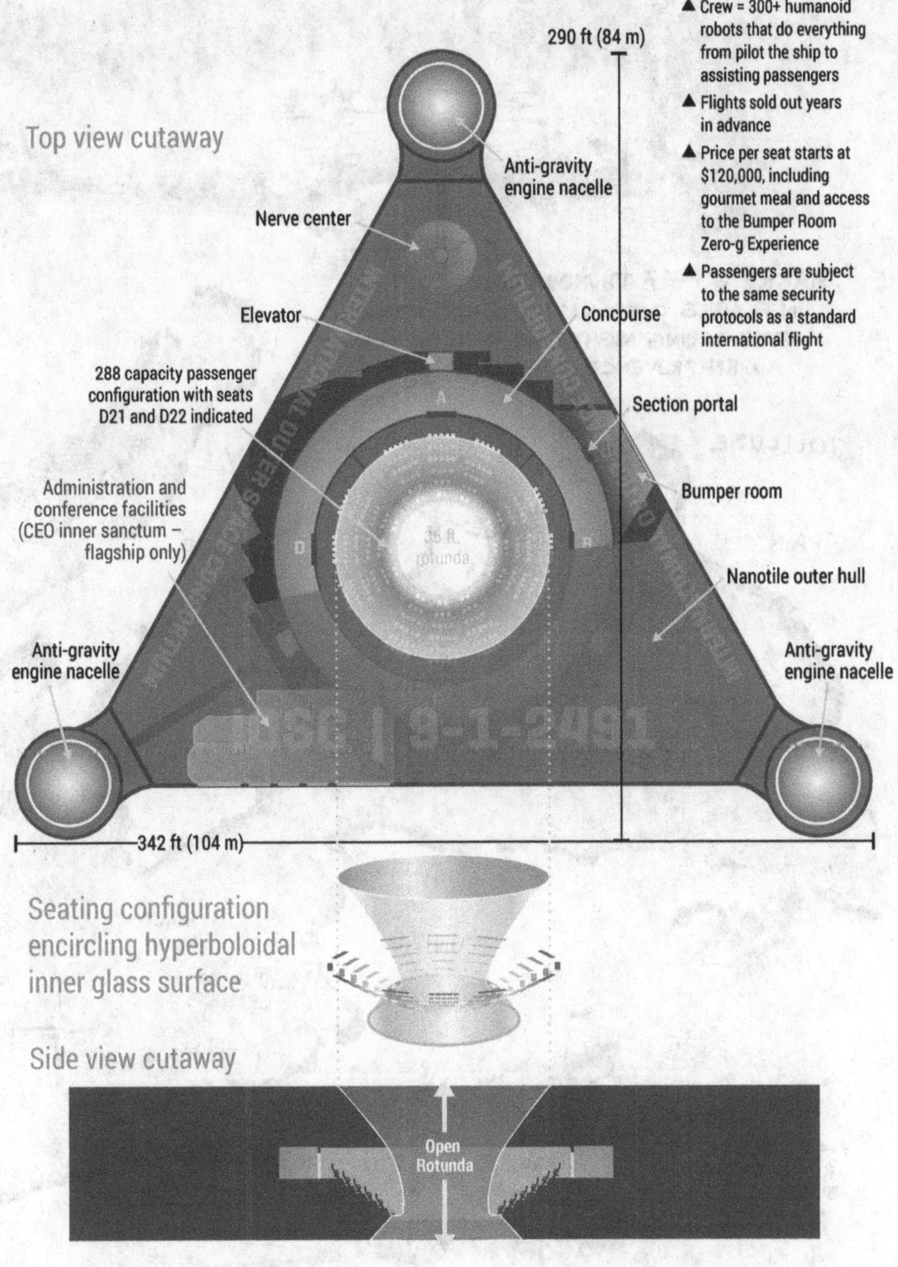

FOO FIGHTERS

HARRY'S P-47 THUNDERBOLT
IN FLAMES OVER NAZI-OCCUPIED FRANCE
AFTER DARING NIGHTTIME RAID ON THE
AIX-EN-PROVENCE RAILYARD

TOULOUSE
MARSEILLE
ITALY
ADRIATIC SEA
SPAIN
ALTO AIRBASE ON CORSICA
ROME
BARCELONA
SARDINIA
TYRRHENIAN SEA
PALMA
MEDITERRANEAN SEA
PALERMO
IONIAN SEA
ALGIERS
TUNIS
MALTA
TUNISIA
GULF OF GABES
N E S W
TRIPOLI
LIBYA

P-40 TOMAHAWKS
FLOWN BY THE
BLACK SCORPIONS
IN NORTH AFRICA

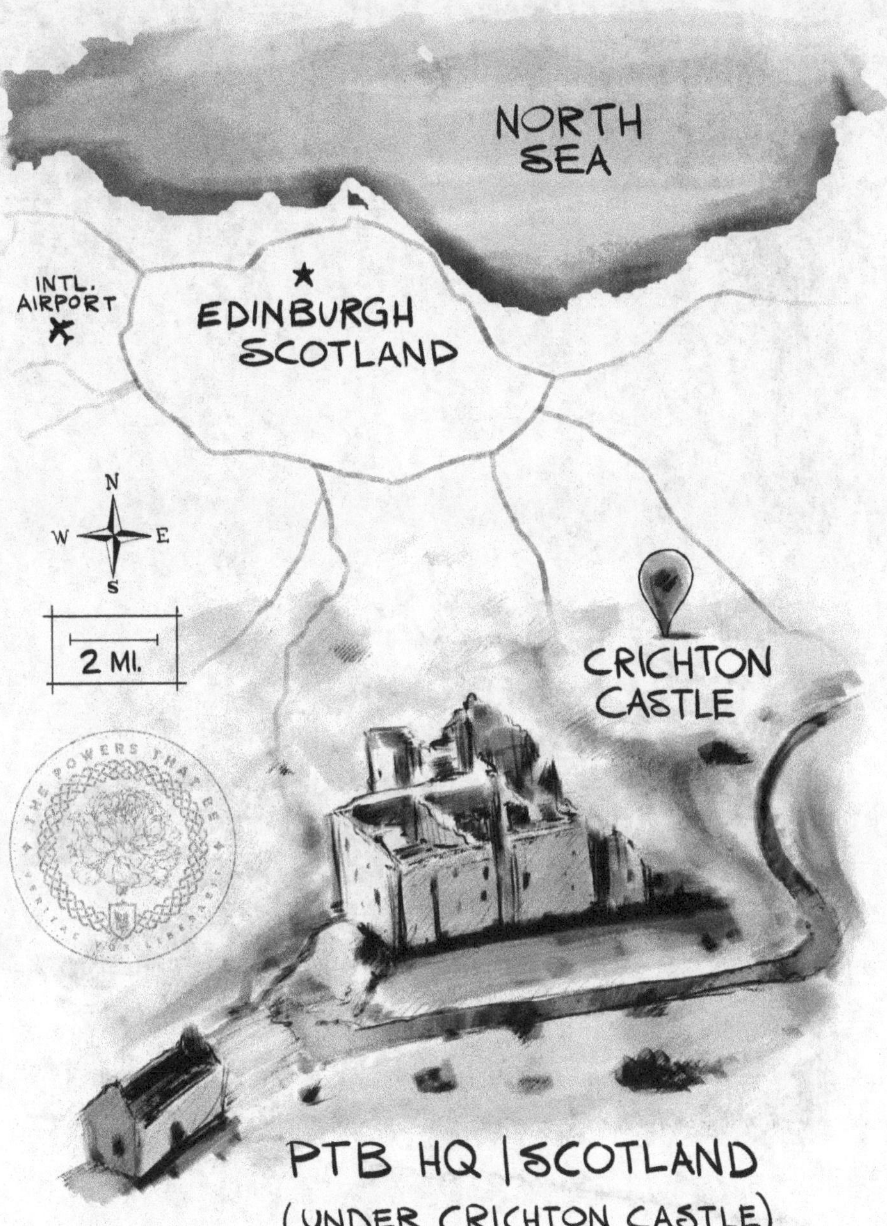

NORTH SEA
INTL. AIRPORT
EDINBURGH SCOTLAND
N
W E
S
2 MI.
THE POWERS THAT BE
VERITAS VOS LIBERABIT
CRICHTON CASTLE
PTB HQ | SCOTLAND
(UNDER CRICHTON CASTLE)

MONTAGNE SAINTE-VICTOIRE

Prologue

Light Specters. The quintessential life forms in a universal hodgepodge of lesser beings burst from the ether over a primeval world. Jettisoning physical shapes eons before, their brilliance and keen, curious intellects compelled their arrival on the third of nine planets orbiting a small star in a spiraling galaxy amongst an infinity in the fickle nebulous cosmos. They came to observe the astonishing wellspring of life thriving in a panoply of ecosystems across quaking landmasses and submerged beneath roiling oceans, flowing rivers, pristine lakes, and turbulent seas.

The ethereal scientists viewed the brutal struggle for existence with dispassionate logic, aware that the Earthbound menagerie trod stratified remains of previous eras wiped out by continental drift, climate change, volcanos, pandemics, and wayward asteroids. A debate ignited over a potential sixth extinction at the hands of the dominant hominid species roaming the planet.

Spectral optimists countered the dour prognostication, arguing that the bipedal creatures were eons removed from many apocalyptic scenarios, self-inflicted or otherwise. The journey from puerile to the sublime is never a trifling matter, and the path of these primitive creatures would prove no exception.

Flying high above an arid savannah, the Light Specters paused over another charnel mess that the cunning and vicious bipedal omnivores instigated. The savage lopsided melee played out in a bloody amphitheater of flattened grasses and dirt. A cacophony of ripping flesh, snapping bones, primal screams, and pathetic gurgles of last breaths echoed across the vastness of what will become known as the Nile River region of North Africa.

Straddling a gory kill, the barbarous ringmaster, drenched in vanquished foes' blood and guts, held a fleshy offering aloft to the strange balls of light hovering in the sky above his thick matted head. A crack of thunder from a fast-approaching storm broke his hypnotized stare. He tossed the dripping mass and fled into the tall grasses, followed by a band of malicious mates, abandoning a trail of bloodshed and mangled body parts in their wake. The electrical storm shrouded the late afternoon sky in dreaded darkness, and the ensuing torrent of pelting rain transformed the grasslands into a swampy marsh. Shifting silt and sand buried the blood-soaked victims in the killing field for eternity.

The species' proclivity for violence and mayhem, unrestrained by their developing self-awareness and intelligence, disappointed the spectral scientists. Anthropological studies of similar warm-blooded vertebrates throughout the universe informed the majority opinion postulating that by this point in their evolution, the latter should modulate the former to a degree.

A vociferous spectral minority made the contentious proposal to abandon aspirations for the wretched beings' future, wipe the slate clean, and start from scratch. Fortunately for humanity, amongst the

Light Specters, cooler heads prevailed.

Marking the end of their study of the small blue planet and its inhabitants as a fleeting instant on a cosmic timeline, the supremely intelligent extraterrestrials were on the cusp of vacating the skies above Earth as if they were never there. However, protecting the rapid ascent of the promising human species compelled deviation from their non-interference mantra. After a frank and heated vetting of various concepts, a plan to construct a proto-pyramidic beacon akin to a cosmic lighthouse won contentious approval.

A survey of the planet revealed that the tamped-down savannah, where they witnessed one of the bloodier melees, proved the optimal construction site. It also served as an ironic rebuke of naysayers within their ranks.

The Light Specters shapeshifted into beings with physical traits necessary for erecting the 73-foot-tall structure from the grassy plain: acquiring an exotic array of materials from Earth and beyond, engineering the sophisticated inner workings, and chiseling a complex matrix across the surfaces. They adhered to a schedule lost to time. Their labors culminated in one final perilous task—installing a mysterious and infinite energy source encapsulated in a simple oval-shaped gold disk.

On a moonless night under a sea of stars, the last Light Specter inhabiting a physical presence blinked large bulbous eyes, bracing against a stiff breeze atop the proto-pyramid beacon. Its nimble four-fingered hands positioned the golden ellipse inches from the shallow concavity at the confluence of a carved matrix just below the northern apex. Unable to distinguish the outward-facing side, the ageless relic glinted with equal intensity, mocking the being's determination to complete the task. On the cusp of completing the circuit, thereby powering the structure perpetually, the engineer recoiled on impulse, unsure and afraid. It knew inverting the volatile golden ellipse would initiate an extinction-level event. The elemental aphorism conveyed through the elliptical lynchpin's unforgiving orientation was not lost on the spectral entity.

Embracing the sheer randomness while acknowledging the gravity of his decision, he flipped the enigmatic power source, repositioned it in a delicate fingertip grasp, released it, and watched it snap in place with a loud metallic clank.

The golden ellipse shimmered to life with a stellar intensity, illuminating the beacon's matrix while a deafening rhythmic hum filled the nighttime sky. Blinded by the incredible brightness, thankful nonetheless not to be blown to sub-atomic particles, the being transmogrified into a swirling mass of lights and dissolved into the night.

A focused beam burst from the tip of the beacon, piercing the night sky, streaming its unmistakable non-intervention message to the far reaches of the universe on an infinite loop.

* * *

A ravenous hunting party skulked along the 118-foot base of the pyramid's northern face, incapable of seeing or hearing the beacon's ethereal lights and sounds. Instead, their primitive gaze fixated beyond the strange, pointed rock onto a beastly herd hunkered in a nearby protective hollow, enduring another terrifying night on the savannah.

* * *

Interstellar explorers and colonizers intercept and translate the beacon's encoded warning, most abiding by the directive: Earth is a quarantine biosphere under Light Specter auspices. Trespassers risk severe punishment and retribution. Conversely, cessation of this warning is tantamount to directive expiration.

The Light Specters exited the fertile world, confident the beacon—a proverbial don't feed the animals sign pinging into space—would dissuade outside influence for perpetuity.

Could the robust humans who outlived, outsmarted, and outlasted the rest of their family tree achieve quintessence as the Light Specters had billions of years ago? Or would the beastly creatures succumb to their violent predilections like similar species throughout the universe had countless times before?

Primitive humans—and every other living organism on Earth—became unwitting beneficiaries of the unsolicited safeguard. However, the Light Specters' motivation stemmed from cold and calculative scientific opportunism to study a species' ascendancy. A rare occurrence requiring unobtrusive oversight and protection, like fostering a seed cast upon the surface of a barren, hostile wasteland. The clumsy grasp for human sentience and relevance before an apathetic universe will play out before their advanced eyes. Fascinating.

The Light Specters acknowledged that the beacon would not thwart extraterrestrial meddling, only full-scale invasion, leading to hyper-advanced human incarnations rising, flourishing, and disappearing, abandoning their less-evolved brethren to wander about archeological enigmas hinting at their fleeting grandeur. Through time, nascent cultures build atop former wonders, adding their legacies to the mystery of human evolution.

While the beacon churned its message into space, bouncing off an exponential number of satellites, unchecked pessimists within the Light Specter ranks remained unimpressed. This hostile faction did not share the hopeful vision for Earth's dominant species. They persisted in an unfavorable opinion of the crude, carbon-based, knuckle-dragging flesh-eaters as a latent threat requiring extermination, not protection. Their strident demands to lay waste to the tiny planet and start over from scratch were denied outright, ratcheting their frustrations—and burgeoning hatred—to cosmic proportions.

Instead of yielding to the plan and accepting their station in the spectral hierarchy, the malcontents splintered from the altruistic majority and became the Dark Specters. Luring a universe of aggressive, malicious monsters to the mineral and water-rich planet through the millennia became an all-consuming obsession. However, the damnable beacon's ceaseless bursts pinging the far reaches of space thwarted attempts to lure invaders to the planet. Even the vilest amongst the crowded field of sentient races understood that contravening the Light Specters' warning would prove ill-advisable. An infinite plunderable expanse is at their disposal. Why disobey a plain-spoken message and risk the vaunted retribution?

Stopping the beacon's ceaseless pings into the cosmos—the axiomatic resolution for the Dark Specters' dilemma—hinged on removing the golden ellipse from the apex. Without its infinite power source, the beacon's silence will beckon alien invaders to ravage the planet to the last remaining seed.

However, nothing is ever quite that simple. Since the Dark Specters participated in every aspect of building the beacon, they knew the essential task of removing the ellipse was a suicide mission. The structure was ensconced behind a protective shield called "the Machine." One-in-a-centillion beings scattered throughout space and time possessed the grace and agility to circumvent the Machine and remove the ellipse. The Dark Specters surmised that someone within their ranks could manifest into a humanoid form and venture an attempt. However, while logic and empathy were blinded by a pervasive enmity for Earth's reigning hominids, the near certainty of a horrible and painful death proved to be a bridge not one of the advanced beings was willing to cross.

The paradoxical solution to the Dark Specters' dilemma was none other than humans. The manipulable sacks of flesh and bones were easy to locate behind rocks and cowering in dark caves. Better yet, the feeble-minded natives succumbed without a flicker of resistance. A refreshing change from obstinate alien races' refusals to violate the Light Specters' preposterous warning beacon. The universe is replete with cowards.

With malicious glee, yet cognizant, the odds of a successful removal were beyond infinitesimal; the Dark Specters coaxed simple-minded humans from primitive dwellings. Stumbling across the open desert to the strange, pointed rock, the addled bipeds climbed. At the literal apex of existence, the recruits gazed upon the shimmering oval disk in their dirty clutches for a nanosecond before the Machine electrified them, launching flaming masses of flesh and bones into midair from the seven-story height. A fetid mass of charred bodies lying scattered around the beacon left scavenging lions, vultures, and hyenas as the sole beneficiaries of every doomed attempt. Insatiable bloodlust, mixed with hateful obsession, transformed the formerly rational pure-energy beings into human torturers. Without remorse, they replicated the grotesque procedure through generations of hapless victims.

Over time, ingrained superstitions and evolving self-awareness compelled the Dark Specters to employ a host of temptations to persuade willing recruits. While every tactic enticed with a unique allure, the splintered aliens discovered that the small golden disk's promise of all-consuming power proved the most seductive bait to lure gullible humans.

Sex came in a close second. Human fascination with procreative pursuits compounded the Dark Specters' revulsion of the wild, unpredictable creatures.

For thousands of years, the incongruous 73-foot beacon near the banks of a mighty north-flowing river emptying into a mysterious sea pulsed its warning into the heavens as human progress ebbed and flowed like the tides.

* * *

The Light Specters' human experiment proceeded apace, albeit with countless indiscreet visitations, flaunting their beacon's directive in plain view of curious and terrified natives. In an unforeseen twist, the human tendency to worship the incomprehensible enriched their nascent cultures, providing primitive societies a purpose beyond hand-to-mouth survival while gleaning alien know-how and using it around the planet. Perhaps human advancement excelled under the deified influence, in which case dissuading extraterrestrial interlopers proved a rare miscalculation. The splintered Dark Specters' nefarious interactions confirmed that their kind remained far from perfection. As long as the visitors behaved, their presence would be tolerated.

Humankind progressed from the knuckle-dragging miscreant studied under a threatening primeval sky in the blood and gore-filled savannah. By the middle of the 26th century BC, various civilizations picked up where their predecessors left off, spreading tendrils into untamed hinterlands.

Resettling over enigmas lost to time, one of the earliest and most successful civilizations flourished along the Nile River's fertile banks in a geographic swath of North Africa where the cosmic lighthouse hid in plain sight for almost 90,000 years. Whether the dynastic Egyptian kingdoms benefitted from proximity to the beacon—or perhaps channeled forebears lost to time—intrigued the Light Specters. An ontological theory given considerable weight posited their interest in safeguarding humanity actuated from a power beyond their comprehension.

Hypothesizing their transcendence while monitoring the complexities of life on Earth was preempted by a more immediate concern: concealing the beacon from a heretofore nonexistent human gaze.

Like their splintered brethren, the Light Specters required human assistance to complete the task. However, instead of gruesome death, their recruit will transcend mortality.

Pharaoh Khufu | Memphis, Egypt
Predawn | 2550 BC

A young Egyptian ruler named Khufu—the second pharaoh of the Fourth Dynasty—was haunted by visions while lying prone atop his royal bed. His thin form trembled, terrified by the apparent origin: a mysterious edifice protruding from a barren valley since before recorded time. Like his predecessors, undocumented reverence of the symmetrical formation was an unexplained facet of his exalted position. The unspoken rule of law forbade accessing the anomalous structure or loitering in its vicinity. Though heeded through the centuries, the punishment of death ensnared unwitting transgressors from time to time.

In return, the enigma out on the desert hardscrabble left the Egyptians alone until now. Out of the blue, it called out to their controversial ruler, invading his psyche and upsetting his posh lifestyle.

Beset by rumors that his reign was invalid due to his questionable birthright, the pampered and healthy yet beanpole-thin young man tossed and turned, suppressing fitful rage, enduring another in a long succession of restless nights. Compounding anxieties at the root of Khufu's insomnia, a hot desert breeze billowed through the sheer drapes covering the open windows of his royal sleep chamber within the palatial complex, like an apparition. Desperate for a peaceful night's rest, he lay flat on his back, pulling the sheet under his goatee chin, and stared at shadows dancing across the painted ceiling above his bed. Out of the periphery of his 20-20 vision, he watched a light pass between the drapes. "Probably a firefly."

The ruler relaxed for a few halted breaths before a heart-pounding dread flooded his senses, watching more lights float through the window. Khufu tried to call his guards as the glowing spheres invaded his quaking personal space, but he couldn't utter a sound, filling him with dreaded fear and confusion.

The spectral intruders acknowledged his presence, merging into a bright pulsating ball of light. The spacious sleep chamber was illuminated in brilliance, forcing his eyes shut behind the soft palms of his clenched royal hands. Regardless, the light pierced his eyelids, rendering him sightless. Blind and mute, he awaited the inevitable, but it never came.

Instead, a coursing river of bizarre people, creatures, machines, and flying craft swirled in his mind, illustrative of a long-forgotten past or an unknowable future.

The nebulous visions ceased, and the royal bedroom plunged into darkness again. Khufu lowered his sweaty hands and squinted into the abyss. Paralyzed with fear, he made out light specks amassing into a glowing sphere. The tingle of a static electric charge stood his hair on end. Still centered on his royal bed, feet pointing at the ceiling under soft cotton sheets, he bolted upright as the orbs spun around his head, morphing into violent streaks of light. The electrified pulses intensified, and Khufu sensed mystifying weightlessness while choking back panic and utter helplessness. The royal bedsheets fell from around his bent waist, fluttering into a heaping pile on the smooth tile floor.

"Do not be alarmed. You are among friends."

"Where are you taking me?"

"You already know, your majesty."

His vision recovering, Khufu squinted through the thrumming mass of energy, holding him aloft, and gasped. He glided past the flapping drapery outside the open window above his palatial estate's moonlit rooftops into the warm night.

The orbs settled the discombobulated ruler upon the hardscape a stone's throw from the northern face of a glowing four-sided pointed structure before vanishing into the night. Khufu stood alone before the pyramid, listening to its orchestral hum while multi-hued lights illuminated the bewildered expression on his smooth, tanned face. Another attempt to shake himself awake proved futile. "I am not dreaming, that much I know."

A desert breeze ruffled his cotton nightshirt as he made a trepidatious barefoot approach toward the pulsating, pointed structure. Reaching the nearest face, he touched the polished surface and felt another static shock permeate his quaking form. Long manicured fingers probed grooves in the beacon's carved maze, eliciting a spectrum of glowing colors mirroring his hand movements. Scanning upward to the apex, he fixated on a mesmerizing golden ellipse sparkling like a human eye. While pondering the small oval shape's supernatural power, a steady light beam resolved, piercing the heavens from the tip with a rhythmic thrum.

"What is this place?"

As Khufu stumbled backward, a sharp pain stabbed his right foot. Hunching down, he noted bone fragments scattered all over the ground. Snatching a whitish shard and examining it close to his scowling face, he cast it into the shadows, "How can it be my eyes have not seen this before now?"

Though the structure existed before recorded time, he looked upon it in stunned silence, witnessing its rhythmic machinations for the first time.

Mindful of the razor-sharp bone fragments scattered among the rocks and buried under the loose gravel and sand, the Egyptian king stepped from the structure's base to clear bright ovals obscuring his vision. A surprised yelp rasped from his mouth as a lean black cat angled out of nowhere, purring against his leg.

Angry and frustrated, Khufu wheeled from the beacon and the cat, seeking solace in the darkness, yearning for someone or something to relieve him of this burdensome fate. A perfect cube, taller than his six-foot frame, manifested out of thin air thirty paces into the desert scrub. Like the beacon, he had never seen its mocking form. Approaching the large shape with the cat following close behind across the bones and rocks, he touched the cube's smooth surface, finding no illuminated patterns, just limestone.

Frowning at his faint reflection in the polished block, anger gave way to confusion, acknowledging that his advisors had made consequential decisions. Despite his misgivings, intuition informed him that this impacted his rule. Overcome by indecision, he plopped in an exhausted heap against the cube, resting his shaved head against the smooth surface, staring in wonderment at the pyramid.

Frightful recognition of venomous creatures lurking in the desert prompted a whispered prayer for the cat to ward off nearby snakes and scorpions.

The black cat slinked to his feet and reclined on the hard ground as if the gods heard his plea. Khufu studied the feline's elegant form silhouetted against the luminous proto-pyramid. The unlikely duo rested, watching the glowing structure's rhythmic bursts into the heavens.

"Impressive. Isn't it?"

Startled, Khufu bumped his head against the solid limestone, "Ouch! Who said that?"

The petite kitty stood and stretched, swinging its long black tail through the air in a gentle arc. Yellow eyes aglow, it spoke in a sultry feminine tone, "Me, of course. In answer to your earlier query, you had not seen the beacon in all its glory because its true nature lay beyond human perception. You are the first to see its infinite machinations. However, humans are advancing beyond our ability to keep it hidden, so it falls on your narrow shoulders to assist us in burying it. Once secured underground, a new pyramid, many times greater in scale, will conceal our beacon, preserving its function and protecting it from human awareness. The scale of the new pyramid, built in your name, will baffle humankind. Conspiracies, legends, and curses will spring from fertile imaginations and persist for millennia. We intend to keep it online until your kind no longer requires protection from a universe of hostile actors."

"Hostile actors?"

"They would have already ravaged your world without this beacon."

"How will I build a pyramid?"

The cryptic kitty reply lingered as its slinky black form transmogrified into a luminous sphere, "You are leaning against the first limestone block. Only 2.3 million more to go."

* * *

For two weeks, nothing happened. Khufu convinced himself the strange episode emanated from a feverish dream. However, lingering doubts juxtaposed with an unusual vitality compelled his secretive return to the ancient edifice. It appeared as it always had, like a big, pointed rock. Laughing at his rampant paranoia, the pharaoh traveled back to his palace. No one of consequence was aware of his absence.

Still, the alien vigor coursing every fiber of his supreme being could not be denied. He felt great. His skin glowed from within in the darkness, and his appearance turned translucent under the bright Egyptian sunshine. Meanwhile, a physical transformation added height and muscle mass, giving him a true ruler's imposing physique.

Another improvement the young lad could previously only dream of manifested in concubinary groupies loitering about the palace, awaiting an audience with their king.

* * *

The Light Specters' feline emissary visited the royal palace in the third week. Bisecting a lush, palm-lined courtyard, the kitty scampered up a flight of tiled steps into lavish living quarters opposite an empty colonnaded throne room. Surmising it must be a holiday, she padded past palace guards and functionaries, too distracted by the inexplicable presence of so many beautiful women to notice one stray cat.

Sniffing the air, the sleek creature stalked to an antechamber hidden behind flowing drapes. Parting thick swathes like the Red Sea, the kitty entered the ornate confines and hopped onto a gilded settee occupied by the Pharaoh Khufu. The king cast a sideways glance from the small animal and back onto the ravishing half-dressed young woman propped on toned arms ringed in gold bands between his legs. The cold stare from the black cat spoke volumes: Playtime was over.

Khufu frowned at the cat, cleared his throat, and tapped his mistress' arm, "Pull yourself together and leave. Now."

The woman's pouting hesitation prompted the pharaoh to repeat his command in a thunderous new voice that sounded as if it came from someone else. Her wide-eyed stare into the frightening translucent countenance of Khufu looming above her sent her scurrying from the room, stumbling half-naked through the drapes.

The reborn Egyptian ruler issued a new command for his guards to expel everyone from the royal palace grounds until further notice.

"I told you this was going to happen, yet you appear surprised to see me again." While grooming dainty jet-black paws, the feline scrutinized the new and improved pharaoh, "I see your transformation is almost complete. That is good. Soon, you will no longer crave that kind of diversion, so I am happy we afforded you time to behave as humans are wont to do."

"Do you expect me to thank you? What did you do to me?" Khufu lifts his muscular right forearm and watches sparkling lights drawn to the surface of his dark skin.

"We adjusted your lifespan, nothing more. You are still a product of your creator. However, your new role requires upgrades to your physical being." Extending a paw in the darkened chamber, "Now, let's get down to business." A holographic representation of a large swath of Egyptian topography glowed in vivid blue and green tones.

Wearing nothing but his semitransparent birthday suit speckled with tiny dancing lights, Khufu leaned forward and studied the three-dimensional image, "Impressive. That is indeed a part of my kingdom."

"Yes, it is. Not a single human can witness the initial phase of our project. Command your generals to cordon off this area to the river and as far into the surrounding desert as possible. Once the beacon is buried and the ground replaced, we will recruit scores of your people to carry out the charade."

"Charade?"

Waving a paw through the air, the image fast-forwarded to a final incarnation illustrating a gleaming white pyramid topped in gold. "It must appear that humans built this in your name. I leave it to your imagination as to why and for what purpose. Now, put on some clothes. There is much work to be done before our guests arrive."

* * *

Khufu's decrees and proclamations filtered down the ranks and were executed without question. Top advisors and generals feared the young ruler like never before. His reign began with disrespectful smirks and eye rolls while derogatory comments and rampant insubordination went unchecked behind his back. Not anymore. No matter how strange, every capricious utterance the pharaoh made was carried out as if lives depended on it. Which they did.

Wielding his army like a blunt instrument, Khufu sealed off a gigantic swath of Egyptian soil under the guise of a leprosy epidemic.

Once the quarantine relocation was complete, Khufu and his feline ambassador welcomed an exotic assemblage of alien contractors.

The first arrival was an eight-foot reptilian engineer, introduced to Khufu as a Gork. No name, just Gork.

An initial planning session between the reptilian and the black cat, while Khufu tried to follow, defined the delicate task: beacon removal from its hallowed placement to a temporary new location. The Gorks' galaxy-wide reputation as world destroyers was well-earned, yet they possessed the right technology to move a large object. The kitty had enlisted worse characters for less critical jobs.

Watching the reptilian offload strange and exotic equipment from his dark-gray block-shaped craft, the pharaoh couldn't resist an obvious gibe, "I know a few Nile crocodiles I could introduce him to."

The cat turned to Khufu, "Are you joking? I can never tell."

"Just trying to help my scaly brother find a date," the pharaoh looked on as the iridescent, green-scaled alien labored in the North

African heat to install large wire-bound anti-gravity cubes around the base of the beacon. "I must say, for such a large, scary creature, he comes across as quite likable."

"Yes. One-on-one, the Gorks are fine. However, our jagged-toothed friend comes from a warrior race. You do not want a whole fleet of their ships to appear above your metropolis unannounced."

With a bulging silver-eyed glance toward his black-haired employer, the Gork indicated he was ready to elevate the massive beacon off the plateau. The odd pair spectated as their alien contractor deftly guided the massive structure off the surface in a cloud of dust via a remote clutched in its clawed hands.

Once the beacon elevated into the hot midday air, the black cat studied the asymmetric hexagonal configuration across its underside. "Interesting."

The pharaoh tried to follow the cat's contemplative gaze, peering at the dark-shaded square constituting the beacon's bottom side, noting some of the shapes were aglow while most of the pattern remained dark. Failing to glean any significance, "What is so interesting? Do the blue-glowing hexagons have a special meaning?"

"Everything means something to someone, my friend. The hexagons are part of the ancient design. The blue-lit ones indicate specific quadrants of the universe where the signal's warning message is received as we speak."

"And you are telling me—based solely on that warning—aliens will avoid coming here and wiping us out? Seems far-fetched."

"It has worked so far. You could at least pretend to be grateful."

Khufu gazes at the blue sky, "We have been worshipping visitors from other places all this time, haven't we?"

Surprised by the pharaoh's dot-connecting ability, "We relented on the zero-tolerance policy long ago; our focus now is on human survival. Your kind made the visitors into gods. Not us. Who knows? Perhaps one day, humankind will be viewed as gods by a gullible race rising from the mud."

The young pharaoh squints through the brightness watching the elevated structure's massive shadow darkening across the uneven hardscape, "You know, I don't see that happening. Humans will likely kill each other long before ever reaching that point."

"Your pessimism is duly noted."

* * *

Day one ebbed to a sweltering close without a human anywhere in sight, and the relocated beacon pinging the sky from its relocated position.

Under a blanket of stars, wide awake and bored to tears, Khufu propped against the original limestone block on a pile of cotton bedding with the cat curled beside him. Feeling the kitty's purr, he watched the golden ellipse sparkle at the top of the brilliant pyramid-shaped maze through the darkness.

Hungry after a long day's work, the Gork headed off the plateau for food, prompting Khufu to call after the scowling reptilian: "Please refrain from eating anyone who looks important."

Chuckling at his dark humorous joke, Khufu's gaze returns to the beacon, "It is too bad my people cannot see the beacon the way I do." After a long pause, he continues, unsure if the cat was awake or off in kitty dreamland, "What if I climbed the beacon and claimed the golden ellipse for myself? Wouldn't that make me all-powerful?"

The cat stretched and yawned, "Purge that thought right now and get some sleep."

Khufu smirked, "I'm not tired. Why can't I take the ellipse?"

"You wouldn't know what to do with it."

* * *

The morning started on the quarantined plateau with the touchdown of a dirty and dented orb propped atop three extended legs in a choking cloud of dust and sand.

Khufu stirred awake, entwined in blankets strewn atop the hardscape, and watched as furry creatures lowered from a hole in the bottom of the spherical craft. The weird sight elicited a throaty chuckle; it looked like a bulbous three-legged animal taking a shit.

The black cat stirred awake and yawned in a husky, sexy morning voice, "The surveyors are here. Right on time."

"What should we call these aliens? Dorks? Sporks? Zorks?"

"That is quite enough. Surveyors will suffice."

Waddling on short stubby legs and dragging long purple capes across the sand, the heat-stricken aliens followed the cat's tour around the site. Khufu curled back up in the covers, wishing he could have brought a friend, overhearing the verbalized beeps, squawks, and burps; the hideous-looking bug-eyed mathematicians took measurements, crunching the numbers and calculating angles.

Unable to sleep, Khufu dragged himself into the new day's heat, trying to follow their work, but gave up watching the creatures establishing spectral points with their elephantine snouts based on dense projected equations. By late afternoon, the extended perimeter of the new and massive pyramid footprint was set with three glowing cubes forming a perfect square with the northwest corner limestone block revealed weeks beforehand.

After a night spent on the uncomfortable dirt and rocks, shivering under a thin sheet, the Gork built a throne furnished with plush palace sofas and bedding in return for fresh local meat.

Khufu quickly realized that the regal bearing exuded by his transformative state prompted unsolicited respect, just like a real king. Nevertheless, his genuine gratitude turned effusive after the lizard man took it upon himself to erect a tent over the throne providing shade from the blistering daytime sun. With the cat perched at his side, the pharaoh allowed the Gork to set up shop in the shaded recess behind the raised throne.

The black cat also enjoyed the comfort, using the heightened position to confer eye-to-eye with the aliens when questions or technical issues arose.

That evening, wind-whipped sand disrupted the proceedings as a sleek white vessel with swept-back wings shimmered out of the star-filled darkness and settled onto the plateau. A ramp lowered near the front of the fuselage, and a quartet of human-like aliens wearing a bare minimum of clothing approached Khufu's raised throne. The fair-skinned Nordic beings flashed telepathic greetings to the cat and the transformed human.

After an inaudible conversation, excluding the king, the handsome group took positions along each surveyed side, staring inward through an invisible centered point where the beacon used to sit. Waving hands through the dry nighttime breeze, they created glowing shapes, twisting, rotating, and resizing in midair and assembling gigantic blocks, row upon row, across the plateau. Through the night, passages and shafts were integrated with mathematical precision extending deep underground. Eschewing sleep, Khufu and the cat watched spellbound as the Designers rendered a full-scale three-dimensional pyramid model into the wee hours of the morning, accounting for over 2.3 million blocks to the nth degree.

As the morning sun colored the eastern horizon into purple and pinkish hues, the radiant alien on the southern side drew Khufu's enthralled gaze with her powerful and mellifluous telepathy: *"This room is for you."*

Entranced, Khufu watched perfect translucent blocks stepping upward at a cosmic angle to the King's Chamber. His chamber.

Sensing an impertinent communication between the mesmerized human and the beautiful alien, the feline vaulted from a perch, padding through the virtual blocks toward the ethereal woman. "Please stop toying with the poor man."

"As you wish."

With a cobweb-clearing headshake, Khufu watched as the unlikely pair's animated conversation concluded. Beaming an effervescent smile, the telekinetic beauty shrugged her sculpted shoulders, wafting an apology to the ruler's ears.

The non-stop extraterrestrial activity continued into the heat of midday. Without ceremony, the overheated furry surveyors completed their assignment and left in the ugly brown ship without saying goodbye. The Gork collected forgotten purple capes the beings shed while baking under the Egyptian heat and folded them in a pile on the off chance they returned to retrieve them. They never did.

The ethereal humanoid architects capped their completed design in solid gold later that evening, approximately one Earth rotation post-arrival. They might have chosen a less tempting element for the capstone if they were more familiar with humans' proclivity for theft.

The radiant Nordic foursome reduced their full-size structural plan into a luminescent pyramidic amulet held in the palm of the other female's lovely right hand. The blond alien beauty led a chanting procession toward the makeshift throne, where the kitty awaited along with the spellbound pharaoh and the bored Gork. With an effervescent smile, she extended a jeweled collar with the one-inch amulet around the black feline's neck and patted its furry head, bowing a solemn farewell.

As the craft lifted off the plateau, ground turbulence ripped the tent from its tethered posts and sent lighter articles into a swirling vortex littering across the desert. The Gork hustled to collect the scattered items and repaired the tent.

The hulking reptilian became an imposing, silent partner in the project, transporting food and supplies to the sight while maintaining the beacon out of view of slack-jawed locals, consuming more than a few of the same.

After the dust settled, the cat curled on a pillow with the crystal pyramid dangling from its neck. Khufu watched the feline breathe before closing his eyes and falling into a deep slumber.

* * *

A horrible grating noise echoed across the plateau, awakening the pharaoh. Already midday and blazing hot, he dabbed his forehead and saw through his skin like never before at tiny lights teeming underneath.

The cat jumped back onto the throne, "They are here."

"Who is here?"

"The miners. Their ship just landed. They are late, as usual."

"Who cares? Is my transformation complete?"

"Yes. And no. You can now alter your form, but I recommend doing so only if necessary. We can talk more later. I must coordinate the next steps with the unpleasant little beings gathering on the plateau."

More concerned with himself, Khufu grabbed a mirror and studied his face. His round-cheeked baby-faced countenance had transmogrified into the chiseled profile of a rugged, handsome adult male. From a certain angle, he now resembled his father, a tyrant like none other.

The loud clank of a ramp hitting the sand and the murmuring of little alien voices carrying across the plateau shook Khufu from his self-rumination. The Egyptian ruler put down his mirror and squinted outside his tented throne at a tubular vessel resolving out of the ether onto the arid plateau in a dusty red cloud. Another ramp dropped from an open hatch, and terraforming alien miners from a distant star spilled out in jabbering groups. The weird little creatures busied themselves offloading equipment from the craft's tail section, including two sparkling crystal formations that caught the Egyptian's eye. The beings crammed everything they could not heft on their tiny shoulders onto anti-gravity carts parked just outside the massive squared-off survey lines. Meanwhile, the pharaoh and cat spectated from a safe distance as the alien contractors eschewed formalities and began excavation.

Menacing black eyeballs dominated the diminutive aliens' smooth, bone-white heads lending physical form to their universal antisocial reputation. Raygun-wielding miners cut precise seams through the ancient strata in 10-foot cubed sections. A second crew moved in and levitated the freed limestone cube, slapping a repositioning symbol onto each section. A third squad guided the floating slabs into the open desert and parked them on the plateau in reverse order.

The excavation of massive cubes of striated rock continued as multiple crews pulled chunks from the deepening hole. The process droned on in blistering hot 12-hour shifts into the fourth day.

The cat was furious with their deliberate pace, but the miners' cutting-edge technology was the only way to dig a deep and precise 132-foot square and refill all 306 feet so no one could tell it was ever there.

Bored beyond measure, Khufu wandered into the desert to clear his head and escape the pasty little bastards roaming the site. The massive scale became evident from a distance, and he was overwhelmed with doubt. Was he doing the right thing? His previous safe life was already a distant memory. The massive pyramid built atop this site will forever cement his name in history in a way his predecessors never dreamt possible. He prayed that their jealous souls would not seek vengeance from the afterlife.

Returning to his throne, the king purged negative thoughts of his angry forebears from his translucent head as a screech from the pit echoed across the plateau. "Finally! They reached the bottom."

***

The whistle interrupted the Gork in the middle of its lunch. Trading the still-wriggling snack for its anti-gravity remote control while picking human flesh from its sharp teeth, the reptilian guided the 73-foot-tall beacon into the shaft. Nearing the bottom, another ear-screeching whistle alerted the Gork to brake. A group of seven miners down below scrambled over the rough-hewn floor to stand up 12-foot support columns, preserving a sublevel underneath the beacon's hexagonal-patterned glowing footprint.

With the beacon safely parked twelve feet off the bottom of the 276-foot shaft, the Gork's job was complete. He collected his supplies and materials and bid the kitty and king farewell.

Noting Khufu's genuine sadness at the Gork's departure, he acknowledged the mutual admiration between man and reptile with bemusement.

Hours after the Gork took flight ensconced within its single-lizard cruiser, a sharp crack rattled the plateau.

Khufu followed from behind. "What was that? Is something wrong?"

"Someone activated the Machine!" The black cat leaped from the throne and sprinted to the shaft's edge, ensuring the golden ellipse remained safe and secure atop the beacon.

The foreman peered over the cat into the dark square abyss with a lackluster shrug.

Khufu tried to follow the high-pitched frequency exchange between the enraged black cat and the shiftless alien.

After the berated supervisor skulked off, shaking its bulbous head, the cat addressed Khufu, "It appears that members of the mining crew tried to sabotage the beacon from underneath. A suicide mission from the start. Those damnable Dark Specters. I wondered when they would try to infiltrate the minds of these simpletons."

"Dark Specters? I am starting to feel like there is a lot you are not telling me."

"The Dark Specters are pure evil. And they use sentient beings to do their bidding."

"Isn't that what you are doing with me?"

The cat transformed into a threatening black deity with a musclebound human body and an elongated canine head with pointed ears, towering over Khufu with a furious growl, "Perhaps we should have brought back your father, instead? We chose you because you are the right human at the right moment. Do not meddle with destiny. The fate of your species is at stake, not just your petty concerns."

* * *

Replacement miners tunneled on a downward angle through the sublevel's southern wall, starting from a claustrophobic vertical tunnel paralleling the shaft, following the plans designed by the good-looking aliens. Activating light from the crystalline instruments situated at the base of the north and south walls, they counted the slain remains of their seven comrades scattered around the blue-cast basement level. Without ceremony for the deceased, they abandoned the in-situ bodies draped under shiny purple cloaks left behind by the heat-stricken furry surveyors.

Back on the surface, work resumed. The miners returned the chunks of strata, one section at a time, to each original position inside the pit. Progress slowed to a crawl fitting angled midsections against the proto-pyramid beacon, set dead center inside the shaft, requiring kid-glove treatment. The seamless perfection of the replaced rock was a critical aspect of the plan. The black kitty ambassador had zero tolerance for the potential of a misaligned gap, cluing some future surveyors to the beacon's hidden subterranean placement.

At the rock bottom of the quarter-filled shaft, the upper 19 feet of the operational beacon, with the golden ellipse oriented north, remained exposed to the stifling air. Next, a 71-foot diameter black granite slab with a 19-foot square cut from its center was lowered into the shaft as the yammering miners scrambled around the periphery, ensuring the cut-out middle of huge black circular mass did not contact the Light Specters' precious pyramid on its descent into the hole.

The limestone slab seated atop the replaced stone deep inside the shaft with a loud whump of hot air that knocked the irascible aliens on their backsides. After the dust cleared and the critical construction phase was completed, a 22-foot-tall black granite dome lid was lowered over the beacon, shrouding it in darkness.

Work stopped, and everybody took a break while the kitty trekked the circumference, double-checking the dome's notched alignment atop the shiny black circular base. Her confirmation of a perfect fit prompted relieved sighs from the hair-trigger-tempered stonecutting crews, unaccustomed to anyone verifying their craftsmanship.

A miner wielding a laser gun climbed to a point eleven feet up the dome's southern side and sliced a two-foot circular hatch into the smooth black granite. The access point is the confluence of shafts and tunnels beneath the Giza Plateau, leading to the surface and the yet-to-be-built Great Pyramid.

With the beacon chamber secure under its black granite half dome, the precision-cut higher strata cubes were returned with pre-cut concavities where ancient limestone butted in perfect alignment against the dome's curvature. Under the black cat's amber-eyed vigilance, the pace of refilling the shaft intensified to a steady rhythm.

At the halfway point in the refilling process, the black cat whistled a halt to work and descended into the shaft, scampering through a side tunnel bored into the southern wall. Keen feline vision guided the tiny animal to the tunnel's pitch-black endpoint. Removing the crystal pyramid from her jeweled collar, she inserted it pointy side down into a small keyhole in the rock and rotated it ninety degrees. With a relieved sigh, she watched a chiseled wall slide aside, exposing an additional thirty feet of claustrophobic tunnel. The kitty proceeded through and reached a precipice at the hollowed-out uppermost reaches of a deep, wide vertical elevator shaft.

The cat strode onto a wooden platform, level with the precipice, and inspected the rope and pulley contraption bolted into the ceiling holding it above the dark abyss. Cursing the sloppy miners' failure to dismantle the elevator before burying it under tons of rock, she cut her losses with the irritable creatures and let it slide. Who knows? Someone might need to use it someday.

Khufu watched his feline partner emerge from the square

tunnel, "Where does that god-forsaken hole lead?"

"It is the only physical passage to the hatch in the beacon chamber. I wanted to confirm its functionality before progressing further."

Visibly annoyed by the cat's meddling, the grumbling miners filled the shaft to the surface, cutting another 26-degree passage northward, connecting the Subterranean Chamber to a planned entry point 56 feet up the north face of the next-phase pyramid project.

Another argument ensued between the black cat and the alien miners when a large asymmetric surface chunk was discovered missing adjacent to the filled shaft. The rock was never found, and the hole became a grotto sandwiched between the ancient plateau and the base layer of limestone blocks forming Khufu's resplendent pyramid. It was later bisected by an ascending escape tunnel used by workers during later phases of pyramid construction.

With the plateau reassembled and the beacon now streaming its message from deep underneath the Giza Plateau, the miners' toils on Earth ended without ceremony.

There would not be a ceremony, and no pleasantries or gifts were exchanged. They collected their pay with overtime and left without so much as a goodbye. Khufu and the black cat watched the vile little beings go, only to discover later that they left their dead saboteur comrades in the twelve-foot-tall expanse under the beacon.

"That is not a problem. The ghastly aliens' demise was recorded and will serve as a warning to future trespassers."

* * *

In 2560 BC, Pharaoh Khufu's pyramid neared completion after years of grueling construction. Seated atop his royal throne, he surveyed the expansive network of buildings and canals surrounding the magnificent limestone and granite structure. Thanking his spectral benefactors for an abundance of musclebound humanoid laborers, he squinted into the midday brightness, beaming at his 480.5-foot-tall creation, covered in polished white limestone, and tipped in gleaming gold. Its 756-foot base aligns with Earth and the stars under the crushing weight of approximately 2.3 million blocks. Deep underneath, the Light Specters' beacon, powered by its golden elliptical power source, continues to ping its message into the heavens.

On the pharaoh's lap, the only creature unafraid of Khufu's transformative state—from a fragile human being who ruled a kingdom to a glimmering translucent guardian of the beacon—purred with contentment.

The Light Specters' role in the design and engineering, not to mention the transport and precise positioning of the massive stones, each weighing an average of 2.5 to 15 tons, kept the project on schedule. Assuming the all-too-human guises of mathematicians, engineers, contractors, and slaves created the monolithic structure's mythology, designed to last for millennia, documented as built by human hands.

Tens of centuries later, baffled explorers stumble across the plateau, hypothesizing massive ramps and rope-and-pulley schemes manned by thousands of slaves acting in concert are the answer, yet fail to budge one pyramid-size block, let alone 2.3 million.

This same curiosity and hubris will take them to the stars in a boisterous, haphazard fit of future ingenuity. Humans are intelligent yet predictable, like those who came before them, and more to follow throughout space and time.

The smaller imitations of Khufu's Great Pyramid—adjacent and across vast oceans—are sources of bemusement amongst the Light Specters. While the stone edifices represent impressive feats of human ingenuity—with assistance from extraterrestrial interlopers—none are as critical as the Great Pyramid of Giza.

Ecstatic with the completion of his pyramid, Khufu's successor, Khafre, commissioned a gigantic limestone monument honoring the cat. The Dark Specters infiltrated his mind with a nightmarish vision forcing him to alter his design and chisel his father's head onto the cat as a lasting rebuke against the entire project.

Hidden far beneath the colossal Giza pyramid within the 71-foot diameter domed expanse, the top nineteen feet of the proto-pyramidic beacon juts from a sea of glassy smooth black granite. At its apex, the golden ellipse powers a hieroglyphic light show while bursting rhythmic energy through the chamber's 22-foot ceiling and the Giza pyramid into the heavens, as it had for millennia.

Obscured from evolving eyeballs, the Light Specters' stern message of non-interference burst heavenward like clockwork, allowing human civilization to continue its unimpeded march toward relevance while surpassing even the more optimistic prognostications.

All was according to plan on the small blue planet.

***

In addition to meddling with Khufu's successors, the Dark Specters never relented from their nefarious schemes. Hiding the damnable structure beneath a massive pyramidic replica elicited derision from malevolent shapeshifting beings. Assuming human forms throughout the centuries, they preyed upon humankind's weaknesses, searching for the perfect foil. Singling out history's megalomaniacal actors and magnifying wretchedness to terrible extremes, they deceived power-hungry fools into believing that possessing the golden ellipse equaled infinite power. However, the who's who of skeletal remains lost in the pitch-black claustrophobic tunnels beneath the Great Pyramid failed to remove the golden ellipse despite centuries of effort. The handful of bad actors who managed to locate the beacon's hidden expanse all succumbed to the Machine. Instead of glorious power and wealth, their ashen remnants were whisked into oblivion.

Despite multitudinous failures from the advent of civilization to almost 1,800 years past the time of Christ, the Dark Specters believed their persistence would one day pay a dividend.

On a sweltering August evening in 1799, the evilness watched a small, petty man, decked out in full uniform, ride his white stallion to the base of the Great Pyramid, right hand stuck under his waistcoat like an idiot.

Napoleon | Giza Plateau, Egypt
07:30 p.m. | August 14, 1799

The late-summer Cairo heat and humidity lingered into the early evening hours. Beyond the pyramids, the last vestiges of sunlight radiated through the cumulus, and stars twinkled overhead in the darkening cobalt sky. General Napoleon Bonaparte, commander of the French Expeditionary Force and self-proclaimed conqueror of Egypt—after his decisive victory over the Ottomans—dismounted and handed the reigns to an attending soldier.

Exuding superiority and purpose, he strode to the base layer of limestone, giving form to the Great Pyramid of Giza, and smiled. Addressing the fawning retinue of generals, lieutenants, soldiers, archeologists, scientists, historians, plus a cadre of pragmatic businessmen and functionaries ingratiating themselves to the victorious French over the vanquished Turks, the diminutive leader found words, for once, escaped him.

Instead, anxious for his transformative adventure full of promise to begin, "Where is Monsieur Dreyfus? Come here at once, Armand!"

Napoleon spied Dreyfus, hidden amidst the crowd, and motioned a short-armed wave for his chief archeologist to join him. Without further ado, the two men climbed prepositioned steps and ladders up the eroded and weather-beaten blocks following a path marked for the occasion. Dreyfus did not share his leader's dogmatic belief; the structure hid undiscovered treasures. He prided himself on his scientific acumen and godless skepticism. Treasures from Khufu's reign, including the pharaoh's mummified remains, fell prey to looters long ago. That is if the ruler was ever entombed in the massive monument in the first place.

Dreyfus served for the past year in the 30,000-plus French expedition unearthing an eye-popping wealth of antiquities from all over the Middle East, including the Rosetta Stone. The revelatory discoveries brought about a new field of study, Egyptology. Despite the Giza Plateau's archeological significance, Dreyfus was thunderstruck when informed of his leader's desire to spend a night inside the crumbling pile of rocks. And the older man wished he could hide under a rock, as opposed to climbing one, when informed as one of the senior archeological experts on the expedition, Napoleon chose him to be his guide. Still, the elder statesman knew one thing; he did not achieve his advanced age by questioning the whimsical, sometimes farcical, ideas of a megalomaniac like Napoleon.

The Frenchmen picked their way up the side of the Great Pyramid of Giza to the main entrance, sixty feet off the plateau. One is a short and stout leader of men; the other is a tall and gangly man of science.

Dreyfus reached the entrance level first. While waiting for his huffing companion, he quickly surveyed chiseled clues indicating where a seamless block concealed the opening from view. "Why go through the trouble of building such a massive structure only to hide the front door? Incredible." Dreyfus had read a Greek geologist named Strabo's eyewitness account from 24 BC, describing the engineering marvel before earthquakes, the elements, and looting Arabs absconded with most of the pyramid's smooth limestone outer casing. The Grecian scientist wrote about a hidden hinged stone that could swivel open, revealing a regal threshold and the Great Pyramid's Descending Passage. Additional eyewitnesses from throughout recorded history corroborated his account.

Eschewing a lower and more readily accessible entrance

tunneled by treasure-seeking eighth-century Arabs—due to its rough-hewn appearance and tragic nickname—Dreyfus wiped his brow and waited for his boss to complete his ascent. "Sir, we could have used the robbers entrance. It is much easier to navigate."

With a final labored push, the world leader hoisted himself atop the last block with a grunted French epithet. Ignoring Dreyfus, Napoleon bent low to peer into the dark four-foot orifice. "Dreyfus, I see my stature has finally become an advantage. And you wanted to lead me through a tunnel dug by grave robbers! We are not thieves, my friend; we are liberators."

"As you wish, sir." Hands resting on his hips, Dreyfus took a deep breath of fresh air. He did not bother to advise his boss to do the same. Instead, without thinking, he gestured the diminutive man across the threshold, like a bride and groom on their wedding night. After a final glimpse at the thinning crowds, he ducked inside, cheek to jowl with Napoleon, "This is awkward."

Dreyfus squeezed past Napoleon in the cramped space, "Watch your head as it is tight quarters in here."

Without waiting for a reply, Dreyfus hunched down the confining passageway. Meanwhile, the general brushed the dust from his royal blue waistcoat and looked down the passage, half-expecting a revelatory experience mere feet inside the entrance.

The experienced antiquities collector knew the scenery would stay the same from the chiseled limestone blocks, dust, and gritted sand at the opening, but the boondoggle must proceed. "If I keep a steady pace, this nightmare will soon end, and I can go home." Weeks from retirement, he looked forward to a much-anticipated return to the south of France.

Halting his sure-footed steps halfway down the claustrophobic 26-degree slope, Dreyfus waited for his fearless leader. Looking back toward the entrance, he watched Napoleon's silhouetted form struggling to descend through the narrow space. The general's leather boots slid from under him on the loose gravel and sand, causing him to fall on his backside and shout a loud expletive, which echoed past the smiling archeologist into the darkness. Stifling an impertinent laugh, the Frenchman mused that Pharaonic ghosts lingering within these walls were undoubtedly aware of their intrusion after that outburst.

Sliding to Dreyfus' bent position, Napoleon pointed a chubby finger at the scientist, a wide-eyed expression distorting his cherubic face, "I'm warning you, Monsieur, the footing in this abysmal passage is treacherous at best. You will do well to slow your pace and not get ahead of your commander again. I say this for your safety, Dreyfus." Napoleon concluded with a dismissive wave. "Now proceed," gesturing his still-pointed finger into the darkness beyond the prepositioned lanterns.

"My apologies, general. I will try to be more careful."

Napoleon could not make out Dreyfus' surreptitious eye roll in the darkness but may have sensed the thin-veiled sarcasm in the measured reply from the experienced antiquities collector.

Surrounded by the suffocating weight of millions of tons of solid rock, the string of lanterns ended after 97 feet at a low square cavity. "Sir, this plugged shaft is the start of what is known as the Ascending Passage. As you can see, it is blocked by solid granite. Who knows why? Fortunately for our endeavors, the Arabs discovered a detour."

"They are a fascinating and resourceful lot, wouldn't you agree, Dreyfus?"

"If you say so, sir."

Dreyfus leads Napoleon a few hunched steps farther down the Descending Passage. Without exposition, he ventures left through a jagged hole chiseled from the wall. The taller man twists and pulls himself across the sharp uneven surface into the Ascending Passage beyond, angling his frame through the softer limestone blocks carved out by treasure-seeking Arabs a thousand years earlier, revealing the once-hidden upward passage.

Gasping and covered in dirty sweat, Dreyfus collapsed on the floor, cursing the arduous detour around the stacked granite plugs, "Only a masochist would build such an inhospitable structure." Probing through the darkness, he located provisions prepositioned for the final push to the King's Chamber: torches, a box of matches, a satchel containing Napoleon's sleepwear, and a single canteen of lukewarm water.

How many intrepid explorers remember to pack their pajamas?

Wriggling through the Arab's workaround tunnel, Napoleon crawled into the Ascending Passage like a calf exiting the birth canal. He settled on the upslope side of Dreyfus and took a breather allowing his companion a few minutes of blessed silence.

"Dreyfus, did the Arabs take everything a thousand years ago?"

"No, sir, the way I understand it, they found nothing of value." Too tired to care, he addressed the elephant in the pyramid, "Neither will we."

The candor was met by more silence in the dark.

Deciding break time was over, Dreyfus struck a match against the rough stone wall, ignited the first torch, and handed it to Napoleon. In his head, he likened it to giving a sparkler to a small boy. Next, the veteran explorer lit his torch, scooped the straps from the satchel and canteen, and flung them over his shoulder. Holding his torch upslope, the flickering light illuminated the claustrophobic passage slanting upward on the same 26-degree angle as the Descending Passage, "Sir, please be mindful of your torch on the way up, so you don't burn yourself or me."

His words fell on deaf ears. Napoleon stared into the abyss without uttering another sound, his torch illuminating the treacherous incline before the two men.

Dreyfus shrugged and began his ascent. Checking ahead into the frightening darkness with the light from his torch, "I apologize, but this is the only known passage to the King's Chamber."

After the scientist's impertinent candor, Napoleon broke from his prolonged silence, "Yes, Dreyfus. The King's Chamber! Lead the way, my friend!"

Ascending the narrow tunnel, the six-foot man trod up the steep incline, bent at the waist with both canteens and his satchel swinging from straps digging into his aching neck and shoulder. Dreyfus feared the torches would flame out from a lack of oxygen as the air grew thinner, abandoning them in the terrifying darkness. He refrained from voicing this concern to his clueless leader.

After 124 grueling feet, enduring scrapes, bruises, obscenities, and a singed boot from Napoleon's torch, the odd pair exited the Ascending Passage onto a horizontal landing at the base of the Grand Gallery. Both men stood erect, stretching sore muscles.

Dreyfus rejoiced in the relative openness after the tight passages and lost focus on the general for a heartbeat before hearing the man cry out in shocked anger.

"Why is there a hole in the damn floor, Dreyfus! I almost broke my leg! Do your job, man!"

Snapping from his momentary lapse in oversight, "That would be the Well Shaft, sir. It exits into a Subterranean Chamber far below the pyramid and connects to the Descending Passage where we started. It was used by laborers to enter and exit this upper area. It is far too narrow and treacherous for us." Seeing the general was not amused after his brush with a broken leg, Dreyfus continued, "Through there, straight ahead, is the Queen's Chamber. And no. There is nothing in there but rock."

Segueing around the dangerous hole-in-the-floor mishap, Dreyfus stepped up a sloped ramp and stood atop the seamless, assembled blocks above the Queen's Chamber entrance. The archeologist elevated his torch high over his head from his vantage point ten feet above Napoleon, still pouting on the horizontal landing. "Behold the majesty of the Grand Gallery."

Napoleon's brush with injury was forgotten as his eyes widened upon the flickering vision of a regal seven-foot-wide corridor towering 28 feet, following the same angle as the Ascending Passage along its 153-foot incline.

Dreyfus turned from the shallow man to the engineering marvel beyond his torch. Exploring the Great Pyramid was more a matter of endurance than discovery, but the Grand Gallery reignited his curiosity regarding ancient Egyptian civilization. It made little sense, yet there it was. Priceless antiquities be damned, mathematical feats such as this incredible passage held the answers. The art of his endeavors was the pursuit of the question. Replaying this conundrum in his balding head, he redirected his torch upon Napoleon, "Sir, without our modern knowledge of mathematics, such as the Pythagorean Theorem, no one can conceive how the Egyptians managed to construct this gallery." With a follow-up chuckle, "Not to mention the rest of the pyramid."

Redirecting his torchlight around the ancient space, he smoothed a bony hand across a corbeled seven-foot limestone slab. Six more corbeled sections pinch inward in three-inch increments to the narrowed 28-foot ceiling. "The engineering and mathematical precision it took to build this, the last of the original Seven Wonders of the World, defies imagination. However, the most advanced country in the history of the modern civilized world is here. We shall soon come to understand all its hidden secrets."

Dreyfus squinted toward Napoleon at the bottom of the Grand Gallery, expecting an inappropriate or ignorant reply. Instead, the small man placed his torch on the floor, adjusted his uniform, and brushed his dirty sleeves and lapels before addressing the taller archeologist.

"Dreyfus, you are misguided in your notion of who built this place."

Without missing a beat, Napoleon continued up the stepped pathway bordered by mysterious slotted ramps on both sides toward the top of the Grand Gallery, leaving his flummoxed chief scientist in his wake.

"I'm getting too old for this," Dreyfus adjusted the straps on his shoulder, marveling at how a nutjob like this guy somehow rose through the ranks and became a world leader. Sweating like a pig, he decided to take a breather and regroup. Ditching his coat, he took a swig from the canteen and stood on the steep incline in his dingy-white, open-collar silk blouse hanging untucked over torn breeches and scuffed and singed leather boots. He swiped his brow using a dirty cloth from the satchel and looked in amazement at Napoleon. Thirty paces ahead, the little man struck a statue-worthy pose, bathed in the flickering light from the torch outstretched in his left hand, staring into the darkness, still sporting his complete, albeit torn and dirty, uniform.

Deciding break time ended, Dreyfus plodded upward to his motionless leader, "We are virtually there, sir. The King's Chamber lies beyond the Great Step at the top."

Frozen in a familiar pose, Napoleon replied in a commanding voice reverberating through the Grand Gallery, "Wouldn't it be glorious if treasures did remain somewhere within these walls? Something greater than trinkets, statues, jewels, and mummies." His laugh had an uncharacteristic derisiveness, "So many damnable mummies!"

Dreyfus sensed the journey had taken a strange turn and proceeded toward his leader, trepidation creeping up his spine. Furrowing his weather-beaten brow, he strained to draw meaning from the maniacal rant.

"Not more worthless junk, dammit all! I want to find something of real value!"

Dreyfus reached Napoleon's side and saw him trembling with frustration. The round-faced little man wheeled toward him, continuing his tirade, "I just don't understand what it's supposed to look like! Is it some kind of tool? Or maybe a weapon?" Napoleon's maniacal eyes darted around the cavernous space as if searching for a lost key. "All I know, Armand, is I was drawn here in the same manner as Alexander the Great! There is a power here for the taking. I can feel it in my bones!

Just think of it, man! A treasure I can use to rule the world would be the greatest archeological discovery in the history of humankind, wouldn't you agree? Of course, you do! Follow me, Armand!"

The general thrust himself from Dreyfus' side and stumbled uphill as if taking the high ground amid a pitched battle. His incoherent exhortations for the scientist to follow echoed through the chamber into the abyss.

Dreyfus embraced his independence from the hapless ranks of the French military. Despite his conscription into babysitting Napoleon, he rebelled against petulant army commands whenever feasible. Standing in the darkness, the fading torch held loose at his side, he shakes his head in wonderment. The maniacal rant elicited an impertinent chuckle, "Armand, is it?" Swiping sweat from his brow, "I'm on a first-name basis with the Conqueror of Egypt—just in time for his complete mental breakdown. How fitting."

The obstinate scientist relented, taking long uphill strides to assist the harried little man before he hurt himself. Peering ahead, he spied what could only be Napoleon Bonaparte. The diminutive fellow made it to the top of the Grand Gallery and now stood atop the Great Step, silhouetted against the inky blackness beyond, uplit by his dim torch.

What manifested before Dreyfus' dilated eyeballs prompted the noted atheist to utter an out-of-character expression: "Dear God in Heaven, what is that?"

An amorphous creature, darker than the inky blackness, shimmering with specks of light, appeared out of the ether over Napoleon's frozen pose. Shocked and horrified, Dreyfus watched the phantasm engulf his stricken leader in its malevolence from head to toe. The lights spun around the dictator's diminutive silhouette in a violent, blurry maelstrom, piercing the quaking man like Swiss cheese. Scared witless yet rapt in a fascinated stare, Dreyfus repeated, "For the love of God, what is that?"

Swallowing back abject fear, Dreyfus attempted to speak as loud as he could muster in the stale air. However, Napoleon vanished from the 8-foot granite landing fronting the knee-height access passage leading to the King's Chamber in the blink of an eye. Stunned by the phantasmagorical display, the scientist shuffled forward, the last dying embers from his flame, the only thing between himself and utter madness; however, his satchel held his box of wooden matches, so not to worry.

* * *

Napoleon proved another terrible disappointment for the Dark Specters, like the power-hungry figures who came and went before him. They met the little general with great expectations on the elevated granite block above the Grand Gallery's high end, feet from the knee-height passage into the King's Chamber. However, the French general panicked instead of embracing their hollow promise of sheer power and control over the civilized world of the late 1700s. The Dark Specters dragged him into the red granite chamber and threw the coward against the lidless granite coffin in an ignominious heap. They considered the efficacy of smothering the shallow man but perceived his fate lay before him. Instead, the malevolent beings who fell from grace eons beforehand abandoned the weeping fool.

Napoleon curled into a fetal repose, cowering in fear, propped against the empty sarcophagus.

Desperate to find a competent human to break the Machine and remove the ellipse atop the beacon, the Dark Specters refocused their evilness onto the elderly fellow who accompanied Napoleon. They watched him climb atop the Great Step outside the King's Chamber, quaking in fear. That is fine; he should be afraid.

* * *

Pulling himself atop the Great Step at the high end of the Grand

Gallery's 153-foot incline, Dreyfus now stood where he saw Napoleon last stand. Trying not to hyperventilate, he peered into the low square portal, hopeful the horrifying vision was a figment of his imagination, "General? Are you in there?" No reply. "Damn. How am I going to explain losing the emperor of France?"

Lowering onto his arthritic knees atop the hard granite, Dreyfus squeezed through the square portal leading into the King's Chamber—where Napoleon must have gone.

A glowing orb greeted him at the portal, hovering before Dreyfus' crooked nose, illuminating his petrified face. Awash in an alien light, the gawky man scrambled onto his feet in a heart-pounding panic. Stumbling backward across the raised platform to the eight-foot-high ledge, an invisible push sent him reeling off the Great Step. Slamming his head and shoulders into the hard limestone at an awkward angle, he tumbled halfway down the stepped corridor before rolling to a stop. Writhing in abject pain, broken and defenseless on his side, his eyes widened onto the light growing into a luminous star-filled apparition above his battered body. Dreyfus' terrorized screams were drowned by the phantasm's explosive release of malevolent energy, casting the ancient corridor in sharp relief before total blackness consumed his stricken form.

Rendered sightless following the explosion, mind-numbing paralysis and an unnerving out-of-body sensation overwhelmed Dreyfus. The man of science felt his body lift off the floor. His torch released from arthritic fingers, clanking to the bottom of the Grand Gallery. Elevating toward the high ceiling inside the chamber, he searched his mind for answers but found it impossible to concentrate, as if drugged. Floating through the nebulous miasma, random thoughts addled his brain. "Am I still inside the pyramid? Hard to say. Am I moving up or down? Impossible to tell the difference."

Dreyfus closed his eyes and thought of his farmhouse outside Aix-en-Provence. How he wished he could experience it one more time. Mere weeks from an idyllic retired life, wry laughter resounded in his ears as if the spiteful chortle came from someone else. His mind tripped over a random lucidity: "I am suffering from oxygen-deprived hallucinations, and reality is now a strange illusion."

Vivid scenes flooded his mind's eye: Civilizations populated not only with humans but bizarre creatures from somewhere else. Machines of war filled the skies. Contemplating whether the visions exposed a war-torn future or an ancient past, he sees a youthful man and woman in strange attire appear from the ether like actors on a cosmic stage. The blond woman clutches a golden elliptical shape against her chest as they flee the same alien phantasm responsible for his current plight.

* * *

Sprawled on a black granite floor polished to a reflective sheen, Dreyfus' eyelids snapped open, revealing rheumy bloodshot eyeballs. His shirt clung to his skin from dried sweat and dust, and thinning hair hung over his dirt-streaked face in gray strands. A foul mixture of drool and sand caked on his stubbled cheeks and chin. He wiped bloody grit from his swollen eyes on a tattered sleeve. "How long was I asleep? What is this place? How did I get here?"

The ambient glow from a triangular edifice pierced his blurred vision. At the top, a bright ovular shape, like the ellipse held by the woman in his dream, held his gaze in an iron grip. Its brilliance dazzled the scientist, overwhelming his soulless bearing with an uncharacteristic wanton craving for its all-consuming power. His cracked skull pounded with the all-too-evident reality before him: the structure's vivid pulsations, symphonic overture, and shimmering ellipse lay beyond his woeful and pathetic human intellect.

Dreyfus struggled onto bruised and battered legs, feeling his way to the base of the top nineteen feet of the beacon's exposed height, like an untold number of recruits back to the prehistoric past. He extended a bony right hand toward the golden brightness piercing his foggy vision, attempting to touch it, "I am standing before the most significant archeological find in human history, and I'm blind as a bat. Damn, my bad fortune."

"Yes, Armand, it is yours for the taking. All you must do is climb the beacon and remove the golden ellipse! The archeological mysteries will all be revealed."

Dreyfus collapsed upon the beacon's north-facing facade. Probing his hands across the carved matrix, he sought handholds to pull himself upward. Electric shocks jolted his form and singed his skin, while rhythmic vibrations permeated his arthritic bones as he willed himself toward the bright, blurry shape. Dreyfus' left boot caught in a deep groove, and one heave later, he pulled his worn-out frame to the elliptical power source.

More malevolent voices filled the old man's head, *"Dreyfus, it is right in front of you! Remove the ellipse and embrace its power."*

The archeologist lay face down, spread-eagled against the beacon, twenty feet off the shiny black floor. Fumbling hands across the glowing shape below his bloody nose, tears of relief welled in his useless eyes when his fingertips felt the curved edge of the elliptical shape. Weeping like a fragile child, he pushed his fingertips underneath as far as they would go and slid them up the sides. With his crooked fingers holding both ends of the oval, he pressed long bony thumbs down onto the brilliant, honeycombed surface to achieve the firmest grip he could muster. After one tentative tug, Dreyfus cried out loud and pulled back as hard as his broken body could muster.

Dreyfus' ignited form was expelled with violent and impenitent force, slamming him into the hieroglyphic-covered black granite dome like a rag doll where he lay sprawled on the smooth granite in a smoking heap of flesh and bone, burned beyond recognition.

Above his smoldering form, the golden ellipse remained functional and secure in its mirrored keep while the Machine resumed its normal operating mode.

* * *

The Dark Specters were not through with Armand Dreyfus. They reappeared out of the charged air inside the hidden chamber underneath the Great Pyramid of Giza, radiating hatred and disgust for the worthless, charred mess littering the stone floor. A powerful gust swirled the burnt, lifeless body into a dark vortex, spiriting him to a faraway place.

Armand Dreyfus awoke to the familiar sounds of rustling leaves and chirping birds. The rich aroma of tobacco smoke wafted to his crooked nose from his favorite pipe nestled in his gnarled hand as he swayed to and fro, slumped in his trusty bent-wood rocking chair. Gazing at the bucolic countryside and the familiar outline of Montagne Sainte-Victoire on the horizon from the vantage of his farmhouse porch in the South of France, he produced a contented smile across his stubbled face.

A disembodied voice invaded his tranquil repose. *"Monsieur Dreyfus, you can remain here for as long as you desire. All we ask in return is your assistance at a point in the future."*

Dreyfus' gaze never left the horizon, "Will it involve the flying machines from my dreams?"

"Yes, Armand, you are correct."

The exhausted Frenchman acquiesced, drifting into a deep slumber. While his consciousness rested, his physical manifestation ebbed into a black silhouette of malevolent stars before returning to the visage of a retired man of science named Armand Dreyfus.

* * *

Hours before sunrise on the morning after Napoleon's ballyhooed night in the pyramid, the general stumbled out of the robbers entrance into the invigorating morning air and collapsed in a heap. Soldiers abandoned their posts, raced to their leader's aid, carried him off the weathered blocks, and placed him on an outstretched blanket. Within minutes, Napoleon's physician arrived on the scene in a harried and disheveled state, thinning gray hair askew and last evening's alcoholic binge still lingering on his breath.

The doctor knelt beside Napoleon and elevated his head so he could drink from a canteen. "What happened inside the pyramid, sir?" Casting his eyes around the scene, he asks the heaving man, "And where is Dreyfus?"

The disheveled general did not reply. Bolting upright, he drained the canteen, oblivious to the gathering crowd, eager to hear about the legendary general's experience inside the infamous pyramid.

Napoleon Bonaparte, the conqueror of Egypt, turned to his physician, "Even If I told you, you would not believe me."

**Space tourism is a logical outgrowth of the
adventure tourist market.**

– Buzz Aldrin

Chapter One:

The Honeymoon

Rachel and Owen | Buzz Aldrin Spaceport, Nevada

08:35 a.m. | August 16, 2044

A Las Vegas taxi glides through stopped traffic and wedges between parked cars along the white curb in front of the brand-new Buzz Aldrin Spaceport Terminal. Honeymooners Rachel and Owen Haig jump out and grab their luggage, waving goodbye—and good riddance—to the lead-footed driver. The e-car whirs into traffic back toward the Strip as the couple rolls their bags onto the curb.

Suppressing concerns that they overpacked, Owen wipes his brow in the early morning desert heat and stares in awe through his mirrored shades at the massive terminal and its soaring glass facade reflecting the cerulean Nevada sky, and produces a broad white smile, "I can't believe we're finally here."

Eager to embark on this iconic chapter in his young and adventurous life that he gets to share with his new bride, he turns and finds her missing. "Rachel?"

Squinting through the crowds outside the terminal, Owen spies Rachel wheeling cumbersome luggage through throngs of travelers around a spectacular water fountain fronting the glass building. His focus shifts onto the spaceport namesake's larger-than-life heavenward gaze cast in bronze, standing atop a chiseled base centered within the 58-foot diameter crystal-clear bubbling waters.

Grappling suitcases under both arms with another wheeled monster in tow, Owen nudges through a group of spry seniors on a day trip to the terminal. Hastening his pace, oblivious to the sour looks while angling toward Rachel, his attention is diverted by a space exploration timeline etched into the fountain's black granite retaining wall—from the 1950s to the revolutionary seed change heralding the advent of space tourism in 2034. Craning over and around the tanned, well-heeled retirees, Owen skims chiseled dates to the last marker commemorating the Nevada IOSC hub's ribbon-cutting ceremony on January 9, 2044, "Wow, a lot has happened in eight short months."

Ignoring his new wife's already familiar hand-on-hip impatient stance, "Hey, Rachel, hold up. I want to take your picture in front of the Buzz Aldrin fountain before we head inside."

Oversized tortoiseshell designer frames conceal her impatient eye roll, "Owen, we're barely out of the cab, and you're already breaking your promise about turning everything into a photo shoot. Plus, what did I say about reading every sign?"

"Don't do it?"

"Bingo."

Deflecting Rachel's annoyed reply, Owen palms his precious credit-card-thin Nikon hi-def holographic camera in his raised right hand and flashes a persuasive dimpled smile, "Just one picture, I swear."

Recalling battles with her little brother on family trips, she acquiesces, but with a caveat, "Okay. But make it quick. All these people are heading in the same direction as us."

"That's true, but there are two liftoffs out of here today, ours and the Sapporo flight. The rest of these tanned snowbirds are here for the nickel tour."

After capturing a photo of his beautiful new bride in hologram mode and a few candid shots for posterity, Owen notes more luggage-bound space tourists crowding past, "Well, what are we waiting for? Let's head to the counter and check our bags. For as much as our luggage cost, I wish I had figured out how to activate the autonomous mode."

Pulling the bulky suitcases, smaller versions stacked atop, Owen readjusts thick straps from a backpack and a satchel on his broad shoulders. With two more bags, Rachel follows her lead blocker through the bustle of spaceport employees, security personnel, and the growing crowd of fellow nascent space tourists.

The natural beauty's lithesome frame and graceful stride draw furtive glances from men, women, and even a few more advanced synthetic humanoids. Rachel is blind to what they see. Although she despises false modesty, her honest self-appraisal details a litany of physical shortcomings: mousy-colored straight hair, too tall, too skinny, and flat-chested. Her wedding day lineup of bridesmaids put her to shame. Those girls she had known since kindergarten had grown into ravishing beauties. She doubted she would see much more of them after her wedding. They remained the same catty group from high school; she was the one who had changed.

Aware of her husband's propensity for posting images without her consent, "I want to approve photos before you share them, Owen."

"No problem, Rachel," laughing while maneuvering his right-hand suitcase around uncooperative strangers, within inches of dead legging a guy, "You never take a bad picture."

"You are not exactly an unbiased observer."

"Trust me; I observe plenty."

Rachel's side-parted dark-blond tresses frame her expressive green eyes and fresh face, cascading in subtle waves over toned shoulders to the small of her back. Sunny highlights and a trace of freckles sprinkled across her straight pert nose are souvenirs from the past two languorous days spent poolside at their posh Vegas hotel, drink in hand. Her idea of a vacation. Now it was Owen's turn.

Rachel tugs at bag straps hanging from the shoulder of her tassel-sleeved, chocolate-brown suede jacket, wondering when the promised fun starts. Matching her athletic husband's long gait, the 24-year-old bites her lower lip sidestepping fellow tourists with a nervous smile. Patting her olive safari shorts, she checks for the tissue-wrapped anxiety pills her mother gave her, just in case.

A tall scarecrow of a man with a long gray beard and a bandana on his weathered noggin notices the vintage Ziggy Stardust t-shirt under Rachel's jacket and shoots her a smiling wink while shuffling past. She stumbled upon the 70s throwback in the Hard Rock Hotel gift shop on the Vegas Strip and decided to wear it in honor of the iconic rocker's space travel fascination.

The new Mrs. Rachel Haig is not alone in loathing what passes for popular culture in 2044. While the topic fails to interest a tin-eared number-cruncher like Owen, she nonetheless favors art, style, and especially the music of the bygone yet easily accessible analog era. Her fortress of solitude is wearing old-fashioned noise-canceling headphones while spinning LP records on the antique turntable her father finally relented and gave to her when he couldn't stop her from borrowing it anyway.

A worn-in pair of vintage brown leather Chelsea boots—her favorite thing—complete her eclectic ensemble, accentuating her long tan legs and taut calves. While far from a health nut, Rachel's daily yoga and on-again, off-again exercise regimen in the lead-up to squeezing into her wedding dress have her honed and ready for anything, she hopes.

Sidling through the sea of humanity within the echoing atrium,

Rachel brushes past an attractive female information attendant. Excusing herself, she wonders: human or synthetic? It is almost impossible to tell the difference. Regardless, all spaceport personnel dressed to the nines in the same military-style space-gray uniforms perform their assigned duties and greet apprehensive space tourism pioneers with confident and courteous *Enjoy the ride* smiles.

When the Haigs' take their turn at the luggage counter, they heft the baggage onto large scales, like any airport check-in counter. Bionic arms grapple the suitcases onto a conveyor rolling through a dark square portal. An observant supervisor realizes the couple has no idea what to do next and motions toward a device, like a miniaturized overhead projector, instructing them how to scan luggage SKUs onto their forearm ticket implants. "You don't want your stuff to end up in Sapporo, right?" Rachel raises a brown eyebrow in agreement with the woman's rhetorical question, watching a greenish beam scan the embedded chip under the smooth skin of her upheld left forearm.

On the cusp of completing the procedure, a distinguished-looking Egyptian in a tailored light-tan suit bumps her arm while grabbing a handful of old-school name tags from the adjacent countertop. After a brief awkward silence, the dark-complexioned man, sporting a clean-shaved head, apologizes with a disarming smile and heavily accented, "Excuse me, madame."

Owen watches the guy meld into the crowd, "Do you know him, Rachel?"

"I've never seen him before, yet he looked at me like he knew me."

"Or maybe he wanted to make your acquaintance, if you get my drift."

"If he is a wealthy sheik. Who knows?"

Owen addresses the smirking supervisor enjoying the conversation from across the counter, "Ma'am, are we through here?"

Double-checking her screen, the smiling lady sends Owen and

Rachel on their way with a rote, "Enjoy the ride." while motioning for the next space tourist to come on down.

Liberated from their cumbersome luggage, the Haigs follow signage pointing toward the security line. Meanwhile, their bulky suitcases embark on an underground journey toward Launch Pad B, bumping, grinding, and twirling across mechanized conveyors through pitch-black tunnels far beneath the broiling Nevada desert.

Parting through the unfinished terminal, Rachel notes a heavy presence of engineers and hard-hatted worker bees with thin-veiled apprehension, worrying her life is in the hands of a not-ready-for-primetime outfit. She hears more than sees drones buzzing about the steel-beam rafters, high overhead in the cavernous glass-enclosed terminal, operated by white-coated technicians consulting holographic site plans. Rounding a corner beyond a row of chic storefronts still touting their grand openings—and a Starbucks—toward security, they trail behind others through a plywood-lined pathway bisecting a construction zone stamped with Coming Soon! Maria's Cantina Bar and Restaurant. Maria's first frozen margarita is still months away if the din from hammering and screeching saws and the incandescent glow of welding torches from the opposite sides of the eight-foot wooden barriers are any indication. That's too bad.

Rachel glances above the planks at the razor-sharp two-story video walls looming high above their heads, morphing through a litany of sponsors, eager to establish a presence in the space tourism arena. "I hope our spaceship is finished by the time we board."

"This is all window dressing, Rachel. The important stuff is fully operational."

Exiting the construction chokepoint dumps them at the back end of a serpentine security line where the couple drops their carry-ons at their feet.

Suppressing a sudden urge to run out into the sweltering parking lot and not look back, Rachel loops a flaxen strand behind her ear, "This is the security line? I feel like a mouse in a maze."

Ignoring the mouse comment, her new husband, with his rakish appearance and short auburn hair, rolls the left sleeve of his mint-green button-down L.L. Bean shirt. Verging on giving the bio-absorbable ticket implant buried in his sinewy forearm a good scratch, Rachel admonishes him to leave it alone.

"You're going to break it."

"The darn thing itches like crazy!" Owen attempts to distract from the palpable anxiety masked behind his beautiful new wife's worried face with a muscular shrug. Raising thick eyebrows while spreading a mischievous smile, dimpling clean-shaven cheeks, he scoots backward to clear a little floor space around their place in line, "How's that? Better?"

"A little." Reciprocating a bright smile, Rachel looks into the compassionate hazel eyes of the man she married, wondering if her life will ever be ordinary. It was hard to believe their ceremony for the ages was just four short days ago. The raucous reception was probably still going on for all she knew.

Accustomed to his wily masculine charms, she plays along with his diversion, "Owen, the implants were your idea. We could have chosen a paper ticket voucher like my friend at the luggage counter and squeezed one thin sheet of paper into our bags."

"I am trying to ensure we fully experience everything possible. We are about to travel into space on the most advanced craft ever built by humankind, not flying coach on a redeye to O'Hare. It's just a little forewarning that my microchip would itch like an SOB could have been nice." Raising a defiant index finger to accentuate the faux seriousness behind his point, "They figured out anti-gravity, but this," pointing at his arm, "is beyond their ability to reverse engineer."

Rolling his sleeve back down, he turns to the eavesdropping woman standing behind him and nods, "How are you doing?" The woman's face reminds him of the actress from the insurance commercials, but he refrains from saying so aloud.

"You'll live, big guy," Rachel concludes, moving on from one of their first and most inconsequential spats. Scanning the line in front of them and beyond the nosy woman to new groups arriving on their heels, she can't help but notice there is no way out.

Catching everyone's attention, a tall and dark man sporting the standard space-gray uniform delineated with thin gold braiding and a triangular medallion on his left breast pocket saunters past their position. A recollection of endless lines waiting to enter Space Mountain and the less-than-unenthusiastic Disneyland ride operators springs into Rachel's active mind.

The man reached the high-tech podium at the front of the cue as if time had no meaning. With every eye upon him in rapt anticipation, he presses a button, and a screen hums to life, reflected in his dark eyes. More agonizing minutes pass, watching him log in and stare at the bright display as if perusing a message from his robot relations union. Finally, an impatient wave moves the first group forward, scanning forearm ticket implants and a smattering of non-itchy paper vouchers at a plodding rhythmic pace.

Slow walking along the line, Rachel can't resist a subtle jab at her new spouse, "We would be much further up in line if not for your impromptu photoshoot outside. If we don't make it onto the next ground shuttle, it can take over an hour for another to return and transport the next load of passengers."

"We'll make it. We have a secret weapon."

"What are you talking about?"

"Check out the folks in front of us; if we can't race past a bunch of them, we're doing something wrong."

A middle-aged man glances over his shoulder at Owen, an irritated expression on his face.

Rachel gestures toward the man, "Indoor voice, Owen."

Winding to the front of the security checkpoint, the

honeymooners shift carry-on bags to their right sides to position their left forearms beneath the scanner under the watchful stare of the stone-faced robot. He cross-checks them on his display and sends them through with a dismissive wave.

Owen can't resist an impertinent snipe, "You know the Starbucks is open back there; perhaps a little caffeine will help you speed things along. It works every time, even for a humanoid."

The cold return stare freaks Owen out, "Bad idea."

Leaving Mr. Personality in their wake, the Haigs race down a long concourse, cutting past the slow family and several other passenger clusters in no apparent rush to wedge into the SRO shuttle ahead.

Owen and Rachel reach the open portal and vault side-by-side through the people mover's glass doors before they slide airtight with a whoosh of air. Forward momentum pushes the couple into fellow passengers jockeying for position inside the 10-wheeled behemoth as it lurches toward Launch Pad B.

Owen emits a relieved sigh, grateful they were not among those awaiting another people mover in the uncomfortable makeshift waiting area at the terminus of the long concourse, enduring Rachel's "I told you so." on an endless loop.

The transport lumbers around a curve in the deep-trodden tracks. Rachel's stance widens, maintaining balance while sensing male and female passengers' sideways glances in her direction. Grabbing the nearest handhold dangling from the ceiling, she shakes an unruly blond lock from her face and glares at a smiling Owen, "You had better lose the shit-eating grin, my friend. You swore I would not regret agreeing to your outer space adventure. So far, I am not impressed. We could be sipping daiquiris by the pool at the Bellagio right now. Margo made them just how I like them, full of alcohol."

"Funny, Rachel. In my defense, I showed you the rendering of the high-speed monorail in the brochure. It's going to replace this bumpy ride out to the launch pads. It will be the ultimate experience.

Since this facility is still under construction, we must grin and bear it. Next time we can stop at Maria's Cantina and have a margarita. How about that?"

"The next time? Let's survive this time first."

A deep voice resonates inside the people mover, *"Greetings, space tourism pioneers! Welcome once again to the Buzz Aldrin International Spaceport. We are at about the halfway point on the short ride out to Launch Pad B. The passenger area is crowded. Please try to make room for everybody. Sorry for the inconvenience. If you can see outside the windows on the left side of the transport, you'll note pillars and track under construction for the monorail scheduled for completion by mid-2045. The International Outer Space Consortium is working hard to make your trip into space a safe, comfortable, and memorable experience for all. Enjoy the ride."*

Angling his view between two bobbing heads silhouetted by the bright sunshine out the tinted windows, the avid photographer zooms onto the most technologically advanced engineering project to hit the Nevada desert since the Hoover Dam. The massive pillars and mesh of interlocking rebar and thin steel beams connecting at the tops of the even-spaced structures jutting out of the scrub and brush, surrounded by cranes, earthmovers, drones, and workers, toiling in the heat to realize the Consortium's aggressive timeline is an impressive sight. For Owen, that is.

In place of the monorail, the enormous people mover gouges a deepening track in the desert hardpan transporting space tourists from the centralized air-conditioned comfort of the terminal across 20 miles of open desert to the awe-inspiring launch pads. On other days, these same transports trundle through the desert to ferry wobbly-knee astronaut arrivals back to the terminal. Though operational, the International Outer Space Consortium's Nevada hub lagged behind other locations, such as the Toulouse, France hub. The destination for all the travelers crowded inside the people mover like a can of sardines.

Owen twists the grasp on his handhold, peering outside to get his first look at the ship resting atop sixteen stories of trestles, girders, and beams as it comes into view over a ridge. The ride speeds up, descending into the deep valley toward their launch pad, one of three in the desert, each approximately 20 miles from the centrally located terminal.

Rachel cannot help but smile at the excited look on her husband's face.

Despite an advertising blitz for the ages, the growing fleet of black triangular spacecraft prompts breathless reports of UFO sightings too numerous to bother counting anymore. The majestic ship sits atop the launch pad superstructure teeming with preflight activity. After a few more bumpy minutes, the people mover reaches a turnaround, jerks to a halt, and reverses into a receiving alcove below a video wall animating Welcome to Launch Pad B in multiple languages. A hexagonal tube telescopes from the terminal structure and attaches to the rear of the dusty transport. A melodious chime and blinking lights indicate it is time to disembark.

The deep disembodied voice repeats: *"Enjoy the ride."*

Standing in front of what is now the exit, the double doors they vaulted through earlier swoosh open, and the couple hefts their bags and hastens to depart with a stampede of eager passengers on their heels. Entering the launch pad receiving area, they follow a marked path allowing fellow travelers to bustle past. Owen ignores a cloned welcome bot, navigating an iron forest of beams, trestles, pipes, and ductwork with an eye out for the nearest lavatory facility, "Not a restroom in sight."

"You are going to have to wait. I'm fine, by the way."

Ignoring his bladder, Owen guides Rachel toward banks of elevators and the promise of facilities somewhere beyond. A perky female humanoid blocks their path, asking to touch Rachel's forearm. Rachel extends her arm, suppressing a mean smile, realizing the lovely bot is delaying a much-needed trip to the loo. "Of course. Here you are. Which way do we need to go?"

"Welcome aboard, Mr. and Mrs. Haig." Twirling with a stiff-arm, mannequin-like pose, she motions toward the bank of elevators farthest to the left.

"You are enjoying this a little too much."

"Why, Owen Haig, whatever do you mean?"

The jolt of the high-speed elevator compounds Rachel's motion sickness from Vegas through the cramped, bumpy ride across the desert. The doors glide open, and they step onto the spaceship's packed promenade deck with fellow disoriented passengers looking for seat assignments farther within the ship's midsection through portals illuminated with large backlit numbers. Rachel scans both directions as far as she can see. "Owen, we are nowhere near our section."

"That's too bad. I gotta pee."

Waiting for Owen to do his business, Rachel breathes the filtered air and takes in the reserved vibe inside the ship, reminiscent of pre-game jitters inside a tense locker room at one of her father's arenas. Her first impressions of the featureless interior are: dull, drab, and unappealing, in that order. The smooth, seamless surfaces lack any human aesthetic. The only visual stimulation comes from muted blue and green lighting. Her inner cynic postulates that the cool-toned palette emanated from an overpaid interior design firm's mission to calm jangled nerves. Armchair psychology would not work in her case. More than a little anxious, she considers abandoning her new husband on the promenade deck before he can exit the restroom.

Instead, Rachel joins a group of disoriented passengers studying a holographic seating chart, searching for the shortest routes to their assigned seats. When it's her turn, she removes her chip arm from her tasseled jacket sleeve and positions it under the scanner. A glowing line animates from You Are Here to Section D on the opposite side of the ship before snaking down to Seats 21 and 22 in the front row, facing inward toward the circular void constituting the middle of the triangular ship.

Her familiarity with the ship's state-of-the-art passenger layout was due to hearing Owen's verbatim recitation from his precious brochure on a loop. Friends and family members—grocery store clerks—anyone showing even a feint amount of interest got the spiel: "It's no different from a theater in the round, except the 36-foot diameter stage is the cold vacuum of space with Earth and a limitless expanse of stars the ultimate backdrop."

The punchline was left to her improvisational skills, which typically went like this: "Hamlet had better be wearing a spacesuit."

The happy thought causes her pouting lips to curve into a slight smile, which Owen, exiting the loo, attributes to her, making eye contact with him.

* * *

Owen exits the restroom with his bladder emptied in the nick of time. He catches Rachel smiling in his direction while conversing with fellow newbie astronauts taking turns using a holographic seating chart. Not wanting to interrupt—and relieved she appears relaxed and enjoying herself—he gestures down the crowded promenade, mouthing, "Stay there; I'll be back in a moment."

Wandering into the crowd, the oblivious new husband misses his wife's pantomimed "What the hell?"

Owen's initial reaction, admiring the ship's relaxing interior ambiance: the blue and green lighting calms jangled nerves—a brilliant choice—and no doubt, money well spent.

Parting a quartet of Asians in blithe conversation, he discovers a paper-thin widescreen display featuring an interactive timeline of space tourism languishing in a forgotten corner. Glancing around, Owen shrugs, a little disappointed but not too surprised by the general apathy toward anything with a whiff of educational content.

Since his homeschooled youth, Owen read every placard or display he encountered, a post-engagement quirk Rachel discovered on an interminable day trip to a natural history museum. In keeping with his reputation, he peruses the touchscreen's interactive navigation while tuning out the commotion behind his wide-legged stance. He selects **Annotated History of Space Exploration** with a firm tap, and a series of conspiracy-fueled Atomic Age newspaper headlines morph across the screen, including the Roswell incident. "One of the worst-kept secrets in modern history."

On borrowed time, Owen fast-forwards from Project Mercury through the space shuttle and the ISS to astronaut, scientist, engineer profiles, the Space Force, and NASA's Artemis Program. As planned, the public and private venture returned humankind to the Moon in 2024. And numerous more times after that, culminating in a permanent base under Chinese auspices. The scheduled mission to Mars in 2030 was shelved when the revelation of a game-changing mode of propulsion was teased. Owen slows his scroll on February 2, 2034, studying a hi-resolution wide-angle image of a V-shaped craft hovering twenty feet above the desert floor. A three-row shoulder-to-shoulder assemblage of 53 world leaders with President Christopher Pratt beaming from the middle of the front row stands in its angular shadow. The politicians are flanked on both sides by an international gathering of white-coated scientists and engineers. Owen zooms in on an older man in an undertaker-style black suit, barely making the crop on the left edge of the image. He notices a cactus-shaped bolo tie gleaming at the man's starched white shirt collar and the jaunty grin on his distinguished face. "One of these things is not like the others."

The caption below the historic image describes the paradigm shift unveiling of the first anti-gravity propulsion craft before an impressive gathering of leaders and a thunderstruck human populace. However, the floating ship—as remarkable as it was—paled next to the real story of the day: disclosure of how, when, and where a clandestine cadre of engineers and scientists came to possess the advanced alien technology. The levitating craft represented the culmination of decades of top-secret work accomplished under strange and mysterious circumstances by multiple generations of individuals from science, industry, and the military, not to mention a few select advisors from more exotic locales.

At the bottom of the screen, he scans a pull quote from Pope John Paul III:

"After decades of secrecy, I pray the revelation we are indeed not alone in the universe will compel all of God's creation to live in peace and harmony."

"Nice try."

The historical event did portend a cascade of consequences for humanity. Owen breezes through the highlights. Some good. Some not so good.

The conspiracy theory crowd was not to be denied in their fanatic attempts to see little green men. On a low simmer since the days of Project Blue Book and sci-fi shows like the X-Files, the UFO subculture ethos boiled over after Disclosure Day in 2034. A groundswell *I KNEW IT* movement went beyond viral, and the southwestern desert environs encompassing Area 51 became ground zero for every attention-seeking freak and lunatic worldwide.

Unfortunately for the vloggers and documentarians, ET selfies were not forthcoming soon. Even for a world marinating in science fiction since H.G. Wells, anti-gravity failed to hold widespread interest post its initial shock value. The jaded public had witnessed so many staged technology announcements by the late twenties that companies like Apple eschewed them altogether. Their first female CEO broke it down ably enough at the time: "Just put it out there, and people will buy it. That simple."

Furthering her point, the levitating black triangle ceremony in the Nevada desert was hardly the first time an invention was made possible with backward-engineered technology. Anyone with half a brain understood that.

Their governments' sudden affinity for candor dumbfounded savvy ufologists, fringe commentators, and conspiracy nuts. A burgeoning group among the commentariat remained skeptical after Disclosure Day. They proposed the unnerving hypothesis that humans were being preconditioned to WE ARE NOT ALONE because something more portentous loomed over the horizon. But what?

In an ironic twist, the iconic photo's location, marked by a well-maintained bronze plaque, is not far from where Owen now stood aboard the spaceship.

Second, the war on terror, ratcheted to an untenable level by the late 20s and early 30s, was squashed in its bloody tracks by the stunning announcement. The dogmatic and hysterical rants of authoritarian terrorist leaders were laid bare by the news that humans were not alone in our crowded universe. Nevertheless, an obstinate group of deniers held sway over large clusters of malleable acolytes in dangerous hotspots worldwide.

For Owen, the most significant aspect of Disclosure Day was announcing a new agency with the all-encompassing moniker of the International Outer Space Consortium. The mission of this noble enterprise? Answering *"What's next?"* and the less sexy yet pragmatic follow-up: *"And how do we pay for it?"*

Owen could answer the second part with his wallet over 200 grand lighter, but he did not care. This trip fulfills his childhood dream of becoming an astronaut, and he gets to experience it with Rachel.

Owen's hand accidentally grazes a button, and a litany of celebrity ruminations, starting with a 71-year-old Brad Pitt, hijacks the screen. Uninterested in celebrity ramblings on the most important date in history, he swipes left and glances over his shoulder, wondering what happened to Rachel. Returning to the screen, he selects the presentation's final section, a non-engineer dissertation on the revolutionary anti-gravity propulsion technology.

"Sorry. Still beyond my pay grade."

Moving on, he sees an animated infographic illustrating how 288 passengers are launched 250 miles above Earth before orbiting a predetermined number of times and touching down at one of five other IOSC sites around the globe.

Avoiding the celebrity tribute button, he taps another icon, opening a cinematic clip of an orbiting triangular ship with the same baritone narration. Owen's mind wanders, trying to identify the actor behind the deep, mellifluous voice.

The video drones on, and Owen refocuses his attention, "… *passenger-carrying spaceship operated by the International Outer Space Consortium is an aeronautical marvel. Measuring over the length of a football field on each equilateral side, the ship's matte-black finish is made from trillions of nano-sized tiles lending its signature undulating visual effect. Comparisons range from a windblown wheat field to the shimmering surface of a lake. However, they appear to your eyes, those tiny tiles are engineered to withstand the immutable physical laws imposed on a spacecraft elevating fragile humans, meaning you (laughs) into the thermosphere. Meanwhile, you and your loved ones are safe and comfortable inside the craft.*"

The video transitions onto a mechanical head with the left side of its handsome facial features missing, revealing a mass of wires, chips, and a gooey, pinkish substance. A human technician enters the frame and installs the missing half of the face, the robot blinking and smiling toward the camera. The narration continues: "*On your voyage into space, you will be in the capable hands of top-of-the-line Kobayashi Corporation synthetic attendants. They are at your disposal, and unlike you and me, they are at ease in the microgravity weightlessness aboard the craft. If you need anything while in orbit, give them a holler; they will float over and attend to your needs. And please remember to be courteous to our robot friends.*"

As the short movie enters its third and final act, a montage of space tourism imagery morphs across the screen. The narrator addresses the salient query from earlier: How to pay for this expensive venture into space. "*… While space tourism is a diversion enjoyed by influential* *movers and shakers, such as yourself, remember that four to fifteen ships filled with space tourists are in orbit daily. From every walk of life, our outreach program to the young and old alike ensures citizens from every continent enjoy a sense of ownership in humanity's mission to the stars. After all, the first astronaut to leave our solar system using this technology exists somewhere out there, even as I speak.*

From our inaugural trips into space a mere two years ago in 2042 through to the tickets you purchased for your trip, the price per seat has reduced from six figures into the high five-digit range, subject to your tier and seat locations, of course. By flying on one of our new spaceships, you contribute to humankind's quest for knowledge, and the International Outer Space Consortium, by purchasing your tickets, upgrades, souvenirs, and generous donations. Even with the giant leap forward provided by the backward-engineered extraterrestrial technology, without the help of space tourists like you, extraplanetary ventures to Mars, for example, would be impossible. So, thanks again for listening, and oh, by the way, enjoy the ride."

Owen produces a rhetorical chuckle, "I didn't realize throwing a huge wad of cash to impress a girl could appear so magnanimous." Owen's splurge on the equivalent of front-row seats directly behind home plate cost a small fortune. "She's worth every penny."

Rachel, ears burning, pokes him in the shoulder, "Who is worth every penny?"

"You are, but you better stop sneaking up like that, or I may change my mind."

Rachel shakes her head, finding her husband getting his inner nerd on reading another widescreen distraction, "I'm having flashbacks to waiting around for you at the Field Museum. If I can pull you from your two-dimensional friend here, I found the best path to our seats. I'd like to sit down and relax with a drink before launching into orbit. Would you care to join me?"

* * *

The pair enter at the upper end of their wedge-shaped Section D and nod past fellow travelers down to front row seats 21 and 22. After stowing carry-ons in sealed under-seat compartments, Rachel perches on the edge of Seat 22 and looks out the floor-to-ceiling window curved around the ship's centered open rotunda. "I'm getting vertigo, and we have not even left the ground."

Peering across the 36-foot circular void, she watches their opposite numbers discovering assigned seats and stowing bags. A little boy holds up a toy replica of the triangle-shaped spaceship, beaming across the vastness with an adorable smile toward Rachel. Owen notes her magnetic charm for the millionth time, watching her reciprocate a friendly wave.

The equilateral spaceship's curved window onto the expansive centered rotunda affords every passenger an unobstructed view of the only home humanity has ever known. One minor detail Rachel failed to glean from Owen's brochure is how the ultra-clear-polymer design bends underneath the innermost circle of seats, broadening the perspective and heightening the sensation of being on the float.

With another bite at her lower lip, she taps the heel of her Chelsea boot on the transparent floor, eliciting a dull thud in return. The dizzying straight-down perspective reminds her of the bridge extending over the Grand Canyon, which she adamantly refused to traverse on an earlier, Owen-inspired trip. Yet here she sits.

"Man, it is a long way down. Can you call over one of those helpful attendants? I need some liquid courage right about now."

A short time later, after the semi-flirtatious sommelier comes and goes, Rachel remains seated with her first pouch of wine while Owen ventures on an impromptu exploration. Sinking her back into seat 22, she glances left across the narrow aisle toward seats 23 and 24, occupied by an older Asian couple. Sipping from the plastic pouch, she surreptitiously watches them holding hands across their middle armrest while smiling out the window. To her right, across from Owen's empty seat, she notices the same distinguished-looking Egyptian man in the light-tan suit hammering away at the keys on his holographic keyboard, "Geez, give it a break."

Rachel contemplates whether the odd fellow recalls cutting in front of her at the counter. The bald man glances like he could read her thoughts, nodding a curt hello, and returns to typing. Watching him tap glowing translucent keys hovering above his lap, she tries to remember when physical devices became obsolete. As if in response, her earphone chimes.

"Hello gorgeous, anybody hit on you while I'm away?"

"Not yet, Owen. But I have my eye on the sommelier. She is quite a charmer."

"That's a new one. I'm almost finished exploring the ship. Can I get you anything before I return?

"Another pouch of chardonnay would be nice."

A few minutes later, Owen plops in his seat and hands his new bride her liquid courage. "Just like the astronauts, don't get drunk and pass out on me. You'll miss the launch!"

"I can assure you, there is not enough alcohol on this entire ship to make me bombed enough to sleep through the liftoff."

The extended preflight time aboard the ship relaxed Rachel's active, what-if imagination, quelling her initial fears of space flight. Envious of Owen's daredevil risk-taking personae—especially if it involves heights—she leans toward more grounded pursuits. Throughout their two-year engagement, nosy family members on both sides of the aisle debate whether they will balance each other's predilections, achieve marital equilibrium, and create great-looking offspring. Time will tell.

From the moment they met at another wedding for someone she barely knew—the daughter of one of her mother's bridge club friends—the scales were tipped in Owen's direction. Rachel found herself doing crazy stuff she never thought she would do. And now, here she sat, sipping wine from a plastic bag with her feet dangling at a perilous height above a threatening mass of girders, beams, wires, and ducts, watching steam and gas venting in all directions, counting down to a controlled liftoff under her well-defined bottom.

The Haig's honeymoon trip consists of hurtling into orbit from the desert two hours north of Las Vegas and performing three-plus breathtaking circuits before touching down in Toulouse, France, seven hours later.

Back on Mother Earth, they will embark upon their French honeymoon. The return journey to their brand-new Manhattan apartment will come via conventional first-class seats on a commercial flight out of Paris.

The couple gazes downward with anticipation and trepidation, watching massive grips at the end of articulated mechanical arms release from the ship and fold into the launch pad like a Swiss Army knife.

"It won't be long now, Rachel," Owen says in an excited, annoying, singsong tone.

"Oh boy," she mutters while sucking the last few drops of crushed grapes from the collapsed wine pouch squeezed tight in her quivering hand.

A razor-thin woman in no-nonsense light-gray suit strides into their section, announcing, "May I please have your attention."

Startled by the abrasive voice coming from up and behind their front row seats, Rachel's eyes widen onto a stern woman with black hair pulled off her prominent forehead into a severe bun framing dark bespectacled eyes, pointed nose, and thin lips.

"Who the hell is this?"

The boisterous passengers fall silent, prompting the woman's lips to curl into a gratuitous smile, "Good. Now that I have your attention, it is time to buckle up. I will check each one of you to ensure your restraints are secure. If you have trouble engaging the buckled apparatus, raise a hand, and I will come by to assist.

Owen's brow furrows onto the tangle of belts and buckles he had ignored until now. "You know, Rach, I don't think 'buckle up' quite describes this rig." Looking at his wife, already halfway buckled for well over two hours, he catches up to her, and together they complete the process. The stern inspector relishes giving Owen's shoulder belt a solid yank.

"Well done, young man."

As the woman moves to check the Asian couple, Owen leans toward Rachel and whispers, "I bet she moonlights at Matilda's House of Perpetual Bondage."

"Owen, sometimes you are too weird for words."

A mechanical voice over the PA interrupts Owen's snarky reply. "All systems go for launch."

Sensing small tremors through their seats, followed by the ship swaying and wobbling, Rachel grabs Owen's arm, "Are we floating off the ground already?"

Owen shrugs, "I'm not sure."

Maybe too much chardonnay. Or not enough.

Never one to overlook life's little ironies, Owen found it amusing that the Nevada hub honored Buzz Aldrin, whose missions into space looked nothing like this: No mission control. No cumbersome tinfoil spacesuits and helmets. No squeezing into a claustrophobic capsule. No dramatic countdown. No radio blackouts. No grainy camera footage. No splashdown and rescue by an aircraft carrier group. No three days of quarantine upon return.

From its nascency in the late 20s as government-subsidized billionaire passion projects competing for rocket-size bragging rights, the notion of space tourism finally came to fruition with the International Outer Space Consortium formation in 2034. A decade later, but just two short years after the first official paid public flights, IOSC quickly became a risk-free diversion for well-heeled patrons like himself. Depending on the hub, the waitlist exceeded a year; with substantial deposits and endless streams of revenue overflowing the coffers, space exploration was full steam ahead.

Aside from pre- and post-flight physical exams, a stunner of a view out the window, and the microgravity, space tourism resembles a ho-hum trans-continental flight. With the confiscatory ticket price and passports, passengers were cleared for takeoff.

The triangular IOSC ships employ a fraction of their astronomical potential, ferrying humans into orbit and back. Engineered around three anti-gravity engines built into streamlined nacelles ball-jointed at each vertex, the omnidirectional craft can hover, accelerate, decelerate, and maneuver on a dime. The backward-engineered ships' flight characteristics would turn fragile human compositions into thick, greasy pools of corpuscular pudding at full throttle.

Early in the test flight phase, The Powers That Be sent one of the expensive ships and a synthetic crew on a Martian trajectory. The entire trip should have taken less than a week to complete at incredible speeds, but the ship vanished into the vacuum of space. The disappointing and expensive loss stymied the PTB engineers and scientists until alien advisors revealed a lurking alien presence destroyed the craft.

Time was running out.

Another well-kept secret is that the periodic table's worth of gasses vented into the atmosphere before, during, and post-launch are due to human engineering limitations. The alien anti-gravity technology has zero effect on its environment. It moves things around for a bit, but they spring right back. Like a good magic trick, it's best not to know too much.

The Gordian knot of ducts and pipelines snaking around the 16-story Platform B recovering every harmful molecule would be much less obtrusive if not for the International Outer Space Consortium's resolute commitment to a green agenda. A requirement for approval in the early years, the mindset permeates every aspect of day-to-day operations, like metastasizing cancerous growth. With the money flowing and everything on fast forward with little to no oversight, why rock the boat?

The Consortium's ET advisors view knee-jerk impulses to modulate advancements with inconsequential environmental add-ons as ridiculous wastes of time and resources. If they could laugh, they most certainly would.

Liftoff | Launch Pad B
01:00 p.m. | August 16, 2044

A rumbling sensation vibrates through hand-sewn leather seats mixed with a chorus of anxious background chatter and an unsettling noise banging in a steady rhythm throughout the ship's interior.

Rachel grabs Owen's left hand, "What the hell is that horrible noise? It sounds like we are inside a giant MRI machine."

"Funny you should say that way, Rachel. An MRI is how the sound is described in the preflight brochure I wanted you to read."

* * *

Beneath the triangular spaceship, anti-gravity propulsion nacelles at each corner generate a warped field, obscuring the launch pad superstructure from view, replaced by shimmering blue light pillars holding the craft aloft high above the desert floor like a three-legged stool. As the black triangle elevates into the Nevada sky, the structure wobbles and distorts back into view.

* * *

Travelogue videos the couple watched with beer and popcorn prove no substitute for the sensorial onslaught coming alive around their restrained positions. A stout fellow sporting a Stetson hat, seated four rows back, shouts an elated whoop-whoop in rhythm with the escalating banging noise. Catching Rachel's pained expression, Owen surmises she would likely relocate the man's hat to where the sun doesn't shine if she could reach him.

The frightening din softens to a rhythmic thumping in 3/4 time as the ship lifts off the pad. As the gigantic black spacecraft shoots into the deep-blue sky, the noise blurs to an inaudible frequency. Meanwhile, Rachel's gaze fixates on the launch pad shrinking to a speck in the southwestern desert below her quivering knees and Chelsea boots.

She is crushing Owen's hand.

The airship accelerates, achieving an altitude of 55,000 feet in no time flat. Suspended at the dizzying, dramatic height, passengers witness Earth's curvature while the crew executes a litany of safety checks. If a life support system malfunctioned or a propulsion engine flashed a warning signal, an emergency return to the same launch pad would be feasible. After ten dramatic minutes, ground control clears a few minor glitches and gives the go-for-orbit command.

Every living soul experiences a brief falling sensation in the pits of their stomachs before the anti-gravitational propulsion sheds Earth's pull with staggering efficiency.

"Here we go, Rachel! Next stop, outer space!"

"I hate you, Owen Haig!"

Pressed into leather seats harder than the brochures would ever admit, every passenger hangs tight to something or someone as the ship vaults to its designated orbit. As the human cargo starts breathing easier and heart rates return to semi-normal, the crew synchs to the nearest ground station far below, transmitting real-time flight data, addressing errors and anomalies, and avoiding the growing ring of space junk. Nothing for the passengers to worry about. "Enjoy the ride."

After the safety checks are completed, seatbelt warning lights switch to OFF; however, many, including Rachel, remain half-belted. Faint murmurs spring forth from passengers expressing varying degrees of awe and trepidation at the fascinating cloud formations and landmasses far below. Meanwhile, attendants float to and fro, taking refreshment orders and attending to apprehensive queries. Unobtrusive janitorial bots dangling hosed vacuum devices suck unfortunate space tourist mishaps and miscellaneous loose articles out of the recycled air.

Adventurous passengers, including Owen, unshackle seconds after the green "You are free to float about the cabin." lights illuminate his section for a preplanned weightless frolic. He asks his new bride to join him, but she passes on the invitation, not wanting to embarrass herself, projectile vomiting in a room full of hovering strangers. An unfortunate soul in her section had already tossed their breakfast; it was not a pretty sight.

Owen Haig floats into the relative darkness within the ship's interior alone, surrounded by a group of kindred daredevils, while the more reserved astronauts remain behind.

* * *

Flying solo after Owen's departure, Rachel tames crazy-hair weightlessness by pulling her flowing locks into a loose-braided ponytail at the nape of her neck. As she finishes, a stylus floats past her face triggering a terrifying self-awareness. Her heart starts to race as vertigo overwhelms her senses.

"Oh no, not now."

Leaning forward, resting her head in her hands, Rachel closes her eyes and inhales recycled air deep into her lungs before a slow and steady exhalation from her mouth. Repeat. A self-taught tried-and-true technique to stave off panic attacks without resorting to the happy pills. Opening her eyes, she concentrates on the confusing mass of greens and blues, splotched with puffy clouds, below her feet. With a mumbled curse, she snatches the floating pen still within reach, shoving it into a Velcro pouch below her left armrest.

Noticing the reflection of her Ziggy Stardust t-shirt in the smooth curved window, a stanza from the iconic song, *Space Oddity*, conjures in her dizzy head, "Well, this is some tin can, and Planet Earth is most definitely blue."

Chastising herself for the sudden panic attack, she recalls her father's wedding speech, which deviated into a commentary on living in a time of such technological achievement. Here she is, experiencing what only a select few in previous generations could imagine doing. No more panic attacks, and that would be the end of it.

* * *

For Owen Haig, the best part of space tourism, and what made it the ultimate thrill ride, comes after the ship settles into orbit. Attendants escort passengers, one section at a time, to an area nicknamed the Bumper Room. Dominated by a massive window facing out from one of the ship's sides, well-heeled Earth dwellers get to play astronaut: experiencing weightlessness, performing acrobatic stunts, and in general, horsing around inside the two-story padded chamber.

The just-as-advertised crazy hair selfies with Earth as the ultimate backdrop, plus frolicking, backflipping, and laughter, leave Owen wistful Rachel demurred when their section's turn came. However, he was surprised she agreed to this unconventional start to their honeymoon in the first place. Best not to push his luck. While enjoying the solo experience upside-down, staring at an unidentifiable landmass outside the large, thick-glass portal, the elderly Asian couple eclipses his view. Extending a tiny camera, beaming from ear to ear, they pantomime for Owen to take their picture.

Accepting the camera with a universally recognized smile, "Okay. No problem. Hang there for a moment while I snap a few shots."

* * *

Comfortable and in complete control, ensconced in her leather-bound astronaut seat, Rachel catches the eyes of the small boy who waved earlier. He smiles at her from across the expanse and gives a thumbs-up. She is about to hand-signal a reply when bright lights burst out of the ether and dance around in the open space rotunda between them, generating surprised gasps from the seated passengers.

While excited space tourists remark on the spectacle, a static electric buzz permeates the weightlessness around Rachel. Wishing Owen could be by her side to witness this real-life space oddity outside the curved viewing window, "He sure has a knack for missing the important stuff."

Rachel oohs with the rest of the seated space tourists while a prickly sensation stimulates goosebumps on her arms and legs.

The orbs glow in a spectacular array of colors and patterns, zooming, bouncing, and spiraling in a synchronized choreography reminiscent of an Esther Williams water ballet from an old MGM movie performed in the cold hard vacuum of space.

As the stunning show continues, a single orb breaks formation and floats to the curved glass opposite Rachel, pulsating on and off like Morse code. Mesmerized, she pushes from her seat to the window, pressing her right hand flat against the glass, attempting to contact the basketball-sized luminous sphere. A strange familial sensation fills her with sheer joy and profound sadness. The light speeds off, rejoining the show, and she snaps from her hypnotic state with the dreadful self-awareness that she is sobbing for no apparent reason.

The show culminates with a spectacular blast of light before dissolving into the ether.

"I believe it tried to communicate with you."

Sensing fellow space tourists catching her dramatic epilogue to the strange lights, Rachel shrinks back to the relative safety of her seat before answering Tan Suit, her new nickname for the Egyptian man across the aisle. "Yeah, it sure looked like it."

Pulling her lap belt secure around her waist, she wipes tears from her eyes and frowns at her reflection, cringing at the handprint she left on the glass.

Tan Suit returned to his typing, oblivious to any societal norm suggesting a polite reply. A man of few words, she surmises, and answers for him under her breath: "Why yes, the strange light did try to communicate with you, Madame. How odd. You look lovely, and I'm so sorry for almost knocking you over at the luggage counter."

Finishing her chardonnay, Rachel crumples the empty plastic pouch into the waste compartment below her left armrest. She would be mortified if it floated off and scared somebody like the pen did to her earlier in the flight.

Scooching her bottom into the seat, Rachel ponders why the International Outer Space Consortium needed an impromptu light show. One would assume hurtling along at over 19,000 miles per hour, sipping French wine, and dining on a gourmet meal through a straw would be entertaining enough. The modern-day consumer is never satisfied. The more advancements humanity achieves, the more jaded they become. How sad. Glancing right, she watches Tan Suit pecking at his holographic keys. The too-cute-for-their-own-good Asian couple to her left and her husband, Mr. Adventure, had yet to return.

* * *

An hour later, with Owen seated, meal service begins with waves of attendants delivering food and taking drink orders. Owen and Rachel checked off their dinner choices months before, and neither could recall their picks for the four-course meal.

"I like surprises."

Rachel counters, "I don't."

A gourmet French cheese sampler came first, followed by tubes of Toulouse-style Cassoulet, designed to acclimate passengers to dining like astronauts so that by the main course, everyone is proficient enough to prevent their dinner from floating out of reach. After the delicious tubes of pureed filet mignon, Gratin Dauphinois, and root vegetables, everyone enjoys a palette-cleansing berry-infused ice cream dessert.

The newlywed couple sucks down their ice cream, watching Earth pass under their shoes a third and final time.

Owen pulls the last precious remnants of the best vanilla ice cream he has ever tasted and decides to address the elephant in the room, "Apparently, I missed quite a performance while I was off floating around like an idiot. I'm slightly disappointed; a light show was not on the flight itinerary. If you want, I can check my brochure and see if it says anything about light shows."

Rachel suppresses an unladylike belch, "Owen, if you take out one of those damn brochures again, I will push you out an airlock myself."

"You know it is unhealthy to keep that inside." Handing his spent ice cream pouch to an attendant over his shoulder, he turns toward his lovely wife, noticing a tiny dab of vanilla on her upper lip's pouty curve. Slightly aroused, he tamps down his male instincts and continues, "I get the message. I'm a lot smarter than I appear. Do you know what I think you experienced? Aliens. They are up here, Rachel!" He peers outside the window, awestruck by the majestic view. "And because of their advanced technology, we can enjoy eating ice cream and goofing around in space. ET is still considered taboo, but they are buzzing around, just like always. My uncle was a Navy pilot; the stories he used to tell were better than a sci-fi movie." Owen's erudite explanation is meant to quell his new wife's unease, but the perplexed expression on her pretty face informs him otherwise, so he decides to change subjects. "Guess what? My bio-whatever ticket implant stopped itching, too."

Laughing despite her misgivings, she turns to her smiling husband, "You are one lucky guy."

Leaning in for a soft vanilla-flavored kiss, "I know." Staring deep into her emerald eyes, "I'm not surprised they reached out to say hello. I can't imagine an alien who wouldn't want to make your acquaintance."

***

Reentry is a fiery inverted nosedive behind the advanced protection of the craft's deployed nanotech heat deflector shields—a miraculous feat of aerospace engineering. However, the sensation of free-falling tens of thousands of feet could not be engineered out of the human body, a fact highlighted in bold on the contract every space tourist consents to with an e-signature John Hancock before finalizing their ticket purchase.

Plummeting through the stratosphere at 55,000 feet, a graceful maneuver reorients the craft upright while the resilient tiles respond to Earth's gravity. With passengers' bottoms pointing toward the solid ground, the controlled descent ensues at an alarming speed.

Peering at the verdant French patchwork below his feet, Owen spies their landing pad destination, along with two others jutting above greenish pastures off in the distance through the early-morning haze. The snake-like elevated rails of a high-speed people mover resolve into view, and he leans over to point this out to his white-knuckled wife. "Rachel, I can see the monorail."

Staring straight ahead, Rachel blurts out, "Great, Owen. Just wonderful." She refrains from casting her eyes downward at the dizzying view.

The ship's flight computer and cybernetic crew execute the final approach via a smooth, decelerating corkscrew descent and set the gigantic spaceship down pillow-soft onto the towering 16-story Landing Pad #3 in a serene valley out in the idyllic French countryside. Rachel confirms with a relieved sigh the comfortable fifteen-minute commute aboard the high-speed monorail to the Space Terminal Hub on the vast acreage of the venerable, reimagined Toulouse Space Center.

In the first few minutes after touchdown, the only sounds aboard the craft are a low crackle of murmuring voices from the control tower through the ship's PA system intermingling with whooshes of air, beeps, whistles, and the clicking and clacking of passengers beginning the process of undoing their restraints. Besides the low background din, the passengers seem in a collective daze. A faint stench of vomit wafts past their noses reminding Rachel it could always be worse.

The Stetson-wearing cowboy breaks the icy silence with a boisterous "Woo-Wee! What a ride!" obliterating the church-like atmosphere inside Passenger Section D. Everyone begins clapping, laughing, and cheering the perfect landing.

Owen leans over to kiss and hug a relieved Rachel. "Thanks for doing this with me. It means a lot."

Their tender moment is shattered by a dizzy passenger faceplanting on the stairs a few rows behind them. A courteous attendant assists the stricken fellow, one-handing him with inhuman strength back into his seat. Suppressing smiles, they look on while the attendant calls for the vacuum squad, admonishing the light-headed fellow, "Careful, Mr. Jones. It may take time to regain your balance."

Rachel turns from eavesdropping on the poor man, shrugging a perfect smile, "Wouldn't miss it for the world, Owen. I love you. And be careful when you stand; I don't want you to fall flat on your ass like the poor fellow a few rows behind us. You'll embarrass me." About to reciprocate Owen's affectionate kiss, she pauses to replay her paranormal experience, "I can't put my finger on it, but something happened in orbit I can't explain. I felt a presence invade my mind."

"You might be overthinking your encounter of the weird kind if you don't mind me saying so."

The dark-blond beauty punches his arm, "You're probably right." Reaching under her seat, she grabs her carry-ons and heads up the stairs, sidestepping the odorous mishap toward the open double doors and the ship's main concourse beyond.

The palpable sense of relief among the departing passengers cannot be denied, giving way to jubilation. Like a tiny yet growing subset of humanity, they broke Earth's surly bonds and all that nonsense. They had all done it now. They were in the astronaut club.

IOSC Spaceport Terminal | Toulouse, France
05:00 a.m. | August 17, 2044

Owen pats a stone-faced attendant on the shoulder while passing through the exit, "Thanks, that was fun!"

Reentering the ship's promenade deck, Rachel turns and catches one last glimpse of their seats and the handprint she left on the curved glass. Trailing behind Owen, she heads to the back of a line waiting on wide elevator doors to slide open. While hefting her bags, she lets out a loud yawn to relieve pressure in her ears.

Crammed into an elevator with fellow wobbly-knee passengers too amped for jet lag, the couple descends to Ground Level. Fresh, clean air greets their senses as the gleaming metal doors open.

"Bienvenue en France." A pleasant fellow in full IOSC uniform smiles, gesturing toward the waiting monorail.

Following the unsolicited directions into early-morning French sunshine, Owen takes a deep breath, "This sure beats the stale air on the ship, especially after mealtime. I think I'll leave a comment regarding the onboard odors."

Rachel laughs, trying to get her leg muscles moving again, "You are one of those people? I didn't know that about you."

"What? It smelled like a bus station toilet in there."

A vision of her mother's persnickety sister springs into her head, "This way to the monorail, Aunt Mildred."

"Was she the one who tried to hit on my Uncle Phil at our reception?"

The whisper-quiet tram whisking passengers between the launch pad and the main terminal is a revelation in comfort and elegance. Water bottles and hot hand towels are arranged on the wide armrests of each plush seat. They collapse into two of the last unoccupied spots across from each other, Rachel facing backward.

Peering at the massive platform outside their spotless window,

"There's our ship atop the launch pad. It's hard to believe we did it."

Rachel nods in agreement but is in full move-on mode, anxious to get on with their trip, "Hey, Owen. Real seats. We are sitting down," goading him into a playful spate.

"Yeah, I get it, Rachel. You hated the people mover in Nevada, and I will never live it down. Got it."

Rachel laughs and smacks him on the knee, "Lighten up; we're here, you dummy!"

"Exactly how many wine pouches did you have on the flight?"

They rehydrate while dabbing the warm towels here and there as the sleek transport whooshes toward the towering French neo-Gothic Main Terminal. Owen notes its stark architectural contrast to the ultra-modern, yet sterile and impersonal, steel and glass edifice they left in the Nevada desert. The spires, flying buttresses, steep-pitched rooflines, and lancet stained glass windows framed by sheer facades of intricate stonework are impressive. And gargoyles, lots of them. A sidebar in one of Owen's brochures hints at locations around the complex where the expressive statues resemble little gray aliens. Cool.

Disembarking from the monorail, Rachel snatches a water bottle and slides it into her satchel. Clones of the attendant at the launch pad usher everyone through heavy ornate doors into the terminal's echoing, cathedral-like interior. Owen gives an appreciative whistle, admiring the attention to detail the International Outer Space Consortium applied to this high-tech homage to Western Civilization's architectural past. The exquisite stained glass and the Michelangelo-inspired murals and frescos depicting space travel and the universe on a grand scale are awe-inspiring. The incredible structure is fast becoming a focal point for the French tourism industry, rivaling the transformative yet controversial Notre Dame Cathedral. Forget space tourism; gate sales for guided tours alone are a revenue boon. The Nevada site, and hubs in Sapporo, Ankara, New Delhi, and Cape Canaveral, struggle to match their success.

After a few minutes exploring the impressive building and

much-needed side trips to the male and female lounges, Owen gestures toward the signs for Ground Transportation, their waiting ride, and the remainder of their honeymoon.

"Hate to burst your bubble, Owen, but you need to reread the fine print on our tickets. We agreed to post-flight physical exams, which IOSC medical staff cross-check against our preflight health data."

"Oh shit, I forgot. Do we have to?" Following Rachel's lovely hand toward a growing queue outside open double doors, he grimaces while watching a nurse escort Stetson, the Yee-Haw Man, across the threshold. "What a buzzkill this is going to be."

"What's the matter? Wasn't this part of the trip highlighted in your brochures?"

"You are purposely trying to push my buttons, young lady."

Stopping at the tail-end of another long line, Owen scratches his head and laughs, "I can't help noticing we always seem to be last."

"Haven't you ever heard the last shall be first?"

"Oh, okay. We're inside this cathedral to the stars, and you get all Bible on me. Is that it?"

"Sometimes, you are just too weird." She scans past Owen to the crowded main terminal and catches Tan Suit excusing himself through a large tour group.

Like most aspects of the Toulouse facility, the post-flight checkup routine is a well-organized affair compared to the Nevada hub. Arrivals are funneled into the adjoining hall, where the exams are administered assembly line-style by teams of robotic physician assistants manning partitioned cubicles.

Rachel is detoured across the hall to another set of draped-off cubes dedicated to the fairer sex. "See you on the other side."

"I hope my HMO covers this."

Owen is greeted by a shiny-faced robot proffering a box of anti-bacterial wipes. With an overt eye roll, he snatches a wet, smelly cloth and navigates to the first checkpoint. He endures a blood pressure check, a cold stethoscope respiratory check, a battery of vision, hearing, and reflex tests administered with blinding penlights, say-ah tongue depressors, and Maxwell's Silver Hammer-style bangs to the kneecap.

At the last cube, the put-upon astronaut named Owen Haig is screened for cognitive and physical impairment via a litany of personal questions by a monotone attendant perched on a metal stool:

"State your name, nationality, and date of birth."

"Owen Haig. American. May 9, 2017."

"Who is the president of the United States?"

"Jackson, uh, Lena Jackson."

"Are you experiencing dizziness?"

"No."

"Do you have a headache?"

"No."

"What about fatigue?"

"No."

"Do you have muscle cramps?"

"No."

"Respiratory issues?"

"No."

"Erectile dysfunction?"

"Excuse Me? I just got off the ship, for Christ's sake. And no. Hell no."

"Last question, which entree did you choose for your in-flight meal?"

"Steak, I guess. Hard to tell since it came out of a tube. Can I go now?"

"Yes."

Exiting the last station, Owen stops before a woman standing behind a cocktail-height counter, double-checking his results and personal information on her handheld display. Noticing his prying gaze, she swipes the screen closed and begins to speak, "Are you …?"

"Stop right there, lady. I feel fine. My wife feels fine. Just pass us the forms promising not to sue the International Outer Space Consortium, and we can get on our way."

The dark-skinned woman gives Owen a brown-eyed frown, adjusting the jet-black bun atop her head. Leaning across the metal counter, a gold cross dangles over a stethoscope draped from the open collar of her lemon-yellow blouse under her white lab coat, "Sir, I'm not sure what you are implying, but just between you and me, I am as human as you are. I would appreciate it if you would treat me with more respect. After all, we need to make sure even an impressive physical specimen, such as yourself, doesn't leave our facility and suffer a brain hemorrhage in the parking structure. It would be bad for our business. Plus, someone would have to clean the mess you leave behind."

Chagrined, he complies with the remainder of the questions and receives a clean bill of health. The last item on the medical list is a prick on his forearm from a handheld appliance administered by the smiling woman.

"Hey, take it easy! Is the chip removal supposed to hurt?"

"Just for you," glancing down at the display with a surreptitious smile, "uh, Mr. Haig." She presents a clear pouch containing Owen's chip updated with the new health screening data. "You may want to pin this to your shirt so it won't get lost. You will need it to retrieve your luggage."

"Thanks a lot, Nurse Ratched. If that is your real name."

"My pleasure. Maybe we'll cross paths again someday."

Owen accepts the baggie, deposits it into his carry-on, and turns to search the crowd for his wife. After a few minutes, shuffling from foot to foot, he spies Rachel smiling back toward somebody while exiting the last cube at the opposite end of the health screening area.

"Boy, Owen, you certainly have a way with people, don't you?"

Owen ignores her snarky observation, "Well, that took forever. I'm starving. We might as well head to the Medieval Times Food Court. It's a long ride to Le Tholonet."

"Hey, big guy, get over it! We're in France. I could eat an authentic French croissant and some strong coffee now." Glancing at a wall clock, "Wait a minute. What about our driver?"

"Our guy will have to cool his jets until we get there. I'm tired of being ordered around by a bunch of robots."

* * *

Breakfasting at a café table beside a gurgling fountain filled with koi fish, Rachel revels in the mid-morning sunlight dappling the bright, cheery interior space, filtering through an ornate glass dome above the food court atrium.

Owen finishes his omelet and spreads local-sourced blackberry jam on his last slice of fresh-baked sourdough. Tearing a corner of the crust and tossing it onto the tiled floor behind Rachel's seat instigates a scrum of screechy, black-feathered birds battling over the crumbly morsel.

"Knock it off! You are attracting the little beggars all around my feet." Distracted by the chirping melee, she spills coffee on the tabletop while spooning it into the French press. "I would drink less coffee if I had to complete this science experiment for every cup."

A solitary feathered creature hops onto the table and bobs its little head from side to side looking at Rachel.

"The little guy is eyeballing you. Your beauty enthralls even birds."

"Yep. I'm a veritable Snow White."

"Not exactly."

"Watch it, Owen."

While finishing their repast, Rachel catches the eye of Tan Suit speaking to someone on his earphone, lingering near the hostess stand, "We should head over to the baggage area and meet our driver out at the Ground Transportation."

Owen finishes his last bite with a sip of tea and dabs at his mouth. Summoning his best Inspector Clouseau-inspired French accent, "Absolutely mademoiselle, let us be on our way."

"Knock it off."

"Okay. Sorry."

* * *

The luggage area bustled with disoriented travelers, helpful robots, and vigilant French security. The efficient IOSC luggage system has the couple at the counter presenting see-through chip baggies to the metal-skinned attendant within minutes.

Rachel notes this vintage humanoid robot has none of the warmth and charm of newer models, but he scans the chips through the clear plastic and presses a button on his display. Thirty seconds later, heavy luggage earmarked for the Haig family autonomously wheels through an opening in the wall and brakes in front of the counter.

Owen is amazed. "How did you get the suitcases to roll on their own? I tried for weeks and could not figure it out. I feared our bags would wander behind a stranger when we weren't paying attention."

The silver-skinned bot replies with a glassy-eye stare, "I synced the bar codes on your luggage to your chips. It is much easier than pulling them yourselves, sir."

"Yeah, that would be true if you could figure out how it works. Thanks."

With a tap near the handles, the suitcases follow the couple to the pick-up curb like well-trained pets.

Owen glances at Rachel with a sheepish smile, expecting a "See? I told you so." to cross her lips.

"What? I didn't say anything. I could not figure it out, either. And we both know I am the smart one."

"Not fair, Rachel. You can't be the good-looking one and the smart one. What's left for me?"

"Goofy sidekick?"

Laughing at their private joke, the pair quicken their pace, eager to get on with the next part of their trip: a luxurious two-week stay at a historic chateau in the picturesque Provence countryside. The lodging comes complete with an attentive staff to assist with sundry details like fiddling with a French press.

The jet-setting honeymooners fail to notice the small orb of light mirroring their path through the Arrival Terminal and outside to a cacophony of honking cabs and buses jockeying for curbside spots along the Pickup Zone. For an inexplicable, only in France reason, Ground Transportation is situated atop the gargantuan five-story parking structure where Louie fumes at the tardiness of his prepaid fare.

Niyo | Above Toulouse Spaceport, France
12:00 p.m. | August 17, 2044

A pill-shaped vessel cloaked against the clear blue French sky hovers 500 feet above the parking garage rooftop. Ensconced inside the stealth ship, an ET freelance operative hired by The Powers That Be maintains a vigilant watch on the chaotic proceedings below. Codenamed Niyo, he awaits the Alexander female's exit from the IOSC terminal. Sifting through throngs of humans heading toward an array of vehicular transports, the child-size alien scratches his smooth head and levers back his seat in the cramped cockpit, "Where is she?"

From the moment the veteran tracker initiated high-altitude surveillance over Rachel Alexander Haig's Las Vegas hotel, his sixth sense was in overdrive. Upon witnessing the Light Specters' orbital spectacle, his intuition was affirmed. While Niyo understood the vaunted pure-energy masters of the universe indeed revealed their radiant presence to a host of lower life forms, their latest grandiose light show had to be for the benefit of none other than Rachel Alexander Haig. Niyo pressed his employer with a renewed sense of urgency: "The presence of Light

Specters has transformed my routine surveillance into a consequential intel-gathering mission with potential Earth-shattering implications. I request permission to continue monitoring the Alexander woman's movements in France. Something else is about to happen. I know it."

Niyo's PTB handler responded with a curt one-word reply: "*Denied.*" Spying on a young couple's honeymoon crossed an ethical line, even for an extra-governmental organization like the PTB.

Hailing from an ancient Gray race, the operative knew that the Light Specters' ultimate vision for humanity hinged on recovering a gold artifact missing for over a century. "Damn those skeptical PTB bureaucrats; time is running out for the good people of Earth."

The Powers That Be circumspect demand for indisputable evidence stemmed from a century's worth of dead-ends and heart-stopping false alarms. Moreover, surveillance of generations of Alexanders had yet to produce anything. A growing chorus of PTB insiders lobbied for an end to trailing Alexanders every time one of them left the house. The freelancer's report of foo fighters floating around an IOSC craft while an Alexander happened to be aboard was the latest in a long line of coincidences, nothing more.

Knowing in his walnut-sized gray heart muscle that he was right but needing tangible proof of the Light Specters' transcendent intentions for the girl, the alien operative peers downward through a magnifying eyepiece and spies his mark. "There she is!" Painting the target, Rachel, with photon pellet trackers, just in case, he watches the blond-headed young woman and her spouse stride on a beeline toward an animated robot chauffeur. Smiling at the driver's consternated body language, gesturing the pair inside the back of his green vehicle, the ET wonders if the robot can squeeze all the couple's luggage into the narrow cargo space, "At least this should prove entertaining."

From his high perch spying on the driver's struggles, Niyo's black oval eyes narrow onto a bright white orb, manifesting out of the ether. A halted breath later, the baseball-sized sphere permeates the robot driver's shiny skin and disappears.

Replaying the incident in slow motion, Niyo witnesses the ball of light entering the robot's cybernetic head.

Seconds after beaming the zoomed movie file to the PTB Scottish nerve center, Niyo receives new orders: *"Clearance granted to proceed with high altitude surveillance into France, but do not attempt to land or contact the humans."*

**We are like butterflies who flutter for a day
and think it is forever.**

– Carl Sagan

Chapter Two:

The Drive

Louie | En route to Le Tholonet, France
05:30 p.m. | August 17, 2044

From the latter part of the 20th century to present-day 2044, wealthy tourists drunk on expensive wines and drop-dead gorgeous scenery have adopted the Provence region of Southern France as their playground. The French impressionist, Paul Cezanne, was so enamored with the sweeping vistas and rugged terrain that he featured one of its signature landmarks, Montagne Sainte-Victoire, in over sixty paintings.

Situated northeast of the ancient town of Aix-en-Provence, the 10 km limestone massif, its arid plains to the south, and verdant hills spreading northward are studded with excavations ranging from prehistorical through the Roman era. Archeologists unearth proto-historical settlements, villa foundations, potsherds, coins, and colorful tiles, piecing together the storied region's narrative by studying the wide range of humans who called it their home over thousands of years.

With a keen yet unexplained interest in the region, The Powers That Be bankrolled an expedition to explore the 3,000-foot limestone landmark's labyrinthine cave system, making headlines upon discovering well-preserved cave paintings chronicling prehistoric life in the region eons before the first cultivated grapevine. Before a redacted tranche of photographs was made public, a heretofore respected archeological journalist leaked a stolen top-secret image depicting the unmistakable shape of an airplane flying over Montagne Sainte-Victoire, the well-preserved cave artwork dating back to 10,000 BC.

* * *

Dominating the horizon through Louie's windshield, Montagne Sainte-Victoire registers as a gigantic waste of space in his Kobayashi-manufactured logic-driven bright-pink brain core.

Louie's synthetic blood boils with inner rage following the last-minute request to reroute onto the backroads of Provence for the final leg into Le Tholonet. "Sacré bleu! Why do they demand I deviate from an ultra-modern elevated tollway onto a rutted country lane?"

From the obnoxious fare's inception at the Toulouse spaceport, the trip turned into a tedious ordeal. The backseat patrons didn't know it yet, but he recalculated their fare based on the ludicrous detour. From the looks of the well-heeled young couple, he assumes they can afford his exponentially increased tip.

Driving the compact two-door fuel cell vehicle hums through the countryside outside Aix-en-Provence, Louie mutters, "almost there," with a crooked smile and an unlit cigarette dangling from his lower lip. Maneuvering the long and winding road's blind corners, hairpin turns, and wandering livestock, Louie's mustached poker-face masks trillions of cybernetic connections and relays pulsating at light speed behind his noble countenance. His heat-seeking eyes identify troublesome road obstacles while keen auditory sensors filter a spectrum of frequencies, listening for dangers. A microchip implanted in his right temple relays geographical information anywhere on the planet with pinpoint accuracy.

Louie, a late-model Kobayashi Corporation C-Class robot, appears human to untrained eyes. Transporting tourists around the South of France, he is accustomed to odd occurrences, awkward interactions, and borderline criminal indiscretions. However, the newlywed couple in his backseat rattled his logic processors down to the silicon, but the reason lay beyond his advanced perception.

A nanosecond after the handsome Americans made their tardy appearance at the white curb atop the IOSC Spaceport's Ground Transportation Center in Toulouse, his programming glitched and reset, glitched, reset, glitched. Someone, or something, wanted in. The persistent entity was not to be denied. Further complicating matters, the detour by the uncouth American tapping his backrest with an annoying patter delays an overdue anti-viral software update and a quart of oil.

Swerving to avoid a black and white cow loitering in the middle of the lane triggers alarm bells, "I failed to identify that organic obstacle ahead of time. I am not right. If I continue driving, it will be dangerous."

The robot chauffeur addresses the ethereal saboteur infiltrating his circuits for the first time. "Should I shut down now?"

A deep male voice echoes inside his head, *"No, Louie, keep driving if you please."*

"Are you the sentient light orb who invaded my circuitry while my distracted passengers struggled into my vehicle back in Toulouse?"

"Yes, Louie."

"I am cognizant you are reprogramming my brain core. I cannot predict how much longer I will maintain control. You have chosen me to transport these humans to a new destination. Correct?"

"That is, indeed, accurate."

"How much longer do I have?"

The cool, calm, collected voice replies, *"Your new programming will initiate in 5…4…3…2…1. Now."*

Louie's head whips back and forth. The harried cabbie attempts to deactivate the unexpected and embarrassing activity, to no avail. His frame stiffens and trembles. The cigarette falls from his mouth as he blurts nonsensical words in 14 languages, like a schizophrenic multilingual chorus.

"Time to reset."

Searching for a byte of clarity in his computerized noggin, Louie's vision becomes static. Blind. To make matters worse, he loses touch with the faux leather-trimmed steering wheel; however, he perceives the car is staying on the road. Relief lasts a millisecond before the strange entity hijacking his circuits accelerates the vehicle.

"Time to reset."

The car veers across the sleepy country road into the path of a pickup truck loaded with clusters of dark-purple grapes. The frantic truck driver lays on his horn and angles right to avoid a head-on collision. Grapes fly out of the bed of his truck. Louie hears screams emanating from behind. "The passengers! Sacré bleu!"

"Time to reset."

"Backup programming, activate! Manual override! What's happening to me?" Louie's reclusive maker neglected to program his defenses against such a cunning, determined foe. At the last possible second, the havoc-wreaking orb rerouting miles of intricate connections takes control, zigzagging around the truck timed with a family of ducks venturing across the narrow road. The robot's blank expression underscores his surrender to the mysterious intruder while parsing his predicament: "My hands are clutching the wheel, and my right foot presses down on the brake. Wait. We're stopping. At last."

After the tint EV fishtails to a neck-wrenching halt, Louie scans his passengers for injuries. "Are they hurt? My insurance is already sky-high."

"No, the Haig couple is fine. Perhaps a wee bit rattled, which is understandable considering they are trapped in the backseat with a malfunctioning robot driver risking their young lives. Shame on you."

"I fail to see the humor here, monsieur."

Satisfied the human passengers are indeed uninjured, the orb in control of Louie jams his sensible brown loafer down hard on what passes for a gas pedal. The hydrogen-powered vehicle's little wheels shoot rocks and gravel into the air before lurching offroad into the tall grass. Vaulting an embankment, the car bounds across a bucolic Provence pasture, scattering panicked sheep in all directions.

"Where are we going?"

"Reset complete."

"Don't worry, Louie. Everything is proceeding according to plan. I will provide information as we veer toward destiny. Watch out for that fence post. Go right. Now!"

Louie steers right. Loud staticky wavelengths in his head resolve into angry, frantic voices ratcheting in his ears from the backseat signaling auditory function back online.

"What do I tell the passengers? They don't understand what I am doing. Neither do I."

"Ignore the passengers for now. Just drive and try not to steer us into that fishpond."

Bumping, weaving, and rolling through the rosemary, juniper, and lavender-filled backcountry, the fuel cell vehicle bounds past the befuddled stares of cud-chewing cows, gophers, and squirrels. Splashing through a creek bed, the pirated taxi rounds a limestone outcropping on a perilous ascent up a little-used fire road to the mystery orb's destination, where it all started 100 years earlier.

Rachel and Owen | IOSC Ground Transportation Pickup Zone
12:00 p.m. (5.5 hours earlier) | August 17, 2044

The newly minted space tourists wedge into the backseat of a two-door, chartreuse, hydrogen-powered e-car. Rachel's latent claustrophobia rears its ugly head, wincing at the vehicular contrast between this clown car and their spacious seats aboard the spaceship. Seated at Owen's right elbow, she watches the heavy robot chauffeur sigh while climbing behind the wheel and blocking her only way out. Great. Just great.

"At least we have plenty of legroom, Rachel," Owen chuckles while tapping the driver-side backrest to a tin-eared beat. Glancing out the side window into the dark garage, he frowns at the confusing mass of red taillights angling toward the exit ramp from all directions, "The drive to our villa should take less than three hours, depending on how long it takes to get out of this parking garage. Our driver comes with a seven-star rating. From what I understand, that is pretty good."

"It is exceptional, Monsieur, and proud of it, too," Louie replies from behind the wheel, laying on his horn to drown out a French profanity.

Rachel ignores the rating remark, "We should have sprung for the rental car." After a long pause, "I know how to drive."

Owen dons his new shades and smiles, "I could learn to drive. It is not a necessary skill anymore. What's the point? Let's not argue. It's a gorgeous mid-August afternoon in Southern France."

The chartreuse e-car wedges between a bus and another bilious-colored gumdrop on wheels, joining a line of cars, cabs, and shuttles funneling into a six-lane artery leading out of the massive parking structure. Eking around a bend, a black SUV with darkened windows and no plates angles in front of them, prompting a silent sigh from Owen, wishing they lingered a while longer in the café to avoid this mad rush.

Louie reports over the backseat: "Pardon, Monsieur et Madame, I understand from the radio that a horrific accident at the exit has narrowed all exiting vehicles down to one lane. I apologize for this inconvenience."

Rachel settles into her passenger-side seat and quells her fear of tight spaces by focusing on the mass of vehicles inching forward. Her mind wanders to the unscheduled light show. "You should have seen it. The lights seemed alive. They moved with such spontaneity! There is no way it was a choreographed show. Plus, they weren't even supposed to be there. As we were leaving, I overheard other passengers talking about it. And what about the light blinking on and off right outside my window? It freaked me out." She pauses as the car lurches forward, gaining another car length toward the exit, "I wish I knew Morse code."

"Maybe it was a long-lost boyfriend. Do-Do-Do-Do - Do-Do-Do-Do…" Owen laughs and delivers a playful tickle to Rachel's ribs.

She squirms away from his wandering hands, "I'm not joking. I can't shake the impression it tried to communicate with me."

"Okay. When we arrive at the villa, I'll call the travel agency and ask if they know of any unannounced light show. My earphone is in my bag in the back, so I can't right now."

"Why did you leave it there?"

Owen puts his arm around her shoulder and pulls her close, "Since you are asking, Mrs. Rachel Haig, this is our honeymoon, and I did not want to be bothered by annoying communications from a bunch of well-wishing relatives and friends. Okay?"

"Okay, Mr. Haig." With a sheepish smile, "Mine is also buried in my purse. I guess we've gone dark until we reach Le Tholonet. Let them all speculate how our space voyage went. It's what they are doing as we speak, anyway."

"That's the spirit, Rachel. If we had perished in a fiery crash, I'm sure they would have heard about it by now."

***

The car snakes out of the structure and peels southeast through the outskirts of Toulouse toward the Mediterranean. Rachel closes her eyes and tries to sleep while Narbonne, Béziers, Montpellier, Nimes, Arles, and Salon-de-Provence whiz by her small window.

Owen peers through the front windshield and compares the fast-approaching road signs to his hand-drawn map, "Okay, Louie. Take the next exit!"

Rachel jostles awake, "Are we there already?"

"No. But we can't see anything from this concrete monstrosity. I like to get off the highway a few exits early and check out the area before arriving in a place I have never been."

"You are an onion. I keep peeling but haven't reached the core yet."

"Onions don't have a core, Rachel. And yes, I am appealing."

A muttering of French wafts over from the front seat.

"What did you say, Louie?"

Louie does not reply. Grumbling under his breath, he detours off the brand-new thoroughfare outside Aix-en-Provence, rerouting onto a bumpy two-lane country road. The destination, a villa behind a gate directly off Route Cezanne in the small commune of Le Tholonet, was only twenty minutes farther on the toll road, but now it will take much longer to reach.

Looking out his side window at Montagne Sainte-Victoire, the majestic limestone ridge towering over the entire region, "Man, this place is truly stunning. I can't wait to plan some hikes and explore, Rachel."

Looking outside at the French landscape passing by her small window, Rachel's disposition brightens. Glancing out the front over Louie's shoulder, she observes his head turning from side to side, like watching a tennis match on fast-forward, "Owen! Something is wrong with our driver! He's freaking out on us! Can robots freak out?"

Unalarmed but wanting a response, Owen grasps Louie's shoulder over the front seat. "What's going on? Are you okay? Pull off the road. Now!"

But Louie can't make out a word and doesn't acknowledge the firm human grip digging into his shoulder.

"He's making horrible noises! It sounds like gibberish! What's going on with him? Did he fry a circuit breaker?"

The car swerves into oncoming traffic, and Owen sees a truck heading for them. "Rachel! Brace yourself! We're going to crash!"

Owen thrusts his right arm in front of Rachel as the lightning-quick scene unfolds in slow motion before his startled eyes. Rachel's hair flies forward before whipping from side to side, her fingertips digging into his right thigh as an eerie humming noise amplifying inside the cramped interior drowns curses and screams. Flinging left, then right, in concert with the car's zigzag past the honking truck's path, clusters of purple grapes splatter the windshield and spill all over the road. A white duck flies past Owen's streaky window, its beady eyes bulging, wings flapping, and its orange beak wide open in midscream. Can ducks scream?

The car screeches to a stop, leaving a long trail of skid marks, smashed grapes, and fluttering white feathers. Louie stares past the spindly windshield wipers smearing smashed grapes off the cracked glass with a squeaky inefficiency before swiveling toward his terrified passengers.

Rachel watches a light beam project from Louie's eyes across her head and chest, "That better not be an x-ray."

"We're not hurt."

Rachel pivots to her dazed husband, "Whom are you talking to?"

"Him, I guess. You didn't hear anything?"

"No."

Satisfied no one is injured, Louie turns toward the wheel and jams on the accelerator.

Bracing like he's on an extreme coaster, "Here we go again, Rachel!"

The car vaults over a wooden fence and bounces into a pasture. Bounding along at breakneck speed, Rachel grabs Owen by the shirt collar, "I thought the scary part of this trip ended when we left the spaceport."

"Apparently not, Rachel."

The car careens upslope, fishtailing around rocky outcroppings, and swerves onto a trail heading toward the tree line. "I wanted to experience the Provence backcountry. Our driver took me literally," shrugging with a sheepish smile.

Bouncing along the rock-strewn trail, proceeding on a steep incline up the mountain's side, the forested slopes darken with lengthening shadows, zooming past their streak-spattered backseat windows.

Rachel watches her new husband lean into a tight turn, catching the glint of a white smile on his face. "You have got to be joking. You are enjoying this, aren't you? I'm scared out of my head, and we'll probably die. But you're grinning like an idiot on an amusement park ride!"

Turning to the blur outside her window, she mutters loud enough to be heard, "Mom was right."

"What about your mom?"

"You never take anything seriously. Everything is just one big joke. Whether hanging off a cliff or paragliding from the side of a building, you're invincible. It must be nice playing Superman all day. I'm just not sure I want to be your Lois Lane for the rest of my life!"

The headlights on the banged-up electric vehicle illuminate the narrowing fire road bisecting the dense forest on the lower slopes below the southerly limestone face of Montagne Sainte-Victoire.

With no way out and an unresponsive Louie going full steam ahead, "There is nothing we can do but wait until this thing runs out of hydrogen or vaults off a cliff, whichever comes first."

Rachel's "There you go again." is cut short as the resilient e-car fishtails to a neck-jolting stop at the foot of a sheer wall of limestone rising high above their ticking car into the dusky sky.

Louie flings his door wide and exits the vehicle without a word of explanation. The shell-shocked couple stares at each other in bewilderment while the open-door warning dings. Snapping to their senses following the nightmarish predicament, they push out of the cramped backseat into the electrified evening air.

Niyo | Montagne Sainte-Victoire
08:00 p.m. | August 17, 2044

Ignoring a direct order, Niyo settles his pill-shaped craft on a narrow spit of grass atop a jagged limestone escarpment just over the ridge from the green taxi's parked position at the base of a sheer cliff wall. After performing a perfunctory system check, he ensures the ship remains cloaked from human eyes before extricating himself from his cramped seat.

Straightening his three-foot frame atop the high-elevation perch, he gathers essentials, including an insect-sized stealth drone, and treks into the thick pine forest, separating his position from the arguing trio. He hears their shouts and insults echoing off high cliff walls and resonating through the woods as he sneaks closer to find a strategic vantage point to see—and record—what comes next. While unsure of what will transpire, he is confident it is critical to finding the golden ellipse.

Traversing a well-trod animal trail crisscrossed with hoof and paw prints through the pine forest in near-total darkness, the being from a far-off world comes face-to-face with a doe and her fawn dining on a thick stand of elderberries. The deer casts a wary eye before returning to her evening feast while her offspring ignores his presence.

Nudging past the local forest dwellers with a stealthy grace, the alien hunkers behind a thick piney trunk with a decent line of sight on the entire glade. He spies the compromised driver standing in a cross-armed recalcitrant pose at the vehicle's tailgate, silhouetted against dull headlights illuminating a limestone cliff base. Meanwhile, the human couple's histrionic display intensifies to embarrassing extremes. Watching the pair yell obscenities and stomp about while laughing hysterically, Niyo can't determine if their enmity is directed at each other, the driver, or all the above. With a disappointed sigh, he reconsiders whether the emotional and uncouth female could hold the key to humanity's destiny. "I may have been a wee bit hasty."

Pondering his apparent miscalculation, a scent of ozone permeates his slitted nostrils moments before a palpable foreboding overwhelms his heightened senses. Cursing his initiative, he decides that retreating to his ship before a storm turns the mountainside into a violent torrent of rain and lightning strikes is prudent. Taking a half step backward, he snaps a fallen pine branch with a loud crack, drawing the Alexander girl's eyes toward his camouflaged position. Standing ramrod still, he awaits her approach with a sullen dread. Right on cue, the doe's survival instincts kick into gear, sending the magnificent animal on a loud and distracting tear through the trees with her fawn following close behind.

Niyo relaxes as the girl's probing eyes pivot onto the robot, breaking into uncontrollable quakes and spasms.

Watching the young couple struggling to aid the stricken chauffeur, Niyo produces a thin smile as familiar luminous orbs stream from the robot, turning night into day. "I knew it all along."

History with its flickering lamp stumbles along the trail of the past, trying to reconstruct its scenes, to revive its echoes, and kindle with pale gleams the passion of former days.

– Winston Churchill

Chapter Three:
The Raid

Neil and Harry | Alto Air Base, Corsica
0930 Hours | August 16, 1944

Operation Dragoon, the code name for the allied invasion of the Provence region of southern France, proceeded apace on D-day plus one. Originally planned to coordinate with the Normandy landings two months earlier, the initial lack of resistance on the beautiful French Riviera landing zones belied the bloody combat awaiting the multi-national assemblage of forces in the following months.

Seaward from the storied beachheads, Corsica's mountainous profile juts above the azure Mediterranean horizon. Napoleon's historic island birthplace became a strategic hub for around-the-clock fighter and bomber operations supporting Southern European liberation forces, like a stationary aircraft carrier, earning the moniker: USS Corsica.

Most of the shell-shocked Corsicans welcomed the Allies with open arms. They looked on through war-weary eyes as the Allies commandeered centuries-old French government buildings and grand villas with sweeping Mediterranean views, until recently, under Axis management. Overnight, tranquil coastal pasturelands terraformed into bustling olive-drab metropolises of tents and prefab structures connected to roads, runways, supply depots, and hospitals for the bureaucratic onslaught of pilots, soldiers, doctors, nurses, support, and administrative personnel.

Near the charming village of Fovelli, nestled between the mountainous island's eastern slopes and the azure sea, Alto Air Base became the new home for the 57th Fighter Group's three squadrons: The Exterminators, Fighting Cocks, and the Black Scorpions. Fresh off the bloody North African campaign, the rumble of brand-new Republic P-47 Thunderbolts replacing obsolete P-40 Tomahawks vibrated everything not nailed down. Relentless waves of takeoffs and landings from the north-south runway bulldozed out of the grassy coastline, rattled war-weary Corsicans' windows, and sent breakables crashing to the floor. Still, it beat the hell out of life under Nazi occupation. The cocksure airmen and their crews ingratiated themselves amongst the welcoming townsfolk, in stark contrast to the defeated Nazis who fled, leaving behind a disastrous mess. An age-old dilemma became an amusing diversion for the locals: minimizing fraternization between their alluring olive-skinned daughters and resourceful American suitors.

* * *

Two pilots sporting well-worn flight suits emblazoned with Black Scorpion squadron patches strode past a bullet-riddled plane parked askew, its damaged engine cowling cast aside on the rock-hard dirt, engine parts lay strewn across a tarpaulin. Wet-behind-the-ears army mechanics tossed a football, awaiting the return of their tough-as-nails sergeant and his sage instructions.

The pilots, Captain Neil Alexander and his wingman, Lieutenant Harry Stark, P-47 Thunderbolt pilots in the 64th Squadron, aka The Black Scorpions, crossed the tarmac under the blazing Mediterranean sunshine toward their commander's office.

A panicked, high-pitched wail disrupted their conversation, "Hey, Captain, heads-up over there!"

Neil intercepted the errant pass in the nick of time before it contacted his head. Gripping the pigskin, he twirled it to the seam and threw a perfect spiral on a bead at the embarrassed mechanic. The pass knocked the mortified kid off his feet, but he caught the ball, eliciting howls of laughter from his buddies in the malingering ground crew.

Straight out of central casting, the six-foot, athletically framed Neil Alexander embodied the image of a dashing fighter pilot. Roman nose, piercing dark-blue eyes, angular cheeks, chiseled jawline, and a debonair shock curling onto his tan forehead from neatly parted jet-black hair. The look prompted good-natured Hollywood gibes from envious squadron mates.

Neil's self-deprecating response: "Carol is the good-looking one in the family, and no, you can't ogle over her photo."

The ground crews' hoots and laughter faded into the background as they continued across the noisy base. With an immodest wink and a perfect grin, Neil brags, "I still have it. I should never have left Yale."

Harry produced an overt eye roll in reply, "Right, Captain, as if you had a choice in the matter."

The trope opposites attract epitomized Neil and Harry's friendship. While Neil possessed an Ivy League pedigree, movie star good looks, and effortless aplomb, a gritty determination personified Harry's young life. Bare-knuckling through a harrowing Bowery orphanage upbringing, a chance encounter with a barnstorming pilot ignited a passion for flight and an opportunity to escape the mean streets of 1930s Brooklyn.

On Harry's US Army enlistment paperwork, he cheated a birth date no one knew anyway, scrapping and over-achieving his way through basic training and on to flight school. Presaging his image as a troublemaker, Harry buzzed the tower in his T-6 trainer during his inaugural solo flight as a tribute to his barnstorming muse. The stunt almost cost him his wings. The next thing the brash, stocky fighter pilot knew, he was battling seasoned Luftwaffe pilots flying mean-looking BF-109s over the blistering Saharan desert in North Africa.

Below his carrot top, maintained in a no-nonsense crew cut, the unrelenting Mediterranean sun freckled the freckles on his fair skin and pudgy cheeks, giving his snub-nosed face a constant rubicund complexion. The pugnacious pilot's breathless and sweaty first impression drew unsolicited advice from unwitting observers to quit smoking, triggering his acidic verbal wrath, "Never smoked a cigarette in my life, pal. Mind your own business, or I'll kick your ass." Or something to that effect.

In its infinite wisdom, the Army Air Corps teamed the straight-shooting Captain Alexander with the mercurial Lieutenant Stark to mitigate the latter's knack for finding himself knee-deep in trouble at the drop of a hat. And while the pair ruled the skies and had the kills to prove it, on the ground, even the affable captain had difficulty keeping his scheming wingman in check.

Neil's typical response regarding Harry's latest shenanigans: "I'm not my brother's keeper."

* * *

Neil slapped his wingman's sweat-stained back and let out a hearty laugh at the comical eye-rolling reaction to his Yale comment. "You're right, Harry. If it's important enough for the Splendid Splinter to put his baseball career on hold and fight the good fight, the least I can do is stick around for a while longer and fight the Nazis."

Harry bit his tongue, denying his handsome friend's attempt to get under his skin. Instead, the pilot swiped a pudgy hand across his face and cast his squinty gaze skyward, "Sure, Captain, whatever you say."

The pilots continued to a line of Quonset huts, entering the relative darkness inside the rounded sheet metal structure situated askew at the far end of the row.

Adjusting their eyes to the darkened interior, Neil and Harry snapped to attention as their Squadron Commander, Colonel William Drake, ubiquitous cigarette hanging from his lower lip, entered from a back room. Grumbling a wearier-than-usual, "At ease, gentleman," the veteran aviator, who flew with Eddie Rickenbacker in the Great War, slipped behind his desk. Settling into his creaking oak chair, he swiveled while scratching the top of his shaved head. Taking the measure of two of his better pilots, he heaved a sigh and gestured for the pair to sit.

Neil and Harry stared across stacks of reports, binders of new regulations, and an unkempt pile of unread Stars and Stripes, waiting for their commander to finish his perusal of a typed dispatch. Growling a curse, Drake coughed while crumpling the thin sheet of paper. Still muttering, "Goddamn," something, he opened a side drawer and pulled out a crinkled manila envelope stamped TOP SECRET. While skimming its classified contents, he coughed again.

Neil looked on as the tip of Drake's cigarette glowed bright orange during a long drag. He noticed his boss stub it in an ashtray decorated with a palm design and the OASIS Hotel-Tripoli logo. An absent thought crossed the pilot's active mind: His only memento from the squadron's bloody stint outside the Libyan city during the North African campaign was a hazy memory of a terrible decision made in the hectic days before the squadron's redeployment to Corsica.

The sound of Drake's raspy voice snapped Neil from his regrettable rumination, "I'm aware you two have flown more than your share of missions over the last few weeks and are overdue for leave, but this request," waving the mustard-yellow envelope, "comes from way up the chain of command. And I doubt we could get half our planes into the air right now if Hitler were flying over in a big red balloon, so I recommended you and Harry for the mission."

He chuckled and coughed again, "Your definition of volunteering is probably not the same one the US Army uses. Plus, since North Africa, you two are leading charmed lives, and your crews manage to keep your planes in air-worthy condition. I've heard the chatter making the rounds, Mr. Stark. You won a lucky golden relic in an unauthorized poker game. It's as if ...." The colonel's conspiratorial hypothesis trailed off, and he reached for his Zippo lighter.

Neil sensed the tension increase and considered setting the record straight regarding the rumors. A sideways glimpse at his hot-headed partner, seething from Drake's intimations, dissuaded him from opening his mouth and inserting his foot.

Following a prolonged silence, Drake shifted gears with a dismissive wave and let out a throaty chuckle, "I guess it's a good thing there is no room for superstition in this man's army." He shut the desk drawer and leaned forward, "I don't give a rat's ass what you won, Stark. Use it in good health if it gives you a fighting edge."

With a distracted glance, Neil caught Harry's pudgy fists unclenching and sensed the tension ease as the colonel finished speaking.

"I would not have volunteered you both, but your names came up, and well, there you are."

Masking his growing annoyance at Drake's reluctance to get to the damn point, "Colonel, if this mission, whatever it entails, helps shorten the war so we can all get home, you can always count on us." A hint of agitation seeps into his voice, "Forgive me for saying so, sir; you have not provided any information as to what this mission does entail?"

The grizzled old fighter pilot lit another cigarette, smoke wafting into the stale air, and turned to a stack of binders, "It's so damned secret, they won't tell me shit." He grabbed the manila envelope again, "This thin sheet of parchment instructs you both to report to the briefing hut and await further instructions. The specific request for your services is all I was told. For some damn reason, the OSS is involved. Those secretive bastards never elaborate ahead of time and will not tolerate tardiness." With a thin-veiled sarcasm, "However, I'm sure they are ready and willing to address all of your questions or concerns."

Drake fired a new cigarette without looking at his two pilots, "Check in with me when you get back."

Halfway out the door, Neil heard Drake's usual send-off, "Oh, and Captain."

"Yes, Colonel?"

"Good hunting."

* * *

Quickening their pace toward the briefing hut, Harry cracked, "The old guy brings a tear to my eyes."

"Probably from all of the smoke."

"He sure does love his cigarettes. I'm relieved he didn't press us harder on the scuttlebutt going around the base about our buried treasure."

On the verge of reprimanding Harry for considering assaulting their commanding officer, a honking Jeep skidded to a stop and blocked their path. The obnoxious interruption superseded his first attempt to address the secret buried in the Libyan desert since their arrival in Corsica.

A gawky corporal yelled from behind the wheel over the Army Jeep's rumbling engine, "Captain Neil Alexander? Lieutenant Harry Stark?"

"Yes, corporal, that's us, but we're already on our way to the briefing."

"Hop in, sirs; I have orders to drive you to a new location!"

The corporal chauffeured the pilots outside the secure perimeter of Alto Air Base into the countryside toward a rustic stone villa nestled atop a precipitous ridgeline in the rugged Corsican mountains and its commanding view of the Mediterranean. Neil admired the cerulean vista speckled with clouds to the far horizon and an impressive armada of cruisers and destroyers protecting merchant marine vessels plying the Med in a zigzagging pattern to flummox U-boats lurking in the deep-blue depths.

Waved past a heavily guarded checkpoint, the Jeep sped along a meandering gravel driveway, braking under the historic villa's porte cochère. The aviators hopped out, and a guard motioned them to the top of the grand stairway, where a baby-faced orderly ushered the pair through thick mahogany arched double doors bookended with rangy potted palms. They proceeded through the echoing tiled foyer into a dim-lit anteroom bereft of accouterments aside from a matte-black rotary telephone atop a spartan desk with a Nazi swastika gouged out of its worn top. The orderly wordlessly vacated the space, leaving Neil and Harry trading bemused expressions on their stubbled faces.

Harry tapped the notorious mark and snickered, "What a bunch of assholes." Pushing the phone aside, he leaned his sweaty frame on the desk, causing it to slide on the tile floor with an obnoxious screech. Oblivious to his social faux pas, "Captain, what the heck did we volunteer for?"

Neil shook his head and berated his wingman, "Are you tired? Just stand there and try not to break anything." Peeking through a small fissure in the blacked-out window shades facing the front portico, "Just once, I'd like to know what we're volunteering for ahead of time."

A nattily dressed older man appeared from the same doorway the orderly vacated, "Ah, you've arrived! Good show!"

Cradling a China cup and saucer, the dashing Brit proffered a handshake, "You Americans hardly ever arrive on schedule. Color me somewhat surprised. Happily, so, I may add. I'm Major General Thompson, representing British Intelligence. I will be briefing both of you on tonight's mission. We appreciate your commander—Colonel Drake, I believe—loaning you and your copilot to us. You see, we are in a bind with our resources stretched rather thin. However, the opportunity before us has the potential to deal a swift and decisive blow to the enemy," he paused and sipped from his cup. "Without further ado, follow me, gentlemen," and gestured for the pair to follow him down a dark corridor.

Matching Thompson's economic pace, Harry glanced through a half-open door on his right, catching a familiar fellow seated in an impressive leather recliner with a brandy snifter on a side table, smoking a signature cigar while reading a newspaper. Bursting at the seams, Harry tugged Neil's sleeve.

Neil turned and winked at his friend, "I saw him too."

The pilots followed Thompson through an open set of double doors at the far end of the mansion into an echoing hall with massive windows blacked out with long opaque drapes taped to the edges of the ornate window moldings. Tiny streams of light seeping through widows were the only clues to the late-afternoon August day outside the thick panes of glass. Instead, wall sconces and festive crystal chandeliers—remnants from bygone happier times—provided lighting inside the cavernous space.

A floor-to-ceiling map of Operation Dragoon landing zones along the Provence coastline, cross-lit with directional lighting mounted on tripods, dominated the room's far end. A mahogany conference table with two of its sixteen chairs pulled askew occupied the parquet floor in front of the map wall. A manila folder, notepad, pen, cups, and saucers were set on the table before each chair with military precision and all-too-British formality. A silver platter heaped with local-grown grapes and dates, French pastries, and a large silver coffee server were within reach of the two seats.

Thompson ensured everything was in order before excusing himself, "I do apologize, gentlemen. There is an unrelated matter requiring my attention before we begin. I will return in a jiffy. In the meantime, relax and enjoy the repast."

Neil and Harry navigated between the opulent furnishings, circumnavigating a trio of chocolate brown leather wingback chairs around a circular coffee table covered with ashtrays, abandoned cups and saucers, and newspapers. Serious-looking men in black suits and ties occupying two chairs glanced at the pilots before returning to their conversation. Still wearing their grubby flight suits, they nodded past the murmuring gentlemen and continued toward the prearranged conference table seating.

Neil poured a coffee, pulled out the chair on the right, and plopped down with a war-weary sigh. Harry slid his seat aside, eliciting another loud groan, leaned forward, and filled a silver plate with grapes and pastries, prompting Neil to shoot an annoyed expression.

Harry noticed the sour expression on his friend's face, "What? I haven't eaten since breakfast. I'm starving."

While Harry wolfed down fruit and pastries, Neil turned toward the far end of the darkened hall where a fair-complexioned brunette in a black turtleneck over a knee-length black dress and nylons sat in a demure cross-legged pose. She appeared nervous, dwarfed on a garish French Provincial settee centered below a gilded gold-framed Tuscan landscape painting.

After making eye contact with Neil, the young woman averted her gaze, concealing a coquettish smile while fidgeting with a red silk scarf.

Harry followed Neil's enrapt gaze onto the girl with a shrug before polishing off another pastry. While Harry exhibited none of the proclivities warranting a swift and ignominious ouster from this man's army, the stocky pilot nonetheless avoided women, precluding swift and embarrassing rejections from the fairer sex. The lone sexual encounter in Harry's sad life ended with half a week's hard-earned pay left atop a shoddy credenza in a dank second-floor apartment in Biloxi,

Mississippi, on a weekend pass. It was also the only time Harry enjoyed a smoke in his entire life. Ashamed and disgusted with himself after the sordid encounter, the mere suggestion that he ever smoked a cigarette triggered his legendary temper.

A Louis XVI clock ticked off four minutes after three atop an unlit French Provincial fireplace mantle ten paces to the right of the door Thompson disappeared through thirty minutes earlier. Her smile faded, and the petite young woman sat in resolute silence, fidgeting with a red scarf in her delicate hands. At the same time, the men in black suits' conspiratorial whispering continued unabated. Neil smirked as his wingman finished off the pile of grapes and his third pastry. Aside from the hushed voices, tick-tocks, and an impertinent belch from Harry, the dark hall was quieter than a library reading room. Neil studied the gigantic wall map of Operation Dragoon with a second cup of coffee and mulled whether they should leave.

Verging on pulling Harry's seat away from the trough, Neil caught Thompson's reappearance from his peripheral vision. Instead of approaching the table, the Brit made a beeline toward the men in black, to his dismay. Never one to suffer fools or have his valuable time wasted, Neil tapped his partner's thick shoulder, "That's it. We're out of here, Harry."

Sensing movement, Thompson turned and saw the two pilots push back from their chairs. He whispered across the echoing space, producing a toothy smile, "Gentlemen, I will be right there! Please sit down."

Harry felt the conspiratorial stare of both black suits pierce his resolve and retook his seat while clearing marzipan from his teeth with his tongue.

After his hour-long absence, Thompson finally took a seat at the head of the table to Neil's right and addressed Harry, "Lieutenant, those two gentlemen would like a word with you after our meeting."

Deep inside, Harry Stark knew what they were after, but they had a snowball's chance in hell of prying it out of his ugly mug. Feigning ignorance with practiced ease, "What do they want? Am I in trouble?"

Thompson interrupts Neil from raising his concern, "Please, Captain Alexander, do not be alarmed. Their interest in Lieutenant Stark is not germane to this briefing. My apologies for the prolonged delay, but I see you availed yourself of the spread. Good show.' Thompson's disarming smile failed to lighten the captain's surly expression, so he cleared his throat and commenced the briefing. "So as not to waste any more of your valuable time, let's get on with it, shall we? Gentlemen, open your folders and hold your questions and concerns to the end if you please."

Realizing the time to protest had passed, Neil broke the seal and opened his folder as the British officer poured a new cup and motioned for the young woman, "Anna, please join us and share the intelligence you valiantly brought to our attention," addressing Neil, "at risk of great personal peril, no less."

Anna stood taller than Neil expected. Shedding her shy demeanor, she moved with confidence before the huge wall map across the table from the flummoxed pilots, tossed the red scarf on the table near Harry, and snatched the wooden pointer stick in her hand.

The striking young woman smiled at the aviators' puzzled expressions before addressing the table with an alluring French-accented English. "Good afternoon, gentlemen. I am here to brief you on the details of an event brought to British intelligence here in Corsica. It concerns an evacuation of Nazi officers and high-level party officials from the south of France via train in the early hours of tomorrow morning under cover of darkness. They plan to travel north to safer Nazi-occupied territory."

Thompson interjected, "We believe this evacuation is part of a broader German retreat. We want to strike the train before …."

Anna interrupted the British officer's exuberance with a sharp crack on the table with her stick, "As Mr. Thompson was about to say, French Resistance obtained the exact time and place." Pirouetting toward the map, Anna stretched the pointer in her left hand, tapping the name Aix-en-Provence, barely legible amidst the topographical lines, directional arrows, pinned notes, and recon photos.

Harry leaned forward and squinted to see the small printed French name on the map, "Jesus, I think I need glasses."

Anna shot daggers at the rude American and cleared her throat in an unmistakable message to shut the hell up, "However, there is a problem: the area is thick with Germans guarding the railyards. Attacking the train from the ground at the optimal time full of Germans and French traitors is not an option. Further complicating matters, the departure will occur under darkness with decoy trains steaming out of town simultaneously to stymie saboteurs."

"Our only hope is for brave patriots to infiltrate the railyard and illuminate the actual train before it departs. This way, the Germans will be lulled into a false sense of security until it's too late."

Neil's Rolex read 1535 hours, "When is this supposed to occur?"

"3:30 a.m."

"Say one thing about the Nazis; they like their trains to run on time."

Anna furrowed her pretty face into a menacing grimace and berated the red-haired comedian, "Do you think this is a joke?"

Taken aback by the hostility, Harry stammered in reply.

Neil knew his partner meant no disrespect and jumped to his defense, but Thompson raised his bony hand to stop him again and took it upon himself to address the emotional French woman, "Calm down, my dear. These men are here to ensure the train never leaves the station. Lieutenant Stark's humor is merely a coping mechanism. I'm sure he meant no offense."

Harry swiveled toward Neil, "Coping mechanism?"

"Harry, don't start ...."

Anna glared at the pilots, her eyes welling with tears, "Look at my scarf! It is stained with the blood of fallen comrades who sacrificed their lives for France. The Germans murdered my family. I barely escaped with my life!" She wiped her dark brown eyes with her sleeve, "This information is not only for your tactical advance into Europe; it is revenge for my countrymen. *Vive la France!*"

Baffled by Anna's outburst, the men stood as she stormed out of the room and slammed the door shut, which sent a priceless Cezanne crashing to the floor.

The Black Suits paused their conversation but remained seated as she made her dramatic exit. The man on the left unfolded a dog-eared map of North Africa and spread it out on the low table while the other made eye contact with Thompson and pointed at his watch.

Thompson acknowledged their signal with a nod. Desperate to salvage the meeting, he turned to the berated pilots, reflexively twisting a waxed end of his mustache between the first two fingers on his left hand, and presented his not-to-worry, toothy grin. Mustering his British knack for understatement, "Anna is a little upset, gentlemen. I do hope you appreciate the risk she accepted in coming here. And the risks her fellow freedom fighters will undertake to illuminate the train in the railyard so you two can swoop in and destroy it at the optimal time."

Finally grasping the crux of the mission, Harry pushed aside his empty plate, "What's this now?"

Thompson stood and moved before the wall map, where Anna's meltdown occurred moments earlier, "I'm gratified to have your full attention, young man." The heat from the blaring cross-directional lamps prompted Thompson to wipe at his bushy brow with a hankie, "These blasted lights." He picked up the pointer and tapped the polished oak surface, "Not to worry, Lieutenant Stark, it's all planned down to the minute in your folder."

Harry picked up his thick folder and produced a sardonic smile, "Well, okay! You had me worried we might have to endure real danger. What am I supposed to do? Throw this at them?"

Neil placed a firm hand on Harry's forearm, "That's enough, Lieutenant."

Thompson dabbed at his forehead, "It's quite all right, Captain. I appreciate your wingman's dark humor."

The dapper English officer pivoted to the map, "Where was I? Oh yes. First, gentlemen, we must maintain the element of surprise." He glanced toward the impatient men and said, "A rare opportunity to kill top German brass in one lethal strike can only work if they don't see it coming. To that end, we are resurrecting a plan whereby resistance fighters infiltrate the railyard and illuminate the target with a fighter bomber attack swooping out of the darkness and delivering Jerry a lethal blow." He smacked the spot on the map with the pointer stick and dabbed his brow, distracted by Harry snatching the last grape and popping it in his mouth, "That's where you two enter the fray."

Thompson returned to his seat, cognizant of the all-too-familiar "you've got to be joking" looks staring him down. Adopting a defensive tone, he conceded the slim odds of success, "In an ideal world, which Lord knows we never have, the planes would be British Typhoons, and the pilots would be RAF. But there is not enough time. There is never enough time. Damn it all." The British officer leaned back and modulated his tone, "Fortunately, gentlemen, a high-level British officer on these premises imposed his will on your high command, which led to getting the both of you on loan."

Neil recalled the cigar-smoking gentleman down the hall.

Thompson noted Captain Alexander's dot-connecting ability, "More coffee, Captain Alexander?" At the snap of long bony fingers, an orderly materialized from the shadows, switched out the pots, and departed.

Harry called into the darkness, "Better keep it coming. It sounds like this is going to be a long night. Right, Captain?"

Over the next hour, Thompson explained the attack plan, starting with the early morning takeoff at 0150 hours. Altitudes, airspeeds, and weather forecasted en route and over the target were described in detail. Neil and Harry took notes and committed the plan to memory to the best of their abilities.

The British intelligence officer cautioned, "The resistance's ability to illuminate the train will be fleeting. After the Krauts realize what is happening under their noses, all bets are off. Adherence to the predetermined time of the attack is imperative. If you follow the flight plan, it should work down to the minute."

Thompson poured more coffee and gestured with the pot. Neil declined. The intelligence officer shrugged and set the silver carafe onto the table with symbolic finality, "Or something will go wrong, and it will be up to you both to determine the best course of action. Bear in mind that the locals despise the Nazi occupiers. Therefore, minimizing collateral damage is paramount, as Anna mentioned earlier."

Flipping through the attack plan, scribbling notes on the leatherbound pad, Neil nodded, a fatalistic grin across his dashing features, "Damned if you haven't figured this one out. I'm impressed."

Harry's beady-eyed stare traced the flight plan on the massive wall map, stretching his stubby frame to get the blood flowing, "Will the resistance fighters have time to escape after they expose the target?"

Thompson studied the stout fellow's ruddy countenance before answering, "Young man, it is a suicide mission for the resistance, and a botched attack will compromise other covert operations." Spreading his hands across the polished mahogany table, "I must say, gentlemen, this mission will be far from a jolly stroll through the park. The railyards in Aix-en-Provence are spiked with antiaircraft manned by sharpshooting SS troops who will throw up flak thick enough to walk across."

"Where have we heard that before? Every time we fly a mission." Harry laughed at his joke.

Thompson closed his folder and finished his cup. "The both of you have my admiration and appreciation—and that of everyone within the confines of this villa." Gesturing toward the hall's double doors,

"Particularly the gentleman down the corridor."

* * *

After parting ways with Thompson via a curt salute, Neil left his partner at the mercy of the black-suited inquisitors. Shifting from foot to foot under the porte cochère, he clutched the leatherbound mission briefing and contemplated why he and his wingman were singled out. Thompson could have leaned on his wing commanders, but he didn't. Why? Corsica is lousy with pilots and planes. "It's that fucking golden ellipse. They want Harry to cough up the Libyan desert coordinates in exchange for being relieved from this suicide mission."

Laughing to himself, "They have no idea whom they're dealing with."

Fifteen minutes later, Harry Stark ambled out the main doors with an inscrutable look and stopped beside Neil without saying a word.

The awkward silence broke as the same gawky corporal steered the Jeep up the drive to chauffeur them back to Alto Air Base.

Careening along the cratered lane hugging the Eastern coastline of Corsica, they bumped past a burned-out column of German tanks and vehicles shoved off the road. From his shotgun seat, Neil marveled at how fast the weeds, vines, and grass overtook the rusting mass of destroyed war machinery decaying under a scrubby stand of oaks and olive trees. Without turning toward the backseat, "Your meeting was short. Aren't you going to share what they wanted? Wait, don't tell me. They're revenue agents after your back taxes if you bite the dust tonight."

Harry produced a devilish grin, gazing at long shadows creeping over the Corsican countryside, holding on as the Jeep swerved around a pothole, "No. I wish it were that simple, Captain. They are OSS agents assigned to track down and secure our contraband." The pudgy man produced a baleful laugh, "That idiot Hodges must have spilled the beans." Checking that the driver couldn't hear him, "It's all hearsay. They have nothing on us. I tried to play dumb, but they didn't buy it.

Lucky for us, this mission, the brainchild of Churchill himself, came along in the nick of time. They had no choice but to let me go on my way. Quite a coincidence, right, Captain?"

"Harry, I don't believe in coincidence."

Neil's recollection of the fateful day they hid the golden ellipse remained shrouded in a nightmarish fog. The mere hint of his culpability sent a chill down his spine. Handwritten coordinates on the back of his wife's photo in Harry's chicken scratch provided the only tangible evidence he was there. And only his conniving wingman knew if the numbers were accurate. The decorated Army Air Corps captain compartmentalized his part in the deceit as a hasty decision made under duress in the chaos of relocating the squadron to Corsica.

Given Harry's account of the OSS involvement, it appeared the black-suited chickens were coming home to roost.

Hot and dry Corsican air whipped through the Jeep as Neil pivoted to meet his partner eye-to-eye and assume the brotherly role foisted upon him by his chain of command, "Drake alluded to the relic earlier today." Recalling Harry's clenched fist response to their commander's impertinent reference to their golden treasure, "I'm worried something is going on inside your thick skull. Anything you want to tell me before we take off on this suicide mission later tonight?"

Noting Harry's chubby face hardened into a stony silence, Neil digs further, "My theory is the OSS strong-armed Drake into singling us out for this raid. They probably thought you would break and offer the coordinates in exchange for getting out of this half-baked mission."

The bouncing vehicle made an abrupt right-handed turn through Alto's main gate. Like a dog guarding its bone, Harry snapped from his trance-like state with a vicious snarl directed at his best friend, "Not a chance, Captain. I'll never give it to them. I won it fair and square. Since we came into possession of the golden ellipse, we are invincible—even old Drake sees it as true. Tonight, let's blast this train full of Nazis and live to fight another day. Nothing has changed, Neil.

The ellipse belongs to us! Your problem is that you worry too much."

Taken aback by Harry's evil, beady-eyed stare, Neil came to a terrible conclusion. This was not the same man he had grown to know over the past couple of years. Brasher. Yes. More confident. Yes. However, Harry's short fuse and careless attitude spell disaster for a fighter pilot. At the root of Harry's negative transformation, a gold elliptical object Neil glimpsed for a fleeting second, as if in a dream.

Unfortunately, confronting self-inflicted burdens would have to wait. The pilots geared up and watched in silence as their ground crews finished mounting 500 lb. bombs under the wings while the heavy aircraft were fueled and armed for this ultra-secret mission from none other than Winston Churchill. Neil checked his watch and spit into the dirt as his crew chief gave him a thumbs-up.

Neil and Harry | Alto Air Base, Corsica
0130 Hours | August 17, 1944

Since early in the North African campaign, Neil and Harry lost too many brothers in arms to count. Like Anna, sweet vengeance in one decisive attack underscored the nighttime mission. And accepting the reality that they might not return applied to every time they were wheels up, not just this time. Even the group meteorologist's CAVU forecast proved a mixed blessing. Flying at treetop level to destroy enemy rail lines, convoys, and gun emplacements was the standard operating procedure for the Black Scorpions of the 64th Squadron. Conversely, if ceiling and visibility were unlimited, sharpshooting Nazis could also target them.

Indeed, a perfect night for flying, Neil thought as he grinned a confident salute to his ground crew and climbed into the cockpit. Winking at his wife's bewitching black and white photo taped aside his instrument panel for good luck, he muses pilots are a superstitious bunch. Flipping switches and powering the plane's Pratt and Whitney engine to life in a cloud of exhaust, he considers how fighter pilots take it to the next level. At least his good luck charm was easy on the eyes.

At 0130 hours, the bomb-laden P-47 Razorback Thunderbolts, dubbed Jugs for their shape and legendary resilience, rumbled down the airstrip in the moonlight and corkscrewed to their assigned altitude above Alto Air Base on their predetermined heading over the Mediterranean, the shimmering French Riviera, and the Allied invasion forces far below. The drone of plane engines drew a predictable scattering of friendly fire. Nothing too close, but a trigger-happy GI's bullet could ruin the mission before it started.

Neil checked his instrument panel and scanned for bogeys. Luftwaffe ME-110 night fighters pouncing on unsuspecting AAF pilots and crews were a constant threat, but they typically preyed on damaged bombers struggling home after a raid and avoided fighter planes. Breathing oxygen through his mask, he contemplated that with any luck, this would be an in-and-out surprise attack, and approximately four hours later, they would be back at Alto drinking warm Italian beer.

The fighter planes rumbled over enemy-held France on a northwesterly heading. Muffled explosions and tracer fire flashed across the war-torn landscape below their wingtips as they flew toward their target. "So far, so good," Neil thought, peering through his canopy into darkness.

Five minutes outside Aix-en-Provence, at precisely 0325, Neil broke radio silence, "Here we go, Harry. I'll take the locomotive and the first car. You take out the rest of the train! Good hunting!"

Harry whooped in reply, "I'm on it, Captain! Lead the way!"

The Thunderbolts swooped low to the treetops dead-on toward the target. Right on cue, a locomotive pulling a train of passenger cars lit up like a Christmas tree amid a confusing knot of boxcars, tankers, Pullmans, and steam engines. Within seconds, chaos reigned throughout the yard; sirens wailed, searchlights pierced the night, and erratic tracer fire arced into the sky. "We caught them with their pants down, Harry! They don't see us!" Neil targeted the locomotive, garishly decorated with red and black swastika banners, and released his bombs while blasting it and the lead Pullman with his eight .50 caliber machine guns, confirming the enemy disintegrating in a fireball as Harry's screechy voice ratcheted in his headset, "Nice shooting, Cap!"

Banking right off Neil's wingtip—still on a sugar-high from the fruit and pastries consumed earlier—Harry skipped his payload into the packed passenger cars while raking them with his blazing wing-mounted guns. Shrapnel, train, and body parts pelted frantic Germans fleeing the hellacious scene as blazes raged throughout the yard.

Squinting through his goggles at the billowing smoke and flames, "So much for minimizing damage to the rest of the yard; war is a messy business."

A thousand pounds lighter without the wing-mounted bombs, Neil streaked over the fires raging below his wingtips and blurted into his oxygen mask mic: "Damn, Harry, the locomotive is still intact. I'm going to come around and try again."

Staticky dead air followed with no reply from his wingman.

The P-47 banked hard for a second run, but vengeful German gunners targeted Neil with a furious barrage of antiaircraft fire. White-hot bullets shattered his canopy, ripping through his cockpit and obliterating his instrument panel. Cursing his careless maneuver, he yanked the useless mask off his face, "In for a penny, in for a pound." Ignoring intense pain throbbing from his bleeding left side, he angled in for a second strafing attack.

Oblivious to the railyard conflagration scorching the undersides of his fighter bomber's wings and dark-olive fuselage, Neil squeezed the firing button on his control stick and watched humans writhing in flames, leaping from the stricken train like rats jumping from a sinking ship. Careening over the chaos, the injured pilot pulled back hard into a steep climb as the billowing fireball from the exploding locomotive lapped at his plane's tail. Managing to maintain control with just his right hand, he leveled off and tried to ignore the terrible pain.

"Let's get out of here, Harry," Neil garbled aloud into his mask before realizing it no longer worked, like most everything else in the cockpit.

Where was Harry?

Wracked with searing pain, Neil searched the chaotic sky while struggling to maintain control of his plane. Air whistled through jagged holes in the blood and oil-spattered canopy. Fearful of a midair collision with Harry's jug amidst columns of acrid smoke rising from the destroyed railyard, he coaxed his plane into a sweeping turn without using his broken left arm. Ignoring sporadic gunfire, he climbed to take one last look at the scene. What he saw sank his heart like a stone. "Harry! What did you do?"

Silhouetted against bright orange flames, the unmistakable shape of Harry's P-47 tail section jutted from a fully engulfed train car. Profound grief overwhelmed the stricken pilot.

The Army Air Force Captain angled his sputtering, smoking P-47 on a heading toward home with the mission accomplished but at a terrible cost. Tracer fire arced toward his damaged Thunderbolt, but he was out of range within half a minute, vanishing into the night, minus his best friend.

Through tear-filled eyes, he spied a white parachute shimmering in the moonlight, fluttering in a dense patch of trees east of town. Realizing Harry managed to bail out buoyed his spirit. He noted the spot and flew on into the inky nighttime sky.

Neil calmed his breathing, taking stock of the damage to his plane and himself. He calculated crossing the thin Allied beachhead and bailing out over the Med, where a friendly destroyer or sub could scoop him out of the drink, provided his best chance for survival. Looking at the blood-spattered photo of his lovely wife, Neil muttered, "Well, sweetheart, looks like I need a little luck, after all."

Letting out a wet raspy groan, he labored to pull back on the stick and ascend through a cloudbank. The jug leveled off at approximately 5,000 feet. Gut instinct, experience, and Army training had to suffice if he were to have any chance. However, nothing prepared Neil Alexander for what came next.

Diaphanous orbs burst out of thin air and swirled around his damaged plane like angry bees. Hypothesizing he must be in the throes of a trauma-induced hallucination, he watched the dancing lights invade his cockpit.

Breathless reports of light balls harassing Allied aircraft seldom made it into official mission debriefs. Nevertheless, most pilots and crew members heard firsthand accounts of the phenomenon. They called them foo fighters. Neil figured they were a German secret weapon or, more likely, pilot fatigue. But here they were, as bright as Times Square on New Year's Eve, inches in front of his bloody face.

Shifting toward more lights entering through the canopy, the Army Air Force captain cried out in agonized pain from shrapnel tearing deeper into his side, realizing he would not make it.

Neither was his plane. The fighter bomber's engine sputtered and quit, the propeller jerked to a stop, and the P-47 dipped sideways into a sickening nosedive. Neil's injuries precluded a bailout. Letting go of the stick, he pulled his wife's photo to his chest and squeezed his eyes shut inside the spiraling aircraft. Accepting death with sadness for a life he would never know, Neil Alexander waited for the inevitable.

But the inevitable never came.

A silent and peaceful drifting sensation proved that death was not so bad. What a relief. Death never strayed far from one's thoughts during wartime. And predicting the experience, a frequent debate topic in the trenches, on the seas, and in the skies.

Another painful jolt forced open bloodshot eyeballs, snapping him back to a new reality. Trying to comprehend what held the damaged plane aloft, the eerie drifting sensation made his head swoon. A pure white light bathed the cramped confines of his blood and gore-smeared cockpit, making it impossible to get his bearings.

"Your injuries are too severe."

"Who are you? Where are you taking me?"

Silence followed.

A sheer stone face reflecting bluish moonlight filled the view outside the broken canopy. Neil's plane floated within feet of the cliff at a dizzying height, ascended over a ledge, and traversed a narrow ridgeline.

He watched in amazement as a fissure gaped out of solid limestone. His P-47 lowered through nose first as if held aloft from its tail by a hook, grazing a rocky outcropping before entering an echoing chasm inside the mountain. The brilliant orbs rested the damaged plane's scorched belly onto the damp cavern floor, settling on its port side next to a gurgling subterranean stream and removing the shattered canopy. With his blood-soaked body lit up by a sheer radiance, Neil Alexander drifted to a faraway place, peering through all-too-human eyes at his wife's smiling face on the crumpled photo still clutched in his bloody fingers. Human concern for his mortal wounds evaporated, replaced by a euphoric sense of wellness.

The specks of light pierced Neil's broken form, separating the man's essence, including his quick-witted charm, curious intellect, and inventive spirit, from his final repose. A deafening hum reverberated through the dark cavern as the orbs transformed the pilot into energized particles, recreating him in a quintessential glowing manifestation floating above his steaming and ticking war-ravaged plane.

The fully realized ethereal effigy of the Army Air Force captain opened new eyes upon his blood-soaked corpse slumped inside the cockpit. "What did you do to me?"

"Your task lies ahead of you. All that you were is gone. Neil Alexander, it is time to go."

Satisfied with their transformative rescue mission, the foo fighters exploded outward in a blinding ball of light, bathing the echoing expanse in silvery radiance and transporting Neil on a spectacular trip across time and space to meet his extraterrestrial benefactors.

Inside the cavern deep within Montagne Sainte-Victoire, the photograph remained clutched in Neil's cold dead hands, where it will stay shrouded in darkness inside the aircraft-cum-coffin for one hundred years.

Harry Stark

Less than one week after the air raid on the Aix-en-Provence railyard, investigators came across the burnt tail section of Lieutenant Harry Stark's P-47 in the charred debris. News of the missing pilot's tattered and singed chute wafting from high branches in a heavily wooded area a few miles outside of town triggered an all-out search for the missing pilot. In a clearing not far from the chute, a rifle platoon made the grisly discovery of a mass grave with the fresher remains of three resistance fighters piled on top.

Inquisitive OSS officers in black suits braved a trek to the dangerous forward area, still crawling with Germans, to interrogate captured Nazis and French locals regarding a stocky red-headed pilot but came up empty. Unsatisfied with the German officers' indignant shrugs alternating with adamant pleas of ignorance; they emptied every file cabinet and safe within the former Nazi headquarters in Aix-en-Provence. They found nothing. The carrot-topped bastard had vanished into thin air.

Unable to locate any blood relations, Colonel William Drake wrote a letter regarding Stark's official MIA status to the man scribbled in as a legal guardian in the lieutenant's personnel file. The famous name, Eddie Angel, was not lost on an old aviator like Drake, "It figures a walking enigma like Harry Stark would list a famous barnstormer as his next-of-kin."

Drake shifted through the lieutenant's meager belongings wholly contained in a shoebox. Reaching under a well-worn Yankees baseball cap, he pulled out a hardcover edition of *The Legend of Sleepy Hollow* by Washington Irving. Never taking Harry for a connoisseur of literature, he noted it was an illustrated edition. "That makes more sense." After a quick puff from his cigarette, Drake leaned back and flipped it open, smirking at the New York Public Library imprimatur stamped in faded cobalt ink on the inside front cover. After another puff, the colonel flipped to the title page and turned cold with fright.

A man who witnessed death up close too many times to count, Drake nonetheless felt an inexplicable chill creep up his spine while studying the childlike drawing of the headless horseman rendered in red crayon filling the negative space beneath the nameplate. Not that unusual; many library books suffered similar fates. An arrow pointing from the headless horseman to the word ME, centered in block letters on the facing page, got under Drake's skin and made it crawl.

Neil Alexander

The most confounding mystery for the OSS investigators assigned to the missing pilot's case involved whatever happened to Captain Neil Alexander after the successful raid. Air and ground searches found no evidence giving any clue in locating the captain's final resting place.

The official record stated: *"The area was searched for impromptu burial sites and wreckage from crashed planes matching the P-47 with negative results. Examination of captured German documents revealed the roster of prominent Nazis killed during the surprise attack on the train but failed to disclose any information about the missing pilot."*

Colonel Drake's heartfelt letter to Neil's distraught wife ended: *"...Captain Neil Alexander overshot the French coastline and crashed into the Mediterranean Sea. However, no floating wreckage was recovered to bolster this theory. Like his wingman, Harry Stark, he just vanished. Hopefully, the Red Cross would inform us if the Germans captured him. In the meantime, I am very sorry for your loss. May God bless you in this time of deep sorrow. All the captain's personal belongings were included along with this letter. If you need anything, please feel free to contact me."*

The terrible news spread like wildfire at Alto Air Base. Two of the best pilots in the 64th Squadron were missing after a late-night raid on a railyard in Southern France. Inseparable since the squadron was formed, the pair were admired amongst their fellow pilots, ground crews, and support staff. Drunken toasts by comrades in arms honored the lost pilots with warm Italian beers held high. After the initial shock wore off, unrelenting wartime events and the tragic loss of more brave pilots and airmen pushed the story of Neil and Harry into the recesses of time.

Neither Alexander nor Stark were liberated from one of the hundreds of P.O.W. camps in the run-up to V-E Day, smashing the Black Suits' last hope of apprehending the pair alive.

Colonel William Drake

Inside the Quonset hut at the end of a long row of ugly metal structures, Colonel Drake sat behind his desk and tried to tune out the early morning Alto Airbase din reverberating through the half-open doorway. The butt of the third cigarette of his morning jutted from the souvenir ashtray, emanating a wisp of blue smoke like the tail section of a downed fighter plane, smashed into an ashen mound.

Opposite Drake's messy desk sat two nattily dressed gentlemen in matching black suits and ties. As the meeting ended, both men stood as if joined at the hip. The man on the left replaced the fedora balanced on a knee, back atop his shaved head, and nodded to his partner. Taking his cue to exit, the other black suit clutched the briefcase containing, over Drake's half-hearted objections, the personnel files of the two missing and presumed dead pilots. Without uttering another word, they walked into the early-morning Mediterranean sunshine.

The war-weary officer lit another cigarette as the door clattered shut behind the two peculiar, humorless men. Alone once more, Drake leaned back in his creaking chair, took a long drag on the cigarette cradled between gnarled fingers, and blew a smoke ring into the stillness. After briefly reflecting on losing more experienced pilots, he returned to the stack of paperwork on his desk and got on with winning the goddamn war.

Carol Alexander

Word of the costly yet successful strike on the railyard in Southern France spread quickly. News accounts of a decisive blow to the enemy and the fiery demise of many Nazis and evil sympathizers inspired rejoicing and countless drunken toasts all around the Allied world.

Meanwhile, Carol Alexander patted her baby boy peacefully asleep on her shoulder and silently grieved the loss of her dear departed husband. She had received the horrible news from an empathetic casualty assistance officer proffering Drake's letter on her front doorstep two weeks after the raid.

One week later, still in shock and mourning Neil's death and the uncertainty of what happened to him on the night of the raid, she endured strange and impertinent questions from two polite yet cold and suspicious agents from the Office of Strategic Services.

The OSS agents sat side-by-side, perched on her living room sofa with cups and saucers on the coffee table beside their opened briefcases.

Though rattled by their accusatory tone, Carol maintained her dignity and decorum from the safety of Neil's favorite rocking chair, reaffirming that she knew nothing about contraband or antiquities, golden or otherwise.

A haunting feeling of being watched persisted throughout the rest of Carol Alexander's long and productive life. Over time she learned to accept it as part of her reality. A smattering of close friends and relatives professed to believe her, or at least told her they did, while others did not.

**The human mind delights in grand conceptions
of supernatural beings.**
– Jules Verne

Chapter Four:

The Reunion

Rachel and Owen | Montagne Sainte-Victoire
08:00 p.m. | August 17, 2044

By the time the compact e-car reaches the fire trail dead-end, the last remnants of dusk ebb into a dark, moonless night. Parked askew in a small clearing in the dense forest, weak headlights shine across jagged boulders strewn along the base of a limestone cliff, towering into the inky night.

Shaken and hopping mad after the dangerous forced detour, the Haigs stomp to and fro across the rocks, dirt, and grass, demanding an explanation from their glitchy driver.

Grabbing her seething husband by the arm to ensure he does not rip Louie's head off, Rachel tries to lower the temperature, "Don't bother, he's not even here. He has fried circuits!"

In contrast to the irate Americans, Louie remains resolute in a cross-armed, defiant pose behind his two-door ride, fixated on a presence lurking beyond the clearing's edge in the dark forest shadows. Never wavering from the inscrutable expression on his long face, his cybernetics determine they are under surveillance.

Following Louie's inattentive stare into the trees, Rachel catches a fleeting glance of something lurking behind a thick trunk. Probably a furry forest dweller disturbed by Owen's booming voice.

Twisting out of his wife's grip, Owen's "Ha-ha!" echoes off the limestone cliff into the night. "Circuits? He's not Robbie the Robot, Rachel. There aren't any circuits to fry. He's had his evil button switched to ON."

"You missed your calling. You should dump high finance and go on the comedy circuit." Rachel swats at a lightning bug, whirring past her face as a distinct tingling sensation creeps up her spine. Something is not right. She tries to adjust her vision in the darkness, peering toward Owen's shape, Louie, barely visible mere feet beyond his silhouette in the fading light.

"Your seven-star rating just took a huge hit, pal! You might as well …" Owen's verbal onslaught is cut short by a strong ozone odor wafting across the darkening meadow, eliciting a sense of imminent danger creeping up his spine. Peering into the evening sky, he sees only stars, but experience and common sense dictate that the side of a mountain is not an ideal place to be in an electrical storm. "Rachel, I think a real whopper of a storm is coming. We need to get off this hunk of rock!"

Perplexed by her husband's dispositional shift from anger to fear, the distinct sound of a broken branch diverts her gaze toward the tree line. Relieved at the sight of a fleeing deer, Rachel turns and finds Louie in the throes of a violent convulsive attack, "When did that start? Owen! Turn around! Louie is having another attack!"

Owen peers toward Louie's spastic form, "Jesus! It looks like he's going to fly apart at the limbs!"

Converging on the stricken robot, Rachel and Owen are knocked on their heels by a symphonic overture pealing to an ear-splitting pitch from somewhere inside the malfunctioning chauffeur.

Ducking a flying mechanical elbow, Rachel trips and staggers backward. Owen maneuvers behind Louie and wrestles him into an armlock, and the synthetic human slumps back into Owen as the shrieking noise abates. "Holy mackerel, he weighs a ton! I don't think I can hold him up much longer."

Without warning, the shrieking noise abates, and Louie freezes in a ramrod-straight stance. Light specks swarmed into the charged air from his eyes, ears, and nose a heartbeat later.

Rachel's green eyes widen in astonishment, "These are the same lights I saw in space; they want something from me!"

Owen pushes from Louie's rigid pose, startled by the ethereal orbs, staggering backward in shock and awe. The lights gather into a single, diaphanous sphere, engulfing his beautiful wife in pure white luminosity before his spellbound eyes.

Horrified at the sight of his wife encompassed by the sparkling, spherical shape, "Rachel, are you okay? What's happening?"

Bathed in lambency, Rachel turns to Owen with a hypnotized vacancy behind her wide green eyes, leaving him uncharacteristically hesitant to act for an anxiety-filled moment. After spewing the lights, Louie goes still and silent behind the car. Still worried about a lightning storm, Owen decides the situation has gone on long enough. Stepping across the loamy clearing to rescue his bride from the mysterious ball of light, he watches the spectral assailant elevate above her staticky hair pose. "That's right! You better back off, whatever you are." The sphere pulses in reply to his stern reprimand before rocketing up the cliff and disappearing over a high ledge.

With the light show gone, Owen rushes to Rachel's side and holds her tight, "I'm sorry I let you down. I'm a little out of my league here."

"It's okay. I'm fine. Those are friendly lights."

"As opposed to what, unfriendly lights? We need to get out of here." Beyond Rachel, Owen watches helplessly as more orbs flutter into the air from Louie's head. "Oh, no. Here they come again."

The light specks amass and expand into a massive, brilliant orb, engulfing the embraced couple and lifting them off the ground in tandem. Owen shoots Rachel a terrified look; she reciprocates with uncharacteristic serenity. Panic overwhelms him as Louie's rigid form recedes in the darkness below his feet.

* * *

Niyo watches luminous orbs engulf the Alexander girl and her hot-headed husband, lifting the petrified couple into thin air. Widening a holographic viewfinder before his face, he records the paranormal event to a digital file for the edification of his doubting Thomas handlers at the PTB. Feeling utter vindication in his assessment of the girl's destiny, he launches a bumblebee-sized stealth drone skyward, mirroring the addled couple's fantastical levitating ascent up the sheer limestone cliff face.

* * *

Owen and Rachel proceed over a ledge at the top of a limestone cliff, feet dangling above the barren ridgeline. The paranormal experience intensifies as a large orifice opens out of solid limestone before their stunned expressions. Through the opening, Rachel spies the shape of a fixed-wing aircraft resolving out of the blackness on the cavern floor far below. "Owen, check it out! It's an old airplane!"

"Man, it is shot to hell. What happened down here?"

Settling onto the slick wet limestone, the sphere shimmers into glowing specks hovering in the cave's clammy interior. Owen confirms his shaky footing, heading toward the well-preserved, war-damaged fighter plane. Rachel follows close behind, hearing his attempted whistle, a nervous tell.

Examining bullet holes riddled along the port side wing, Owen puts a hand inside a large, ragged gash, ensuring it is not an illusion. Clearing his throat in the dampness, "I wish I knew more about aircraft, but I believe it is a World War Two-era fighter plane."

Rachel smooths her hand across the engine's cowling, noting the scorch marks streaked along the fuselage. "It doesn't take an expert to tell this old warbird went through quite a battle." Tilting her head toward the sliver of nighttime sky visible through the opened orifice far above, she watches the lights dance like fireflies.

Owen follows his wife's gaze, calling out the mischievous lights, "Is this why you brought us down here? Well, the joke's on all of you! We don't know squat about vintage aircraft!"

"Not to worry, young man, I do." The sonorous voice echoes from deeper inside the cavern. Startled, the couple spin and watch a man approach, accompanied by a squadron of small white orbs. As if things could not get any weirder, a flickering, candle-like illumination glows from under his skin, flight suit, and leather pilot's jacket, emblazoned with a black scorpion insignia.

The man offers a warm smile from his ethereal appearance, "That's my old aircraft. A P-47 Thunderbolt, although warbird has a nice ring to it. I last sat in the cockpit 100 years ago to the day. My name is Captain Neil Alexander. Rachel, I'm your Great-Great-Grandfather. My physical body perished," referencing the orbs of light floating around his illuminated presence while ignoring the eavesdropping drone, "but these miracle workers rescued me at death's door a century ago, inside this cavern."

Tears well in her eyes as the same familial recognition she experienced in space draws the stunned young woman to stumble across a subterranean stream closer to her long-lost relative's radiance.

Owen hurries to follow her impulsive decision to sprint from the plane across the slippery cavern floor. Placing a protective hand around her waist in a defensive posture, "I'm sure this is more than a family reunion. Why did you bring us down here?"

"I'm glad you asked. Inside my cockpit rests a photograph of Rachel's great-great-grandmother. I want her to have it. Would you retrieve it for us? I believe it should be resting on the seat where I last left it."

The befuddled broker turns back toward the war-damaged fighter plane, retracing his steps over the uneven surface with helpful orbs lighting the way.

"Rachel, I understand you have no idea who I am or why I brought you here," with a devilish smile, "and on your honeymoon of all times. But I know what a thoughtful and intelligent young woman you have become."

"Thanks, I guess. But if you followed my whole life story, you must know I am far from perfect."

"Honesty and humility serve you well, my dear, but you have nothing to be ashamed of. I have been there for the family through good times and bad, watching over generations of Alexanders." Neil pauses to let his words sink in, "I guess you could say I'm the family guardian angel, for lack of a better description." With an evasive smile, Neil adds, "You know you are special. Right?"

"Me? Special? You have the wrong girl."

Looking into the distance toward the glowing orbs lighting Owen's way as he hoists onto the wing to peer into the cockpit, "I'm sure your new husband wholeheartedly agrees."

Rachel can't resist a derisive laugh, "Are you sure my parents didn't put you up to this?" Following her impertinence, she blurts out a nagging thought. "You aren't old and gray. You look younger than me."

"I was only 26 years old, Rachel. I appear before you in my human form to help you understand my former self. What I am now is beyond explanation." Neil gestures behind Rachel into the darkness,

"Ah! Your husband found the photo."

Rachel notes Owen's stunned expression uplit by accompanying orbs, extending the photograph in his trembling hand for Rachel to see.

"Is that your remains inside the cockpit?"

Neil's reply is interrupted by a loud gasp from Rachel.

"She looked just like me!"

"You bear a remarkable resemblance to Carol. She was an incredible woman, and I was privileged to see her through her grief to the ripe old age of 98 years young." With a wink and a nod, "I helped a little, but bragging is frowned upon among my kind."

Meeting Rachel's emerald eyes, Neil's amiable demeanor ends: "Yes, Owen. That is my physical body, but my spirit is with you now. However, the immense energy it took to bring you down here was not for a pleasant family reunion. Rachel, flip the photo over if you please."

With the assistance of an orb of light, Owen peers closer at a series of barely legible numbers written in faded fountain ink scrawled across the creases and ruddy stains, "Are those map coordinates?"

"Affirmative. The coordinates mark where two naïve young airmen buried a prehistoric artifact of great consequence to all humanity."

Owen is about to follow up with another query, but Rachel beats him to the punch, "Hold on a second. Let me get a word in here. How did you obtain the coordinates?"

"It's a long story, Rachel. However, I will start by admitting I was one of the two naïve young airmen who hid it. The other was my friend and wingman, Harry Stark."

The bewildered looks on the newlyweds' faces speak volumes. "Why did you and your wingman bury it?"

* * *

Light specks illuminate the threesome standing atop a slight rise above the clear bubbling waters opposite the plane's repose in the deep cavern. The gurgle of the fast-flowing stream pervades the dank interior, drowning the tinny whine of the alien spy drone hovering in the shadows.

Neil's radiance increases as he assembles the golden ellipse backstory into coherent chunks. "In early 1943, a Nazi spy stationed in Cairo became obsessed with the legend of a beacon erected by Star People eons before our current human civilization. Since no archeological evidence or written history was discovered to corroborate the tale, it was added to a long list of legends attributed to the pyramids. However, the Germans focused on tales describing the structure's mystical power source, known only as the golden ellipse."

Owen mutters, "Nazis. We hate those guys."

Rachel rolls her eyes at Owen's arcane reference, "How did this Nazi spy see beyond the ghost story when no one else could?"

"Under the British and Egyptians' noses, the spy, Hans Gruber, was lured inside the Great Pyramid to the King's Chamber by a modern incarnation of Cleopatra. Once inside, she shapeshifted back into the Dark Specters—a splintered faction cast off from my kind millennia ago."

"Dark Specters? Are they still around?"

"Oh, yes. We must stay vigilant at all times." Sensing the couple is managing to keep up, Neil smiles, "Don't worry. You will be fine."

"So, then what happened?"

"Right. Anyway, they transported Gruber through solid rock to a secret beacon chamber constructed by a pharaoh under our influential guise over 2,500 years ago."

"His name was Khufu, if I'm not mistaken."

"You are right, Owen. Most impressive."

Rachel rests her toned left arm on his shoulder, "That's my new husband, full of useless trivia."

Neil continues without skipping a beat, "After eons of failures, the Dark Specters were stunned that the German survived the removal of the golden ellipse. Unaware of the cosmic randomness of his success, the Nazi shoved his prize into an attaché, and the Dark Specters expelled him from the pyramid."

Owen notes that every mention of the Dark Specters agitates the bright specks surrounding Neil's glowing form.

"The Dark Specters basked in the bitter irony of a human being unleashing a torrent of destruction on humanity. The Nazi spy was the last recruit in a line of self-possessed egomaniacs duped into penetrating the Great Pyramid to the hidden beacon chamber and the prized golden ellipse. We built the beacon to broadcast a warning into space to leave Earth alone. Since Gruber's successful extraction a century ago, the deafening silence communicates the opposite message."

"Open season on Earth?"

"Precisely, Owen."

"What happened next, Grandpa?"

Neil produces a wan smile at the familial reference, "Gruber awoke face down in a gutter in Cairo, still clutching the attaché. However, his lucky streak ended when he made a deadly miscalculation."

"What did he do?"

"Gruber showed the golden ellipse to his commander, who shot him between the eyes and took the golden ellipse. Stupid move. The enigmatic artifact was packed inside a crate burnished with a single swastika alongside a trove of stolen antiquities and loaded onto a convoy bound for a Luftwaffe airstrip."

Rachel resists the urge to reach out and pass her hand through Neil's holographic form, afraid of what she may discover.

Neil senses her reticence, "This is where Harry and I enter the picture. An advancing U.S. Army battalion stopped the German convoy dead in its tracks. The recovered contraband, including the golden ellipse, ended up at a captured airbase outside Tripoli, Libya, where my Black Scorpions squadron was stationed. A few days later, my wingman, Harry Stark, sat in on a late-night poker game organized by a corruptible quartermaster named Hodges. The Dark Specters stacked the deck in Harry's favor. He walked away from that poker game with the golden ellipse and never looked back. I regret not seeing how much his prize changed him until it was too late."

Turning wistful, despite his other-worldly appearance, "Neither of us had any clue of the importance of the nine-inch oval relic beyond its weight in gold. Stationed in the middle of nowhere during wartime, material things had no long-term value. We probably would have traded it for a bottle of Kentucky bourbon." Neil hesitates, "At least it's what I would have done. Before I could do anything to alter the situation, I realized Harry's agenda had a dark and sinister endgame. Had I known …."

Neil finishes the story with a heavy sigh, "Before our Fighter Group shipped off to a new airbase on Corsica, Harry schemed to bury the artifact in the Libyan desert. Ensuring we both had skin in the game, he transcribed the coordinates onto the reverse side of my wife's photograph you are now holding."

Rachel cast her eyes on her great-great grandmother's faded black-and-white image she held in her still-trembling hand.

"My wingman was a gambler, always taking chances. I did not understand until it was too late that the Dark Specters corrupted him. We both conspired to hide the relic, but only Harry knew humanity would pay the ultimate price. You may ask how I managed to evade their dark influence. In hindsight, I was too self-involved and did not comprehend how far Harry had slipped until our last day. Greed shaped my decisions. We all have regrets, Rachel."

He produces an irony-laced smile, "But fate had other plans for both of us. An early-morning air raid on a railyard not far from here exactly 100 years ago on a night like tonight stopped any delusions either of us had about selling the golden ellipse for millions. It was the end of the life I had known and loved and the beginning of something new and transcendently wonderful."

"What happened to Harry?"

"I know he managed to bail out before his plane crashed and could have escaped to friendly territory. However, instead of a hero's welcome, he would be greeted by OSS officers demanding the whereabouts of the golden ellipse. For many years I assumed he died from his injuries. But now it appears that the Dark Specters are using him."

"Poor Harry."

"Indeed. Poor Harry." Neil pauses, remembering his pugnacious friend the way he was before winning the golden ellipse.

Swaying on her feet, Rachel pinches the bridge of her nose to halt a bout of vertigo, "Let me get this straight; to turn off this ancient beacon—a cosmic lighthouse to the stars—all one needed to do was remove an elliptically-shaped power source? How come nobody managed to accomplish this before Hans Gruber came along?"

Neil passes through Rachel's startled body and proceeds toward his plane through the darkness.

Caught off guard, Owen catches his wife and stops her from reeling backward. "I hate to keep asking this, but are you all right, Rachel?"

Shaking from his grip, the flustered young woman spins on her heels and follows her grandfather's glowing figure, splashing through the subterranean stream. Skidding to a stop, inches before Neil's radiant form at the starboard wingtip of his shot-up Thunderbolt, "Answer the question. How did the Nazi spy accomplish what countless others throughout history tried and failed?"

A look of consternation crosses Neil's radiance. "Sheer randomness, my dear."

Following Rachel's path, Owen scampers from behind in time to catch her fainting backward into his arms.

"Good catch," Neil sighs with relief. "In more ways than one."

Resting his wife's limp form on the damp cavern floor, Owen glares at the ghostly figure, "I'm not sure what or who you are, but if anything happens to her, I will hunt you down and kill you and all your foo fighter friends."

"Foo fighters? That's a name I haven't heard in a long time. Rachel will be fine. You must trust me when I tell you my goal is to keep you and humanity safe from harm."

Owen replies with palpable frustration, "Why all the subterfuge? I understand a hunk of gold exists to power an ancient alien beacon. And since the Nazi spy stole it, the world is exposed to space invaders. But can you cut to the chase? It's been an extremely long day."

"You are right, too much information. I get it now. 21st-century humans are doers and not much for all the dirty details."

"You could say that old man, or whatever you are." Reclining on the smooth limestone, cradling Rachel's head in his lap, "Okay, please proceed. I'm all ears."

Neil reads Owen's unspoken reminiscence of campfire stories and is heartened to discover the put-upon fellow used to be in the Scouts. In a former life, Neil was an Eagle Scout, one of his many human accomplishments. "All right, let's get on with it, shall we?

"This guy is a walking, talking History Channel show."

Neil reads the impertinent thought right out of Owen's mind. "The History Channel would turn this story down as too far-fetched."

"You can read minds. Of course, you can."

Neil shines a deferential smile, giving Owen a slight shoulder shrug.

"So, just to be clear, this is not the second coming of King Tut. It's a nine-inch ellipse with golden dimensions—sounds like it would make a nice salad plate."

Rachel jabs Owen with a sharp elbow, "Don't interrupt, let him finish." She props herself on the hard, rocky floor.

"There you are, back amongst the living."

"You gave us a bit of a scare; take a moment before you try to stand."

Owen synopsizes the unbelievable story, "Let me see if I understand what you are asking. You want us to track down a relic, this golden ellipse, hidden in the god-forsaken Libyan desert. Travel to Egypt, locate a beacon underneath the Great Pyramid of Giza and reattach it, so the thing starts working again. All because hordes of alien invaders are coming to destroy humanity. But wait, there's more: no one on Earth knows this beacon exists, but Rachel and I, noted archeologists that we are, waltz right up and find it. Do you understand how crazy that sounds?" Gesturing around the cavern, "even now."

Neil proffers a deferential nod, "Of course, you are right. You two are not our first attempt at recruiting human help. However, despite our abilities, success has taken exactly 100 years, a mere whisper in the fabric of time. Without the beacon, my kind fears what is coming will not bode well for humankind."

Alarmed at the gravity of Neil's last statement, "What do you mean? Who are these ETs? Forgive me, but aren't you one as well? Maybe we should take this to the UN and let them handle it."

Neil brightens to a blinding glow. Wheeling on the pragmatic young man, the stern echo of his voice reverberates into the darkness, "Owen Haig! If you bring those corrupt, paper-pushing bureaucrats into this, my retribution will be swift and severe! Trust only yourselves. The dark forces who compelled the Nazis to steal the golden ellipse desire an end to the human experiment. If not for a fortuitous attack on that Nazi convoy, the golden ellipse would have made it to Berlin. The successive chain reaction of events would have resulted in the decimation of every living thing on this planet."

Still reeling from the ominous remonstration, the pair watch in awe as their illuminated counterpart segues to Owen's alien remark. Spreading his arms wide, Neil's glowing form transitions into a tall, gray being with elongated limbs and bulbous eyes dominating an egg-shaped head. The frightening visage looms over the pair, reflecting their terrified expressions in its gleaming black eyes. While its slit-shaped mouth never moves, Neil's familiar voice communicates from its eerie face. "Calling us aliens, like this amiable fellow, is a crude over-simplification. An endless variety of beings in all shapes and sizes populates every corner of our universe. We are all aliens to each other. You are, too. However, amongst my kind, the belief in a unifying higher power persists, so take heart." Lowering his smooth gray face nose-to-nose with a startled Owen, "To be more precise, we prefer Light Specters, or, if you prefer, you can call us angels. And in every religion, there are good angels …."

Owen nods, "… and bad angels. The Dark Specters. I am starting to understand."

Reverting to human form, the Light Specter emulates Neil's disarming smile, "Excellent! You are an intelligent young man, Owen Haig, and a credit to your species."

Addressing Rachel in a much softer voice, "You do indeed bear a striking resemblance to my Carol. Your destiny was determined before birth—only now is it coming to pass."

"Are you referring to what happened when I was 18?"

"That event foreshadowed your abilities. Trust yourself."

"I don't want to go further down the rabbit hole, but can't you handle this yourself? After all, your kind constructed the beacon. Didn't it come with a warranty and spare parts?"

Neil starts to fade but can't resist a chuckle at Owen's dry, "No. We cannot alter the course of human history without affecting the outcome. The Dark Specters damaged our experiment by recruiting humans to destroy the future of their own species. Now, it falls to both of you to make it right, or every living thing on the planet will face the ultimate consequence. A sixth extinction." Referencing the imminent alien invasion, "I wish you all the luck in the world in returning the ellipse atop the beacon before time runs out."

The glowing apparition, formerly known as Neil Alexander, transforms before their eyes into a frail human being in a blood-soaked flight suit. The long-lost aviator struggles to speak, appearing in his final mortal state of existence, "Rachel. Follow your intuition in the coming days. You will make the right decisions. You always have. Take extreme caution in your travels to the coordinates and trust only yourselves." Gazing at the pair with a longing sadness in his watery, bloodshot eyes, "My commander always ended a conversation with an overused expression; however, it seems appropriate given the circumstances: Good hunting."

Neil's human appearance transforms into specks of light and disappears into a spiraling void.

Rachel mumbles to herself, "Let the Machine do the work."

Watching the remainder of the lights elevate out of the cavern, Owen raises an eyebrow, "What did you say?"

Fetching, despite the current dilemma, Rachel turns the photograph over in her hand, "Huh? Nothing. Some random thought. What should we do?"

"Well, first things first; let's get out of this cave."

Out of the darkness, orbs lift them out of the cavern.

The drone follows from a distance.

Captain Neil Alexander's P-47 Thunderbolt plunges into the inky blackness, serenaded by the gurgling subterranean stream.

Louie | Montagne Sainte-Victoire
12:30 a.m. | August 18, 2044

Louie watches as what began as another day's fare descends the sheer cliff before his synthetic eyes. The attractive couple settles onto the solid ground a few paces distant from the rear bumper of his battered vehicle. He watches them gulp deep breaths of air, trying to regain their composure after the eerie experience. The tall woman, Rachel, recovers first and moves toward him.

Louie, feeling none the worse for wear, begins apologizing

for his inexplicable actions, but with a raised left hand, she stops his mea culpa before he can get a word out. He focuses on her right hand, extending a crumpled old photograph between her thumb and index finger by a dog-eared corner.

"Louie, read the numbers on the flip side. Are you able to decipher these coordinates and pinpoint the exact location?"

Owen steps forward on shaky legs, "Yeah, what do you make of it?"

Louie accepts the photo and notes the resemblance with a cheeky smile and an over-animated back-and-forth overreaction. Seeing his robot humor fall flat, he shrugs and flips it over, scanning the numbers penned onto the backside of the silver gelatin print. Pulling a new cigarette from his deep shirt pocket, relishing the attention, he pauses before returning the photo to the trembling and disheveled woman. The smile disappears below his thin French mustache, "This is south of Tripoli, Libya? Monsieur et Madame, why would you want to go there?"

Niyo | Montagne Sainte-Victoire
12:30 a.m. | August 18, 2044

The bumblebee drone whirs down the cliff, swerving into the dark forest adjacent to the clearing. With his unauthorized intel-gathering mission a success, Niyo catches the tiny drone and hesitates. The alien knows the cave incident recording is a game-changer. But then again, it is the PTB. Who knows how they will interpret the paranormal family reunion? The presence of an entity claiming to be the infamous Neil Alexander will draw even more intense scrutiny and a hefty dose of skepticism.

After recording a brief native tongue explanation of his insubordinate actions, the alien opts to instead present the hi-def digital movie file to his PTB handlers upon his return. After watching his stunning surveillance footage, the doubters will come to their senses and acknowledge the Alexander girl's destiny. As a bonus, any threat of punishment for violating direct orders will be rendered moot. With a heady sense of accomplishment, Niyo packs the drone in a pocket and retraces his path through the dense forest toward the escarpment where his cloaked ship is parked.

Although Niyo's acute night vision allows him to pick his way back along the treacherous path in absolute darkness, he overlooks a thick root in his exuberance. As if in slow motion, unable to quantify the severity of his misstep before it is too late, Niyo tumbles head-over-heels thirty feet down a steep embankment. Covered in cuts and bruises, he crumples to a stop in a cascade of loose limestone shards, pine bark, and needles after striking his head into the side of a boulder.

Unconscious for an indeterminate amount of time, the alien awakens and struggles onto his feet. He reaches a long finger to his head and feels aqua-colored blood seeping from a deep gash in his gray noggin.

A chorus of grunts and snorts from the shadowed tree line interrupts Niyo's string of ET epithets crackling across the steep ridge. Injured, exposed, and vulnerable, a sense of danger pricks the nape of his thin gray neck seconds before an ear-piercing squeal bellows out of the darkness.

The hapless alien wheels in terror as a wild boar charges and gores Niyo on its long protruding tusks before flinging the three-foot, 52-pound alien's slackened form farther down the steep, rocky embankment toward three piglets spilling from the undergrowth, ripping and gnawing at the exotic late-night feast.

* * *

Hours later, the bumblebee drone crawls from Niyo's ripped matte-silver bloodstained jersey and rises off his mutilated remains scattered amongst the detritus. After documenting the alien's demise, the drone returns to the cloaked ship. Preset to autonomous mode by

Niyo before vacating the meadow's edge, the AI drone syncs to the ship's auto-pilot and navigational systems, elevating the invisible craft straight up into the starry night sky to 60,000 feet, handshakes with a PTB cloud storage site and uploads a half-terabyte of the paranormal cave incident hi-def feed along with Niyo's pre-recorded message in his ancient native tongue. The translated version begins with a simple statement: *"It is Rachel Alexander …."*

**Don't try to solve serious matters in the middle
of the night.**

– Philip K. Dick

Chapter Five:

The Imposter

**Rachel and Owen | Port of Tunis, Tunisia
07:00 a.m. | August 20, 2044**

Rachel Haig awakens with a start, facing a cream-colored wall. Shivering beneath the full-blast AC vent inside a veranda stateroom aboard the Mediterranean Star, she curls into a fetal repose and shifts onto her left side. With a silent sigh, the 24-year-old lifts her toned right arm and tugs a flaxen mess of hair from her face, acknowledging slumber time is over. Twisting into an over-the-shoulder glance toward her new husband, she sees him sleeping like a baby, cocooned in all the bedding. Meanwhile, she lays twisted into a pretzel, wearing a thin smiley-face t-shirt and underwear to shield her goose-bumped skin from the refrigerated air.

This is her new life. From now on, controlling the covers will be a constant struggle, but she loves Owen. And despite his current cozy repose, she knows he loves her, too. Rubbing the sleep from her eyes, the weight of their current predicament floods her mind. Did she possess the mental fortitude to see their strange new journey to a successful resolution? Her long-lost ancestor's confidence exceeded what she had in herself by leaps and bounds. It's just the fate of the world.

No pressure.

Wide awake, Rachel rewinds her life from her preemie birth through her teens as a sliver of morning sunshine sneaks through closed shades, angling across the bed. Throughout her adolescence and into her rebellious and experimental teenage years, family, friends, acquaintances, and complete strangers gravitated to her effortless aplomb. She tried to flip the annoying paradigm, but no matter how bad her behavior or outlandish her appearance, nattering nurturers responded with sympathetic hugs and forgiveness. The younger version of Rachel Alexander wanted to be left alone, but something embedded within her essence made anonymity impossible.

Staring at the ceiling, Rachel could not believe six years had come and gone since the night of her violent sexual assault at the tender age of eighteen. The paradigm shift she desperately tried to make arrived without warning in a crescendo of lascivious violence that extinguished her light and destroyed her once-promising future in a singular act of evil.

Depression, self-loathing, and uncontrollable panic attacks followed in the disastrous wake of the horrible event. Rachel's distraught parents paid for well-intentioned therapists and a litany of prescribed treatments, but nothing quelled her disgust for herself. The hubris of her naive youth spent pushing nothing bad ever happens to me past its limits left the precocious teen vulnerable to the scenario everyone warned against, and she knew it.

Taking stock of the last two years since meeting her snoring spouse, she thanks God for Owen Haig, jostling the thin mattress.

Without his help, she would never have vanquished the demons and restored some of the charismatic charms she radiated from the day she was born three months premature.

Rachel checks that her prince is asleep and smooths her hand across the raised scar on her left side before slipping into a light sleep. In a recurring nightmare, she relives the night she was raped for the zillionth time as the lascivious face of her knife-wielding assailant projects in her subconsciousness.

Like experiencing a violent car crash, the whole episode happened in a frenzied blur. Parting from a large group of inebriated revelers, Rachel snuck out a back door at an eighteen-and-over nightclub to steal a smoke. In her altered state, she failed to notice the shadowy figure who followed her outside. Shoved to the ground from behind, her initial shock turned to helplessness, unable to fend off the depraved attacker. Sobbing for her life, her resolve crumbled, pinned beneath his terrible weight on the graveled macadam in the trash-strewn alley behind the club. The creep held a gleaming nine-inch blade to her throat—dripping with blood from the three-inch incision he carved into her exposed left midriff—and warned her to hush. Unable to escape the horrible closeness of the guy's stinking hot breath, he proceeded to have his way.

Consumed with rage, guilt, and fear, Rachel closed her eyes tight, seeking refuge from within. A halted breath later, a white-hot flash of light pierced her smoky eyeshade, and latent energy surged through every fiber of her being. Forcing her eyes open, she saw her attacker's face contorting into a startled, wide-eyed panic. Bloody spittle gurgled from his ugly mouth, and an acrid smell of burnt flesh wafted into the dankness from where Rachel grasped the knife handle, penetrating through his chest past the titanium hilt. The knife tip jutted out his back through the garish pattern of his sweaty silk shirt.

Her rapist bled to death like a stuck pig, slumped across her body with his dirty trousers pulled down pasty-white legs. She lost consciousness, still gripping the knife as the supernatural ambiance underneath her skin, generated from the incredible burst of energy, faded to normal long before help arrived.

Rachel awoke, handcuffed to a hospital bed. Her head pounded with a dreadful hangover. Focusing bleary and bloodshot green eyes on the IV catheter taped to her forearm, she noticed a ruddy patchwork across her exposed skin mixed with an antiseptic odor.

A stone-faced Providence policewoman noted her movement, uncuffed her wrist, and escorted her to the bathroom. Rachel felt violated again as the leering dyke failed to avert her gaze while she peeled out of the stiff hospital gown, stark naked. Seeing her sad reflection in the bathroom mirror, covered in bloodstains, bruises, and a three-inch gash stitched closed on her left side, smeared in orange iodine, she vomited into the sink. The uniformed woman made no move to help. Her cold stare made Rachel feel like a criminal. Maybe she was. Stepping behind the semi-transparent mildewed shower curtain, the distraught 18-year-old washed back-alley grit from her hair and scrubbed her skin raw under the tepid jets. Staring at the reddish water swirling into the drain between her black paint-chipped toes, she angled her throbbing head under the spray and broke into uncontrollable sobs.

* * *

Lying next to her snoring husband aboard the ship, an unquantifiable facet lingered beyond Rachel's memory of the six-year-old episode. Pondering the paranormal reunion in the French cave, she wonders if Grandpa Neil caused the flash of energy that saved her from certain death on that horrible night. He seemed to relish his role as the Alexander family guardian angel. Where was he now?

* * *

The manslaughter charge was dropped once the rape kit testing came through, but the media circled like sharks. Rachel Alexander became the poor little rich girl who got away with murder. Her rapist was the son of a Rhode Island state senator who championed herself as an advocate for women's rights. Yeah, right.

The traumatic experience derailed Rachel's college and medical school plans. Instead, she made the safer choice to sequester herself inside the family's Rhode Island mansion. When her small group of friends left for the hallowed ivy-covered halls of academia—and nonstop partying—she morphed into a homebody. Her parents worried about her drinking, but she assured them her partying days were in the rearview.

* * *

Hobbes Rare Books was her sanctuary, a hole-in-the-wall used bookstore juxtaposed between an over-priced antique shop and a maritime art gallery in downtown Newport. The proprietor, a human fireplug in a pilled maroon sweater named Stanley Hobbes, was a constant in her life. A regular at birthdays and graduations for as far back as she could recall, the little man reveled in her achievements like a proud uncle and a shoulder to cry on when things went awry.

Following the attack, she spent copious amounts of time in his shop while he sat perched on a stool behind a countertop stacked with old volumes listening to her wide-ranging ramblings. Perusing bookshelves crammed with unread gems by authors who slipped the mortal coil long ago, she gravitated toward reads reflective of her ordeal. The more fantastical the subject matter, the more engrossed she became in the brittle dog-eared pages.

Sneaking back through a side entrance, new paperback in hand, she draped across a chair or, on warm summer days, out by the pool, immersed in mysteries and sci-fi yarns published decades earlier.

Aside from sporadic and failed attempts to conjure the same energy from the night she was raped, another new obsession came after discovering her father's antique record player and his extensive collection of LP records. Rachel spent her evenings curled up with a drink in her father's study, listening to 70s and 80s rock, punk, and new wave bands through noise-canceling headphones while pouring over the lost art of record album covers and liner notes.

Her mother's concerns turned into heated arguments, followed by days of the silent treatment. Mrs. Alexander blinked first every time, "Rachel, you'll never meet anyone if you refuse to leave the house! Why don't you marry Mr. Hobbes and get it over with, young lady? Even your goofball younger brother has a steady girlfriend, for Chrissake!"

One month after her 22nd birthday—four long years after the assault—Rachel's desperate mother cajoled her recalcitrant daughter into attending the wedding of her bridge club friend's stuck-up daughter.

Rachel acquiesced to her mother's constant pleading with an eye-rolling frown, "I barely know them, Mom. They are your stupid friends."

"Do it for me, Rachel. You might meet somebody."

After finishing a rueful laugh at her Mom's wishful thinking, "Oh, now that would be special."

"Yes. It would."

In an otherwise empty pew at the back of the church, wearing a knee-length black cocktail dress and high heels, dark blond hair curled in an elegant ponytail, Rachel exuded aloofness. She successfully walled off the other wedding guests but could feel their prying eyes upon her. As the ceremony started, she perked up at the sight of the third groomsman—the most handsome man she had ever seen. "Huh. Maybe Mom was not so dumb after all."

The bubble burst quickly as Rachel was introduced to the guy's boyfriend at the glitzy reception at Rosecliff, a Gatsbyesque venue in Newport, Rhode Island. Oh well. The party carried well into the night to the silly portion, where drunken people made embarrassing decisions to stand up and groove to a pulsating beat. Meanwhile, she sat alone, as far from the dance floor as she could manage, hidden behind a gaudy centerpiece at a massive table filled with empty plates, glasses, and bottles.

Peering through her champagne flute, she watched a guy in a blue tailored suit head toward her around the tables and chairs. "Uh-oh." He introduced himself as Owen Haig and asked her to dance. She declined. However, from that magical moment onward, they talked.

After the reception wound to a hazed conclusion around 02:00 a.m., the pair moved outside, sharing a bottle by the hotel pool. Pants rolled to the knees and feet dangling in the water, Owen told her about his life, where he grew up, and what he did for a living.

A cheeky "Sounds boring." was her reaction to hearing he worked in the financial industry.

A dimpled, smiling "It has its moments," his comeback.

Not the most handsome man she had ever seen, Owen possessed a rugged yet boyish charm that won her over before she could conjure an excuse to push him away.

After regaling her with his weekend adventurer exploits, it was her turn. Owen knew she was the infamous trust fund murderess but allowed her to tell the tale. Aside from Hobbes, it was the first time anyone listened to her side of the story. Everyone was too focused on her looks and the Alexander family fortune. Nobody cared enough to notice she was dying inside until this guy entered her life. Owen was different. He saw through her untouchable veneer to the carefree and intelligent young woman she was before the attack.

The promise of a new day glowed across the eastern horizon as she finished her life story through the ripe old age of 22. He held her in a warm embrace and kissed her on the cheek. And then he whispered the words no one else would say, "The sonofabitch got off easy."

She was hooked.

* * *

Following a luxurious hot shower, Rachel pads barefoot across the darkened cabin past her slumbering husband in beige shorts and an olive-green tank top with her clean and brushed hair pulled in a damp towel over her left shoulder. Sliding open the glass door without making a sound, hot Tunisian morning air instantly warms her body, stepping onto the small private veranda. "Ah, that's more like it."

Following their hasty departure from the docks in Marseilles the previous morning aboard the Mediterranean Star, Rachel, and her snoring bedmate crashed in their well-appointed stateroom. While they caught up on much-needed sleep, the passenger ferry made its 22-hour Mediterranean crossing and slipped into the Port of Tunis before dawn over North Africa.

The troubled young woman blows steam from the rim of her paper coffee cup, compliments of the wonky, single-serve brewer perched atop a tiny shelf in the stateroom. Observing the beehive of activity on the wharf far below, she ponders hints and clues embedded in her restless dreams since parting ways with Neil inside the cave, "The Machine reference must be related to the buried golden artifact. But how?"

Owen breaks the quietude with a loud yawn, flinging the slider open and pushing aside one of the cheap wicker chairs while rubbing the sleep from his bleary eyes. Moving next to Rachel along the narrow rail, he gives her a playful pat on the bottom. "Morning, sunshine. So, you are talking gibberish in your sleep and having conversations with yourself. Good stuff, Rachel."

Rachel sips her coffee, "Good morning." Ignoring his comment with a sly sideways glance, "Sleep well?"

His affirmative grunt and unkempt early-morning Neanderthal appearance gave her the usual private chuckle.

Leaning over the rail on his forearms, staring into the murky water lapping between the side of the ship and the barnacle-encrusted pilings of the dock, "Here we are. I felt ridiculous fabricating a story for our families about how we upended our honeymoon midstream and detoured to North Africa. My mother was not happy when she heard the news."

"She was probably unhappy before your call, so you have that going for you."

"Careful, Rachel, my humor is starting to rub off on you."

* * *

Local Tunisian vendors prepare for another disembarking crowd of tourists, students, and government functionaries in the Mediterranean Star's shadow along the blistering hot wharf. They rush to assemble tents, stands, and tables, rife with an exotic array of comestibles, trinkets, and quasi-legal services, for the boatload of free-spending foreigners.

A motorcyclist decked out in black leather from head to toe slowly guides his sleek, black, two-wheel machine down the wharf, parting the crowd of pedestrians, oblivious to the indignant stammering and shaking fists in his wake. Nearing the end of the dock, he applies the brakes and stops. The Mediterranean Star reflects in his candy-apple red helmet's mirrored face shield, surveilling the passengers disembarking down the gangway in the Tunisian heat. He ignores the cursing shopkeepers and disoriented arrivals, searching for a newlywed couple thrust on a journey to locate an ancient relic before the extraterrestrial shit hits the proverbial fan.

* * *

Owen takes a noisy slurp from Rachel's morning coffee, "That hits the spot. I want a cup." Angling through the sliding door, he stares at the arcane, miniaturized coffeemaker for a flummoxed instant before calling for guidance. "How does this thing work?"

"Check the drawer below the coffeemaker," Rachel smiles, listening to the loud, clanking sounds of her husband wrestling with the single-cup IQ test. Realizing he was making little to no progress, she peers through the half-open slider, "Find the box of Moroccan coffee cubes. That's what I'm drinking." Staring into his befuddled face with an empty paper cup crumpled in his right hand, "For God's sake, Owen. Press the button on the side, and the lid will pop open."

"Oh. Okay. Thanks."

He returns with a steaming cup, "What a piece of crap, coffeemaker."

"You are hopeless around machines."

They look beyond the frenzy of activity on the wharf toward the ultra-modern skyline encircling the vast port juxtaposed with the golden vista of the ancient city of Tunis, peaking between the imposing glass and steel megastructures.

Breaking the silence with another obnoxious yawn, he sloshes coffee onto his hand, "Man, it is hot out here."

Rachel faces her new husband, a wry smirk crinkling her cute, freckled nose, "Nothing gets past you. You are going to make one hell of a detective."

"I'll be happy to survive long enough to return to my normal day job, international spy."

Rachel laughs, avoiding a coffee spit take over the rail, "I thought you were some sort of banker. That's what you put on your dating app bio. What a big liar you are, Owen Haig!"

Owen's zinger of a reply is cut short as their new traveling companion pushes the door open and steps onto the veranda: the new and improved Louie.

Louie | Le Tholonet, France
12:30 a.m. | August 18, 2044 (54.5 hours earlier)

Illuminated by the electric car's dim headlights at the base of the precipitous limestone cliff on the forested shoulder of Montagne Sainte-Victoire, the dazed couple showed the faded, handwritten coordinates on the reverse side of the blood-stained photo to their confused driver.

The sentient orbs of light covertly shadowing the pair from space and manifesting into Rachel's long-lost great-great-grandfather had vanished into the ether. They vacated Louie, too. His profane reaction to the coordinates was a dead giveaway; the irascible French robot was back online.

Louie's miraculous reset was insufficient to placate Owen. The 27-year-old investment banker's thrill-seeking, superhero-sized ego took a colossal hit from the paranormal event. For the bumpy drive down the mountain, the humanoid acquiesced with a dramatic eye roll, muttering more French profanity while angling his lanky frame into the back seat. Rachel stared through the bug-smeared and dirt-spattered windshield from the shotgun seat, dead tired but feeling equal measures of confusion, anxiety, and exhilaration coursing her racing mind. Satisfied with the seating arrangements—reeling from the whole experience—Owen wedged himself behind the wheel for the tense drive to their villa.

After a few wrong turns and a heated exchange about which way to turn at a fork in the road, Rachel hears the run-flat donut tires crunching over gravel through the gate of the honeymoon chateau in Le Tholonet in the early-morning darkness at 2:00 a.m.

With an unlit cigarette dangling from his lower lip, Louie helped the couple port luggage inside, stacked in a precarious heap at the bottom of an elegant, curved staircase at the far side of the chateau's spacious foyer.

Everyone was exhausted, even Louie. Since leaving their hotel on the Vegas strip for the Buzz Aldrin International Spaceport—which seemed like a million years ago but was only a little over a day earlier—the newlyweds had not slept a wink.

After the luggage and carry-on bags were inside, Owen grabbed Rachel's most cumbersome monster and trudged up the staircase. Meanwhile, she waded zombie-like into the pile of bags, unable to focus. She considered curling atop the stack in her exhausted state of mind, but the tempting idea was interrupted by a weird murmuring noise inside the chateau. Her bleary eyes peered up the curved flight, but Owen was out of sight.

Concentrating on the faint sound, she determined it came from an arched passageway on the opposite side of the expansive foyer beyond an exquisite French Provincial console arrayed with pictures, candles, and a clipboard holding the owner's contact information and house rules. Against her better judgment, she tiptoed and peered down the unexplored corridor. Halfway down the dark, picture-lined hallway, she saw Louie, nose-to-nose with a life-sized oil portrait of a somber, patriarchal figure, mumbling different languages in unison, like he did when the whole thing started.

"Louie! What is the matter with you? You promised everything was fine, and you were back to normal mode, or whatever you called it! Snap out of it!"

Louie turned from the portrait with a glassy-eyed vacancy, staring through the distraught young woman.

"Owen! Can you come down here, please?"

"What now, Rachel?"

"It's Louie. He's acting strange again."

"How can you tell?"

"Just get down here, dammit!"

Coaxing Louie out of the shadows, the exhausted couple sat their wonky driver in an upholstered accent chair and told him to stay put.

Meanwhile, Rachel called Louie's employer, expecting to leave a terse message, but a live person made the innocent mistake of picking up the phone. Owen stood guard, half asleep, half-listening to his new wife, dressing down the apologetic after-hours helpline operator.

An hour later, at 4:00 a.m., Owen mused the adage, the squeaky wheel gets the oil, is accurate indeed. The human technician standing in the early-morning darkness at the chateau's wrought-iron front gate was living proof.

Leading the taciturn technician onto the estate, red toolbox grasped in his hairy meathook hands, Rachel expressed how terrible she felt disrupting Louie's carefree existence chauffeuring tourists around France. Entering the foyer, where the stare-eyed Louie waited, the tech proffered a creepy, gap-toothed smile and gestured for the talkative woman to stand beside Owen, arms crossed, struggling to keep his eyes open.

The tech settled on the tile floor before Louie, expanding his multi-tiered box of tools and gadgets to its fully open position. He hummed aloud, perusing the contents, and finally removed a digital gauge with a long red cord uncoiling from the bottom. Turning his attention to the addlepated android, he probed rough, stubby fingers under the side-parted mass of straight, black hair on the left side of Louie's head. Locating the desired port, he connected the male lead, and the gauge activated with a rhythmic ping. Allowing himself a demonstrative sigh, the swarthy fellow watched numbers scroll across the instrument's readout. To Rachel, the whole process appeared low-tech for a complicated cybernetic repair. She flinched as the pudgy man yanked the plug from Louie's noggin and tossed it in his box. With a smirk, she surmised he did not miss many meals, watching him stand, stretch kinks from his fireplug frame, and scratch his scraggly beard. Pray, that was all she saw him scratching.

"Madame, whatever caused Louie to malfunction had nothing to do with you. He is well past his refurb date. These late models are so lifelike it is easy to forget they are machines and eventually break down, like a washing machine. You're familiar with those, right?"

Despite craving sleep more than he could remember since college, Owen forced himself to wake up and stretch his right arm to his fuming wife's side. He sensed her desire to rip the horrible little man's head from his stubby body in response to the chauvinistic remark.

He also noted with an inexplicable uneasiness that the technician, who went by Francois, never asked what caused Louie's meltdown. An esoteric house call repair to this remote village at such an odd hour would typically ring alarm bells in Owen's head. However, it never went beyond a benign curiosity in his sleep-deprived psyche.

Eschewing further explanation, Francois proceeded to open Louie's head, akin to the toolbox unfolding open, exposing a bundle of wires suspended in a pinkish ball. Circular scorched marks, like cigarette burns, peppered the glimmering surface, "Here is your problem, my friend." He yanked the mass and tossed the ruined hardware into his box. Wiping an oily residue from his thick, calloused hands, the tech informed the couple he would return with a cart to wheel the non-functioning robot to his van.

Making his way out the front door, Rachel rushes to block his path, "You are going to fix him, right?"

Francois replied over his shoulder, never breaking stride, "No, mademoiselle, he will be disassembled, and his parts will go toward newer models. We are a business, not a nursing home for fellows like Louie."

After the tech exited, Rachel stepped across a scattering of tools and parts on the floor toward the haphazard pile of luggage by the curved staircase. After a brief, foggy-eyed search, she pulled the dog-eared photo from a side pocket on a designer bag. Holding it to Owen's drowsy face, she flipped it to reveal the faded handwritten numbers, "Louie recognized these coordinates at a glance. He is a walking GPS. We need him to help us locate the golden ellipse."

"Rachel, are you insane? Do you seriously believe we should drop everything and go to Libya based on what your dead relative told us in that damn cave? It must be a collective hallucination; space travel may have radiated our brains. The whole thing is crazy! Not to mention, it means a trip to Libya, of all places. Louie was right about one thing: it's not a nice place. Even though the war on terror officially ended in the 30s, bad actors remain all over the Middle East. That victory parade down Pennsylvania Avenue was full of crap, and everyone knew it! If you ever watched anything other than cooking shows, maybe you would understand what's happening." Owen proffers a sheepish shrug, realizing he may have crossed a line.

"That's a bunch of crap, and you know it. I know more about this world than you do, and I have the scars to prove it."

"Rachel, at the risk of angering your Grandpa Neil, maybe we should impart what we learned to the nearest embassy and let them figure it out. They will likely humor us but laugh their asses off the minute we leave. At least our consciences will be clear."

"This stinky bastard wants to tear Louie apart. However, if we flash enough cash in his greedy face, I bet he will install a new wad of wires in Louie's noggin. I'll pay for it. Please!"

"Rachel, we had this all planned out. What about the rest of our honeymoon? I thought you wanted to relax and do nothing for a few weeks, not set out on an ill-advised adventure into the unknown."

Rachel held the stained and wrinkled photo to her husband's stubbled face, "It's a good thing my Great-Great-Grandpa could not hear you."

"I don't know, Rachel. He's probably listening and laughing with the rest of his foo-fighting buddies."

Rachel gives Owen her best sad-eyed stare.

Owen snatches the photo with a surrendering nod, "Okay, Rachel, you win. You always do. I guess you bought yourself a robot friend."

"I'll try to keep it platonic."

"You want to go there?"

"I'm joking, Owen. You are a real grouch when you miss your beauty rest."

"Well, I'm sure Louie will be very thankful we saved him from ending up in a box of spare parts."

"It's not about rescuing Louie; we must save the world for our children."

Rachel and Owen | Port of Tunis, Tunisia
08:30 a.m.| August 20, 2044 (Back to present time)

Rachel beams with a sense of accomplishment as Louie, showing no ill effects post his impromptu brain core replacement a little over 48 hours earlier, steps onto the crowded balcony. "Good morning. We can't thank you enough for agreeing to accompany us here to North Africa."

"Yeah, Louie, thanks a lot."

Louie admires the view from the high veranda on the passenger ferry, "What a splendid morning!" Turning to face his new friends, he bows his head with a curt nod, "Think nothing of it. I'm more than happy to accompany you on this expedition." Gesturing through the open slider, "The porter delivered your breakfasts. Don't let your eggs get cold, Master Owen. Ms. Rachel, I'm afraid they only had blueberry scones; I hope it meets with your approval."

"A blueberry scone sounds great, Louie. Thanks."

After Louie retreats into the stateroom and slides the door shut behind him, Rachel turns with a mischievous smile, "I still can't believe we have an English butler. Would he mind if we changed his name to Alfred?"

"Alfred?"

"As in Alfred Pennyworth."

Owen responds with a blank stare.

"Are you telling me you never watched a Batman movie or read the comic?"

"For someone born in 2020, you're a walking encyclopedia of old-school pop culture trivia." Looking at the ancient North African city's skyline in the shimmering early morning heat, "If you want to reference a pertinent blast from the past, how about something from an old Harrison Ford movie."

"Indiana Jones didn't have a manservant."

Owen swats at a big fly crawling along the rail, "Huh. I guess you're right. I stopped watching those movies after that CGI Indy fiasco. Not good."

"Speaking of imposters, I'm still getting used to Louie's new English accent. I miss his snarky French personae. Too bad the repairman didn't have another French brain core thingy in his van."

"Your old Grandpa did quite a number on Louie's cybernetics." Owen laughs and glances through the glass slider at the humanlike entity situating meals on a small coffee table, "And somehow, we managed to get a house call at four in the morning. I'm still trying to square that circle. But yeah, I agree with you; Louie was designed and engineered to be a rude Frenchman. The pudgy guy installed a new brain core from what he had on hand, an English butler. The other choice was a German diplomat." continuing in an exaggerated baritone voice, "We chose wisely."

Rachel looks askance in response to another obscure, regurgitated movie quote, "On that odd note, let's put a cork in our little conversation. Louie's employer's loss is our gain. And I am happy he is through toiling as an underpaid driver. We'll take good care of him." Rachel drains the last few drops of coffee from her cup and retreats from the Tunisian heat into the relative comfort inside the stateroom.

Owen blocks her path, a seriousness darkening his chiseled face, "Rachel, Louie is not a puppy. If an advanced alien race infiltrated his circuits once, there is nothing to say they won't try again." Lowering his voice, "Just be careful around him is all I'm saying."

Rachel nods in agreement, acknowledging the magnitude of their task and the warning about Louie. Pangs of hunger rustling her stomach, she places her hands atop Owen's shoulders and leans close, touching her body against him, "I get it. Bruce Wayne could not have said it better himself." Her towel unravels from drying hair, and seductive feminine wiles deploy with a delicate kiss on her transfixed husband's scruffy cheek while guiding him out of her path into the stateroom where blueberry scones await.

A flummoxed Owen is left standing on the veranda, Rachel's empty coffee cup somehow finding its way into his hand.

* * *

After breakfast, they reorganized daypacks, already pared to the bare necessities before leaving the villa in Le Tholonet. Inspired by how many essentials Rachel could forgo, Owen pulls a tin of hair goo from his pack and tosses it into the bathroom wastebasket. Glancing into the mirror, he notices Louie in the background looking his way. Raising an index finger to his lips, as in hush, the banker flings the incrementally lightened pack over his shoulder and opens the cabin door. The trio follows other departing passengers through the ship and onto the wharf. With her first steps off the boat, Rachel scans the scene with a confident smile, masking anxiety she can never leave behind.

Halfway down the wharf, they purchase a bag of dates and move down the row to Ahmed's Jeep Rental.

Owen picks up a flyer, "I guess we need some kind of vehicle."

Behind a sun-faded banner with his name in a bold typeset situated alongside a goofball caricature of himself, Ahmed widens a gap-toothed grin across his whiskered frying pan face, sidling around a rickety table in a flowing Tunisian tunic draped over his rotundness. Sidestepping before Owen, he doffs the red fez atop his balding head, "My friend, will you need a vehicle for your wonderful time here in Tunis? It is scorching here, and public transportation is very shoddy and dangerous. I can rent you a Jeep, and you will be delighted, my friend, because it is inexpensive, and the fresh air hitting your face keeps you cool. What a bargain I can give to you!"

Rachel steps between Owen and Louie, "Ahmed? Right? Okay,

I'll bite. How much?"

Taken aback by the aggressive young woman, "How many days will you need a rental, Madame?"

"Tell you what, Ahmed. We don't want to rent. We want to buy one of your Jeeps."

The gears turning beneath his red fez, Ahmed negotiates, "I will tell you what. I have a special Jeep you can buy for one thousand American dollars. An excellent deal, my friend." Ahmed shoots a nervous glance between a poker-faced Owen and the precocious and pretty young American woman.

Rachel pulls her pack off her shoulder and removes a satchel full of bills from a zippered pocket. "Let's see the car; we'll talk turkey afterward."

"I do not deal in turkeys, Madame. I believe Salaam has monkey steaks if you want a barbecue."

"Just the Jeep, Ahmed."

The Tunisian businessman leads the trio off the wharf to a gravel lot behind an old seafood packing plant where a row of late-model four-wheel-drive EVs bakes under the sun behind a rusted chain-link fence cordoning off Ahmed's property. Approaching the main gate, the salesman pushes a button on a fob produced from a pocket in his tunic, parting screechy, chain-link gates like a fez-wearing Moses. He motions for his new customers to enter, and the group moves into the compound, passing a small shack, aka Ahmed's rental office. Jeeps, pickup trucks, mopeds, and bicycles are parked askew in various states of repair scattered around the dilapidated, teal-painted, clapboard structure. With his customers in tow, the salesman ignores his grease-covered mechanic, hunched under the hood of a broken-down Toyota pickup truck, yelling a profanity-riddled tirade in French at some wonky engine part. The group reaches the far corner of the oil and grease-stained premises with more profane insults and curses wafting through the hot, dry air. Squeezing single file past a flatbed truck, they halt before the front grille of a weather-beaten old Jeep with its large, circular headlights staring at them.

Ahmed exclaims triumphantly, "Here it is, my friends, a vintage 1983 Jeep CJ-7. I challenge you to find another vehicle like this anywhere in Tunis!"

The couple stares in wide-eyed disbelief at the four-wheel-drive refugee from the latter part of the last century. Louie's poker face remains unchanged, and the mechanic's tantrum pierces the prolonged silence. Sensing his customers' unimpressed reactions, Ahmed dispenses with decorum, shouting over his shoulder at his ill-tempered mechanic to shut his pie hole.

Addressing the American couple, "My apologies. It is a monumental challenge to find good help these days." Gesturing toward Louie, he comments wryly, "What I would give to have an army of these cool-headed fellows."

The couple shares a knowing smile after their initial shock at seeing the four-wheeled relic fades.

"He has his moments."

The brutal Saharan Desert sandblasted the original tan paint off most of the metal body. In addition to enduring the harsh North African climate with the scars to prove it, the enigmatic vehicle survived primitive Tunisian roads and a litany of owners and renters over its lifespan.

Owen shrugs, "Well, we're here. May as well check her out." Stepping forward to kick the old girl's tires, he raps his knuckles on the rust pattern resembling an ancient mariner's world map spread across the iconic, rounded hood and front grille. Pretending he knows anything about cars, he winces at the hollow sound and produces a low whistle, as in, "That 'ain't good."

Ahmed reads Owen's apprehension, "Sir, she is sound, I assure you. And in excellent shape under the hood, where it counts. The tires have many, many miles left on them! My friend, it even comes with a brand-new spare mounted on the back. And most important, it may appear a little worse for wear, but it runs like a top and will get you to your destination without drawing unwanted attention to yourselves along the way." He pauses and squints through the brightness toward the mysterious American couple, "I can also take care of the paperwork. No one will know you were ever here. Do I have that about right, my friends?"

Ignoring the salesman's perceptive comment, Owen addresses his better half, "What is your opinion, Rachel?"

The hot woman removes her sunglasses and peers through the wide-open driver-side window. Arching an eyebrow, Rachel leans under the weather-beaten, safari-brown soft top and inspects the ad-hoc patchwork of duct tape holding the decades-old vinyl in place. "Does it come with an extra roll of tape?"

Sensing his customers are getting cold feet, the Tunisian businessman discloses to the outspoken woman that the soft top's zipped plastic windows are missing. "Trust me, you would not be zipping the side windows in this heat, plus the breeze will keep you plenty cool; it's like having air conditioning!"

"Ahmed, a thousand dollars is a little steep considering it's seen better days, decades ago." Rachel unsnaps the driver's side door, brushes gritty sand off the cracked, brown vinyl front bucket seat with the side of her hand, and climbs in, shooing a fly from the faded plastic Jeep logo centered on the worn steering wheel. Inspecting the rest of the dash, she produces a subtle smirk, noticing the headlight knob is also missing. Placing her right hand on the aftermarket, bright yellow happy face shift knob, she calls for the salesman to give her the key while pressing the clutch pedal under her left boot to the firewall. Ahmed presents her with the keyring, which includes a souvenir plastic surfboard screen-printed with his cheesy logo. Inserting an old-school metal key into an ignition switch for the first time in her life, she gives it a hard turn. As advertised, the Jeep immediately roars to life, prompting Ahmed to wipe his brow with relief and yell a compliment toward his harried mechanic over the noisy engine.

Rachel leans out the window, "I'll give you 800 dollars and not a penny more."

"Done!"

Unusually silent during the negotiation, Louie sticks his head inside the back of the Jeep from the passenger side, scanning the tight confines illuminated by yellowy light filtering through the soft top's filmy, wrap-around thick, plastic window. Angling into the back, he swats a fly off the plywood bench screwed in place with a threadbare maroon seat cushion atop its splintery surface. Looking backward, where the seatback would typically lend support, a red metallic storage container is screwed into the wood in its place. Owen passes him their packs, which he manages to stow side-by-side into the narrow box. Tight fit. He inserts a new cigarette between thin lips, ignoring a synthetic déjà vu of another life spent shoving passenger bags into tiny vehicle compartments.

Louie scoots to center his seated position between the front bucket seats, drumming long fingers on the thin pad. Peering inside the grimy drink holders molded into the cracked plastic middle console, he sees a gigantic, iridescent beetle hunkered in the sticky well. Scooping it out of the holder, he flings it out the passenger side window before anyone notices, especially Miss Rachel.

"Did you just toss something out the window?" Rachel calls over her shoulder, wiping grime from the rear- and side-view mirrors with a wad of tissues and well-aimed spit.

"A candy wrapper, Madame. Nothing more." Science fiction bullshit regarding a robotic inability to lie does not apply to higher-end synthesized humans, such as himself. He wonders if Miss Rachel and her suspicious husband know that fact. It is in his manual that nobody bothers to read.

Owen finalizes the transaction with Ahmed while Rachel

familiarizes herself with the spartan instrument cluster and adjusts the streaky mirrors. Louie closes his eyes and places his right hand on Jeep's metal frame, sensing the rebuilt six-cylinder engine's vibrations. Opening his eyes, he produces a familiar, crooked grin, confident the classic vehicle is indeed roadworthy.

Rachel slides her left hand along the steering wheel and gives the old girl some gas, ready to go. Owen hops into the shotgun seat and turns to check on Louie, centered atop the unforgiving plywood backseat.

The old Jeep rumbles out of the rental lot, following Ahmed's circuitous directions on navigating through the labyrinthine waterfront district to an eastbound on-ramp for the Trans-African Highway.

Ahmed watches them go, clutching a wad of American currency alongside his mercurial mechanic.

* * *

"This isn't bad at all." Rachel checks the side view mirror, one-handing a bend in the road, right hand atop the shift knob, winding along the narrow lane. "It's a good thing one of us knows how to drive a stick," glancing sideways at Owen through her Ray-Bans, "unlike some people in the car."

"At least I have a driver's license. Most people don't bother anymore."

"Don't be so defensive."

Owen ignores the comment and tests the battery in a cheap, plastic, pocket-sized flashlight he found rifling through the glove compartment.

Louie's head angles between the hot front-seat passengers, "Miss Rachel, if you become fatigued, please don't hesitate to avail yourself of my services. I am quite proficient in driving manual-shift automobiles."

"She's going to do just fine, Louie. Just relax; your time will come."

Rachel maneuvers through a bustling roundabout, shifting into third gear, and shoots a stern glance at Owen, "Don't be mean to Louie."

Downshifting into second at a steep incline, she swerves halfway to the top to avoid smacking into an ancient-looking shepherd and his flock, stepping into their path like refugees from a forgotten era, "They appeared out of nowhere!"

"I never cared for mutton."

Rachel hangs a right at the summit, entering an ancient commercial district where the locals conduct their daily affairs. The chipped paint, plaster, weathered awnings, and broken windows give the street a charming old-world vibe.

Owen catches an occasional English word or phrase amongst the French and Farsi signage advertising every kind of merchant, service, and eatery under the Tunisian sun.

With practiced patience, the young blond guides the Jeep through a traffic snarl of cars, trucks, taxis, pedestrians, bicyclists, wandering livestock, and scooters of all shapes and sizes, looking sixteen ways at once as she presses onward down the crowded boulevard.

Approaching another insane roundabout, Louie interjects at the last second, "Take the second turn-off to the right."

"A little more warning next time, Louie!"

"My apologies, Madame, it won't happen again."

"And don't forget to call me Rachel."

Rachel | Trans-African Highway
10:15 a.m. | August 20, 2044

"I hope this bucket of bolts holds together," Rachel jokes while shifting into fourth gear. The speedometer pegs sixty miles per hour, merging with light mid-morning traffic onto the six-lane Trans-African Highway. Heading southeast out of town, the Jeep ascends a ridgeline, and the threesome takes in the expansive Tunisian coastline and the Mediterranean Sea sweeping into view.

"Wow! Quite a magnificent view. We should pull over and take some pictures. Right, Rachel?" Owen chuckles with a mischievous wink toward his camera-shy wife and commits one of his married life's first little white lies. "Don't worry; I left my camera at the villa."

Rachel does not take the bait and continues peering ahead down the highway.

Louie announces from the cramped confines of the makeshift backseat, "From here, we are looking at an approximate nine-hour drive time to Tripoli."

Owen shifts his position on the hard-as-nails, cracked leather passenger seat, "Nine hours? Can we go any faster, Rachel?"

"No. Maybe downhill."

* * *

Blazing sunshine beats down from the cloudless sky, baking the North African landscape as far as the eye can see. Intense heat radiates off four lanes of macadam, creating a road mirage evaporating over the horizon. Heading south on the well-maintained highway, the Mediterranean Sea comes back into view beyond barren escarpments punctuated by palm-filled hamlets and small fishing villages hugging the coast. Owen produces a dimpled, fatalistic sigh, raising thick brown eyebrows above his mirrored shades, realizing it was mid-morning, still hours before the hottest point of the day.

The wind whips under the vintage Jeep's soft top. Duct tape pulls loose, noisily flapping in the breeze. Grabbing the bag of dates from his pack, he feeds one to Rachel, happy to see her in the zone, driving in the slipstream of a large delivery truck four car lengths ahead.

Rachel washes down the chewy sweet date with the last drops from her water and deposits the crunched plastic bottle in the middle console drink holder, whispering, "Let the Machine do the work."

"What did you say, Rachel?"

"Nothing."

As a delivery truck rumbles past at over 85 mph, Rachel notices the oval logo adorning its dented and rusted rear hatch: Oasis Produce.

"Can I have another date?"

Miles farther down the highway, Rachel checks her rearview mirror, and her heart skips a beat seeing a motorcyclist zooming out of nowhere at breakneck speed. The sleek, black motorbike accelerates behind the Jeep within inches of the spare tire mounted on the tailgate. "If I tap the brakes, the guy will fly over our Jeep."

"Maintain your speed, Rachel; it's just some jerk showing off."

Owen and Louie watch as the daredevil swerves into oncoming traffic, sidling close enough for Rachel to reach out and touch his candy-apple red motorcycle helmet. Clad in a black leather jacket, chaps, and boots, the rider mirrors alongside until an oncoming truck prompts the daredevil to accelerate down the highway, disappearing around a bend as fast as he came.

Angered by the two-wheeled exhibitionist, Owen places a reassuring hand on Rachel's shoulder, "Are you all right, Rachel? Probably a local nut unaccustomed to seeing a woman driver, even in this progressive-minded day and age."

The ceaseless flapping noise from the duct tape and a hot vortex whipping under the old soft top make normal conversation impossible. Louie raises his voice to be heard above the din. "Master Owen, a recently published Oxford University paper, contains data on local populations' evolving opinions on gender since the war on terror ended. I am happy to recite the statistics if you like …."

"No, thanks, Louie! Nothing ended as far as I can tell; this is still a dangerous part of the world."

"I'm fine. The motorcycle rider didn't mean to scare us." Rachel steers around a tight bend in the serpentine highway while casting a sideways smile directed at her fellow travelers.

Still fuming regarding the close call, "Let me guess. Another one of your crazy premonitions?" Owen instantly regrets his sarcasm.

Sensing the friction between his traveling companions, Louie changes the subject, intent on interrupting their repartee, before one of them says something regrettable, "Perhaps we should focus our attention on more pressing concerns looming approximately three hours ahead. The Libyan border."

Owen | Shell Station, Gabes, Tunisia
02:45 p.m. | August 20, 2044

Outside Gabes, Tunisia, the trio rolls into a gas station across the cracked, oil-stained pavement. Rachel and Louie quickly traverse the sunbaked lot and enter the ramshackle market to peruse the vacuum-packed comestibles.

"I hope they have pretzels." Volunteering to fill up the Jeep in the triple-degree heat, Owen's stomach growls, shifting from foot to foot, trying to avoid melting the soles of his shoes. Waiting on the slow pump, he notices a rip in the sunbaked soft top and decides he has had enough of the windy vortex the covering creates inside the old vehicle. He unsnaps the flappy, threadbare material without considering the potential for calamity. However, the minute he does this, he realizes he has made a mistake as the over-half-century-old vinyl crumbles in his hands. Standing in the incredible heat, he can do nothing but laugh and hope his traveling companions don't mind a little extra sunshine and wind in their hair. Pulling off the remainder of the ruined top, the filthy interior, roll bar, and plywood bench seat are bathed in sunshine. Looking at his handiwork, he shrugs, "On the plus side, the backseat should be less claustrophobic, and no more flapping tape."

Looking toward the market, Owen spots a large trash bin around the right side of the dilapidated structure. Dragging the ruined soft top remnants across the lot, a shadow in the shape of a motorcycle comes into view beyond the bin. Squinting through his tinted shades in the blinding midday sun, the overheated man moves toward the corner of the building, not expecting to see the same motorcycle from earlier. Repressing nascent paranoia unlike any experienced over his 27 years, he shoves the ruined soft top into the dumpster. Furtively peering toward the bike-shaped shadow, the same sleek motorbike from earlier comes into view. But where was the rider? He wants a word with this dangerous road hazard and marches around the corner toward the storefront.

* * *

The whir from an oscillating fan on the crowded Formica countertop inside the gas station market does little but push around the hot, dry, dusty air. However, when Rachel slides open the refrigerated case along the market's rear wall, cold air hits her square in the face. Lingering in front of the open door under the pretense of shopping for cold drinks, Rachel feels her body temperature drop. "Oh, yeah, Louie. This is the ticket."

"I am gratified you are cooling down, Madame."

A burly fellow operating the cash register, sporting gold chains around his thick, stubbled neck and a tangled matte of black hair pouring out his open-collar polo shirt, stubs a cigarette out in a bowl. With a bombastic voice in English, he yells at the establishment's lone customers, "Hey, you, back there! Make your selection and close the case! You are letting my cold air escape! We are barely able to keep the lights on as it is."

Rachel closes the freezer door, turns toward her companion, and smiles, "Busted."

Louie casts a glance over his shoulder, "Indeed."

"Watch and learn, my friend."

Rachel saunters toward the gruff cashier, sweating soft drink bottles held by the necks at strategic positions in both hands, channeling a cheesy beer commercial she endured while watching last year's Super Bowl with Owen. Setting the dripping bottles onto the counter, she leans forward and slides them toward the flustered man, "I'm so sorry for wasting your precious electricity, sir. It must be so hard to maintain such a fine little shop."

"Madame, it is I who should apologize. Please make use of the cooler some more if you like. It would be my pleasure to watch you; I mean, do you require anything else?"

Rachel wheels around and winks at Louie, "I'm fine. Thanks anyway."

Louie suppresses a smile and places water bottles, chips, and pretzels on the counter without making eye contact with the gobsmacked man who never stood a chance.

Jangling from the bell hanging on the market's grimy glass door diverts Louie's attention as it slams open while Rachel completes the transaction with the addled cashier. Owen brushes past without speaking in the narrow storefront area, ignoring his traveling companions.

Louie spectates with mild curiosity as Owen searches each aisle inside the darkened store.

The loud revving of a motorbike engine fills the market from outside, followed by the screech of thick tires throwing sand and gravel as the mystery rider speeds onto the highway.

Cursing under his breath, Owen rushes to the glass door and watches through the sun-faded cigarette and soft drink window-cling advertisements as the bike disappears. "Damn! I wanted to have a word with that guy."

Removing his sunglasses, Owen's eyes adjust to the market's dark interior onto a surprised Louie, Rachel, standing before a large, hairy cashier staring mouth agape from behind the counter. Realizing he made a scene, he proffers a sheepish grin and gestures at the cold soft drinks sweating pools of water on the narrow countertop, "I could go for a beer."

Rachel smiles at her stressed husband, "You're not driving. Why don't you grab a six-pack and meet us at the Jeep?"

"About the Jeep …."

Louie | Tunisia and Libya Border
06:45 p.m. | August 20, 2044

A short time later, they slowed to a crawl behind the bumper-to-bumper line of honking cars and trucks inching toward the under-staffed border checkpoint between Tunisia and Libya.

"Let's review our story again before we get to the front of the line."

Rachel recites their story in a sing-song voice, "We are on assignment for National Geographic, covering the turmoil continuing in and around Tripoli. However, thieves absconded with our cameras, equipment, and official paperwork. All we have are our passports."

"Boy, you had me believing our cover story, but what about Louie? He doesn't have a passport."

"Do robots need a passport?" Rachel asks as she quickly puts out her hand to stop Louie from interrupting the debate between herself and her new mate. "No one asked in Marseille when we boarded the ferry."

Owen counts down the dwindling line of vehicles in their lane with growing trepidation, "Yeah, well, they weren't going to shoot us or throw us in a dark prison cell if we didn't have the proper paperwork, either."

"Are you capable of playing it cool, Owen? Don't be such a worrywart."

"Maybe your motorcycle boyfriend put in a good word for us. He must have passed through here at some point."

Louie considers their current situation, "Master Owen, you

may be more right than you know."

Multiple lines of vehicles move apace. "Why are so many people trying to get into Libya?" Owen throws up a hand to stifle Louie's answer to his rhetorical question.

The pickup truck in front of them lurches onto Libyan soil, and it's their turn to pull forward to a yellow and black striped gate. A thickset security guard sporting a black beret and sweat-stained, army-green uniform motions toward Rachel with an impatient hand wave, "Halt right there!"

The din of idling motors and noxious fumes swirling under the super-heated arched checkpoint spanning the highway causes their ears to ring and eyes to water.

Owen watches the gruff Libyan border official strutting around the Jeep's tailgate, noticing the man pause and glance under the spare tire.

Sitting erect on the exposed backseat, Louie greets the suspicious officer with a genial English-accented, "Hello, sir."

Rachel watches the guard approach in her side-view mirror, her right hand sliding from the wheel to the happy-faced shift knob, ready to throw it in gear, just in case.

The guard taps the side of the Jeep with his thick, hairy hand, "Travel documents, please."

Rachel produces her passport for the man giving it a cursory glance, bending it in his thick, hairy, meat hook hand while gesturing for Owen's travel documents.

"I'll be back."

"I've got a bad feeling about this," unconsciously repeating another overused movie line of dialog.

The guard disappears inside a small office, slamming the door behind him. The hot, sweaty trio watches the Libyan's silhouette gesticulate in an over-animated fashion before a seated individual behind a desk through slanted window blinds.

Louie produces a concerned frown, "It appears they are arguing, but I cannot determine what they are saying over the engine noise."

Owen notices the man pantomime a stamping motion before returning the passports to the guard.

The door flings open, and the security guard stomps outside, muttering to himself, and tosses the passports to the nervous couple in the Jeep.

"You are welcome to continue on your way into Libya." The border guard gives a small wave, a wicked, gap-toothed smile widening across his broad, dark features, "Drive safely."

"Thank you, sir."

The striped gate angles open, and Rachel reties her ponytail while steering one-handed, following Louie's detailed directions to the Libyan Coastal Highway. A briny sea breeze blasting through the open-air vehicle motoring on a southeastern heading replaces the prevailing desert wind. Paralleling the deep blue waters of the Med outside the Jeep's port side, Rachel's tanned hand rests on the happy-faced shift knob in fourth gear averaging a steady 60 mph on the last 2.5 hours toward Tripoli.

"Interesting," Louie says from the backseat. "It appears as though we have the answer to one mystery."

"And what would that be, Louie?"

"Whether or not I required a passport."

Rachel swerves past a slow-moving truck and laughs, "Someone should alert Ray Bradbury."

"You mean Isaac Asimov. He wrote, *I Robot*."

"I'm sure good-old Ray had robots in his books, too."

Owen deadpans, "We probably shouldn't argue about science fiction in front of Louie."

Rachel tries to suppress a fit of laughter but lets out a hearty chuckle upon seeing Louie's puzzled reaction in the rearview mirror.

Louie's nonplussed: "I fail to see the humor." elicits more good-natured laughs.

Owen opens his passport, careful not to let it go in the vortex, and inspects the stamp. "That was a little too easy. What do you think, Rachel? Any more names you would like to drop."

She grips the wheel, staring out the dirty front windshield, "All joking aside, I believe we are pawns in a three-dimensional chess game, and someone just made a move in our favor."

* * *

A remote tracking device attached to the tailgate in a wad of sticky goo by the mystery rider on the highway blinks red. The bribed border guard noted the unobtrusive device stuck under the Jeep's spare tire and granted passage onto Libyan soil, despite the passportless android, a clear border violation. Protestations from his fellow guards fell on deaf ears.

Easy money.

* * *

Farther along the monotonous drive, silence turns to boredom. The setting sun lengthens shadows across the sandy topography pocked with dirt-poor villages, swaying palms, and ubiquitous mosques of all shapes and sizes crowded along the azure sea. Minarets jut into the darkening sky along the more populated stretches of highway, echoing the sunset call to prayers across the land, audible over the cooling air whipping through the open vehicle.

The grumbling in Owen's stomach is the equivalent of his evening call to dinner. Crumpling an empty pretzel bag in his hands, "I have driven across the most backwater places in the good old USA, and even in the middle of nowhere, you will find a McDonalds or a Taco Bell, or something, Fred's Diner for crying out loud. We should have bought more to eat at the gas station in Tunisia." He glances at Rachel, still sporting her shades well after the blistering sun sunk below the western horizon behind them. He watches her staring out the windscreen with a two-fisted grip on the wheel, deep in concentration.

"Our camping trip in Montana was epic, right, Rachel? Rachel, are you listening? Rachel! Wake up!"

Louie places a firm hand on Rachel's shoulder, giving her a gentle nudge. "Miss Rachel, wake up if you please."

Rachel's bleary gaze widens onto a disorienting blur of red taillights and yellow-striped macadam whizzing past, startling her awake with a frightened gasp, "Okay! Okay! I'm awake now!"

Pulling off the highway, the Jeep skids to a stop on a wide gravel strip. "Wow. I am so sorry, guys. I've never fallen asleep at the wheel before. I must have been more tired than I thought and starving."

Removing her sunglasses, she rubs her eyes and yawns. I need to get out of this seat and stretch my legs."

"Sure, Rachel, it will do us all good to get out and stretch our legs."

They stroll up a sandy berm as the last remnants of sunlight ebbs behind storm clouds on the horizon and the North African sky fills with stars.

With a loud yawn, Rachel stretches her back, gazing skyward, "Look at all the stars."

"Hard to believe we were up there just a few short days ago." Owen pulls her close and makes a command decision.

* * *

The temperature plummets into the seventies after sundown, a welcome reprieve for the Jeep's weary travelers who endured triple-digits throughout the day. Back in his element for the first time since France, Louie navigates scant traffic using his night vision mode, clenching an unlit cigarette between thin lips at a jaunty angle for the final stretch into Tripoli.

In the Jeep's cramped backseat, Rachel and Owen jostle for

comfortable positions underneath a black wool blanket emblazoned with the International Outer Space Consortium logo. After squirming and innocent elbows, Rachel falls asleep in her husband's embrace. Meanwhile, wide awake in Libya, Owen rests his head on a bundled pullover sweatshirt from his pack and feels something jabbing into his lower back, "I'm going to pay for this."

The Jeep's dim headlights guide the way, bumping along the Libyan Coastal Highway under a blanket of stars. Owen counts the vehicles and military trucks hurtling past, enduring Rachel's incoherent mumbles and restless leg kicks. "This will never replace counting sheep."

Louie speeds along in fourth gear, passing slower traffic, avoiding the military trucks, and maneuvering around looming asphalt fissures with his acute sensory detection in full operating mode, just as advertised.

Staring at the back of Louie's head of deep-black hair blowing in the evening air, Owen recalls the first meeting in Toulouse, "He comes with a seven-star rating."

Holding Rachel tight, his chin resting atop her sleepy head, Owen spies a bright light standing out in the field of stars. His semi-comfortable repose vanishes, replaced by an overwhelming dread, "Could the bright spot be one of the ET invaders Neil warned us about?" Carefully extricating his left hand from under the blanket, trying not to awaken Rachel, he edges forward and taps Louie's shoulder, "Is there anything you can do to make this thing go faster?"

Louie replies over his shoulder without moving a synthetic muscle, "No worries, Master Owen! I have the vehicle to sixty-eight miles per hour. We will be inside Tripoli city limits in a little over an hour. I advise you to get some rest."

Against his better judgment, he settles next to his slumbering wife, casts one more worried glance at the bright star overhead, closes his eyes, and falls asleep.

Louie | Outskirts of Tripoli, Libya
09:35 p.m. | August 20, 2044

The staccato of automatic gunfire reverberating in the distance stirs Owen from a deep slumber. Bolting upright with a start, he grimaces in pain from his awkward sleeping position in the back of the Jeep, throbbing from his tailbone to his head. Stretching to get the blood flowing to his extremities, he peers into the darkness around their parked position. Like flipping a switch, the day's events flood back into his frontal lobe. "Oh yeah, we're on the road to nowhere."

Rachel glances over the front passenger seat and tries not to laugh at his flummoxed state, offering a riposte to lighten his mood, "Road to nowhere? Is that referencing the classic Talking Heads song or an old Hope and Crosby road picture?"

Ignoring another volley of Rachel's obscure references, "My back is killing me! Why are we parked here?"

Flipping on the souvenir flashlight from the glove compartment, Rachel shifts to face the back of the Jeep and her husband's discombobulated repose, "You needed sleep." Shining the light in his groggy face, "I woke up only a short while ago and climbed into the front to help Louie navigate. We are inside Tripoli city limits. It is chaos, just like you warned. Louie pulled over a few minutes ago to map a route toward a safer part of town so we can find a place to crash for the night."

More gunfire erupts near their parked location in the shadows of a crumbled building.

Louie snatches the torch from Rachel, flicking it to the off position, "Madame, let's not advertise our arrival in Tripoli any more than necessary if it's all the same to you."

**Is it better to out-monster the monster
or to be quietly devoured?**

– Friedrich Nietzsche

Chapter Six:

The Agent

Rachel | Outskirts of Tripoli, Libya
09:35 p.m. | August 20, 2044

Ahead of the idling Jeep, nestled alongside the rutted curb of the potholed boulevard, war-ravaged buildings hulk against the darkened evening sky through the grimy bug-spattered windscreen. Louie's night vision acquires heat signatures of six individuals lying in wait behind an overturned bus. Intuiting their likely hostile intentions, the anglicized android formulates an escape route.

The palpable sense of anarchy mixed with sporadic high-caliber gunfire far exceeds Louie's worst fears. Concluding discretion is the better part of valor; he warns his passengers it's going to get a little weird, "This is going to be close. Get as low as possible and hold on tight!" Slamming the CJ-7 through its gearbox, he accelerates down the middle of the trash-strewn thoroughfare, swerving to avoid the bus and the mass of humans in its shadows.

Vigilant for lurking dangers impeding his chosen route, Louie peels around a bend and careens onto another cratered street, hearing Owen, loud and clear, yelling from the back, "Louie! What are you doing?"

Ignoring his sore neck and back, Owen stows loose articles and the precious wool blanket while trying not to fly out himself, "Helluva way to wake up from a nap!"

Resisting centrifugal force through an impossible hairpin maneuver, Rachel swings into her seat. Louie floors it over a rise, and the Jeep goes airborne before bouncing downhill past a blur of cars parked along the narrow residential street. Sensors working overtime, he coolly activates his turn signal at the bottom of the steep incline and makes a legal right turn onto a thoroughfare heading out of the rebel-held district.

Allowing a quick glance at the receding chaos in his rearview mirror, Louie produces a satisfied grin, expertly shifting up and down the resilient Jeep's gears while veering around potholes and roadblocks, "I do apologize for the abruptness of our escape. The preponderance of malcontents wielding automatic weapons in the rebel-held section of Tripoli left me with no time to explain."

Merging onto a bustling avenue illuminated by LED streetlights casting a greenish hue on the nighthawkish city-dwellers, Louie conjures memories from a past life driving busy metro streets, "We should be much safer in this part of town as long as we don't draw attention to ourselves. This section of Tripoli is insulated from the strife we escaped a few miles back."

"Well, that is a relief." Owen scans locals mingling in sidewalk cafes and hookah lounges exhibiting a carefree elan while others loiter in front of apartment buildings and markets, haggling with vendors hawking everything from exotic delicacies and Chinese-made electronics to black-market contraband. "War? What war? You're right, Louie. We must have crossed the imaginary border from crazy into mildly insane town."

Rachel snickers, "I'm starting to get used to it. Does that make me insane?"

"Probably."

Louie taps the brakes at the back of a long line of cars at a Libyan army checkpoint. Rachel watches the yelling guards waving arms in a crazed windmill motion, directing honking vehicles unchecked through the intersection. "Those men appear disenchanted with their chosen line of work."

Owen makes inadvertent eye contact with a serious-faced officer standing at attention as they stop and go through another government checkpoint. "Man, this shit is more serious than you'll ever hear back in the states. Careful, Louie, we need to blend in."

"Point well taken, Master Owen," Louie nods at a passing soldier with a courteous smile. "The preponderance of military personnel illustrates the tenuous hold the Libyan government maintains in this upscale Tripoli district."

Looking ahead at the overlapping mass of neon signage hanging from buildings along both sides of the street in this festive section of the ancient city, Rachel notices the name OASIS illuminating one letter at a time on a loop. A recurring keyword in the weird dreams disturbing her sleep since the cave incident; she knows it is significant but refrains from saying so aloud.

As they start and stop past the establishment under the neon OASIS signage, Rachel realizes it is a nightclub jam-packed with sweaty grinding young people. Like the shady joints frequented in her rebellious youth, she suppresses cringe-worthy memories, "Given the oppressive heat, this balmy evening air gives the locals a chance to get out and socialize. Good for them."

More staccato gunfire echoes off the buildings, like July 4th on steroids, but the nighttime populace appears unfazed.

Owen finger drums to the hypnotic Middle Eastern beat thumping from bars and restaurants up and down the bumper-to-bumper avenue. "As long as you don't mind a little intermittent gunfire while you're out partying, buying groceries, or whatever, it's not a bad place to live."

Pulling her tired gaze from more soldiers shouting commands at a swarthy group of agitators at the next bustling intersection, Rachel decides to air the vexing word rattling inside her head, "Louie? What if there is a hotel called, let's say, The OASIS. I can provide you the name, and you drive us to its location, right?" With a self-conscious chuckle, "I mean, if there is one."

Louie glances in Rachel's direction, steering through the bustle and smiling like a kid caught with his hand in the cookie jar, "Why yes, you are correct."

He brakes behind an empty troop transport and faces her, Owen leaning between the seats, "I confess, while driving here, I could not help overhearing your muttered references to an oasis, among other things. Ironically, the word oasis is commonplace in this part of the world; however, I deduced you were referencing a historic Tripoli hotel. I made it our destination since we needed a place to stay. Neither of you suggested anywhere else since our arrival, so it seemed prudent to stick a pin in The OASIS Hotel - Tripoli."

Owen places a comforting hand on Rachel's shoulder from the backseat, "Oasis. Machine. You said so many things in your sleep over the past few days; I lost track. Let's go with Louie's hotel theory. In the morning, we can set out to the exact location from the coordinates on the photo and see whether it leads to an oasis."

Rachel clasps her ring hand atop Owen's, the pricey rock diffracting streetlights in a rainbow of colors drawing their collective gaze. She turns to Louie, biding his time until their romantic moment passes, "Okay, let's get a move on; I could use a shower and a stiff drink."

"A good plan, Madame."

"For the millionth time, it's Rachel."

A nagging thought invades Rachel's overactive mind: Did Louie's new and improved English butler version come with pinpoint navigation like his previous French programming? Only time will tell. Owen suggested purchasing a GPS locator as an insurance policy, but Rachel balked at his apprehension, "Owen, when did you become such a worrywart? Louie is our GPS."

Praying she does not regret her brash confidence in Louie's new noggin, Rachel watches the robot drive while Owen people-watches from the back. Like a rat in a maze, Louie indeed navigates Tripoli's confounding network of checkpoints, one-way streets, roundabouts, dead-ends, detours, late-night traffic snarls, and scattered gunfire without incident.

Rachel's lips curl into a triumphant smile, and she thinks, "I knew he could do it."

Louie | OASIS Hotel, Tripoli, Libya
10:35 p.m. | August 20, 2044

The battered ride squeaks to a stop at the curb in front of the historic landmark edifice wedged between ultra-modern, glass, and steel monstrosities, quadrupling the hotel's seven-stories of cracked brick and stucco. Rachel lets out a whoop and embraces a surprised Louie with a kiss on his cheek. He reciprocates with a raised eyebrow and a polite nod, gesturing toward the 1940s-style, scripted logo for The OASIS Hotel - Tripoli. Right out of an old Humphrey Bogart movie, the sun-faded, hand-painted moniker decorates the stucco facade at eye level next to the double set of revolving glass doors.

"Here we are," Louie declares with a triumphant grin.

Owen vaults his aching body from the Jeep, sticking the landing on the worn red carpet beneath the hotel's front awning.

A fresh-faced bellboy, Hassan, greets the new arrivals, fidgeting with his name badge hanging askew from an ill-fitting maroon uniform.

Before the bellboy can recite his practiced welcome speech in English, Owen calls to Rachel, "Well, that was a little too exciting."

Despite the monotonous journey across a scorching desert ending with a harrowing gauntlet of gunfire through war-torn city streets, Rachel sweeps blond locks over her shoulder and glides out of the Jeep with effortless grace.

Reaching for the sky and stretching kinks from her svelte feminine form, Rachel overlooks the firecracker of cognitive stimuli going off inside the thunderstruck bellboy's prefrontal cortex.

Turning to Owen with an effervescent smile, "Why don't we check in," with a wink at the addled teenager, "and let Louie and this handsome young man handle the Jeep."

While working his first shift as the late-night bellman at the OASIS Hotel, Hassan cannot tear his eyes from the stunning woman. Mouth agape, he watches her push through the revolving doors and calms his beating heart after she enters the hotel. Emitting a low whistle, he turns toward the vehicle to get on with his humdrum job, coming nose-to-nose with Louie's inscrutable countenance. The startled kid suppresses a cough, waving a hand through smoke wafting from the driver's lit cigarette.

"Close your mouth, young man; flies will get in." Louie gestures toward the rear of the Jeep, "The red metal box contains my colleagues' bags. You may also check underneath the bench seat." Pausing while the harried bellboy pries the thick packs jammed inside the narrow box, "What are the parking arrangements for this establishment?"

Hassan stops mid-pull to answer the strange man, "Uh sir, yes, sir. There is short-term self-parking behind the hotel. Otherwise, I can take your Jeep across the street to the Hyatt and give you a voucher. We share their parking garage for our valet services."

Indecisiveness clouds Louie's cybernetics. He bonded with the bucket of bolts on the highway, and now an illogical paranoia won't allow him to relinquish the metal key to the polite, albeit puberty-stricken, kid. "I will avail myself of your establishment's short-term parking." With his decision made, he peers through the glass doors and spies Owen and Rachel standing in front of the check-in counter. "Also, if you can round up some digging implements before I return, I will be much obliged."

"Sir? Digging implements?"

"A pick and a shovel, boy! Now see to it like your tip depends on it!"

Ignoring the ridiculous struggle to extricate bags from the Jeep, Louie slides behind the wheel, turns the key, engages the clutch, and drives around the corner to the self-parking lot. The befuddled hotel employee is left standing on the carpet with crumpled daypacks swinging from straps clenched in both hands.

Hassan tosses the bags onto a luggage carrier, waving a hand in front of his face to clear the smoky cloud lingering in the hot nighttime air, and notices an odd blinking light under the vintage Jeep's spare tire as it heads for the lot. "Where am I going to find a shovel around here?"

Recalling his grandfather's words when he told him about his new job at The OASIS Hotel: "That old hotel was reduced to rubble during World War Two, and though it was rebuilt, its ghosts remain. Don't you get it, boy? It's haunted! Do I have to paint you a picture? If you accept the bellman position, you will witness strange occurrences you will never forget." Pushing the squeaky cart toward the shiny gold elevator doors, Hassan smiles at the irascible old man's words.

Leaning in to push the oversized luggage carrier, he stares down at the light backpacks and frets whether a certain someone may erroneously assume he is too puny to deliver them by hand. With escalating self-awareness and a sudden urge to present himself as manly as possible in his loose-fitting uniform, he abandons the cart. Checking his reflection, he hefts both bags and taps the button for the sixth floor.

Half a minute later, still waiting for the doors to open, he taps the button nonstop until the stupid doors open with a resounding ding.

* * *

Hearing the knock on the door, Owen hurries from the bathroom and slants the door to Room 642 open enough to accept the bags from the disappointed bellboy and gives him a generous tip. The young man's olive-skinned, hairless face spoke volumes; he hoped to see Rachel.

After tossing the backpacks on the bed, Owen pauses to appreciate the graceful arc of his wife's backside as she peers out the dirty window in her underwear. Her filthy, stinky t-shirt and shorts are already on the queen-size bed. Breaking the silence, trying not to stare like the slack-jawed youngster, "You sure had our bellboy's attention."

Rachel ignores the bellboy comment, rubbing her hand across the three-inch vertical scar on her left side just above her waist, "Are you tired?"

Owen pretends not to notice her tell, smoothing a hand across the scar from her assault signals anxiety. "No. I'm too wired. I doubt I would fall asleep. I'm not used to getting shot at during a high-speed chase. However, I might like to take a shower. And since it appears Louie prefers the company of our old Jeep, we have this shabby little hotel room all to ourselves for the foreseeable future."

Rachel peeks through messy golden locks with a sensual green-eyed smile.

* * *

Around the corner of The OASIS Hotel, down a trash-strewn alley, Louie stares into the darkness, hands gripped on the steering wheel, seated ramrod straight inside the parked Jeep. Only two other vehicles occupy diagonal spaces in the short-term parking lot behind the old hotel: a jet-black sedan with tinted windows and a sleek motorcycle with its engine still ticking and cooling after a long ride.

A hungry rat finds a discarded pizza slice inside a dumpster and drags the cheesy prize under the sedan to nibble away at the triangle.

An ominous presence materializes out of the shadows in the passenger seat beside Louie. The wraith's eyes glower with venomous resolve from under a hooded camouflage sweatshirt emblazoned with a skull design beneath a black trench coat. The entity mutters a monotone binary code hacked like a hot knife through butter from the maker's firewall-protected, encrypted server farm. The series of letters and numbers trigger a self-destruction countdown designed by the Kobayashi Corporation as a last resort to discourage intellectual property theft, i.e., kidnap his pricey robots.

With the malicious code activated within Louie's nuclear-powered cybernetics, the ethereal presence extends a skeletal hand from an oversized cuff and presses a bony fingertip to Louie's right temple. A secret microchip compartment springs open, and the being switches the chip with a counterfeit before rebooting the robot. Louie goes dark. The cigarette dropped from his lower lip, off his left thigh, and out the side of the Jeep into a fetid puddle.

Immobilized with the blank stare of a crash-test dummy in the driver's seat, the robot's hands clutch the wheel at ten and two o'clock, bathed in the dimness of a lone LED floodlight.

Its malevolent task completed, the stranger transmogrifies into a dark specter shimmering with lights and vanishes into the night.

Ninety seconds later, Louie's miles of chips, wires, and goo restart. Back to normal functioning mode, he swivels to address the hooded apparition, finding nothing but an empty seat.

Having consumed most of the Neapolitan feast, the rat curled its long tail and fell asleep under the sedan, satiated and satisfied.

Flynn | OASIS Hotel Bar
12:10 p.m. | August 21, 2044

Also satiated and satisfied but too wired for sleep, Rachel steps from the elevator in white tennis shoes, turquoise capris, and unkempt blond hair pulled into a damp ponytail cascading down the back of a loose-fitting, white linen blouse. Leading the way, her investment-banker-turned-adventure-seeker husband struts out of the elevator in a too-tight, light-gray polo untucked over safari-style khaki pants and his trusty Adidas sneakers, sans socks. Not what Bogey and Bacall would wear under similar circumstances, but it will have to do.

Room service would suffice for Rachel, but the front desk clerk promised Owen the bar would remain open until 04:00 a.m., and since it was just a little after midnight, he convinced her the night was young.

Hassan is surprised and delighted to catch another glimpse of the young woman exiting the elevator from behind the bell desk adjacent to the revolving doors.

The American couple head in the opposite direction toward the OASIS Lounge, the historic hotel's venerable old watering hole at the main lobby's far end. The pair stroll through an asymmetric assemblage of antique furniture from a bygone era: Queen Anne wingback armchairs and sofas upholstered in worn, dark-brown leather with nailhead trims, coffee tables displaying local pottery and large bowls of oranges and end tables centered with flickering, French Empire, candelabra-base lamps with yellowed shades. The furniture is situated on ornate Moroccan rugs and surrounded by tall, rangy palms bursting from colorful Algerian ceramic pots. Palms bookend double doors inset with jewel-toned stained-glass patterns obscuring the darkened lounge beyond.

Parting the heavy inlaid doors, Owen gestures for his bride to cross the threshold, whispering as she passes, "That shower was amazing! I had dirt and dust in places I ought not to mention."

Rachel winces a smile, "Yeah, I know. Next time, let's shower first."

Laughing like carefree newlyweds for one of the few times since leaving Las Vegas, they enter the bar's low-lit ambiance. Pushing half-past midnight, they note barflies and hotel guests filling red leather booths and even-spaced barstools around the circular bar. Owen takes Rachel's hand, making a beeline toward two empty stools.

Looping a strand of long, damp hair behind her left ear, she slides onto a seat, casting a furtive glance at the mixed patronage. Noting a preponderance of men with the raucous exception of a large gaggle of ladies laughing, joking, and imbibing neon cocktails across the bar, she smiles toward the dark-skinned bartender with a bushy beard.

Flinging two palm logo coasters atop the bar, he speaks in a thick Nigerian accent, "What can I get you?"

"Macallan on the rocks, please."

Rachel punches Owen's arm, "Whatever happened to ladies first?" With a quick and easy smile, she nods, "I'll have the same, but make mine neat."

The bartender returns with two tumblers, plopping a large cube in one, pours the whisky and replaces the bottle back in line on an under-lit glass shelf.

Out of view on the highest shelf above the aligned liquor bottles, a collection of vintage World War Two era photographs propped up in simple metal frames collect dust. Among the old photos is a group shot of the 64th Army Air Corps Squadron, the Black Scorpions. In the wide-angle image, pilots and crews are aligned wingtip to wingtip along the front and atop the wings of a mean-looking P-40 Tomahawk fighter plane. Standing on the fighter plane's starboard wing, the smiling faces of Neil Alexander and Harry Stark beam toward the Life Magazine photographer's camera lens.

Gesturing his upheld glass toward the bartender, tending to another new arrival across the low-lit circular bar, "Well, Rachel, apparently your wily feminine charms don't impress everybody."

She clinks his glass and takes a tentative sip with one eye on the ladies peppering the brusque fellow with another round of fancy drink orders, "I'm suffering guilt by association."

Swiveling on her stool in the opposite direction, past Owen's bent left elbow resting, she notices an ashtray emblazoned with the OASIS Hotel logo. "Whoa, I just had a massive déjà vu."

"Deja vu? Come on, Rachel. I need ten minutes of normal."

Finishing her drink, she grabs Owen by the leg, "I figured out what's happening to me. When Neil passed through me in the cave, he left a lifetime of memories in my subconscious and activated something inside my brain. His experiences appear in my dreams. It's what you hear when I talk in my sleep. Neil was at this hotel. He guided us here for a reason."

Catching the bartender's eye, she gestures for a refill.

Owen indicates he is okay before addressing Rachel's mea culpa, "I'm glad you got that off your chest. We are in the middle of something fantastical, but we made it this far. Whatever we need to do from here, I'm your man."

Rachel takes a long drink from the new glass, "I'm glad you are my husband, Owen." Pausing to gather her thoughts, "We need to gather our stuff and head out to the desert tonight, locate the golden ellipse, and get to Cairo on the next flight out of here." She takes his hand in hers, "Neil led us here, but now I can't shake the feeling a terrible presence matched our every move. And despite his thoughts rattling inside my head, I have no clue what to do once we get to Cairo."

Casting a paranoid eye around the bar, Owen leans forward and whispers, "Maybe Neil arranged to have Indiana Jones meet us at the airport?" Laughing at his small joke, he stops mid-chuckle upon seeing her aggravated frown.

Reaching for her glass, Rachel gives Owen a sly sideways look, "What is it with you and Indiana Jones?"

The bawdy group of ladies breaks out in a drunken chorus of

happy birthdays followed by whoops and laughter. Rachel watches the revelry with a weird, misplaced resentment before swiveling nose-to-nose with a perplexed Owen, "You and I are going to return the golden ellipse atop that alien beacon underneath the Great Pyramid." Downing her drink, she clacks the glass onto the bar, "There. I said it."

Owen motions for a refill, hellbent on confronting the elephant in the room for the first time since France. "Are you serious, Rachel? I agree, Neil wants us to do that, but he was pretty stingy on the details. I can wrap my brain around going to the coordinates and locating the buried treasure, but the rest of it?" Shaking his head, he glances around the bar to ensure no one is eavesdropping, "Do you have any idea how ridiculous the rest of the plan sounds?" A look of incredulity spreads across his face to bolster his rhetorical question. "Neil wants you and me, Rachel, to walk past armed guards, enter the Seventh Wonder of World, and without any guidance whatsoever, locate a chamber every archeologist since Howard Carter did not know even existed. That is fucking impossible. I am truly sorry to be the one to tell you, but it is."

Sighing at his wife's tearful reaction, "Rachel, please don't cry. I assumed we would come to our senses and drop the damn thing at our embassy and let the whole matter become someone else's problem— even though a ghost named Neil threatened to kick my ass if we did."

The bartender slides Owen's new glass across the bar's smooth surface and pours a new shot over the ice.

Rachel stops Owen from reaching for his glass, "Think about it, Owen. Why did the foo fighters rescue Neil? He had the photo with the coordinates with him in the plane. Now we have it." Lowering her voice to a whisper, "The ellipse changes people for the worst. Neil trusts us and no one else. We have to do it."

"If true, how do you know I won't take the thing for myself and leave you stranded in the desert?"

With his point made, Owen lifts his glass, and again, Rachel stops him before it reaches his chapped lips. "It's a risk I need to take.

Neil used Louie to guide us to the cave, and he probably cleared the way for us to reach this point." Rachel wipes a tear from her cheek and gives her partner a reassuring smile, "You agreed to rescue Louie from the scrap heap. He is working out fine. This will, too, if we keep the faith and stay the course."

Owen sets the tumbler atop the bar without a sip and proffers an easy dimpled smile toward the love of his life, "Well then, I better keep my wits about me. By the way, where is Louie? We haven't seen him since we got here." Glancing at silhouetted barflies seated around him, his gaze fixes on a familiar-looking presence on the opposite side of the bar. With a jolt of recognition, he notices the shadowed figure is wearing a familiar-looking motorcycle jacket. Never much for coincidence, despite their current predicament, "Hang here for a second, Rachel, I'll be right back."

The man acknowledges Owen's approach, placing a Coke bottle on a sopping coaster. "Can I help you, mate?"

"Why are you following us?"

With an amused grin reciprocated toward the stern countenance of the fist-clenched younger man, the rider swivels face-to-face with Owen, his smile widening across his dark features while raising his hands in mock surrender, "You spied me from clear across the bar. Good for you, mate." Finishing the 16-ounce bottle with a final swig, "Ah! I do enjoy a frosty beverage after a long ride!" Sliding the empty across the slick wooden bar, "Owen Haig, it's time for us to have a proper chat."

Noting the black man's British accent, Owen musters a sarcastic reply, "No shit, Sherlock."

"Yeah. No, shit. How about you slow your roll, grab your better half, and let's move to a booth and take a proper meeting." Slapping a dog-eared 50-dinar note on the bar, "There. I just paid for my Coke and that overpriced Scottish swill you two were drinking."

Tipping his empty bottle toward the puzzled young woman across the bar, he smiles, "Cheers, Miss."

Rachel looks from the stranger and back at Owen, reading his puzzled expression.

The mystery rider rises off the stool, matching Owen's height and build, but with a toughened, "don't fuck with me" edge to his steely-eyed stare.

Owen feels like an idiot—unsure whether to acquiesce to the suave fellow's suggestion or take him outside and beat the crap out of the guy. Further complicating his dilemma, the outcome of a physical altercation is far from certain after standing toe-to-toe with the Brit.

Rather than ratchet up the tension, the man lets out a burp and assumes a friendlier posture, "I get it, mate. You want to take me outside and teach me a lesson for scaring you and the missus back on the highway." Chuckling at the notion, he continues, "let me explain, and if you don't like what I have to say, we can have a go, right?"

Stepping backward, Owen gestures toward an empty booth.

Rachel carries her glass to the table and scoots across the red leather bench seat. Owen angles beside her, unclenching his right fist with a head-shaking sigh, "Man, what's next?"

The man plops down across from the couple, unzipping a pocket inside his black leather jacket. Opening a bifold wallet, he pushes his ID across the table without a preamble.

"Did you get this from a cereal box?"

"That's spot on! Good for you, Owen. Actually, it required six box tops, and I had to scribble out my name and address on an index card and post it to Buckingham Palace."

Rachel can't resist snickering at the dry English sense of humor, thinking she somehow stumbled into one of those British mystery shows her mother liked to watch. Wiping a tear from her eye, "Speaking only for myself, I would not recognize a fake ID if it bit me in the ass," glancing at the long name, Terrence Omari Flynn Gilliam on the ID, "uh, Mr. Gilliam."

Steering clear of any reference to the lovely lady's fit arse, "I appreciate your candor, Mrs. Haig." The agent drapes his right arm over the booth's red leather backrest with practiced nonchalance, evaluating the dishy American couple with feigned indifference. Hearing another squeak of his leather jacket against the red leather booth, he hopes the impertinent noise doesn't bollocks his suave outward demeanor. First impressions are essential in his line of work.

The rugged yet erudite black man seated across the table tests Rachel's uncanny eye for sizing people up at a glance. First, the obvious, his world-weary smile and the hint of gray at the temples of his short-cropped thick black hair indicate he is older than his beaming ID headshot. The Brit's deep-set gray eyes glint in the bar's low lighting, piercing below his expressive brow. A day's growth of beard peppers his mocha-brown, angular jawline below prominent chiseled cheekbones. Dark puffs under his eyes and a trace of wrinkles are probably remnants of his long day squinting at a blur of pavement trailing the Jeep across North Africa.

Noting the couple's disheveled appearance, the rider breaks the awkward silence, "Right. You two have been through a lot these past few days. Your heads must be ready to explode, yeah? I get it; believe me, this shit is not easy to take in."

Owen slides the ID back across the table, "Mister, you don't know half of it."

Deciding time was running short for all of them, the mystery rider breaks the ice, "My name is Flynn." With a playful wink at Rachel, "Without the mister, just Flynn. Like a pop star. Never cared for my Gilliam surname. Long story, I suppose. I won't bore you with it. Life is a messy affair, isn't it?" With a huff, he widens his eyes on the nonplussed pair staring at him, "Right then, let's get on with it. I work for a clandestine organization that has carried on for quite some time. And yes, I have been tracking your movements since you left Marseilles on the passenger ferry."

Focusing his keen gaze on Owen, "I apologize for our little

dust-up out on the Trans-African Highway in Tunisia. I was unsure how you planned to get to Tripoli, and I didn't want to lose your trail on that god-forsaken stretch of desert highway. It was the only way to attach a tracker to your Jeep before the Libyan border. The tracker also signaled my guy at the Libyan border to let you pass." Reading their poker-faced reactions elicits a genuine chuckle, "What? You thought it was dumb luck or divine intervention?" Sliding the ID back inside his jacket, he arches his dark eyebrows, "Might I inquire why you didn't fly to Tripoli from France? Plane fare a bit too high?"

Rachel clears her throat to come up with a reply that doesn't sound completely insane, "Uh, Flynn, we decided to make the drive from Tunis to stay below the radar and enter Libya as anonymously as possible." A suspicious smile crossing her tanned symmetrical features signals she is ready to go on offense, "I guess our plan failed since you were one step ahead the entire time."

Owen gloms onto her line of questioning, "Spot on, Rachel. Enough with the bullshit, Mr. Flynn. Why are you following us, and how do you know so much about our travels?"

Shunning polite banter, Flynn quells the couple's suspicions by cutting straight to the point, "Owen, your wife is a direct descendant of a Captain Neil Alexander. Not a day in her life or the lives of other Alexander family members passed without the vigilant oversight of my organization for well over the last century." The agent addresses Rachel's puzzled expression with an empathetic grin, "Ever feel like you're being watched, Mrs. Haig?"

Rachel replies, "All the time."

"Well, for the first time in your life, you know why. Your ancestor, Neil Alexander, and his wingman unwittingly hid an Egyptian artifact with the power to alter human history. When the US government learned of its existence and realized it landed in a supply dump run by an incompetent moron named Hodges, they sent in a couple of OSS agents to retrieve it, but the men in black were too late."

Owen's eyes widen, "That's right. The men in black were part of the clandestine services."

Jabbing the tip of his right index finger into the tabletop for emphasis, Flynn corrects the familiar stereotype, "Not the point, mate. I last wore a black suit at my Mum's funeral. God rest her soul. What is important is that it all happened one hundred years ago. I'm one man in a long line of agents who have carried this torch through the years. During World War Two and a short time afterward, OSS agents handled the matter. By the way, OSS stands for the Office of Strategic Services. I understand history is not taught in American schools anymore."

Rachel's well-intentioned rationalization of her homeland's dumbed-down standards sounded worse spoken aloud than it did in her tired head, "Blissful ignorance is better than the shit show riots we used to endure."

Distancing himself from the idiot class running the world, Owen remembers another trivial morsel gleaned on a field trip to DC with his mom back during his homeschooled youth, "The OSS became the CIA, if I'm not mistaken."

Rachel shakes her head, amazed for the zillionth time by her husband's propensity to pull factoids out of a proverbial hat, "Owen, when this is over, we have to get you on Jeopardy."

Relieved the attractive pair are not a couple of trust-fund idiots, Flynn decides to jump in with a dig of his own, "America could just admit their 250-plus year mistake. We'd welcome you all back with open arms and a spot of tea."

"Not happening, Flynn."

"I get it. Where was I? Oh yeah. After the war, the CIA focused on the Red Menace. More, shall we say, arcane missions—such as locating a pilfered Egyptian antiquity—were left to my organization."

Rachel folds her hands, leaning forward, "Now, who are you associated with again."

"Oh, the name? Right. It's uh, it's called The Powers That Be."

Flynn clears his throat, "Ever hear of it?"

"Nope. Can't say that I have. And that comes from the guy who knows what OSS stood for." Owen senses they are dealing with a loose nut and starts to squirm while nudging Rachel under the tabletop, "The phrase 'powers that be' is a common expression, but I never heard it attached to any formal organization." Noting the time, Owen tries to conjure a disarming smile, suddenly dead tired. "Look, buddy. Just leave us alone, and we can go our separate ways, okay?"

Holding her tumbler, Rachel smiles at the black man's unflinching grin, "Thanks for the drink."

Flynn notes the time with a raised eyebrow—beyond the fact it was pushing 2:00 a.m. "There's a reason why you never heard of The Powers That Be."

Owen halts his slide from the booth mid-scooch, "go on, we're listening."

"The organization exists beyond the scope of normal everyday life. For over three hundred years, our service to humanity has opened doors and pathways with the assistance of off-worlders."

"You mean aliens?"

"Yeah, aliens. Like in the movies, only these fuckers don't mess around, Owen." Raising a finger for emphasis, "However, after the US government threw this case in our lap, our ET advisors drew a straight line between the missing relic and our survival as a species."

Owen settles back half in and half out of the booth onto the thick upholstered seat, catching Rachel's subtle nod affirmative. "All right. What do we have to lose?"

Rachel whispers across the table, "I think the artifact you refer to is called the golden ellipse. Ever hear of it?"

"Why, yes, I have. We are on the same page, after all. Good show. Jolly good show. Correct me if I am wrong, but from what I was told, you two have the exact coordinates to its location outside Tripoli?"

"Agent Flynn …."

"Just Flynn, my dear."

"Okay, Flynn. We already know the rest through our exotic source. We recognize that the golden ellipse must be returned to some alien beacon."

"Rachel, I don't know if you should say much more."

Flynn abruptly scoots out of the booth and stands over the couple. "Owen is right. We are all in the same boat. Plus, time is not our ally. What's say we pool our knowledge and resources, find the golden ellipse, and return it to where it belongs before it's too late."

As soon as Flynn finishes his pitch, a presence looms behind him from the darkness inside the bar, catching him uncharacteristically off guard. It's Louie.

"There you are, Master Owen and Miss Rachel! I have been searching for you everywhere." Turning to face the British agent, Louie continues, "You, sir, are the motorcyclist who trailed us since we left Marseilles. Nice to make your acquaintance." Smiling at the surprised faces staring at him, "I have taken the liberty of expediting checkout. The Jeep is gassed-up, packed, and ready to go under the watchful eye of the bellboy." Gesturing toward the door, he concludes, "Shall we go?"

Louie | Tripoli, Libya
01:55 a.m. | August 21, 2044

Now carrying a foursome, Louie steers the Jeep around a sharp bend, swerving to avoid late-night jaywalkers, accelerating back toward the dangerous part of town.

Flynn hangs on and addresses the group from the backseat bench next to Owen, "When The Powers That Be assign a new case, it's best not to ask questions." Tapping Rachel's shoulder, "By the way, Rachel, I am sorry the Alexander family has lived under this shadow for so long."

"Was anyone in my family aware of the surveillance?"

"That is above my pay grade, but I doubt it."

Louie slaloms around burning obstacles scattered in the road, "Since time is of the essence, the two-hour detour constituting a safer route out of the city and doubling back in the direction of the coordinates would take too long. Not to worry, I know this vehicle like the back of my manmade hand."

Flynn taps Louie's shoulder as they hurtle through a darkened underpass, "You are a Kobayashi product if I'm not mistaken. Let's see, I'll guess a C-Class android. Am I right?"

"I'm impressed, Master Flynn. You know your androids."

"The Kobayashi Corporation is another in a long line of shell corporations owned by The Powers That Be," Flynn smiles toward Owen, looking for a reaction, but gets nothing.

Cramped beside Flynn on the narrow wooden plank behind Louie, Owen searches into the darkness for signs of trouble while listening to the back and forth over the Jeep's rumbling engine.

Flynn presses his new friends with a rhetorical question, "Haven't you all wondered how we went from clumsy, metal automatons to human-looking robots within a decade?" With a hearty chuckle, "Blimey, the modern world is so bloody gullible. It's scary how little the vast majority knows and understands."

"I guess Owen and I are in the minority."

Owen watches Flynn produce a sleek, dark-gray handgun from his jacket, "I hope we won't need to shoot our way out of Tripoli."

"Better safe than sorry, mate." Flynn checks the magazine in the Belgian-made, lightweight polymer weapon's grip, and hands it to a surprised Owen. "Can you handle one of these?"

Owen correctly accepts the hi-tech pistol and replies with a solemn-faced nod.

Reciprocating the young man's seriousness with a "Good show," Flynn slides another case from his jacket. Snapping it open, he adroitly screws three parts together without averting his gaze from Owen's inquisitive expression. Assembled, the odd-looking weapon resembles a miniature chain gun. Cradling it in his right hand with the muzzle pointing skyward, "For this piece, it helps if you can memorize the field manual and recall it to the letter under severe duress." Noting Owen's consternation, "Packing a little heat comes with the territory."

Louie wills the vehicle around another hairpin, zigging left and zagging right. "I apologize, but here we go again! There are hostiles on the second floor to our right! Madame! Get down!"

A staccato of automatic gunfire explodes around the Jeep. Bright flashes ricochet off wrecked cars and crumpled buildings, and a narrowing line of flaming oil barrels and overturned vehicles pinch their forward progression toward a makeshift kill box at the end of the block. Standing with his legs braced against the backseat, Flynn repeats Louie's firm admonition for Rachel to stay low, laying down a withering cover fire of pulsating energy blasts from his advanced weapon toward muzzle flashes emanating from the broken windows looming ahead.

"Hang tight, everyone!" At the last second, Louie foils the insurgent trap, busting through a gap in the blazing cans and accelerating out of the perilous situation.

Flynn checks his balance to remain inside the Jeep while Owen fumbles to remove the gun's safety in his shaking hands. The satisfying sensation of hammering away over the fiery trail of toppled trash barrels and tires in their wake proves what the doctor ordered to snap Owen from his early morning funk.

The smoking gun still pointed in a two-hand grip at the receding scene, ablaze in a fiery glow, "All right! Take that, you bastards!"

"Geez, Owen, how long have you kept that pent-up aggression inside?"

Owen glances at Flynn with a mean grin, "You have no idea."

Surprised by the devastating energy blasts and Owen's covering fire, the terrorists scurry into the shadows like cockroaches. The Jeep zigzags around more obstacles with three fragile humans and an indomitable robotic stunt driver, shaken but uninjured. The resilient Jeep lost a headlight and absorbed a few direct hits, but otherwise, motors onward unaffected.

Rounding the next darkened corner, their lucky streak ends with a bang. A sniper round holes the windshield, hitting Louie in the right shoulder with a terrifying thump, "Heavens! I've been shot!"

Louie's right side goes limp, and his hand drops from the happy-face shift knob while his leg presses the gas pedal to the firewall. Stuck in third gear, hurtling toward the black expanse ahead, the transmission whines in agony, pleading for an upshift. Realizing what is happening, Rachel yells, "Louie! Press the clutch! I'll shift us into fourth!"

The resilient Jeep lurches into fourth gear, careening through long-abandoned, war-ravaged neighborhoods. Rachel acts as Louie's literal right-hand man, working the manual shift as Owen and Flynn watch for further ambushes and snipers. Fifteen minutes later, the foursome dashes out of the last shadowy vestiges of the Libyan port city's rebel-held outer limits on a southeastern heading into the open desert beyond under a dome of stars.

***

A lone functioning headlight pierces the early-morning darkness hours before another sweltering northern Libya day. Bouncing along a remote agricultural road into the rugged, sparsely populated hill country south of Tripoli, Louie wheels off the gravel onto the dry grassy shoulder and screeches the shot-up vehicle to a creaky stop. Rachel pulls the vibrating shift knob into neutral.

"Time to reset."

Rachel glances at Louie, "What did you say?"

Ignoring Rachel's puzzled query, the injured robot lifts his left leg from the Jeep and pulls his useless right half out of the vehicle. Pirouetting to face his companions, he grabs the steering wheel with his functioning left hand to maintain balance. Intentionally swinging at the waist from side to side, he observes his right arm swaying at his side like a limp noodle. Checking the bullet hole in his favorite light-blue, polyester, short-sleeve, button-down shirt, "I apologize for getting shot, but gratified you are all unharmed." Training his glassy-eye stare onto Flynn, "Even you, sir." Catching himself and adjusting his precarious balance as the steering wheel pulls left, "the bullet severed a connection which obviously provides motor functionality for my right side. I don't normally lean left, but I currently have little ch- ch- choice in the matter."

Louie meets their blank stares and attempts a brave smile, but the crooked, mustached grin distorts his expression into a distorted grimace. His next utterance is an incoherent jumble: "That is is mmmyyy Bri-, Bri-tttttish stiff uuppppeer lipppp in f-f-f-ace of of of adddvvverrrs, adversity. Ggggooodd ssshhhhowwww… jjollly good sh sh sh show."

Flynn notices Louie's expression freeze to a blank stare and vaults from the Jeep to lend support before the inert, cumbersome robot collapses in a heap beside the idling car. Owen shoves the gun in his belt and rushes to help Flynn hoist their heavy comrade into the front passenger seat, Rachel coaching every step as if they are moving a priceless antique settee.

After angling Louie into Rachel's front passenger seat, the stricken, synthetic man stares through the cracked windscreen, "I need to perform diagnostics to ascertain the extent of d-damage to my neural and motor malfunctions. I mean functions. Shut down now? Yes, I believe I will." Louie slumps forward against the Jeep's dashboard with a hollow thump.

After Louie's theatrics, a dejected Rachel crawls behind the all-too-familiar steering wheel while Owen and Flynn reassume their backseat positions. The trio contemplates their next move on the side of the remote road in the darkness. The sad noise of an animal yelping in pain breaks the silence, muffling to low whimpers before ending with a painful, animalistic scream.

"At least someone is having a nice dinner."

Rachel yawns aloud, scaring a tiny nocturnal creature into the tall brush.

"These hills are alive."

"With the sound of music?"

"Yeah, Owen. That's what I meant."

"Bloody hell, play nice. Marriage counseling is not part of my training."

Owen ignores the remark, scrutinizing the leather-clad agent, "You wouldn't happen to have a GPS locator in your magic jacket?"

"Sorry mate, but no." Seeing the youthful American's disappointment, "Cheer up, Owen, we have the coordinates and three functioning earphones. In theory, we should be able to triangulate the burial site. It will be far from exact, like finding a needle in a haystack once we locate the spot. But it's our only option with Louie out of commission."

***

Four-wheeling into the rocky heights beyond Tripoli, following the Jeep's lone functioning headlight, Rachel picks a circuitous path around jagged outcroppings and escarpments in the barren landscape. Enduring another twenty minutes of gravel-strewn switchbacks, they scrape past boulders and crisscross a dry creek bed. Their path leads up a perilous ledge with a near-vertical drop on the driver's side, causing Rachel to tamp down her fear of heights in front of the group.

They screech to a halt atop an eastern ridge overlooking the box canyon they traversed to reach the point indicated by the coordinates. To her right, Rachel notes a silhouetted rock formation jutting into the night sky in the distance. "That would make a great landmark." A chill permeates her spine, peering at the imposing edifice, barely visible through the darkness. In her adrenaline-fueled state, the incongruent formation resembles an erstwhile monument to a past civilization, but she refrains from saying so aloud.

Owen repeats the coordinates for the umpteenth time: "32 degrees, 33 minutes, 48.1 seconds north and 13 degrees, 31 minutes, 18.1 seconds east" and receives an affirmative chime through his earphone. "This is the place, all right."

Flynn scopes the desolate area with the first glow of the morning sun over an hour beyond the Eastern horizon. He frowns at the formation looming a few hundred yards in the distance, "You could be spot-on about that being a landmark, but it's almost too obvious."

Rachel yawns a maybe, in reply.

Shining his pocket-sized torchlight over the rocks, boulders, dried-out grasses, and gnarled, spiky trees, he concludes, "Even if we brought a backhoe, finding the exact burial spot is going to be damn near impossible. Man, if only we had that famous Kobayashi pinpoint accuracy at our disposal."

"Screw it; let's just start digging," Owen replies while scanning the topography for visual cues, potentially marking the exact spot. Peering into a rocky piling, he glimpses something skitter across the sandstone before vanishing into a crevice. "Not good."

Rachel sees Flynn's powerful torch and remembers the cheap, plastic flashlight inside the Jeep. Rushing to the passenger seat, she pushes the inert, blank-staring head aside and pops open the glove box, "Sorry, Louie."

Wielding the pick and a shovel that Louie had the foresight to pack, the trio chips into the rock-hard ground at several of their best-guess spots inside a generous thirty-foot perimeter. They are rewarded with blisters, sand, rocks, and scorpions for their backbreaking efforts.

Owen swings the pick, golfing aside another black-plated beast with its poisonous tail curled menacingly upward and its pincers ready to strike. "Damn these things!" Planting his tool in the dirt, he reaches the end of his rope, "I'm sorry, everyone. I hate to admit this, but I need a break."

Rachel stumbles over a rock, waving her light athwart the pockmarked ground, "I'm with you, Owen. We should have stayed at the hotel. This turned out to be a disaster."

In the dark, Flynn hears, more than sees, his colleagues' morale nosedive, "Take heart, I have just the remedy."

The agent produces a satchel from a hidden lining inside his belt. Unsnapping an end, he pours a thimble-sized pile of silver pellets on a flat spot of dirt. Owen and Rachel watch with mild curiosity as he jogs toward a desiccated carob tree and drags back a rangy leafless branch. The resourceful agent breaks two-foot sections of bone-dry wood under his boot, stacking the kindling into a teepee directly over the pellets. With the campfire built to his satisfaction, he brushes bark and dirt from his hands in an over-animated motion and moves beside the couple, arms crossed, admiring his handiwork.

Owen deadpans, "Don't we need a match?"

"Wait for it." Flynn smiles.

The pellets combust in a deep blue flame and glow to life under the branches. Seconds later, the teepee is fully engulfed, casting the monotone landscape of rocks, boulders, and scrub surrounding their site in deep, cerulean shades, reaching all the way to the towering sandstone formation, flickering like a giant apparition through the darkness.

Owen notes the branches are fully engulfed, yet they do not burn into embers like a normal fire.

"Grab your pilfered IOSC blanket and make yourselves comfortable by the fire." Gesturing toward his odd-burning creation, "Not a single self-respecting beastie will come near that flame, so you can enjoy some shut-eye without a scorpion crawling up your knickers."

Rachel replies, "I would ask why, but I am too tired to give a damn."

Flynn chuckles in reaction to her weary reply. As the attractive pair nod off under the wool space blanket—the agent moves to examine their Kobayashi-built friend.

The blaze flickers and crackles, popping blue sparks into the crisp desert air. The Haig's peaceful repose is bathed in the otherworldly fire's ethereal bluish lambency while anesthetizing wisps of smoke trick their brains into compressing six hours of sleep into an hour-long power nap. A Powers That Be agent would never embark on a mission without combustible pellets laced with a generous sprinkle of magic sleep dust, and Flynn was no exception.

Hearing Owen's snoring assures Flynn that his companions are enjoying their trip to slumberland. He steps through the darkness, upwind of the campfire, to the Jeep, where Louie's slumped form stares out the windshield. Adjusting his torch to illuminate the motionless robot's bullet-holed shoulder, the resourceful Brit produces a thin sheath of precision tools from his leather jacket. After laying them in a precise order atop the vehicle's scorched and damaged hood, he concentrates deep within his photographic memory, recalling a Kobayashi manual with detailed C-Class schematics. Some folks devour pulpy paperbacks for relaxation; Flynn enjoys reading manuals.

In the early-morning stillness, with only the crackling fire and Owen's rhythmic sound breaking the silence, he hears a dreaming Rachel's utterance, "Let the Machine do the work."

"Good advice, my dear," he muses while pressing a hidden button at Louie's neck. The manmade head mechanically splits apart, revealing, to his surprise, what appears to be a cheap third-party brain core. The spherical baseball-sized mass of chips and wires suspended in a pinkish goo under a translucent membrane perplexes and surprises the man, unaccustomed to either reaction, "My dear fellow, what in the bloody hell happened to your original brain core?"

Flynn | Libyan Desert
07:00 a.m. | August 21, 2044

"Monsieur, it is time to wake up."

Crusty eyelids snap open like roller blinds, revealing Louie's long, odd face inches from Owen's nose. "Back off, Louie. One of us has the world's worst case of morning breath, and I think it's me."

Pushing upright on the dirt, he snatches a jagged rock from under his bottom and flings it into the bushes with the wool space blanket draped over his shoulders like an Indian chief. A ponytailed Rachel strolls past with an effervescent smile in a clean, olive-colored t-shirt, Bermuda shorts, and her ever-present Chelsea boots. The coffee aroma wafting across the pleasant morning air reaches Owen before noticing the paper cup cradled in her lovely hands.

Refreshed from her power nap for the ages, courtesy of the still-smoldering, alien-tech campfire, she greets her husband with a too-peppy, "Morning, sunshine."

The whole ordeal floods back into Owen's addled head. Twisting sideways like a pretzel on the dirt, Owen sees the athletic profile of Agent Flynn, dressed down to a black tank tee stretched over his broad physique, untucked over his khakis. Noting the motorcycle jacket draped aside the imposing man's hunched position, he rubs gritty sand from his eyes.

Acknowledging Owen's grumpy morning persona, the agent hoists a steaming paper cup in a white-gloved hand, "It's 7:00 a.m., top of the morning to you, sleepyhead." After an animated sip of coffee, Flynn refocuses on a pinkish sphere glistening in the morning sun atop his makeshift workstation on the Jeep's opened tailgate.

Registering the time, Owen scrambles onto his feet, checking for creepy crawlers in his khakis, and complains to no one in particular, "Why am I always the last guy to wake up? Next time, I am setting the alarm an hour ahead!" His voice echoes off rocks and boulders into the box canyon below the ridge, scaring a flock of birds into the deep-blue early morning sky.

Pausing to let the echoes fade, he focuses on Louie's signature grin widening under his thin mustache.

Owen cannot hide his amazement at the sight of Louie. Somehow, while he slept, Louie reverted to his original French persona. Gesturing at the smiling robot, striking a cocky pose with arms crossed and right leg planted forward from the left, cigarette smoke wafting in the breeze, Owen demands, "When the hell did that happen?"

With an amused smile, Rachel hands her incredulous husband an instant joe in her recycled cup, all courtesy of Flynn's magic jacket, "While we slept, Flynn brought him back online. But that's not the best part; he returned him to the French chauffeur we know and love." Gesturing toward Louie with her coffee, "And get this! Louie is standing atop the exact spot. So, can you pull yourself together if it's not too much to ask? We didn't want you to miss the groundbreaking."

Downing the warm cup of coffee in a single chug, rejuvenated after his accelerated sleep cycle, "Flynn, toss me the shovel; let's get this party started."

Wearing his bullet-holed shirt, Louie scuffs an X in the dirt with his shoe, takes two long steps backward, and announces in his best French accent, "Gentlemen, and the lady, I give you the precise spot indicated by your coordinates."

* * *

Flynn's roundhouse swing of the dull-bladed pick strikes the sunbaked surface, sending rocks and dirt flying everywhere. Rachel and Louie watch with bated breath, clear of the swinging blades and dirt. After a few more swings, Owen uses the shovel to excavate the loosened debris, piling it alongside the widening hole. Within minutes, both men take a breather in the early-morning heat.

After a small swig, Owen passes the canteen to Flynn and addresses the back-turned robot, standing apart from the group, staring into the canyon, "Louie, are you positive we are digging in the right spot? The hole is at least two feet deep, and I don't see a sign of anything.

It is a nine-inch fucking disk. We could be off by less than an inch and never know it."

Offering the water to Rachel, who declines, he shrugs and addresses another nagging possibility, "I hate to mention this out loud, but are the coordinates accurate? Depending on those numbers, we could be five feet, ten feet, or a mile from the actual spot."

Rachel sighs out loud in abject frustration, "You have got to be kidding."

Owen sees Louie collapse face down in the dirt seconds before an ear-piercing screech erupts from the replicant's sabotaged cybernetics, assaulting the auditory senses of every creature for miles into the surrounding desert.

"Fuck me! How did that happen?" Flynn's curses are drowned in the blaring wail as he tosses the canteen and rushes to aid their distressed synthetic friend.

Owen sprints behind Flynn and yells at the agent over the shrill noise, "Now what? I thought you fixed him?"

Ignoring the panicked peanut gallery, Flynn grapples the seizing robot from flying apart, pressing dirty fingers into Louie's right temple to open a compartment and remove an exposed chip pressed between his thumb and index finger. Louie's spasms ebb as he examines it in the sunlight looking for a tell-tale marker. A look of fear crosses the unflappable agent's face, "Bloody hell! No wonder we can't locate the ellipse. Louie's fucking microchip is a worthless piece of shit! Someone rigged him to self-destruct."

"Self-destruct? How did that happen? Can you shut it off?"

"There is no time to explain! Run upwind as far away as possible! I will try to deactivate the self-destruct, but it might involve opening him again, and I may run out of time before he detonates into a million pieces. This Kobayashi model contains radioactive material that will disperse over a wide area if he blows! Get out of here! Now!"

Rachel starts to protest, but Owen grabs her by the arm, "It's not up for debate, Rachel! Someone turned your robot into a dirty bomb! Let's go!"

Pulling a distraught Rachel from the chaos, they break into a dead run into the desert. Sidestepping scrub brush and vaulting rocks and boulders, the heaving pair skid to a stop, bent at the waist, hands-on-hips after the two-football-field-long dash across the scorching desert hardpan they peer back across the scrub to see what is happening.

Out of breath, Owen squints across the barren landscape toward Flynn and Louie, "No mushroom cloud, that's a good sign."

"Man, can we ever catch a damn break?" Rachel wipes her brow with her sweaty forearm and retwists her messy hair into a ponytail.

From across the expanse of desert, they wait in helpless anticipation watching Flynn and Louie standing face-to-face and performing calisthenics near the parked Jeep.

Owen laughs to ease the tension, "Why didn't we take the damn Jeep?"

Shading her eyes from the brightness, "Next time."

The weird Simon-says routine stops as Flynn closes up the hidden compartment at Louie's shiny temple, and the screeching noise stops.

"I knew he could do it."

"That makes one of us."

The couple zigzags back, eager for an explanation, "What was that all about?"

Louie lifts his right hand, stopping Flynn's reply, "I was booby-trapped to explode." Checking Rachel's expression, the synthetic Frenchman winces at his potential indiscretion, "Pardon my language, Madame."

"It's a common expression, Louie, don't worry about it."

Louie steps forward, "As fate would have it, Monsieur Flynn enjoys reading manuals. And he recalled a specific section in mine relating to a physical sequence designed to terminate a C-Class synthetic human in mid-function."

Flynn interjects, "It's like yanking the cord to give your computer a hard reboot."

"Indeed. A sequence used primarily as a tool for law enforcement to subdue rogue synths. Agent Flynn's quick-thinking action may be the first time somebody ever used the tactic to disarm a self-destruct countdown. There is a first time for everything."

Approaching Louie, still trying to calm her heart rate, she glances at Flynn, "In other words, you made a lucky guess?"

Flynn retreats to his workstation in the back of the Jeep, "Sounds about right. But wait, there's more. Tell them the rest, Louie."

"That was a malware-infected knock-off microchip that sabotaged my GPS. I'm afraid I am no help for our purpose here this morning. To further complicate our situation, my memories as your English butler remain locked inside the brain core Flynn removed. Therefore, in my present state, I cannot locate the coordinates or recall who did this to me."

Flynn walks to the back of the Jeep and returns with the pink knock-off brain core, "I'm an intelligence operative, not a robotics engineer, but I can spot a counterfeit brain core when I see one."

Owen cannot hide his surprise and puzzlement, "Hey! We paid a lot of money for that brain core! How is Louie even functioning? We watched a technician from his company replace his damaged core with a new pink glob at our villa in Le Tholonet on the night of the cave incident. Right, Rachel?"

Rachel studies the pink mass and nods, "That is right. How can he function as his normal French personality without the original brain core?"

Flynn replies with a good-humored laugh while tossing the gooey ball into the air, "C-Class cyborgs don't require these dodgy hunks of wire in their noggins. It's nothing more than a redundant processor. In Louie's case, all it did was paper over his factory-installed French chauffeur OS with an English butler. It is a common practice on the secondary market, but I'm surprised the cheap knock-off core your guy installed even worked. I bet he was a little quirky. The cheeky bloke took the both of you for a ride, right, Louie?"

"That is indeed correct, Monsieur Flynn. However, part of my English butler modification included strict deference to my new owners on matters relating to my acquisition." Louie smiles at his friends, "And you never asked."

Owen cannot believe what he is hearing, "You mean to say we drove from Tunis to Tripoli for over ten hours with a walking, talking, radioactive time bomb since leaving our villa in France?"

"Yes and no. The new brain core you bought had nothing to do with turning Louie into a dirty bomb." Tapping Louie at the temple. "The bogus GPS microchip caused the self-destruct. It's quite ingenious, really. The clock triggered as we entered a predetermined radius around the coordinates. Someone tried to turn this patch of desert into a radioactive dead zone, like Chernobyl, ensuring the ellipse would remain hidden."

Owen connects the dots, "So the real question is: who else knew the coordinates?"

Rachel places her hands on her hips and stares into the distance, "Aside from my Grandpa Neil, only one other person knew the coordinates. Harry Stark."

Owen rolls his eyes, "Okay, here we go. Come on, Rachel, let's reel back in the paranormal crap."

Flynn winces at the tangible nerve struck in response to his original question. Changing the subject, he pats Louie on the back, "It was a close call, yeah. Whoever it was, if they knew Louie would start wailing like a fire engine after the countdown, they could have switched that off too and bollocksed the whole area."

A baby scorpion ambles through their group like it owns the place. The agent nudges it aside with his boot, "It's in the manual."

"You mean the one nobody reads?"

"Precisely."

With her ears still ringing from the alarm, Rachel breaks from the group and strides to the edge of the desolate canyon, "Well, what do we do now?"

Flynn tosses the brain core at Owen, who juggles it before cradling it in his hands, "We improvise."

* * *

The tolerable morning temperature rises toward less-than-livable triple digits as the group huddles at Flynn's makeshift workbench behind the Jeep. Owen returns the brain core to Flynn, who tosses it in his hand and launches into his plan. "This knock-off brain core—that altered Louie's identity to a loyal subject of King George—can work in place of his sabotaged GPS microchip.

Flynn smiles back at the blank human stares while Louie nods his approval.

"Now, how the hell is that supposed to work?"

Flynn turns the brain core in his hand and smiles at Louie, "Well, we will establish a direct connection between this pink ball and the hard drive where your GPS application is stored."

"First things first, Louie, if you would be so kind, open your hidden compartment so we can destroy the fake microchip."

Louie presses his right index finger to his temple, exposing the malicious chip. Flynn grinds it into the hard ground under the heel of his boot.

Flynn smiles, "Now then, Louie, hold out your right hand, palm down."

Louie follows the direction with unnerving passivity.

The agent produces a scalpel from his belt of tricks and slices into the top of Louie's hand, exposing synthetic muscles, tendons, and an eerily human-looking bone structure.

Rachel protests, but Louie quells her worried look, "It's all right, Madame. I see where this is going. It just might work."

Flynn parts sinewy muscles in Louie's hand with forceps, revealing a matchbook-sized hard drive attached to a coil of delicate wires no thicker than human hairs. "There it is."

Averting his gaze to the horizon, Owen attempts to quell queasiness even while witnessing a non-human surgical procedure.

Flynn looks at each of them in turn, "When Louie says he knows something like the back of his manmade hand, it is not just an expression." Nudging the square black wafer with the scalpel blade, "This small hard drive contains the programs and apps that control Louie's high-level C-Class functionality, like linguistics. Why Kobayashi embedded it in the right hand is a mystery."

"Maybe it is a reference to a right-hand man?"

"Good show, Rachel; I never thought of that. Whatever the reasoning, pinpoint GPS is a hallmark of Kobayashi's C-Class robots, so it stands to reason the GPS programming location is in his hand. Here comes the fun part, since Louie's original microchip is not an option, we will utilize the redundant brain core you purchased in its place."

Flynn gestures toward the reflective pinkish mass, taking a deep breath and focusing on the task, "We are ready to attach it to this small hard drive." Flynn taps the incision atop Louie's hand.

Louie remains as still as a statue.

"Does your arm ever get tired?"

"Not as such, Madame. However, I may have to swat at the scorpion on the back of my pants leg unless I can impose upon one of you to do it for me."

They all stare in unison at the black monster perched at the lower back of Louie's left thigh.

"Remain still, everyone. I got this." Owen sends the scorpion flying from Louie's leg with a roundhouse kick. "Man, those creepy things are everywhere."

Flynn's focus never wavers from the incision, utilizing pick and forceps to uncoil long filaments attached to the one-inch black square in the mechanical, downturned hand. "Nice kick, Owen. You take lessons?"

"A little Krav Maga back in the states, just to let off some steam."

Rachel rolls her eyes, "Owen, modesty does not suit you at all." Looking at the impromptu surgery, fascinated by the complexities inside the synthetic hand, "Owen is at the Black Belt level."

Flynn glances toward his whip-smart and attractive new friend, "Rachel, please scoop up the brain core and hold it next to Louie's hand."

Returning his focus to the narrow incision, Flynn attempts to ease the tension, "A black belt in Krav Maga? Your mother must be proud of you."

"Word of advice, Flynn, the less mentioned about my mother in front of Rachel, the better."

Flynn smiles at the radiant beauty, balancing the brain core next to Louie's opened mechanical hand. "What's the matter, Rachel? Don't you and Owen's Mum get along?" While making the impertinent query, the resourceful agent lifts the translucent filaments from the shallow opening atop Louie's hand and guides them with the forceps to the brain core. The filaments respond to the new host by wriggling apart and snaking along the core's pink membrane, penetrating like a root system on steroids.

Rachel is distracted from her oft-repeated mother-in-law rebuttal argument, watching the filaments snaking apart on the pinkish surface, piercing the membrane, and connecting to the processor's inner workings. The pink mass thrums to life in her hands, lights pulsing from under the slippery surface.

"Is it supposed to vibrate?"

"Considering what you are cradling in your hands was designed to be activated inside a protective skull surrounded by viscous fluid similar to motor oil. It's not surprising that you can feel it doing its thing."

"It feels kind of nice, like a purring cat."

Fearful of becoming a proverbial third wheel, Owen clears his throat to enter the discussion, "What can I do to help?"

"Our new connection is fragile; Rachel must hold the brain core next to Louie's hand as still as possible. Owen, I need your help syncing our makeshift computer to a monitor." Supporting the thin wires with precision forceps, Flynn shields the fragile connection as a slight breeze picks up across the plateau as his mind races to the next step, "Okay, Owen, reach into my jacket."

"What am I looking for?"

"A holographic keyboard, and you won't even have to buy me dinner later."

Owen hesitates before reaching into the deep pockets inside Flynn's jacket, "Nothing will bite my hand, right?"

"No. But I could go for another caffeine jolt if you find another instant coffee."

Owen reaches into the agent's leather jacket, probing for an opening in the lining, and pulls out a thin, lozenge-shaped object.

Flynn glances sideways toward the item Owen places before his field of view, "Nope. Try again."

Owen slides his hand back inside the man's leather jacket and removes a silver object, slightly larger than a sugar cube but with an embedded lens on one face. Flynn casts another sideways glance, "Eureka! You found it. Since you pulled out my eyeglass case the first time, I assume you have no idea how to operate a holographic keyboard."

Rachel chuckles softly, careful not to move her hands, "Owen still uses his Dad's antique iMac."

Owen defensively replies, "Hey, it works, doesn't it? I used it to purchase our tickets into space."

"I don't want to get into a marital spat about which of you is more tech-savvy, so let me walk you through it. First, orient the cube, so the lens faces up; next, press firmly two times on the sides."

Owen complies. Nothing happens.

"Okay, press and hold for a beat, wait for a second, and repeat. Bloody hell, this is like describing how to ride a bike."

"Hah-hah! Success!" Owen looks through a bluish 18-inch, V-shaped display projecting a granular, noisy pattern in search of a digital connection from the silver cube. "I've seen these things at trade shows, but you rarely see one in use out in public."

Flynn ignores Owen's latent fascination with alien technology and studies the display, "Owen. Focus. Now twirl your index finger counterclockwise on the side to adjust the display as large and bright as possible."

After a throat-clearing cough, Flynn commands: "Keyboard."

A keyboard springs open in front of the conical display. "Okay, now it's Louie's turn. What's your C-code?"

Quiet throughout the procedure, Louie stares into the desert without moving a synthetic muscle and replies in an unsettling robotic tone, "I cannot comply. It is against my programming to divulge proprietary information."

"You C-Class blokes are an obstinate lot! My holographic display needs it to gain access to your processor. I'm not sure how long this connection will hold."

"I'm sorry, Agent Flynn."

Flynn abandons his attempt to reason with unyielding robot logic, addressing Owen, fresh off his first tech success, "Move behind Louie and press firmly on the nape of his neck. Just be careful not to push too hard."

"What will happen?"

Rachel chimes in, "Owen, just do it!"

"Okay. Hang on a second." In a lower voice, while moving behind Louie, he mutters, "That's enough caffeine, Rachel."

"I heard that."

Owen follows the instructions, and indeed, Louie's head splits open into four sections, as it did back at the villa.

"On the bottom left, there should be a small plate with a series of numbers and letters; that's his C-code. All you have to do is type it using the keyboard."

Owen holds the cube projecting the cutting-edge keyboard and display combo above the back of Louie's opened head in his right hand while hunting and pecking the 32-digit code on glowing keys with his left index finger. The noise-filled display comes to life with a high-definition, bluish-hued view of the Libyan desert, mirroring Louie's view looking straight ahead.

Owen is simultaneously relieved and amazed at his handiwork, "This is incredible!"

Flynn steals a glance at the screen, "Jolly good! Now close Louie's head like you opened it, and don't drop the cube. Okay. Just so you both understand, the screen shows what Louie sees, but technically, he is blind. We will guide him, so he does not walk off a cliff."

Flynn and Rachel maintain the tenuous connection, flanking Louie's outstretched hand as he lurches 180 degrees, resembling Frankenstein's first tenuous steps. Owen leads the hunched band across the uneven desert hardscrabble under a cloudless scorcher of a day, searching for the actual coordinate location.

Peering through the holographic viewer, Owen sees another black scorpion out of his peripheral vision and kicks it aside, causing the display to raster in and out of focus. "Watch it, Owen! You are screwing up the connection!"

Rachel struggles to hold on to the slippery, vibrating ball in her sweaty hands. Her nose starts to itch. "Damn!"

Flynn, attuned to his cohorts' fragile states of mind, asks, "What's the matter."

"Nothing. I'm fine."

The less-than-merry band shuffles forward, "How will we know if this is working?"

A fly buzzes and lands on Flynn's nose, crawling across his cheek. Scrunching his face, careful not to upset the filamentous connection in his hands, Flynn tries not to sound like a know-it-all. "Louie's cybernetics are offline except for his motor functions and GPS. For all intents and purposes, he is a walking zombie robot."

Owen swats away a fly with his free hand, "I think I binge-watched that show."

Flynn repeats the coordinates from memory, prompting Louie's stumbling path left toward the canyon's rim.

"I hope he is not taking us over the cliff."

"Payback's a bitch, Rachel."

"Not funny, Owen."

Louie angles right, paralleling the canyon on their collective left side. They move through a patch of razor-sharp thorn bushes toward the towering rock formation jutting over ten stories into the deep blue sky.

The view again pixelates into noise, prompting Owen to readjust the cube's handheld position to regain an image of what Louie sees inside the V-shaped holographic screen. While struggling to steady the tiny cube's projection, he also avoids the odd trio stepping on his heels.

Rachel winces in pain, "Damn! That's going to leave a scar!" as her right leg drags across a dried-out thorn bush.

Searching the landscape through the holographic monitor, Owen sees a white pushpin shape animate into view near the top of the sheer rock wall. "Hey! Is that what it looks like?"

Rachel peers through the screen, "Holy shit! Why did they hide it way up there?"

Flynn studies the elevated location through the wavering screen, "I think you just answered your own question, Rachel."

Owen widens a grin across his dirt and sweat-smeared face, "I'll make the climb."

Rachel breaks from her concentrated gaze, "Can I let go now?

My back is killing me, and if I don't scratch my nose soon, I will lose it."

Looking through the display at the dancing pushpin, Flynn commits the spot to memory, "Yes, Rachel, we did it. Talk about a group effort."

Flynn severs the connection between Louie's hand and the brain core processor and directs him to sit atop the nearest boulder.

Louie winces, "I could fry an egg on this rock."

Rachel hands the inert, pinkish ball to the PTB agent, "That was fun. Let's not do it again anytime soon."

"Deal." Flynn flips the brain core in his hand, "I'll bring the Jeep over here."

As the resourceful agent treks across the plateau to the Jeep, Rachel turns and finds Owen already scouting his free climb up the sheer rock wall.

Owen catches his wife's tired gaze in his direction, "It had better be up there, or I quit."

Moving to Owen's side, she crosses her arms and stares upward, "You will get no argument from me. It has to be over 100 degrees out here. I want you to rest and drink water before doing this, okay?" With a soft kiss on his cheek, she adds, "For me."

"Since you put it that way, I guess I could use a little sip of water." Looking toward Flynn, approaching the parked Jeep baking in the midday sun off in the distance, "And by the way, I am tech-savvy. And now I can even operate an alien holographic computer."

"Would you like a merit badge?"

"Maybe I would."

* * *

Screeching to a halt along the base of the steep rock formation, Flynn hops out of the driver's seat on a beeline to Louie. The sightless robot, still waiting for repair on the blistering-hot rock, hears his approach. The agent spreads his tools on the smooth rock aside his patient and remarks with a tin-ear bedside manner, "I hope I can put Humpty back together again."

Louie, blind as a bat, looks right through the sweltering agent's whirlwind of activity, "Me too, monsieur."

While Flynn proceeds with Humpty, Owen and Rachel make themselves useful, stowing dirty packs, the shovel and pick, and the space blanket into the Jeep's narrow compartment and the dark recess beneath the wooden plank.

Noting the dwindling water supply, Owen surveys the area with an audible sigh. Catching a glimpse of Rachel arranging and rearranging the bags and gear inside the Jeep elicits a private chuckle. After watching her pack and repack luggage for two weeks before leaving for Las Vegas, the new husband understands it is his wife's method of expelling nervous energy. Better than pills.

Owen stands over Flynn's shoulder, watching the agent stitch up Louie's hand.

"Looking good. How do you feel, Louie?"

"My vision is back online, but I am far from perfect. Please accept my apology for everything I put you and Rachel through during our journey. And for neglecting to warn you about the repairman back in France." He looks off into the distance blinking his dark eyes, testing his restored vision, "I was not myself."

Owen ignores the unsolicited and unnecessary apology, "Well, it's good to have you back."

Tamping down lingering fears, Owen assumes a brave façade and announces, "I have had my fill of water, the Jeep is ready to go, and Louie's vision is back online. The only thing left is for me to free-climb this rock and liberate the damned hunk of gold from its hiding place so we can put this God-forsaken place in the rearview." Glancing from person to person to robot, "Okay, here I go!"

"Be careful and watch out where you place your hands. Those scorpions are all over this damn place."

Overhearing Rachel's admonition, Flynn jogs over and produces a pair of leather gloves, handing them to Owen, "Try these on for size. They should offer some protection."

Owen shoves his right hand into the glove and laughs, "They don't fit. You must acquit." The trio returns a blank stare at his long-forgotten historical reference.

Realizing his belated attempt at humor fell on deaf ears, "You wouldn't happen to have these in an extra-large, would you?"

"Maybe in my other jacket."

Rachel fails to suppress a nervous laugh.

"You laugh at his joke? Sure, Rachel, I see where this is going." Handing the hi-tech gloves back to Flynn, "Keep them. I like to maintain the sensation of touch as I climb rocks." Casting a brave grin toward his worried wife, seeing a tear streaming down her face, "Among other things."

Owen starts to climb his pre-planned route, economizing movements in the blazing heat. Rachel, Louie, and Flynn spectate from below with bated breath, straining their necks as Owen, with practiced patience, confirms his next handhold before releasing his last narrow purchase.

Louie breaks the tense silence on the ground, "I just realized this whole area is crawling with Black Scorpions, and Neil Alexander's squadron was also called the Black Scorpions. Quite a coincidence."

Rachel's green eyes widen as ominous chills creep along her spine.

Flynn wheels toward Louie, "What did you say?"

"I said …."

Rachel quells a panic attack and cuts him off, "Owen, how is it going up there?"

"Just dandy, Rachel!"

Squinting at the death-defying weekend rock climber and all-around daredevil, Flynn comments, "Bloody hell, this bloke is for real."

* * *

"No self-respecting creepy-crawly would be caught dead up here," Owen grunts, straining to reach for the next handhold. Plastered against the vertical rock face like a bug on a wall, he summons core strength and pushes higher from the secure purchase under his right shoe.

Sliding his fingertips into a cracked groove, sweat pouring off his brow, he probes a perilous narrow fissure above his head and locates a handhold. Swinging from the wall, he hooks his right leg over the ledge and hoists himself atop in a heart-pounding motion. Scrambling to his feet, relieved he did not fall to certain death, he calls to his companions from the dizzying height, "I'm here!"

Surveying the four-foot ledge, Owen squints upward, noting his proximity to the summit. Adjusting his eyes to the brightness, he examines the sun-scorched sandstone banded with rusty brown and ochre covered with primitive pictograms. Swiping a swollen hand across his forehead and squatting before the crude renderings, Owen searches for clues amid the stick-figure representations of man and beast in an epic conflict. His gaze lands on a drawing depicting a human thrusting a spear through another human. "This is useless. Where is the goddamn crevice we saw through Louie's eyes?"

Verging on heatstroke—and an expletive-laced tantrum for the ages—Owen finds a chiseled scorpion rendering waist-level in the rock at the leftmost section of the ledge. Putting his tirade on pause, he sidesteps along the narrow purchase to examine the more detailed rock art with the lowest expectations. To his astonishment, the shift in vantage point reveals a fissure wide enough to squeeze through right below the scorpion's curved tail. "Huh, another optical illusion, like the cavern entrance where we met Neil back in France."

Shifting from agony to elation makes his head swoon under the blazing sun. Regathering his wits, Owen gulps from the plastic water bottle tied at his waist and pours the rest over his dirty, matted hair.

Tossing aside the spent bottle, Owen hunches down on his knees and scooches through the opening, thankful he brought Flynn's powerful torch. Casting the light inside, darkness swallows the beam of light.

Veering back to disappointment, Owen mutters, "Of course, the damn thing couldn't be right here at the opening." Pulling himself through the narrow rocky hole into blackness, swollen hands probing across graveled stone and sand. Belly crawling forward, he feels the rock give way to nothingness, "Huh, what the hell?"

Grasping around, looking for a further purchase, his vision adjusts to the darkness. Training the flashlight straight down, his heart sinks, "Another cavern. Great. I'm beginning to hate spelunking."

Propped on his elbows at the edge of a tall, circular shaft, he heaves a labored sigh. An all-time favorite movie quote pops into his head, "Snakes. Why did it have to be snakes?" Laughing at his private joke, he is nevertheless cognizant of slithering dangers.

Widening the light on the shaft's sandy bottom far below his gaze, "No snakes. Life does not always imitate art. Thank God."

Repositioning himself in the narrow void, Owen sits on the hard rock and looks past his dangling feet, catching a metallic glint in the stone an arm's length below his purchase.

For an ecstatic second, he thinks he found the ellipse before discovering the metal object is an old, rusty piton with a tattered rope tied through it in a knot, hanging in a lazy, coiling sweep to the sandy bottom.

"Okay. Someone hid the ellipse down there and left the rope behind. Makes sense."

Owen pauses to consider his next move. On the one hand, he could trust the rope, rappel the thirty feet to the cave floor, grab the ellipse, and climb back out. Yanking it with as much downward force as he can muster in the confined area, he curses his indecision. "The piton seems stable, but it seems too convenient not to be a trap."

Racked with indecision, Owen checks the shaft, finding precious few handholds, "Okay, a free climb is out of the question; the rope wins."

Clenching the torch in his mouth, he inches forward, giving the rope another firm tug and double-checking the knot for good measure. "Here goes nothing."

Rolling onto his stomach in the confined space, he edges into the dark, feet first. Contorting sideways to grab the rope, he knocks the torch from his mouth. Stopping cold, he cringes, listening to his only source of light clattering to the shaft floor. "Damn! I am off to a great start."

Checking his grip on the course old rope, "I wish I had the gloves. Too late now." With a fatalistic glimpse outside the small fissure at the blue sky beyond, he takes a breath and allows his weight to pull him over the side, rappelling into the darkness. The strain on his arms is more than anticipated, and he hangs on for dear life. Tenuous, frightening minutes later, fearful of what may be lurking at the bottom waiting for him to fall, he glances down and realizes the torch is lying in the sand scant feet below his dangling boots. Laughing despite the pain, thankful the rope held, he hangs a moment longer before dropping into the sand, "What is this place?"

He scoops the glowing torch in full Indiana Jones mode, blows gritty sand from the lens, and widens the beam to illuminate the 10-foot diameter expanse. "Okay, let's get started." Dropping to his knees, he plants the flashlight and smooths his hands through the loose sand with successive sweeps, like searching for a lost ring after a day at the beach. His patience fading after an initial, systematic approach, he throws sand in every direction with maniacal abandon. Pebbled grit sticks to Owen's sweat-drenched clothes and filthy, rope-burned skin. Relenting with an exhausted sigh, he plops his weary body down, repositions the torch, and tries to clean sand from bloody scrapes and sores on his hands, "My kingdom for a metal detector. Where is the golden ellipse? It has to be here."

Owen stands and brushes his shirt and pants, "Shit. So much for that theory." Directing the light around the tall, narrow shaft, he sees nothing but the jagged outcroppings, cracks, and fissures he scraped across on the way down.

On the brink of abandoning the search, a revelation permeates his exhausted mind: the rope focuses his attention downward. It never occurred to him to check above the opening. Owen narrows the powerful beam, training it into the natural domed ceiling, elevated another ten feet above the knee-height entrance. "Come on. Come on." Steadying Flynn's hi-tech torch in his shaking hands, he watches the circular patch of light move across the darkened expanse.

The beam reflects off a shimmering brilliance piercing the darkness and illuminating his wide-eyed gaze.

"Well, shit, there it is!"

Overwhelmed by his discovery, Owen shutters the torch and jams it into a side pocket on his khakis. Grabbing the rope like a crazed lunatic, he struggles to shimmy off the floor and hears a loud crack echo off the walls. Before realizing what happened, he crumples flat on his back into the sand with a resounding thump and shields his head out of reflex as the piton clatters down in a hail of rocks and debris, with the old rope landing in uneven loops tangling over his aching form.

Unsure of who or what may be laughing at his misfortune, he lies flat on his back, gazing at the ellipse far above, taking stock of his injured body. "Good thing I was only a few feet off the sand." He stands and gathers the rope, coiling its length to the piton tied at one end, and loops it over his right shoulder. With a determination born out of three torturous days of ancient aliens, a rattling Jeep, extreme temperatures, getting shot at, scorpions, and, oh yeah, almost being reduced to atoms by a walking, talking dirty bomb, Owen finds his first tenuous handhold in the thirty-foot shaft and wills himself toward the light.

After a few aborted attempts and painful falls, Owen climbs, grunting, cursing, and willing himself upward through the echoing darkness. Exuding sheer willpower, unwilling to surrender to his fate, he thrusts his swollen and bloody right hand toward the ledge at the entrance, groping for the spot where the piton gave way. Establishing a firm grip, he pulls with all his might and slides his torso forward over sharp rocks and pebbles, heaving and gasping for air while his legs and feet dangle into the darkness.

Quelling an unusual panic, the urbanized, city-dwelling investment banker suppresses idle thoughts on his brush with death at the bottom of a dark hole in the middle of nowhere, pulling himself back into the blessed sunshine. Rising shaky-legged, he peers down at his companions far below.

* * *

Louie is the first to spot Owen's head peeking over the ledge. "There he is! Monsieur, were you able to locate the golden ellipse?"

Owen's raspy voice echoes from above, "Yes. And no."

Rachel and Flynn cast a perplexed glance at each other, "Now what?"

* * *

"I found it, but I can't reach it." Mulling the potentialities in his addled mind, "If you don't see my shining face peeking over this ledge in the next fifteen minutes, it means I'm dead, and one of you will need to give it a try." Owen pivots toward the opening with crazed abandon and a determined look in his eyes.

* * *

The threesome stands on the rock-hard dirt under the ridiculous midday heat without a hint of shade.

"Did he just say what I thought I heard him say?" Covered in sweat and worried beyond measure, Rachel wheels toward the man and robot with a pleading look.

"Don't worry, Rachel. He'll be fine. He knows what he is doing." Flynn considers his many talents and the terrible admission that rock climbing was not among them, "Louie, check fifteen minutes from right now."

"Oui Monsieur, consider it done."

* * *

After looping his rope line over a jagged projection in a hasty knot under the hot sun, Owen uncoils it through the opening while scooching forward on his hands and knees. Without waiting for his vision to adjust from light to dark, he positions his feet on the inner precipice and stands on shaky legs with the rope around his arm. His throbbing head bumps an unseen outcropping in the dark. "Dammit!"

Hunched under the obstruction, he slants forward, trusting the rope, and shines the light on the domed ceiling. The glint from the ellipse, centered like a light fixture, shines with a mocking brilliance.

"Damn! So close, yet out of reach!"

The taught rope digs into his forearm as he leans out and strains his free hand upward. Swaying over the abyss, grappling with his next move, a single orb of light appears in front of his face.

One of two humans on Earth familiar with the orbs, he assumes it came to help him reach the ellipse. "Hey, Neil, better late than never."

His grip on the rope slackens as the orb elevates the surprised man above the void within reach of the golden ellipse.

"Take it, Owen Haig. It is right in front of you."

The enticing words reverberate in Owen's addled mind, weakening his fragile resolve. Fighting the temptation to give in to the evil elevating his prone figure above the deep, dark shaft, "This is too easy. Now I understand how it got here. You are the Dark Specters. You lured Harry Stark to this spot to hide it for eternity, but now I can reach out and take it? I don't think so. You are the bad angels and can go to hell where you belong." Using his refusal to buy time, Owen twists a rope length around his right arm and holds on tight.

You are a fool, like all of the others.

The orb vanishes into the ether, leaving Owen's form floating in midair for a tremulous heartbeat before dropping like a stone. The rope strains under the stress of his freefalling weight, crashing his left side into the wall midway down the shaft. Thrashing in feverish terror, Owen yells, twisting on his lifeline in the dark before forcing himself to calm down, realizing he is still alive and in one piece. Adjusting his grip with beaten and battered hands, regretting not taking Flynn's gloves, another light below his feet gives him a start before realizing it is Flynn's torch lying useless in the sand. "Shit! Now I will lose my deposit."

Chuckling at his joke, the determined man wills himself hand over hand back up the rope. Scowling like a dog and cursing a blue streak, he hurries back into the sunshine.

* * *

Flynn waves up at Owen, overcome with relief, knowing his fifteen-minute countdown has come and gone. "What can we do to help, Owen?"

A rope cascades down the cliff in reply.

"I need the pick! And don't ask any stupid questions."

Louie turns to Flynn, "Where did Monsieur Owen acquire the rope?"

* * *

Resting on the sundrenched ledge, Owen takes stock of his injuries while waiting for the group to attach the pick and a new water bottle to the rope. Nothing too serious. Just a lot of cuts, bruises, and a swollen left eye.

Hearing Rachel's voice yelling the okay and feeling a tug on the rope, he starts to hoist the requested items and almost passes out from a new pain piercing his left torso. "I hope that is not a broken rib." He grimaces, pulling the heavy metal pick and a new water bottle to his elevated, narrow purchase.

Owen secures the frayed line around the rock outside the opening and pulls it taut, wincing at the horrible pain in his ribcage. "It's a miracle that held my weight. What was I thinking?" Chastising himself for rushing headfirst into the abyss, he ties the rope in a harness instead of twisting it around his skinned left forearm. "A rookie mistake."

Ready for action with the water gulped in one long pull, he grabs the pick in his right hand and stoops low to reenter the darkness.

Smirking at the flashlight lying useless in the sand, Owen checks for malicious balls of light, "Nothing in here but us ghosts." His chuckle echoes across the shaft as he squirms through the narrow slot and stands on shaky legs with his backside flattened against the near-vertical rock wall. Sliding his left hand from his side, he reaches toward the same shelf he banged his head on earlier, feeling for a handhold he can trust. "There it is!" Testing his weight against it, he finds it a perfect handhold. "Better to be lucky than good, I guess."

Switching focus to his right side, he loosens his grip to the end of the pick handle to gain as much length as possible. "Don't drop it, idiot!"

Estimating the distance to the ellipse in the dark, Owen takes a deep breath and arcs from the wall while supporting his weight from his left-handed purchase in the rock. Much closer but still an agonizing distance from the prize. He makes a tentative lunge with the pick: swing and a miss. Strike one. Stretching aching muscles and tendons beyond their limits like a sadistic chiropractor, he tries again, hitting nothing but air. Strike two. Realizing he cannot maintain his weakening fingertip grip in the handhold, he tries to think of another way. No matter what he tries, he is over a foot shy of hitting the ceiling, let alone knocking the ellipse free from its entrenched position. Owen is at the end of his rope.

* * *

Rachel collapses to the ground in a heap as Flynn rushes to her side, "Louie, bring the blanket and what's left of their water. She is suffering from a heat stroke."

* * *

"Okay. This is it." Owen ignores the intense pain throbbing in his side and angles himself from the interior shaft wall as far as his body will stretch. In a continual motion, the desperate man lowers the pick to the limit of his reach, closes his eyes to quell the unfathomable pain, and flings the rudimentary digging tool upward with all his might. Releasing the handle at the apex of his underhand follow-through, he opens his crusted eyes as the dull metal blade clanks off the ceiling in a sea of sparks.

Raising his right arm to shield himself from the spinning pick handle and a cascade of loosened rock raining past his swaying form, he spots a glint of metal and snatches it out of the air by the tips of his swollen fingers.

The startling sight of his crazed reflection shimmers across the elliptical artifact held in his tenuous grasp.

Sheer terror eclipses Owen's moment of triumph as his left-handed purchase slips free. Freefalling into the shaft yet again, he hears the pick banging and clanging ahead of his fall. With a gut-wrenching jolt, the harness comes close to turning him into a soprano as the rope strains past its frayed limit, slamming him upside-down into the shaft wall like a suicidal acrobat.

Swaying upside-down midway down the shaft from the rope's end, Owen holds the shimmering golden ellipse before his swollen eyes, "You better be worth it." Fearful of passing out, he shoves the relic into his pants and pulls back up the rope with one beat-up hand over the other.

* * *

"Wake up down there! I have it!"

Louie scans to the top of the cliff in time to see the frayed, dirty rope hurled from the high ledge, uncoiling in midair. He jogs to catch it, securing the frayed end at the base of the rock wall.

A wholly relieved Flynn surprises Louie with a celebratory smack on the back, sending the hefty robot stumbling forward. Both spy Owen high above on the ledge, silhouetted against the sky, thrust the gleaming artifact high above his head.

* * *

Owen laughs with maniacal weariness, recreating the iconic scene from an old Disney flick. Knowing the crew below failed to get his sight gag. Right now, he could care less.

* * *

The golden ellipse reflects the blue sky while communicating its liberation to the Machine.

* * *

Nursing half a bottle of lukewarm water under a makeshift canopy made from the space blanket, Rachel hears the whoops of joy and cries like a baby. From her covered position in the Jeep front seat, she cannot see Owen, so she gains control of her pent-up emotional state and musters a strong enough voice to call out, "Great job, honey! Now quit goofing around and get your ass down here!"

Watching Owen rappel the sandstone precipice with the most iconic artifact in the history of humankind shoved down the front of his torn and tattered khakis, Louie turns to Flynn with a straight-faced seriousness, "Things are about to get interesting."

Louie | Libyan desert south of Tripoli

05:20 p.m. | August 21, 2044

Elongating late afternoon shadows provide no respite from the desert heat bearing down on the exhausted quartet. Louie slides his patched-up robot frame behind the repacked Jeep's wide steering wheel and produces a weird robot sigh, "Huh, that's odd."

Agent Flynn wipes his brow from the shotgun seat and turns to Louie, "What? What's odd, Louie? I am too shagged out to jury rig another connection in your fucking noggin, mate."

Avoiding eye contact with the agitated PTB agent, Louie produces a half-smile and replies, "I don't have the key."

Wheeling toward the Haigs, Flynn winces at Owen's battered form for the umpteenth time, slumped beside Rachel on the back seat bench. "Bloody hell, Rachel, I hope my alien dust helps your partner. There is a limit to what the white powder can do, but at least it should mitigate his pain."

Eyes swollen shut on his black and blue face, Owen hears the PTB agent loud and clear, "I'd trade your magic pixie dust for an ice-cold beer, Flynn."

"Me too, mate." Turning to Owen's better half, "Now Rachel, Louie here tells me we lost the key to this bucket of bolts. I could have sworn I left it in the ignition."

Owen emits a loud wail, "Ah, for God's sake, don't tell me you guys lost the key?"

Still combating wooziness after suffering the onset of heatstroke, Rachel leans forward and pulls the surfboard keychain from a deep pocket in her shorts, "Keep your pants on, all of you; here's the fucking key. What a bunch of babies." Rekindling her newfound swagger, the former trust fund murderess tosses the key over the seat, "Now listen up, boys. Owen is banged up pretty bad. I feel like shit, and Flynn appears three shades darker than when I first met him. Louie, get us the hell out of here!"

"Oui, Madame, it will be my pleasure."

Flynn shakes his head and smiles broadly toward the ever-alluring Mrs. Haig. "You heard the lady, Louie. Set a course for the Tripoli airport." Checking an extraction protocol programmed into his earphone, he continues, "I will work on getting us a ride from there."

Louie bumps and spins the resilient Jeep on a reverse heading off the arid plateau, "We will be there in 72 minutes, barring any more terrorists."

"It is too early for that lot to be out and about, we should be fine, but just in case," Flynn brandishes his reloaded sidearm. Bounding around a hairpin turn, the PTB agent scans the darkening Saharan sky, "We are running out of time."

**Never interrupt someone doing
what you said couldn't be done.**

– Amelia Earhart

Chapter Seven:

The Interrogation

**Rachel | 36,000 feet above the Mediterranean Sea
09:20 p.m. | August 21, 2044**

Rachel's fingers squeeze into her high-tech armrests inside the well-appointed cabin as the wedge-shaped commuter jet swoops through the turbulence like a kite. Exhausted but unable to sleep, she presses her dirty blond head into the brushed-leather seatback and peeks out her first-row port side window at the threatening skies churning above the white-capped Mediterranean Sea. A persistent rattle from the aft galley heightens her anxiety. Attempting to calm her jangled nerves, she hums the melody to *Space Oddity*, to no avail.

Closing her window, she looks across the aisle at Owen's banged-up profile clutching an empty tumbler in his bandaged left hand. Envious of her snoozing mate, she reaches out and touches his purplish left forearm, unable to resist a smile as his head slumps forward, resting his stubbled chin against the open collar of a snug neon pink polo shirt Flynn discovered in a box of cheesy corporate gear before takeoff, replacing his stinky, bloody, and tattered safari shirt. The thin cotton polo is embroidered across the left breast with a gaudy teal logo depicting a butterfly with a field of stars in its spread wingspan. The same mark adorns the tail section of the stealthy, V-shaped business jet operated by Chrysalis Air, a PTB shell company.

The flying wing completes a gut-churning bank to port. Detouring majestic storm clouds towering above the Egyptian coastline, the flight proceeds on the final forty minutes of its two-hour route out of chaotic Tripoli toward the relative orderliness of Cairo's bustling airport.

Levering her seat to its fully reclined position, Rachel stares at the air and light controls on the false ceiling above her and startles at Louie's upside-down countenance eclipsing her view from the row behind her.

"Hello, Madame. There are still 38 minutes before we land. It would be my pleasure to bring you another chardonnay."

"It's okay, Louie. I have reached the point of saturation where another sip will do more harm than good."

"Understood. Our colleagues are fast asleep. I am troubled you are unable to follow suit."

Rachel's reply is cut short as the aircraft dips and sways. A nerve-wracking flash of lightning illuminates the dim interior from the starboard windows. The tiny craft, dwarfed by the thunderhead, vectors on a southeasterly heading around the roiling clouds.

"Not to worry. I'm starting to enjoy this."

Louie relaxes into his second-row seat and appears to smile at something outside the window.

A snoring Agent Flynn slumps against the third-row window on the starboard side with two empty travel-sized Hendrick's gin bottles and a mess of peanut shells vibrating across his brushed-metal tray table.

The plane dips into a descent. For a harrowing second, Rachel thinks they are going down before realizing they are initiating a gliding approach toward Cairo after outrunning the storm front with the last thirty minutes bumpy yet tolerable.

Rachel unbuckles and looks over her seat at the unflappable Louie, staring at passing clouds. Making a loud throat-clearing sound, she disrupts his reverie, "Louie, sorry to bother you, but does the phrase, Let the Machine do the work, mean anything to you?"

"Madame, aside from hearing you repeat it exactly 13 times since departing from France, I have never heard it before."

"Thanks anyway, Louie." Twisting forward, she scoots to get comfortable in her clean but wrinkled shorts and cotton blouse, the last two articles of unworn clothing from her bag. Clasping her trusty safety belt, she glances across the aisle and sees her husband's black and blue gaze upon her.

In a drugged, sleepy voice, courtesy of Flynn's pharmacological supply, Owen struggles to form words from his cottony mouth, "Are we there yet?"

"Not yet, pinkie. We still have another 20 minutes. Go back to sleep."

A tapestry of city lights twinkles in the rainy late afternoon gloom across the darkening Egyptian topography, marking their return to civilization. Rachel peers out her rain-spattered window and mutters, "Let the Machine do the work."

* * *

A turbulent jolt nudges Flynn from slumberland. Rubbing the sleep from his eyes, the veteran PTB agent awakens from a power nap courtesy of a preflight whiff from his alien-supplied stash. A quick one-eyed peek across the aisle finds his blue canvas bag lying crumpled on the seat containing a meager assortment of personal effects: clothes, razor, coffee cubes, a small arsenal of exotic weaponry, and one ancient power source wrapped in a clean pink hand towel from the jet's cramped lavatory.

On the broiling airport tarmac back in Tripoli before hustling aboard the Chrysalis flight to Cairo, Flynn insisted on transporting the ellipse in his bag over the super-heated objections of an irate Owen. Rachel and Louie restored peace between the two men, calming the out-of-character banker's angst to a grudging acceptance of Flynn's plan to carry the relic to Cairo.

Flynn noted the gold elliptical relic's mental hold on the headstrong American with curiosity and alarm. Though they had just met, the perceptive agent noticed a shift in Owen Haig's demeanor since liberating the golden ellipse.

Flynn | Cairo International Airport
10:00 p.m. | August 21, 2044

The jet dips below the low cloud cover and lands in the unusual late-August thunderstorm—a welcome reprieve for the bone-dry environs around the Cairo International Airport. The flying wing, often mistaken for an old B-2 bomber, taxis away from the main terminals, wheeling toward a private hangar complex tucked into a sleepy corner of the massive airport. Navigating a circuitous path across the puddled tarmac, the sleek flying wing rolls to a stop outside the gaping maw of an enormous hangar.

Owen leans forward in his seat and stretches out the kinks. The sleep-inducing elixir, coupled with a shot of rye, did the trick. Once again, he is completely rested and alert. If only he could accelerate the healing of his bruises, scrapes, and cuts, he would be fit as a fiddle. Even the pain in his ribs was tolerable if he did not make sudden movements. Smiling at his lovely partner's come-hither, messy-haired appearance, his dimpled expression causes the swelling around his right eye to flare with pain. "Damn, it hurts like hell."

"Just tell anyone who asks you were beat up for wearing your ugly pink shirt."

"Hilarious, Rachel. Now, who is the comedian?"

Rising too fast from her seat, she falls into Owen's embrace, "I'm a veritable laugh riot."

Louie stands, sigh-rolling between the couple's repartee to open the hatch. "You two should get a room."

"We tried that; it was rather short-lived."

Outside, mobile light standards switch on, illuminating the dripping port side fuselage reflection in the wet tarmac as Chrysalis Air mechanics in gray coveralls silkscreened with the butterfly logo wheel a short stairway to the opened hatch. Louie clanks down the metal stairs and proceeds toward the cover of the hangar through the light rain. He is followed by Rachel with her well-traveled daypack slung over her shoulder. Fighting dizziness from the stomach-churning flight, she accepts the man's extended hand on the right. Louie watches her jog to the cover of the hangar, noting her avoidance of the pavement cracks.

Next comes Owen, looking like a prizefighter, bounding down the metal steps. Swinging the remnants of his dirty daypack over his shoulder, regretting tossing the tin of hair gel way back in Tunis, he smiles at the ground crewmen staring at his bruised face. "You should see the other guy."

Jogging under the shelter of the hangar, Owen takes a position next to Louie and Rachel. "Whew! That rain felt pretty good."

Glad to have her Chelsea boots planted on solid ground, Rachel adjusts the dusty pack on her shoulder, "So, now what?"

Louie deadpans, "I guess we wait for Agent Flynn, Madame."

* * *

Flynn stretches across the narrow aisle, grabs his duffel by the strap, and removes the tight-wrapped ancient relic. Whisking aside peanut shells from his open tray table, he places the bundled object on the brush-metal surface, unfolding the cloth until the prize within is revealed in all its glory juxtaposed atop the Pepto Bismol-colored towel.

Resting inert and exposed on the soft terry cloth, the timeless artifact refracts bright spotlights outside the starboard window onto his face. Fascinated by its elegant simplicity, he glides roughened fingertips along both sides of the nine-inch oval and angles it off the cloth. Startled by his reflection, dark eyebrows raise, and his delicate hold lets go like it's on fire. Chiding himself for letting it get to him, "Blimey! This thing is legit. What the hell just happened?"

Inspecting the ellipse from different angles, he catches a brief glimpse of ovals spinning together and flying apart in mesmerizing formations over the smooth gold surface like old-timey Spirograph drawings rendered in disappearing ink. "What the fuck was that?"

He tries to replicate the optical effect to no avail. Another mystery added to the relic's legendary power-generating ability that defies any rational scientific explanation. Flynn wonders if the PTB advisor waiting inside the Chrysalis hangar will fare better in unlocking the elliptical enigma's hidden secrets.

"I better get moving. Don't want to piss off Owen any more than he already is."

Flynn takes a series of images with a tiny camera from his jacket and flips the golden ellipse to record the opposite side. "Fuck me, this thing is weird."

Setting the camera to overlay precise measurements on the quantum-def digital images, he notes the ellipse's major axis at 226.52 mm. The minor axis measures 140 mm. "Blimey, this thing matches Fibonacci's Golden Ratio to a scintilla of a millimeter. Even the one-inch thickness rounding down to a sublime curved edge radiates perfection."

Satisfied with his impromptu photoshoot, Flynn uploads the contents in an encrypted folder to a lunar server farm for posterity. Common practice, just in case something dreadful happened on Earth.

Hearing a familiar chime, Flynn taps his earphone, "Yes, sir, we made it to Cairo …. Not too bad. The young man sustained some injuries, but he'll be fine." The agent tucks the camera back into his jacket and folds the pink towel back over the ellipse while listening to his boss on the other end of the call. "No, sir. Bad idea. Need I remind you of the woman's family connection?"

Flynn glances out the window, half-listening to the long-winded reply, "Okay. Thank you, sir. Yes, I know it's unusual. One hundred years is a long time. I know what is at stake. I have a family out there, too." Raising his left eyebrow, "I will ensure the Advisor gets his long fingers on the relic. I just hope he gives it back. The fucking thing has a way about it, that's for damn sure."

Terminating the connection, Flynn mutters, "The Advisor creeps the shit out of me." while repacking the ellipse in the duffel. Brushing peanut shells from his leather jacket, he moves toward the exit and pauses between the open hatch and the cockpit doorway on his right before deciding to knock.

The door swings wide, revealing two attractive female pilots dressed to the nines in chic powder-blue uniforms. The copilot's expressive brown eyes sparkle with delight, and a brilliant smile widens across her smooth tawny features seeing the sight-for-sore-eyes bowing at the door.

Flynn knows the exotic beauty well, reciprocating a friendly smile. "Hello, Astrid; how are things?"

The copilot's effervescent smile never wavers, looking from her pilot to Flynn and back again. She breaks the ice in a lilting Scottish accent, "Nicole! Look what the cat dragged in! What a pleasant surprise." With a shrug, she turns back toward the agent, wedged at the door, "We're fine, thank you. Your looking fit."

"Thanks, Astrid. You changed your hair. It used to be much longer, yeah?" Not waiting for Astrid's lengthy reply about losing her famous Afro in favor of short-cropped, tight-black curls, Flynn turns to address the pilot, "Nicole, I would have …."

Ignoring Flynn, she leans sideways, reaching a pale left hand to flip a switch on a console above her chestnut-brown pageboy hairstyle. "Astrid, I'll need you to contact the tower; we leave as soon as this asshole is out the door."

"Right. Now I'm an asshole." With a sighing glance out the narrow rain-flecked windscreen, "What a bloody mistake this was."

Nicole Weiss, a trailblazing woman who grew up rustling cattle on the family ranch in Wyoming before joining the US Space Force out of college, turns with a sad and pained expression distorting her fair-skinned, attractive face, "I have not heard from you in over a year. What the hell is the matter with you? On second thought, forget it. I don't want or need your lame excuses."

"A year? It hasn't been that long, has it? Let's see, the last time I saw you, I guess, was after my emergency extraction from the Siberian crash site," wincing at his inadvertent confirmation, "last year." With a wink, he flashes a roguish smile, "That whole operation was bollocksed from the start. The doctor warned against strenuous activity during my recuperation." Flynn's smile fades as his little joke falls flat. Imagining the weight of the ellipse in his duffel pulling him down, "I was assigned this case soon after my return to active duty. It's important, Nicole." Trying to mend hurt feelings, he promises, "Once this is over, we can take an extended holiday. Just the two of us. You can fly me anywhere you want."

Astrid is listening while inputting a series of commands into a terminal. "Nicole, how about the Moon? You can dump him there."

Flynn forces an awkward laugh at Astrid's inside joke, "Well, ladies, people are waiting on me, so I better get going."

Avoiding eye contact, Nicole answers, "Yes. You should leave. It's what you do best."

"We'll see how it goes here in Cairo. It is the end of the world, or I will see you both in a few days. Cheers!"

The copilot turns and waves goodbye, "Cheers, Flynn!"

Nicole watches her on-again, off-again romantic dalliance jogging through the rain toward the hangar and the waiting group, "He has the temerity to use *The end of the world* as an excuse and gets away with it every time."

Astrid follows her gaze out the window, "One of these times, he may not be full of shit."

Owen | Chrysalis Air hangar
10:45 p.m. | August 21, 2044

Owen watches a chastised Agent Flynn traverse the tarmac in the steady rainfall, zeroing in on the duffel bag and the hard-won relic tucked inside, "Hey Flynn, what took so long? We were starting to worry something was wrong."

Flynn walks straight up to a surprised Owen and pats him on the shoulder, "You are a lucky man, Owen Haig. Don't screw it up."

Watching two grown men commiserate, Rachel turns to Louie and feigns comical, teary-eyed empathy.

Louie wheels to hide a cheeky laugh.

A loud, throat-clearing redirects their attention toward a tall skinny man with thick horn-rimmed glasses, dressed in a lime-green and burgundy shirt and tie combo under a nerdy white lab coat. The no-nonsense man stands under a jet fighter nose cone, "May I have your attention. My instructions are to escort your group through the hangar. Stay inside the yellow lines on the floor, and refrain from touching anything. Eyes forward, follow me."

The bedraggled foursome hoists their bags and follows the white-coated technician with a tablet tucked under his right arm through the cavernous hangar.

While not an aviation enthusiast, Owen's interest in aircraft was piqued after his up close and personal experience with Grandpa Neil's P-47 Thunderbolt in France. He gawks at the assemblage of vintage aeronautical marvels parked at odd angles throughout the massive hangar space. "This is quite a collection; I bet the Smithsonian would like to get their hands on these old aircraft."

Toward the back of the echoing hangar over two football fields long, a sizable section is concealed behind massive swaths of opaque, light-colored fabric hanging from the rafters high overhead to the sealed concrete floor. Owen glimpses scientists operating an exotic array of instrumentation staged around a floating, dull-gray craft through a gap in the drapery. "Huh." A second glance causes his heart to race as a diminutive humanoid alien, conferring with two white coats, comes into view through another gap in the cloth. The being's bulbous head swivels, focusing piercing-black saucer-shaped eyes right through a flummoxed Owen.

Suppressing a total freak out, and not for the first time in the last day, the 27-year-old banker quickens his pace to rejoin his group. He is bursting at the seams to say something.

Rachel cuts him off with a raised hand, "Not now, Owen. Quit screwing around."

Flynn seizes on the diversion to pass the towel-wrapped golden ellipse to a technician standing in the shadow of a vintage stealth fighter. Relieved of its weighty contents, Flynn swings the duffel over his shoulder and jogs to rejoin his group's hasty passage through the Chrysalis Air hangar complex.

Catching up and matching Owen's long strides, the PTB agent offers some sage words of wisdom to the excitable American: "I would refrain from joking around with these blokes, mate. They have no sense of humor."

Rachel adds, "Yeah, Owen. Do you want to get beat up by a bunch of nerds? Hasn't your rugged masculinity taken enough blows for one day?"

"Perhaps." Unable to resist another furtive peek toward the draped-off area, "I need to change out of this pinky shirt."

A little gassed after the forced march through the dark shadowy hangar, they reach the back end and pause to catch their breaths before an oversized door centered with a reinforced window. Through the glass, Rachel sees an antiseptic, fluorescent-lit hallway culminating at a bank of elevators beyond a water fountain and a few side doors.

The nerd proceeds through the door without bothering to hold it open for the rest of the group. Louie darts forward and grabs the handle before it slams shut, gesturing for the human trio to pass through.

Rachel bows, "Thank you, Louie."

"Chivalry is not dead, Madame. It's just lost in a sea of technological advancements."

Flynn nods and smiles, angling past Louie.

Bringing up the rear, Owen can't resist a backward glance, prompting Rachel to tap his shoulder and whisper, "I saw him too."

* * *

With the below-his-paygrade task of escorting the bedraggled group completed, the technician abandons them in the hallway and proceeds to the elevators, repeatedly pressing the down arrow. As the elevator doors slide open, the nerd advises them to wait; someone will be along within a few minutes.

Flynn mimics the accommodating flack, "Can I get you two anything while we wait? A coffee or a Coke? How about a Snickers bar?" Blank tired stares return his gaze, "Lighten up! You Americans, always with your knickers in a tight-wound knot." Flinging open the second door on the right, he gestures toward a bank of vending machines positioned along the left wall inside the windowless breakroom, "Voila! Pick your poison."

From left to right, Rachel surveys her choices: one for snacks, a second for cold refreshments, and a third machine with a spigot for water, coffee, or hot chocolate. Great.

A white-coated nerd blocks Rachel's view, staring zombielike through the SNACK machine's streaky glass, perusing its packaged comestibles. She peers over his shoulder, spies a package of donuts, and waits for the guy to choose something while her stomach growls in protest.

Owen proceeds past the sticky linoleum tables, plastic chairs askew, and the vending machines. He is drawn like a moth to the flame toward a bulletin board on the far wall, covered in yellowed newspaper clippings of Far Side cartoons.

Rachel sticks her tongue out at the oblivious technician and plops onto a cheap plastic chair at the first table. With a frowning sigh, she attempts to pull her husband from the antiquated comic collection push-pinned to the board, "Owen, grab me a coffee and a package of powder donuts."

"Heh-heh, how I love a good comic strip." Turning to his frowning wife, "Funny thing, Rachel. I lost my wallet during our search for the golden ellipse. It must be at the bottom of the shaft in the Libyan desert next to Flynn's fancy flashlight, but you'll be happy to know my passport is in my bag."

The technician springs to life, fishing a bag of cheese doodles from the slatted opening at the bottom of the vending machine and beating a hasty exit.

Owen watches the door slam in his wake, "Was it something I said?"

Louie preempts Flynn's reply, "Monsieur, we should refrain from mentioning the ellipse."

"What he said." Flynn produces a wad of bills from his jacket and turns to the ravenous woman, "Rachel, allow me to purchase your coffee and donuts. It is the least I can do."

Owen turns from the board, focusing on Flynn's duffel lying on a table littered with crumbs, coffee rings, and foil candy wrappers,

"I have not seen the ellipse since we left Tripoli. Let's have another look while we wait."

Louie's left eyebrow arches, looking from the bag to his bruised and battered friend and back again as he sits to watch the imminent fireworks.

Flynn gives Louie a curious, "How do you know that?" look, allowing Owen's suggestion to linger while he turns to insert a bill in the machine. The slot accepts the dog-eared currency on the third try, and he makes a black coffee selection. With a sheepish expression across his stubbled face, he shrugs toward the young American in the bright pink shirt, "It is no longer in my duffel."

The coffee machine whines and whirs before the sound of dark, piping-hot liquid hitting a cheap paper cup percolates through the palpable tension filling the room.

Breaking the awkward silence, Owen's stern voice sends a chill along Rachel's spine, "Where is it?"

Before Flynn can reply, the door opens, and a well-dressed woman peeks inside the snack room, "Ah! Here you all are." Her pale blue eyes meet the agent's relieved face, "Hello, Flynn. Are you taking good care of our guests?" Casting her gaze upon the rugged man in the pink shirt, the Kobayashi creation, and finally, the attractive young woman seated on a hard plastic chair with long legs crossed and elbow rested on the sticky tabletop, "Mrs. Haig? I presume. Please, dear, come with me."

Surprised beyond measure, Rachel leans forward, "Who, me?"

Appealing for guidance but receiving none from her fuming mate, she turns to Agent Flynn.

"Looks like the principal's office for you, young lady."

Rachel stands, unsure of herself and wary of separating from the group. She never even got to eat her donuts. This is beginning to feel too real.

Turning from the peanut gallery, Rachel assesses the new player in their little psychodrama. The woman's disarming, authoritative presence quells her initial anxieties like a cool, hip, fashion-forward grandmother unaffected by the ravages of age. Natural, charcoal-gray hair is styled in a full-bang pixie cut, framing her striking good looks. Her pale and smooth complexion requires minimal makeup and a hint of wrinkles for gravitas. Shorter than Rachel, she is nonetheless blessed with an enviable figure for a woman of any age. Rachel's fashion sense is also piqued, admiring her trendy yet business-like, tailored black suit, with an elegant cream blouse and patent-leather, square-toe red pumps. She surmises the shoes are Prada, and the ensemble is Chanel; however, it would be uncouth to ask out loud. Regaining her composure, wearing her olive-green t-shirt and khaki shorts ensemble—compliments of a downtown Manhattan sporting goods store—she turns to her husband. "It's alright. We are all on the same side, I think."

Placing a manicured hand on her hip over the chic Coco Chanel suit jacket, the fashion plate bolsters Rachel's remark, "That's right, Mrs. Haig. We just want a word with you." Guiding the young woman toward the door, she flashes a disarming smile, "Nothing more. I promise."

Owen watches his lovely wife mouth goodbye before the door swings shut.

Flynn lifts the paper coffee cup from under the recessed spigot in the machine. Owen moves to stand beside the PTB agent but refrains from talking. Louie's heavy frame bows his cheap plastic chair into a saddle, staring toward the bulletin board with a raised eyebrow, biding time while reading the cartoons from across the room.

The agent takes a sip from the steaming cup, prompting Owen to break the silence, "That was Rachel's."

Lowering the cup, Flynn pivots toward the fuming American, "Honestly, Owen. Everything will be fine. I'm not freelancing alone, and what happens next has real-world consequences. The way I understand it, you wanted to hand the ellipse over to the authorities yourself."

"How do you know that?"

"I can read lips. I read your conversation in the OASIS Hotel bar before we met." Reading the unamused expression contorting Owen's bruised face, "Come on, mate. There is someone I want you to meet. Louie, wait here in case Rachel returns before we come back."

"Oui, Monsieur."

Flynn opens the door leading into the hangar, and Owen halts in his tracks, realizing who it is he wants him to meet, "Uh, Flynn. Let's go back and wait inside. I could go for that Snickers bar after all."

"Nonsense, Owen. Whether you like it or not, you are one of us now." The agent makes a beeline for the sectioned-off hangar floor space, motioning for his reticent companion to enter through a parted drape.

Owen ducks through the opening and sees the strange craft, but the white-coated techs and the little gray man are absent. In their place, an old man in a director's chair reclines in a cross-legged pose. Light from somewhere reflects off the man's angular features and thinning gray hair combed back on his prominent forehead.

Owen's first reaction upon seeing the man is he reminds him of a Shakespearean stage performer now well into his twilight years. Comparing new acquaintances to famous people is a social crutch he employs in stressful situations. The whole picturing them naked routine never worked for him. However, his harried mental state refuses to conjure the actor's name. Damn.

Wearing a saguaro cactus-shaped silver bolo tie at the collar of his crisp white shirt tucked into dark wool pants and polished black shoes, he points his cane at a dumbfounded Owen, "Owen Haig, it is a pleasure to finally make your acquaintance! We are thrilled you agreed to join us." The man leans forward and coughs, distorting his holographic image before the signal autocorrects to a lifelike focus. Turning to address an off-camera assistant, "I am off my mark? Bloody hell, Andrew."

"I regret we cannot meet in person. This blasted holographic technology has its shortcomings. It almost makes me nostalgic for Zoom meetings. My doting physician warned against unnecessary travel. Pity. I do miss being in the field. I was an exceptional scrapper in my day." The patriarchal figure's attention wanders to a rheumy-eyed memory conjured in his mind.

Unable to mask growing incredulity, Owen glances from Flynn's stubbled cocoa-brown poker face to the three-dimensional projection and the floating spacecraft beyond. Erupting with pent-up frustration, he reaches his wit's end, "Who the hell are you people?"

The outburst breaks the man's reverie, and he coughs again, causing his projection to warp in and out. Motioning at an unseen functionary to back off, he faces forward and clears his throat, "Where are my manners? My name is Artemus Pennywell. I am the CEO of The Powers That Be. And Flynn here is one of our top agents."

The feed cuts in and out as Pennywell adjusts his position in the director-style chair, "And you, sir, along with your wonderful wife, possess the key to our survival." More coughs. "Flynn will work with our folks in Cairo to coordinate your accommodations and travel needs. Once again, I regret my absence, but I congratulate you and Mrs. Haig on finding the golden ellipse. You accomplished what trained field agents failed to do for decades. I hope it can be restored to its proper place before our time runs out. Goodbye for now."

The vision of the man distorts again as he leans forward in his chair to stand with the help of his cane, his graveled voice echoing into the hangar before the session terminates, "Dammit, Andrew, this thing …"

With a jolt of recognition, Owen realizes Pennywell is the man at the cropped edge of the famous Disclosure Day group photo in the Nevada desert—and the distinctive voice-over from the video presentation.

Known throughout The Powers That Be as Ping, the Gray alien Advisor settles his 300-plus-year-old body into a biometrics-enabled seat within the floating craft's circular cockpit. Activating a virtual screen, he reads the pink-shirted human outside the ship's curved hull, standing next to the PTB agent. Ruminating on the agitated young human's wild and uneven thought patterns, his wise old eyes narrow as the pair recedes back into the hangar through the draped canopy.

Ping's wrinkled, pale gray form straightens as the viewscreen transitions onto the troubled countenance of his 134-year-old protégé, Artemus Pennywell, reflecting in his deep-black intelligent gaze.

Pennywell gets right to the issue, dispensing with formalities, "Ping, I need your unbiased opinion of the young couple based on your experiences with the Light Specters. Do they stand a chance?"

Hailing from a peaceful offshoot of an otherwise malicious Gray race spreading evil tendrils across the universe, the Advisor contemplates a digital translation of the question. After a contemplative pause, he taps a response on a holographic keyboard: "Without question, the man named Owen will fail, like every other human throughout time. The female, Rachel, is an enigma. Following her ancestor's miraculous transformation, he advised the Light Specters of the experimental treatment your group injected into her pre and post-natal developing brain."

Pennywell's face darkens with shame, "Yes. The blue spark. Professor Richard King's plan to accelerate human evolution. It is unsettling that Rachel's father volunteered his premature baby girl for our drug trial in exchange for some prime real estate."

"Regardless, Artemus, the Alexander woman's blue spark may prove providential."

The cryptic answer translated into a tinny English-accented

monotone fails to assuage Pennywell's guilt and the burdensome knowledge of the invasion fleet looming toward Earth, "I let this play out, and now I am beginning to regret it. I wish Paddy was here."

"Artemus, your mentor, Paddy McCoy, was a good man but lacked your mental fortitude. We altered your DNA to prolong your lifespan so you would live long enough to meet this moment. That is why I am troubled by your lack of confidence in the girl. I understand the gravity of your situation, but you must resist the temptation to meddle. If the one called Rachel succeeds, it will usher in a new age for humanity. If she fails, the Dark Specters will claim vindication and celebrate humanity's demise. Regardless of the outcome, it was meant to be."

Ping reads the pained expression on his old friend's face. While sadness and trepidation are foreign emotions, the alien understands Pennywell's concerns and, what's more, the efficacy of maintaining a fractional representation of the human species.

"Not to worry, Artemus. I have convinced my associates to extract enough of you to preserve humanity from extinction."

"Thanks. I think. You and I know most people on the list will not make it onto a ship in time."

Millions of years farther advanced than his human counterpart, Ping ignores the pessimistic remark and holds up the golden ellipse in his long fingers for Pennywell to see, "Please send a technician to retrieve the ellipse. Its function is beyond my comprehension, and I no longer trust myself in possession of it."

Rachel | Chrysalis Air, Sub-Level 15
11:35 p.m. | August 21, 2044

A buzzer sounds as elevator doors swoosh open, revealing another fluorescent hallway after a stomach-dropping descent through fifteen levels of ancient Egyptian strata beneath the bustling airport. Rachel can't help noticing it is identical to the ground-level corridor.

"Do you ever get lost in these hallways? Maybe a breadcrumb trail might help?"

"No, that wouldn't work with the rats and all."

"I was joking."

Chanel, Rachel's nickname for her fashionable new friend, turns with an amiable smile, "I know you were, dear. Now, right this way, Mrs. Haig. Our people want a candid, one-on-one conversation away from the rest of your group before sending you on your way."

"Can I tell them anything they don't already know?"

Rachel's worn leather boots match the economical click-clack of expensive designer heels, echoing in the long hallway past drab, unadorned, eggshell-colored walls bathed in a greenish glow from extra-long, daisy-chained, fluorescent light fixtures. Stopping at the sixth door on the left, "Honest answers work every time."

Without knocking, Chanel ushers Rachel inside an expansive, wood-paneled conference room. A video wall at the far end loops a screensaver of generic deep-space images. Nothing special. At the far end of the table, a mature Asian man is seated with his back to the screens, pouring over a sea of binders and papers, scribbling notes on an old-school pad of paper with a fountain pen. How quaint. His striped bow tie and button-down shirt under a houndstooth jacket with suede elbow patches, wisps of gray hair, and wire-rim spectacles give him a professorial gravitas.

Two assistants, a woman seated on his right and a man seated to his left, are Rachel's age and presumably scientists, judging by the ill-fitting white lab coats concealing their drab outfits du jour. The petite woman has short-cropped, dull-brown hair and the sallow complexion of someone rarely exposed to sunshine. Otherwise, she is unremarkable in every way, a real plain jane. The guy is a typical nerd, also pale as a ghost, with uneven stubble peppering his narrow chin and a receding hairline of short-cropped dark hair.

Inside the room, a pin drop could be heard. The trio ignores Rachel's sleep-deprived presence, and Chanel does not bother with formal introductions. Instead, she unbuttons her jacket, steps to the table, and pulls out a comfortable leather chair near the end of the room, gesturing for the young interviewee to sit.

Looking down the polished wood surface toward the preoccupied trio, Rachel shrugs and plops into the chair. Folding her hands on the tabletop, she awaits the third degree from the three losers, separated by three empty seats between herself and their end of the table—the rule of thirds.

Plain Jane glances toward Rachel without losing focus on her stack of papers. She removes a sheet from the pile and slides it before the professor.

Rachel watches the riveting activity before glancing over her right shoulder toward the door. Finding Chanel gone and the door shut tight, she wonders how the woman managed to sneak away in those heels.

Plain Jane's nerdy counterpart lifts his eyes from the thick pile of papers and glances toward the captivating beauty who just entered the room. Rachel suppresses a smile, witnessing his surprised, too-obvious doubletake. Well-acquainted with the phenomenon, she long-ago accepted impertinent stares as part of her life. However, a new wrinkle is the invisible daggers shooting across the table from Plain Jane in response to his overt heterosexual reaction.

After Plain Jane's silent rebuke of the young male scientist, dubbed Doubletake in Rachel's head, the twosome returned to their binders and papers. The Professor had yet to cast his eyes in her direction at all. The silence is deafening and unnerving. With a growing sense of anxiety and claustrophobia—fifteen stories underground in the conference room's formal setting—Rachel's tired mind wanders, concluding she is underdressed for the occasion. Wrinkled, grungy t-shirt and shorts ensembles were de rigueur when driving the rickety Jeep, sleeping in the dirt with the scorpions and dodging gunfire, especially juxtaposed with her cohorts' tattered appearance. However, this is the first instance since leaving the villa in France when she missed having access to her extensive wardrobe and shoe collection. My God, the shoes! And the jewelry. And the makeup case. Not to mention a pile of elegant purses and accessories. She had to get out. Now!

Rachel's pulse quickens, and the room closes inward before her eyes.

"Mrs. Haig? Rachel? Hello? Is anybody home?"

A snap of the fingers returns Rachel to the here and now. Looking toward the trio without focusing on any of them, "I'm sorry, what did you say?"

Plain Jane repeats her initial query from the left side of the long table, "I asked if you experienced hallucinations over the past few days. Perhaps you are undergoing one right now."

"Hallucinations? No. Why?"

"Are you aware of the significant nature of the artifact you and your colleagues brought to our attention?"

"Yes, I am. Are you?"

Plain Jane ignores the shot across her bow. "Mrs. Haig, The Powers That Be started following the case of Captain Neil Alexander—your grandfather twice-removed—after he was reported MIA in Southern France during the Second World War, one-hundred years plus five days ago. We understand there is a possibility, however remote, that you contacted him over the last few days." She pauses for effect and glances at her frowning superior, "Or, you made contact with an entity you believed was your relation."

On a hunch, Rachel decides not to play along, "I'm sorry, but is there a question in that statement? Agent Flynn asked if I felt like I was being watched. Nothing like a little confirmation. However, my family has nothing to do with why I am here. They should all be left alone."

Plain Jane winces at the obfuscation. "Agent Flynn tends to speak out of turn."

Slapping a notepad onto the table harder than he meant to, Doubletake adds his two cents to the impromptu interrogation. He clears his throat and casts a wary glance toward Plain Jane, "Rachel. May I call you by your first name? Do you believe in ghosts?"

"Okay, let's go down the rabbit hole." Curious where the nerdy guy is going with his out-of-the-blue query, "Rachel is fine, and yes, I believe in them. Do you?"

Doubletake swivels to face her, alarmed by her recalcitrance, "Please, Rachel, do not be defensive. We are on your side. We all believe in your story and want to help. First, we want to understand more about your meeting with Captain Neil Alexander." Glancing at his notes, "I'm going to ask you a series of yes or no questions, okay?"

Rachel pauses, taking note of Doubletake's kind eyes, "Yes."

The relieved, nerdy man chuckles, "Good one. Okay, first question: Did Neil's form appear human during your time with him?

"Uh, No." Rachel hesitates, realizing these people possess more information than they can divulge. How are they aware of what happened in the cave?

"Was he translucent? Could you see objects through him?"

"Yes, he was. And I understand what translucent means."

"Did he project light outward from his form?"

"Yes."

"Were any other... How do I put this? Did other orbs of light assist him?"

"Yes."

"Did those lights ever attempt to communicate with you, or was all communication through his form?" His voice cracks at the end of the sentence, flustered by her come-hither appearance.

"No. Well, kind of. It depends."

Plain Jane, sensing a slight hesitation in the young woman's resolute demeanor, cuts to the chase, "Did the person who claimed to be your ancestor possess specific family information an imposter would have difficulty knowing? For instance, did the subject of your sexual assault at eighteen come up during your paranormal conversations?"

Tired, hungry, and desperate for a shower, Rachel breaks, "If you are asking whether the ghost of Neil Alexander put a knife in my hand so I could stab it through the heart of a rapist bastard who was going to kill me, I do not know. But if you want to know if he instructed my husband and me to cancel our honeymoon, travel to the Libyan desert, and dig up an ancient relic, the answer is yes! You know that already. Am I fit to continue, or has my traumatic past and the weirdness of the last few days left me verging on insanity? I can put your minds at ease. I'm fine. So is Owen. We are wasting valuable time."

Upon clearing the air, Rachel realizes she has nothing to fear from these eggheads. Commanding the room, she goes for broke, "Neil Alexander is part of an intelligent race beyond our comprehension. Have you people heard of foo fighters? Not the old-timey rock band, but the little orbs of light freaked-out fighter and airline pilots never report. They are one and the same." Directing her gaze at the older man in the middle, she continues, "I don't want to waste more time rehashing shit you people already understand better than I do. Earth is under a terrible threat, and I don't mean the typical global warming bullshit."

Rachel leans back and takes a deep breath, tickled by Plain Jane's perceptible wince at the cutting remark.

Doubletake's hangdog expression transforms into a forced smile, "Can I get you anything, water perhaps?"

Rachel ignores the offer, "I should be at the pyramid with the golden ellipse right now."

Plain Jane frowns with an exasperated sigh, drumming her fingers on the table, "Mrs. Haig, are you familiar with the pyramid complex? It is immense. How will you know where to go or what to do when you get there? Is there more you are not telling us? I advise against holding back information. What if you are incapacitated? Don't you think you owe it to the world to tell us your plan? You do have a plan, don't you?"

The callous reference to a plan was the last straw. Rachel stands and hears herself speaking six simple words, burrowed deep within her psyche, in one iconic sentence, "Let the Machine do the work!"

Slumping down into the seat, she follows with a weak utterance from her heart, "That's my goddamn plan."

Swiveling in her expensive chair, Rachel acknowledges Chanel's reappearance in the opened doorway, a pained expression on her face. Defying the grave solemnity in the room, Rachel starts to laugh, "My husband wanted to turn this whole thing over to the authorities after we found the ellipse. Of course, my Grandpa warned against it. Now I understand why. You are all talk and no action. And that's on a good day." In full command of the room, with the Professor, Plain Jane, and Doubletake, as well as Chanel, hanging on every word, she smooths her hands across the fancy mahogany tabletop, "Well, I have news for you all, you're not as smart as you think. Things are happening under your noses; you are too blind to see!"

After a brief pause, Doubletake chimes in, "What kinds of things, Rachel?"

"Oh, I don't know. Perhaps aliens will land on the White House lawn, chop the president into pieces and sprinkle her on a salad? They are not coming to welcome us into the community of planets or any nerdy Star Trek bullshit." Noting Doubletake visibly recoiling at the cutting remark, she softens, "No offense."

His blushing, schoolboy grin prompts Plain Jane to erupt in frustration, "For crying out loud, Roy! She is playing you; can't you see what she is doing here?"

"Enough!"

Rachel and the two sniping bureaucrats snap to attention at the bellicose outburst from the Professor.

He closes his binder, pushes back in his chair, and stands. Adjusting his jacket, he steps behind Plain Jane and pats her on the shoulder, "No more coffee for you tonight, Greta." Moving to the empty spot beside Rachel, he gestures at the seat, "Do you mind?"

Shaking her head, Rachel laughs, "This is your party. Go right ahead."

He reaches into his jacket and produces a remote. Pointing it at the video wall, the screensaver switches to an animated solar system view. Rachel stares at the screen and sees three red circles, one within Saturn's circumsolar orbit, another somewhat askew within the orbital range of Mars, and a third half the distance between Earth and the red planet.

The Professor presents Rachel with an uneasy smile, "All three circles indicate current positions of armadas of ships within our solar system. They all have cloaking technologies beyond our capacity, obscuring their approach. Our advisors provided a filter allowing us to monitor their progress. Any of them could be on us in a flash. To be honest, we don't know the cause of their delay. Perhaps they are arguing amongst themselves. Or drawing lots to decide who gets what.

While not every alien race wants to destroy us, we are sitting ducks in a large pond. After Disclosure Day in 2034, it was decided that humanity required a mental buffer separating real-life ET from real-life War of the Worlds. This facility was built as a base of operations to search for the ellipse and the legendary beacon. It is our only hope of stopping the imminent invasion. Two generations of archeologists, scientists, and mathematicians here in Cairo and operatives in the field have come up bone dry. During the Cold War, we thought the Soviets recovered the golden ellipse. We almost came to blows. The effort since the end of the War on Terror has been more unified. The invaders will not play favorites; they will wipe us out, regardless of race, sex, politics, or creed."

The Professor eases back in his seat and frowns at the stunned woman over the rim of his glasses, "Now we are on the same page, young lady." He positions his remote in front of Rachel, adjusting its angle with a nudge, "My colleague wishes to speak to you," and taps the device.

A holographic image springs to life, inches off the table, projecting an elderly man leaning on a cane. "Hello, my name is Artemus Pennywell. Earlier, I had the pleasure of meeting Owen, and I'm impressed by everything you managed thus far," chuckling and pointing his cane at the poker-faced Asian man, "with the help of one of Mr. Kobayashi's headstrong creations, no less." While pausing to gather his thoughts, Rachel leans closer, "I am placing our Cairo staff at your disposal. You hold the key to averting this disaster. I understand any attempt to change the course of events would have deleterious consequences. We are not prone to hyperbole at The Powers That Be, Mrs. Haig, but destiny best describes your arrival on our doorstep." Pausing again, "I wish you and your husband good luck and good hunting."

The Asian professor, outed as the famous recluse, Mr. Kobayashi, ends the transmission and angles past Rachel to address Chanel, standing by the door, "This interview is over. Please escort the others in now."

Minutes later, Chanel reenters the conference room with Flynn, Owen, and Louie. Seeing the famous Mr. Kobayashi seated beside Rachel, Flynn turns to his synthetic friend, "Hey Louie, this is as good a time as any to meet your maker."

Louie's eyes alight, seeing the Asian man beaming in his direction, "It is indeed an honor, sir."

Kobayashi glides around the table, unable to look away from his discombobulated masterpiece. "I see you have been through a lot; follow me." The pair exit through the door, and Chanel hastens to follow, calling over her shoulder, "I will make sure he does not take too long."

Owen's weary gaze leads to the far end of the table, past the two nerds returning to their binders of notes and equations to the solar system on the big screen and the pulsating red spots. "Are those what I think they are?"

"Bloody hell, now there are three of them? When did the new fleet show up?"

Plain Jane's deadpan reply, "About a week ago, Agent Flynn."

Doubletake pushes from his chair and moves to address Rachel, "I apologize for all of the subterfuge and prying questions. It was a pleasure, Mrs. Haig. And good luck. Needless to say, we are all counting on you."

While winking at Rachel, Owen reaches to shake the young scientist's hand, "I see you made a new friend."

Rachel beams while grabbing the harried man's other hand and whispers in his ear, "You can do better."

Doubletake turns beet red.

Plain Jane remains seated, ignoring the pleasantries. Seizing the opportunity with everyone distracted by the too-perfect American couple, she transmits the latest developments to her outside contact.

Professor Tarek Hamed | The Cairo Museum
01:10 a.m. | August 22, 2044

Amber light escaping from a cracked doorway pierces the darkened corridor at the far end of a row of shuddered offices along an administrative wing inside the venerable Museum of Egyptian Antiquities, aka the Cairo Museum. Post the midnight hour, inside his cramped office, Professor Tarek Hamed drums thick, calloused fingertips atop a stack of papers, staring across the room at the empty desk belonging to a colleague he has never met. Emitting a loud sigh, he summons patience, waiting for the promised call from Greta, his well-paid source, employed as a statistician at a sham outfit called Chrysalis Air. The woman's excited message instructed him to await her inside scoop regarding his metaphorical white whale: the golden ellipse.

Tarek Hamed persevered through decades of universal derision from narrow-minded colleagues, mocking his belief in a legendary structure hidden far below the Giza Plateau for thousands of years before recorded time. While fellow academics laughed in his face, benefactors and employers viewed the otherwise brilliant archeologist's quixotic hypothesis as a festering source of embarrassment: "Professor Tarek Hamed, you have turned your once-promising career in Egyptology into a joke. The pyramids are replete with legends, curses, and ghost stories designed to keep the masses in line. Your theories fall within that spectrum. Cease any further investigations into your ridiculous research, or your grants and privileges will be revoked."

Well, the joke is on them. Hamed's desk drawer holds the key to accessing the ancient structure. And with the golden ellipse now within his grasp, his life's work will be complete. Ruminating his reliance on unpleasant individuals—such as the nasty woman who is late with her phone call—he muses it is a small price to pay for immortality. His earphone chimes; it's Greta.

Tuning out the annoying woman's report after hearing the magic words: *The elusive golden ellipse is in Cairo, recovered by an annoying American couple who plan to return it to the pyramid.* He forwards the call to a secure recording device. The dapper Oxford-educated Egyptian heard all he needed to hear. He can listen to the rest of her blow-by-blow bitch-a-thon another time. "Good job, Greta."

An anticipatory tingle courses Hamed's spine envisioning the culmination of his life's work. First, he must relieve the hapless Americans of their incredible burden with the assistance of a host of unsavory co-conspirators.

Yasmine Sardouk | The Cairo Museum
10:35 a.m. | September 24, 2043 | (Eleven months earlier)

Still acclimating to his new position at the Cairo Museum, Professor Tarek Hamed's morning is interrupted by an abrupt knock on his office door.

A breathless young woman bursts inside, introducing herself as a new research assistant with information that sounded too good to be true: "Professor, I have a key to unlock your theories on par with the Rosetta Stone. All you have to do is follow me, and you will finally have the evidence to silence your critics once and for all."

The dark-complexioned petite young lady in tight jeans and a Cairo University t-shirt under a lab coat, with her jet-black hair bobby-pinned behind her ears, ensured the hallway was empty before pushing Hamed's office door shut. "I work downstairs in the research department and have access to a climate-controlled storeroom filled with mummified animals. What if I told you one of them—a non-descript wooden cat sarcophagus—holds the key to your theory of an ancient structure buried deep underneath the Great Pyramid?"

Hamed stood from behind his desk and leaned forward to check the photo ID hanging from a lanyard around the girl's neck. Yasmine Sardouk. Smoothing his thick mustache, he flashed his gap-toothed smile, "The first thing I would say, young lady, is who put you up to do this? Was it Cartwright? No matter. Go back and tell the fat bastard I don't appreciate his sense of humor. Good day."

Hamed returned to his seat, but the young lady did not budge. Her stare unsettled the archeologist to no end.

"Really? I am a very busy man. Please leave, or I will be forced to call security."

"You are skeptical. I assure you, no one put me up to anything. Well …."

Hamed catches a strange look distorting her attractive features for a heartbeat.

"I must insist that you follow me right now. Time is of the essence."

Her insistent tone sets off alarm bells in Hamed's mind, assuming she is off her rocker, on drugs, or both. Nevertheless, given the hoop-jumping and ass-kissing it took to land his new position at the world-renowned museum, he decided discretion was the better part of valor. "Okay. You win. I will play along. I can spike Cartwright's coffee later, I guess."

Following her through a maze of corridors to a little-used pre-renovation elevator, he watched her press the button multiple times with palpable impatience.

"Young lady, the cache of mummies you refer to has awaited study for over a year. I think they can wait five more minutes."

She turned and gave Hamed a relieved smile while stepping through the still-opening doors. "Come on."

He watched the girl tap her ID on an access pad, and 3LL lit up the display. "That is a sub-basement level. There is nothing down there of value. Miss Sardouk, what is going on here?"

After a gut-churning plummet, the gold doors slid apart onto a darkened space. Hamed looked into the darkness and heard the tell-tale skitter of rodents scurrying for cover. Expecting a surprise party or a blunt object up the side of his head, Hamed stepped off the elevator, "This better be good."

The woman moved with a familiar purpose to a bank of switches partially obscured behind a long row of overstuffed file cabinets. Low-wattage incandescent bulbs strung across the ceiling flickered on, and Hamed found himself face-to-face with a ridiculous gold-trimmed sarcophagus prop fabricated for a long-forgotten show. Wrapping knuckles on the cheap resin prop, he looked into the vast space at row upon row of overloaded shelves stuffed with a panoply of long-forgotten curiosities and ephemera from past dioramas, exhibits, and museum events, all cast in the dim yellowy light.

"This way, Professor."

Not finding party hats and balloons—or a mugger lurking in the shadows—Hamed shrugged and followed the fit young woman down the aisles. His wandering eyes shifted from the shelves onto Yasmine's pert backside, moving the seam on her thin white jacket from side to side. Unexpected arousal prompted a cheeky jest from the affirmed bachelor, "This would be a great place for a little midday rendezvous."

Yasmine ignored the impertinent comment, turned a corner, and stopped before a row of high shelves filled with Egyptian cat sarcophagus replicas. Though more authentic looking than most of the crap in the basement, he recognized them from a charity gala he attended. The cat statues were used as paperweight decorations on silent auction tables. Case closed.

Chagrined by Yasmine's lack of interest, he grabbed a fake kitty statue off the shelf, channeling his best Bond impersonation,

"So, you invited me down here for a little pussy, after all."

"Trust me when I tell you, Professor, that will not happen."

Sliding the ridiculous hunk of resin back in line with its kitty mates on the shelf, he heaved a frustrated sigh, "Look. I'm not sure who put you up to this, but these are worthless replicas of a famous British museum antiquity sealed inside a glass-enclosed case for over a century. I studied it for a paper I wrote when I was your age." With a growing incredulity at her recalcitrance, "There is a mummy inside the real one. These are filled with nothing but air, like your head."

"Tarek, I can assure you, the statue in the British Museum is fake. I made the switch myself."

Taken aback by her use of his first name, Hamed's tanned brow furrowed, watching the woman stretch her lissome frame to the highest kitty-lined shelf to access another replica sarcophagus.

On the cusp of advising the young woman to seek mental help, the archeologist observed that the kitty statue cradled in her arms had a signature crack at a precise spot between its pointy ears. A detail left off the replicas and something only a practiced eye would notice.

Hamed's eyes widened in surprise, "This is the genuine artifact? How did it get here? I cannot be a party to this kind of theft, young lady. I have a responsibility …."

"Old man, you talk too much."

Before he can stop her, Yasmine grips the cat by its neck and smashes the sarcophagus headfirst into the leading edge of the gray metal shelving, splintering the dried-out head and shoulders of the exquisite feline antiquity into jagged wooden bits.

"My God, woman! What in the hell did you just do?"

With a mischievous smile, she turned the headless statue upside down, giving it a vigorous shake. The crumpled and tattered mummified remains shook apart inside the exposed cavity, and a small object fell to the floor and bounced into the cobwebbed recess underneath the lowest shelf.

"I promised you a Rosetta Stone, remember? It is now resting beneath this shelf unit."

Still reeling after watching the priceless antiquity smashed to pieces, Hamed failed to notice Yasmine's body fading into a terrifying visage. Instead, he fell onto his knees in his white pants, bent low to the floor, and peered under the shelf. With an audible sigh and a fear of spiders on high alert, he reached his right hand into the shadowed darkness. Groping through the cobwebbed recess, his index finger stabbed into something sharp. "Ow! What the hell!" Grasping the small, pointed object, he pulled it into the yellow light. Studying the small crystal pyramid held betwixt his thumb and pricked index finger, a smile crossed Hamed's face, "You can buy one of these in the museum gift shop. Now I know Cartwright is behind this …."

While pulling himself back onto his feet, a small red droplet bled from the tiny fingertip puncture wound onto the crystalline shape, eliciting a brief luminous blue glow. Shaking his head at the hallucination, he realized the young lady had vanished. "Ms. Sardouck? Yasmine? Are you there?"

Brushing dust from his clothes, Hamed scooted the broken pieces of wooden kitty head and shoulders under the shelf. Picking up the headless sarcophagus still holding the mummified remains, he addressed the relevant deity, "My apologies, Bast. I would have opened this sacred piece with care and finesse." The perplexed man tossed the ruined artifact onto the highest shelf. It landed on its chipped and cracked wooden base like a cat.

Wrapped in well-preserved ancient Egyptian cotton swaths, the feline head protruded from the broken kitty-shaped coffin. Dainty pointed ears twitched in the shadows atop the shelf.

Surprised his new friend was not waiting by the elevator, Hamed pressed the button and turned out the lights. Regardless of whether the tiny treasure in his sweaty hand proved significant to his lifelong cause, he made a resolute promise to thank Yasmine and advise her to seek treatment for whatever it was that ailed her. Or perhaps they would bump elbows in the breakroom and share a private laugh. Who knew?

Hamed's show of gratitude would have to wait. Following the strange incident, he holed up in his one-bedroom flat, spending the following week hell-bent on solving the riddle behind the trinket. Eating and sleeping became secondary pursuits, and his position at the museum hung by a thread.

He witnessed the crystal pyramid alight when he first held it, but nothing since then. Not to mention, he had no clue what it was supposed to do.

A 2:00 a.m. amphetamine and caffeine-fueled epiphany led to a breakthrough. The sharp tip of the crystal shape had pricked his finger under the shelf. Could it be that simple? Grabbing the least dull knife from a messy kitchen drawer, he sliced it into his forefinger, producing a copious amount of blood. Holding his finger above the one-inch crystal pyramid centered on a stack of magazines atop his cheap IKEA coffee table, he dripped syrupy red blood down all four faces. Nothing happened other than his damn finger bled like a stuck pig.

Perched on the edge of his sofa, about to call it quits and go in search of a band-aid, a beam of bright blue light burst from the tiny apex. He vaulted backward in surprise, smashing into the threadbare seatback couch cushions.

Before his addled vision, a detailed wireframe materialized in vivid detail inside the low-lit open space of his spartan apartment. As the familiar structure manifested into view in a complicated maze of glowing blue lines and shapes, he realized he was looking at a three-dimensional blueprint of the Great Pyramid in its original form. Leaning forward, trying to take in everything at once, he stroked his square stubbled jawline, oblivious of his bloodied fingers. Scratching his wiry head of hair with his other hand, he stood up and angled around the volumizing model, noting the pointed top disappeared beyond his paint-chipped ceiling. Looking through the web of blocks locked together in perfect symmetry, his sleep-deprived gaze followed the precise 26-degree angle of the Descending Passage. To his dismay, it disappeared into the stack of archeology journals, sandwiching a vintage issue men's magazine atop his coffee table.

Dropping onto his knees in gray Oxford University sweatpants, Hamed's head and shoulders illuminated as he moved inside the intricate linework. Bending low to peer under the pine table, he watched the Descending Passage continue to the Subterranean Chamber inches above the worn Berber carpeting. At the opposite end of the Chamber, he found the narrow 30-foot tunnel bored into solid rock—the Southern Shaft. The enigmatic tunnel piqued his curiosity through the years. Now, it was viewable in a scaled form, right inside his living room.

"This is interesting, but I could find a 3D pyramid model from a simple Google search."

Hamed contemplated the enigmatic crystal perched on the stack of magazines until five in the morning. "Damn this thing! There must be something more." Out of coffee and patience, his frustration boiled over. He risked picking up the crystal to ensure Made in China was not etched on the bottom.

* * *

In the early-morning hours, within the quiet confines of the apartment below Hamed's rented domicile, the lower sections of the blueprint burst through the ceiling. The ancient beacon's domed chamber and complex tunnel system delineate downward in a brilliant blue ambiance.

Curled atop a worn sofa pillow, a short-hair mutt emits a low growl, watching the strange lights animate downward before stopping a foot off the floor.

The dog's sleepy owner stumbles into his kitchen for a glass of dirty Cairo tap water, catching a fleeting glimpse of the strange lights rising through the ceiling. Standing in the darkened room, the man scratched himself, poured the water down the kitchen sink, and went back to bed.

The dog rested its chin on petite front paws, keeping a wary eye trained on the ceiling.

* * *

Lifting the three-dimensional pyramid diagram proved Hamed's revelatory *Rosetta Stone* moment, staring thunderstruck at myriad tunnels and shafts through solid rock to a beacon chamber constructed by *his* Star People. And, of course, they built the Great Pyramid, too. He was right all along, and now he had the proof.

Hamed discovered that rotating the pyramid in midair scaled the entire projection up and down. Remarkable. Tempted to create an actual size projection from right inside his living room, he sized it to fit within his apartment with plenty of room to spare. More adept at manipulating the blueprint without losing it, he turned the crystal shape over in his hands. Noticing the intensity starting to fade, he coaxed more blood from his sliced fingertip, brightening the virtual representation, "Cheaper than buying batteries."

Perched on his sofa, he studied the reduced version of the pyramid down to the beacon chamber, discovering hand gestures that magnified details too small for the naked eye. Summoning his years of research and knowledge, Hamed enlarged the tunnel at the Subterranean Chamber's south end. Searching the carved space, he looked for clues. Near the end of the shaft, a plot point pulsed on and off: You are here.

Leaning forward, the archeologist widened onto a blinking V-shaped recess. An animated vision sprung to life, showing a four-fingered hand inserting his crystal pyramid, pointy side first, into the keyhole with a quarter-turn. The rock wall at the end of the passage slid aside, revealing the tunnel continuing to the precipice of a bottomless shaft.

Flabbergasted and beyond giddy after his eureka moment, Tarek Hamed finally understood what Yasmine meant by his personal Rosetta Stone: "The crystal is not just a blueprint of the Great Pyramid; it is also the key to unlock a map leading to its real purpose on Earth."

* * *

Flush with a sense of accomplishment, Hamed made his triumphant return to the Cairo Museum as the promise of a new day brightened the eastern horizon. Bounding down the halls in his tailored white suit, searching for his pretty muse, he stumbled across his rotund colleague, Cartwright.

"Cartwright, my friend. Have you seen a young research assistant named Yasmine Sardouk? I have something for her."

Cartwright grabbed Hamed by the white jacket sleeve and pulled him aside, "Tarek, where have you been? The young woman disappeared last week without a trace. Interpol field agents are poking around and asking a lot of questions. Quite a scandal."

"Oh, no. I have been under the weather, my friend," sensing the bullshit meter pinging in Cartwright's fat head, he added, "and the router in my apartment finally bit the dust. I have been in the dark."

"Huh. Really?" On the cusp of continuing to the promise of fresh donuts in the breakroom down the hall, Cartwright wheeled on the stunned Hamed with a conspiratorial look on his pudgy face,

"She started here around the same time you did. Why were you looking for her?"

Tarek Hamed went cold inside, "What? Uh, well, I offered to help her with a research project. No big deal."

Cartwright replied with a suspicious smirk before breaking into a hearty laugh, "Research project? Yeah, sure." Ambling closer to Hamed, in a voice just above a whisper, "By the way, Tarek, it is a good thing you two did not get close. She was also implicated in a theft at the British Museum. She replaced a cat sarcophagus on display with a cheap fake. They have the whole thing on the closed circuit." Cartwright scratches his beard, deep in thought, "There are cemeteries full of those things. What would an attractive young woman with her whole career before her want with a dead cat?"

Sweating bullets on the inside, Hamed forced a laughed reply, "Maybe she was lonely and wanted a pet?"

Cartwright's poker-faced stare flummoxed Hamed before the rotund professor broke into a hearty guffaw and ambled down the hall in search of his morning donut, his bellicose laughter echoing off the walls.

Hamed hurried to his office and locked the door behind him. Thankful his office mate was still on a spelunking expedition in Asia Minor, he collapsed behind his desk and buried his head in his hands. His personal Rosetta Stone refracted morning light across his coffee-stained desk blotter, mocking his concern for the deceased young woman.

Thinking fast, he opened his side drawer and shuffled through the mix of contents. Finding a black velvet pouch containing an airline-sized Scotch, he removed the bottle and placed it on the desk. Next, he dropped the incriminating pyramid inside, buried it in the cluttered drawer, and slid it closed.

After a brief hesitation, Hamed unscrewed the cheap plastic lid from the whisky bottle and downed it in one long pull. Swiping his shirt sleeve across his mouth, a terrifying thought crosses his frontal lobe, "What happened to Yasmine? I bet she is dead." A chill shivered up his spine. "Oh God, it wasn't me, was it?"

* * *

After Professor Tarek Hamed's fateful meeting with the murdered research assistant—her crystal pyramid discovery hidden in a messy desk drawer—his focus morphed into an all-consuming pursuit of the golden ellipse.

His well-paid mole inside The Powers That Be, Greta Thornberry, fed him blow-by-blow accounts of the intensified quest for the missing elliptical power source. She also shared the Earth-shattering reason behind the frantic desperation underlying the search.

Double-checking the veracity of Greta's intelligence through an astronomer employed by the International Outer Space Consortium, Hamed focused on a detailed 3D projection of the beacon's northern face. The stunning ancient alien architecture was indeed in a non-functioning state. "The golden ellipse powers the beacon, which acts like a lighthouse warning ships to stay clear of Earth. Fascinating. I guess this answers Fermi's Paradox."

Examining the empty oval-shaped cradle where the missing power source is supposed to rest, an evil smile crosses his tanned face, "Restoration of the golden ellipse would turn the beacon on again and ward off an apocalypse. Hmm, decisions, decisions."

Professor Tarek Hamed | The Cairo Museum
01:10 a.m. | August 22, 2044 (Back to present time)

Greta's last communique, detailing the bumbling Americans' late-night interrogation and the latest positions of the fast-approaching alien ships, meant his decision time drew near. He alone would save the world or not. His choice. Not theirs.

After reading Greta's last message, Hamed glides open his side drawer, removing the small black velvet satchel cinched closed with a red drawstring. Edging around the desk toward the office door, he grabs his Panama hat and white suit jacket from the rack. Taking one last look around his cramped office, he drops the satchel into an inside jacket pocket. With an anticipatory gap-toothed smile, the archeologist flips the light switch off, closes the office door, and exits the museum.

Nina | Chrysalis Air hangar
01:20 a.m. | August 22, 2044

Inside the glass-enclosed lobby, lit up like broad daylight, the foursome awaits their ride into Cairo at the administrative end of the immense hangar. The three humans try to get comfortable, slumping on ridiculous-looking, ultra-modern furniture with garish pink rectangular cushions. Meanwhile, Louie perches wide awake on the edge of his gleaming, metallic chair, fit as a fiddle with circuitry fine-tuned, software updated, and a new microchip installed in his noggin, compliments of Mr. Kobayashi. Leaning forward, he scrolls through archeology journals on a tablet atop the knee-height glass table.

Rachel looks across at her manmade friend, noting his brand-new clothes. She surmises his wrinkle-free, light-blue polyester shirt, with oversized, buttoned pockets, worn untucked over creased, tan trousers, and no-nonsense, polished, black leather shoes must be standard-issue

Kobayashi robot attire. It is virtually identical to his ensemble from their first meeting atop the parking garage in Toulouse.

Reclining uncomfortably in the ridiculous metal furniture, toned left arm entwined with her somnolent husband's bruised and bandaged arm, Rachel casts a furtive glance at Flynn's lanky form, draped over a chair with his scuffed boots crossed atop the glass coffee table, a new duffel containing the ellipse perched on his lap. She surmises the agent makes himself comfortable in just about any situation—quite a talent.

Time passes at a snail's pace into the early morning hours of August 22. They wait in blessed silence, decompressing. Headlights appear out of the night beyond mirrored group reflections in the floor-to-ceiling window facade. Darkened silhouettes of date palms swaying in the post-rainfall, balmy air greets a jet-black Tesla SUV, pulling to the curb at the end of the sidewalk.

Flynn jumps out of his seat, swatting Owen's leg, "Look alive, you two, our ride is here."

Seconds later, the familiar click-clack of Chanel's heels precedes her arrival in the marble-floored lobby. Looking as fresh as a daisy, she proceeds to the weary group, clutching a brown leather attaché, "This contains your hotel reservations, a stack of Egyptian pounds, and two company cards." With a good-natured chuckle directed at the disheveled couple, "You can't stay at the Ritz Carlton looking like a bunch of vagrants. I added a suitcase with new clothes and toiletries to the rest of your gear in the SUV. I am pretty good at guessing sizes, so you should be fine. However, please put it on the cards if you need anything else."

Owen rubs his eyes, accepting the proffered attaché, "The Ritz Carlton? Well, I guess it will have to do."

Flynn gives Chanel a light kiss on her cheek, "Nina, my love, it has been a pleasure."

Turning on her expensive heels to ponder the agent's usual flair for disarming a tense scene and lightening the mood, "Flynn, one day, a woman is going to come along and make an honest man out of you."

Rachel scrunches her tired and pretty face at Chanel, "Nina? All night long, I never got your name."

"The less known about us, the better, my dear. However, if all goes well, we will meet again." After a brief awkward silence—a tacit acknowledgment of the enormity of the situation—she recovers her upbeat, polished demeanor, "Godspeed."

Rachel watches the woman, who goes by Nina, spin on her red Prada heels to avoid revealing tears welling in her eyes, click-clacking through a side door into the hangar's maze of offices and conference rooms.

Don't spend time beating on a wall,

hoping to transform it into a door.

– Coco Chanel

Chapter Eight:

The Pyramid

Rachel | Nile Ritz Carlton, Cairo, Egypt

02:35 a.m. | August 22, 2044

Wedged into an expanded third-row seat inside the black SUV, Flynn watches the rain-slickened thoroughfare streak past through dark-tinted windows en route to the hotel. His bushy right eyebrow arches at a random thought, *Zero percent is the average summertime precipitation in Cairo*. Perhaps the freakish late-summer rainstorm foreshadowed oddities yet to come.

The young SUV driver cast furtive glances at the strange man in the front passenger seat but refrained from speaking. Peeking at his rearview mirror, he checks the good-looking couple entwined in a somnambulant repose in the second row.

Louie stares out the windshield past the headlights piercing the damp early-morning stillness along the Nile Corniche. Gorgeous vistas of the famous river reflect city lights around every bend along the palm-lined street, passing hotels, restaurants, and high-end retail establishments, hours removed from another day catering to well-heeled patrons.

The SUV hangs a left, bounding up a driveway, and brakes under the porte cochère fronting the Nile Ritz Carlton. Louie compliments the chauffeur, pushes his door wide, and hops from the front passenger seat at the guest drop-off area outside the glitzy hotel's pristine, glass-enclosed front lobby.

A nightshift bellman opens the tailgate, porting filthy daypacks from the vehicle onto a luggage cart alongside a portmanteau containing handpicked clothing for the group, courtesy of Nina.

Rachel swipes a circle in the fogged-up backseat window, taking a gauzy peek at the deserted early morning arrival area in front of the Ritz, nudging her sleeping husband, "Wake up, we're here."

Flynn leans forward from the cramped, third-row seat, "Oh, for fuck's sake, will one of you please get out! I'm suffocating back here."

Owen turns to Rachel with a sleepy smile, "Where have I heard that before?"

Rachel | The Nile Ritz Carlton, Cairo, Egypt
06:39 a.m. | August 22, 2044

The golden ellipse tantalizes Rachel from just beyond her outstretched fingertips. Its brilliance mirrors a sea of licking flames encroaching on Owen's spreadeagle form, languishing atop a polished black surface far below her altered state. The bedlam rattling her troubled mind is punctuated by high-pitched churlish laughter spewing from a round-faced maleficence morphing from a spinning dark cloud above her quaking form.

The horrifying man's bulging eyeballs pop from burnt sockets, stretching on long sinewy fibers snaking around Rachel and violating her space, "Look at me, damn you! Look at me!"

Acquiescing to the petulant monster, she watches his leering eyeballs recoil, hanging loose from the sockets. Pustules ooze and mix with blood and sweat, dribbling down his grotesque, cartoonish face, crackling and sizzling in thick rivulets over burnt, blistered skin. Mortified by his stomach-churning appearance, Rachel vomits and bursts into uncontrollable panicked sobs.

Teetering on insanity, she watches helpless and confused as charred skin peels and flakes up to the man's elbows in tattered strips while he stretches like pulled taffy and grasps the ellipse. With a triumphant laugh, he yanks the oval relic close to his exposed chest and caresses it in his skeletonized hands. "Mine! It is mine!"

Despite her disgust, she watches as he taunts her by flipping the ellipse, animating reflections of swirling fires juxtaposed with huddled masses of humanity suffocating in the throes of death.

Struggling to maintain her tenuous grip on reason and logic, Rachel appeals to the man her assailant was before embodying pure evil, "Harry, why are you doing this to me?"

Swiping at her tear-streaked soot-covered cheeks, she waits for him to speak, but with his prized possession in hand, he no longer wishes to play. Instead, he transmogrifies into a succession of victims from pre-civilizational to failed ellipse looters through the centuries. The final manifestation is a tall, fair-haired man sporting a Gestapo uniform with a bullet hole centered on his forehead. The Nazi spy lingers for a heartbeat before churning into a spiral-shaped blackness coruscating with malicious stars. Rachel watches as it vanishes into the ether.

Abandoned in the netherworld abyss, Rachel realizes the ellipse is also gone. Searching where Owen's prone form lay, she screams in agonizing sadness at the sight of his burnt carcass.

A harrowing future manifests in her psyche of unquenchable fires billowing thick acrid smoke into a cast-iron sky blotted out by armadas of alien ships. Wind-whipped ashen debris scatters across the barren landscape *marking the ignominious end of human civilization.*

A calm disembodied voice speaks over her apocalyptic vision, "This is what the sky will look like."

* * *

"Rachel, wake up!"

Sleep-crusted emerald eyes blink open, focusing on the worried expression across Owen's battered face. Shifting to extricate herself from the knot of luxurious hotel bedding twisted around her form, she heaves a relieved sigh, "I was having a nightmare." Looking sideways at the bright morning view outside the expansive suite's floor-to-ceiling bedroom window, she stretches her lissome body and yawns, "Thanks for waking me up."

"Your voice carried throughout the suite and probably into the hallway. I kind of had no choice. Flynn, Louie, and I woke up and dressed over an hour ago, drinking coffee and hanging in the living room when we heard your screams."

Ignoring his blow-by-blow account—a little embarrassed she subjected the group to her nightmarish shrieks—Rachel switches subjects, "Look at you, Owen Haig! Not the last bloke to wake your ass out of bed. I bet that felt good." Swiping at her red nose, she produces an unintentionally sexy smile, "Nice new duds, by the way."

"Bloke? You've been hanging around Flynn too much." Owen poses in olive-green travel pants with seamless, zipped pockets on both legs, advertised on the hangtag as pickpocket-proof. "To answer your question: Yes, it did." A light-tan Patagonia shirt with the sleeves rolled twice draped at the perfect spot over the pants with a form-fitting black t-shirt tucked underneath. A new pair of Timberland boots complete his ensemble. "Nina did good, don't you think?" He finishes a playful turn before his sleepy wife.

Rachel props upright with one hand holding the sheets and the other scratching her messy bed hair, noting Owen's prizefighter face, bruised arms, and clean-bandaged hands. "You look great, but are you in pain?"

"What? Hell no. I'm fine. Our bed with real sheets and covers did the trick, especially after another sniff of Flynn's magic sleep dust. I was out like a light."

Squirming to adjust her underwear beneath the sheets, "I thought of something. We included Egyptian cotton bedding on our wedding gift registry, and here I am, rolled up in them like a mummy."

"If mummies looked like you, necrophilia would run rampant in these parts."

"Thanks. I think." Unwound from the last corner of bedding, "Now, get out of here, and let me have some privacy.

* * *

Rachel exits the well-appointed suite to join the boys' club downstairs, hatching a plan of attack over breakfast in the Ritz Carlton diner. Heading toward the elevators, she double-checks her room key in a zipped hip pocket in her new traveler khakis. At the end of the opulent hallway, she taps the down button while taking her measure in the full-length mirrored doors. The pants fit perfectly, thanks to Nina's uncanny knack for guessing clothing sizes. The breathable, stretched cotton, narrow leg style suits her figure from hips to toes. Biting her lip, Rachel checks the untucked drape of her dusty-brown soft-linen safari-style shirt with the sleeves rolled at the cuff and the open-collar revealing a hint of a soft pink Lululemon sports bra underneath. Reveling in cleanliness for the first time since leaving France, she could not believe the Saharan sand and grit washed out of her long hair down the shower drain. Flinging brushed and blown, dark-blond tresses across her back from side to side, she loops a golden lock behind her right ear, feeling like she just stepped out of a European shampoo commercial.

The brand-new hikers Nina chose to complete her ensemble were left behind in the shoebox back in the room. The elevators ping open, and Rachel steps into the mirrored space with the scuffed toes of her Chelsea boots peaking below the cuffs of her new pants. They got her this far, and if anyone asked, she could get all Nancy Sinatra on their ass if they pressed too hard on the subject. In reality, she is traveling with two guys and a robot. If they noticed her shoes at all, she would be surprised.

"Ma'am! Can you hold the door, please!"

Rachel taps the door-open button repeatedly, and within seconds, a large, sweaty man vaults into the elevator. Rachel offers a fetching smile toward the older man wearing a sky-blue fanny-pack cinched at the waist of his Bermuda shorts with vintage 35 mm cameras swinging from thick Nikon straps across the front of his tent-sized Hawaiian-style shirt covered in a World War Two airplane motif.

"Thanks kindly. I sure do appreciate it. Some folks around here can be downright rude."

Rachel manages a genial smiled reply, noticing an aircraft on the man's voluminous shirt matches Grandpa Neil's P-47. Coincidence? God only knows. Tamping down anxiety, she recovers her wits, "Full disclosure, I was going for the close button, but I pressed the wrong one."

Silence as the man stares at Rachel's poker-faced expression.

"I'm joking, sir. I would never do that to a fellow American traveler."

The man breathes a relieved sigh, "Woo-wee. You had me going there, little lady. I'm Reverend Earl Warren, but you can call me Earl. I need to get downstairs and meet my better half for breakfast before our tour packs up and leaves without us. That is why I was frantically waving at you from down the hall."

"A tour? Where to?"

"The pyramids. The only way onto the premises these days is with a sanctioned tour group. My wife and I signed up last night. For some darn reason, they are ratcheting way back on the number of visitors and guarding the place like Fort Knox. It's funny, considering it's just a big pile of rocks, but you know what they say, 'When in Rome, do as the Romans do.' Anyway, I think the bus leaves in an hour, and I want to grab a bite here beforehand." He gestures for Rachel to exit first as the doors slide open. "Lord knows what they are selling from those cockroach carts out by the pyramids. Fried scorpions and the like, from what I gather."

"Sounds delightful."

Another long stare.

"Kidding. I'm a kidder, Mr. Warren."

"Nice talking with you, Ma'am. Take care, and God bless!" The hungry man sets off down the wide corridor lined with Egyptian antiquities on loan from the Cairo Museum displayed atop marble pedestals inside glass enclosures. Rachel watches him go, hearing the oversized cameras clanking together across his girth as he trundles toward the main lobby and the dining area beyond.

"Mr. Warren? Can I ask you a quick question?"

Pausing adjacent to a display containing a wood-carved feline sarcophagus dating from the Fourth Dynasty, he turns, half-expectant of another query from the polite and attractive young woman, "Yes, ma'am?"

"Is there room for a few more people in your group?"

* * *

Owen spots Rachel and waves her to their window table on the far side of the bustling dining area overlooking the traffic-clogged thoroughfare and the Nile River beyond.

Acknowledging his wave, Rachel is distracted by billowing sails from boats floating up and down the Nile. It is a bright and sunny Egyptian morning outside the climate-controlled establishment; however, inside Rachel's head, Mr. Warren's off-handed Fort Knox comment regarding enhanced security at the pyramids echoes as she angles past tables toward her group.

Agent Flynn stands from his continental breakfast and watches the young woman navigate the tight table layout, drawing the usual glances. He muses it is like meeting the American woman for the first time, minus layers of dust, dirt, bug bites, knotted hair, torn clothing, and unbrushed teeth.

She accepts the proffered seat, courtesy of Owen, and flashes a pearly-white smile, "Good morning, everyone. How did we all sleep last night?"

Flynn is about to voice a carefully worded compliment, but Owen interrupts, "What happened with the new boots Nina picked out?"

"Owen, you never cease to surprise the shit out of me. No. I just wanted something of my own to go with Nina's breaching-the-pyramid-to-save-humanity outfit."

Oblivious to her intentional snark factor, Louie chimes in, "Good call, Madame. Nothing beats a well-worn pair of shoes."

Seated across from the stunning beauty beside her well-built husband, Flynn shelves his attempted compliment altogether, blurting out instead, "I hope the amenities are to your liking."

Rachel nods with faux seriousness, "Yes, sir. The room is fine."

After a pregnant pause, she laughs, "Lighten up, Flynn. You clean up nice, yourself. I'm glad to see you in something other than leather biker wear."

The agent glances down at his untucked safari-style shirt and khakis, which take the hidden pocket routine to another level, "It's a little warm out for the leather jacket. However, I had to jettison a few items I hope we won't need."

"Okay, let's agree we are the cool kids table." Taking a sip from the freshly poured cup of black coffee placed before her, Rachel leans back with an over-animated orgasmic moan. "Oh, man! No offense to your jacket coffee, Flynn, but this is the best coffee I have ever tasted."

Blowing steam from her cup, she searches the dining area, "See that man in the Hawaiian shirt over there? I met him in the elevator. He told me we must sign up for a tour to get anywhere near the pyramids."

Owen swipes his last corner of burnt toast through bright yellow yolk along the rim of his plate, "Huh."

Flynn stuffs a last bite of Danish into his mouth, washing it down with a swig from his cup, "That's not a bad idea."

Rachel steals a slice of cantaloupe from Owen's plate, "I'm glad you think so because we are leaving with his tour group in thirty minutes."

Rachel | The Nile Ritz Carlton, Cairo, Egypt
09:30 a.m. | August 22, 2044

Pushy foreigners, traffic jams, and an overbearing bureaucracy favoring the only game in town, tourism, are the legacy of an impoverished modern-day Cairo populace in 2044. The pittance garnered from a litany of unfulfilling tourist-focused service industry jobs only aggravates resentments. Dirt-poor locals look askance at wealthy foreigners who willingly abandon posh establishments, like the Ritz, to gawk at ancient piles of rocks and crumbling statues under the North African heat on a desolate plateau. Most Egyptians curse their antiquated past and despise outsiders for their passionate interest and curiosity. The Ptolemy Dynasty and the Egyptian Empire ended with a snake-bitten Cleopatra over two millennia ago. For the vast majority, it's been nothing but a colossal pain in the ass ever since.

* * *

Evidence of the previous night's rainfall evaporated into the oppressive Cairo morning air as the diverse assemblage of tourists turned wannabe Egyptologists board the electric motor coach under the Ritz

Carlton porte cochère.

"No turning back now." Rachel takes her turn, stepping up and into the air-conditioned bus, flashing a nervous smile toward the hairy bus driver, who returns her smile with a curious recognition.

* * *

With a busload of eager visitors seated and ready, the gruff driver pauses to type a cryptic message to a mysterious benefactor waiting at the opposite end of the route. With the message sent, he tucks the device into his shirt pocket, anticipating the windfall bonus awaiting him for just doing his stupid job. Still grinning, he checks a side mirror and wheels the bus onto the Nile Corniche, merging with a conga line of cars, trucks, coaches, and bikes of every kind.

* * *

Quelling anxiety by taking a mental roll call of her fellow tourists on the bus, Rachel starts with Reverend Earl and his lovely wife, Mabel, with her crimson pageboy swaying to the start and stop movements in the first row. A boisterous Spanish clan, including grandparents, parental types, and unruly children, occupy the next five rows. Rachel glances past Owen toward their cohorts, seated across her narrow aisle. Flynn appears bored, though his gears are no doubt turning. Louie stares outside from the window seat, taking in the passing scene. She hears more than sees the exuberant Korean contingent over the high seatbacks filling the remaining rows to the back of the well-appointed motorcoach. To paraphrase Owen's comment while waiting to board, "Yep, it's a good group."

The pyramids loom in the hazy brightness outside her tinted bus window. "Are we really doing this?"

"Try to relax. I have a good feeling about this." Owen balances a dark-green Fjallraven daypack like a newborn baby on his lap. The high-end bag contains water bottles, a Swiss Army knife, hand towels courtesy of the Ritz, the cheap plastic souvenir flashlight from the old Jeep's glove box, and one golden ellipse. Tugging the sales tag still cinched to a zippered side pocket, he turns to his partner in life, "Should we leave the tag attached? We might decide to return it after we're through here."

"Sometimes, I wish you would just be serious."

Bouncing the bag on his lap, "Well, excuse me for projecting beyond the next few hours."

Romanticized notions of traversing windswept dunes and exotic oases en route to the last remaining wonder of the world vanish like a mirage in short order. The view outside the elevated bus windows is an encroaching sea of humanity surrounding the Giza Plateau, complete with honking vehicles of every kind, tenements, run-down businesses, souvenir stands, tourist-trap museums, and sidewalk chefs peddling local comestibles from greasy carts.

Rachel sees a street vendor below her high window. "I wonder if he has fried scorpions in his cart?" The man's leathery countenance locks onto her green eyes for an unsettling moment before the bus lurches forward, leaving the toothless fellow coughing in a reddish cloud of fine dust.

Successfully navigating another tedious day's route, the driver makes a sweeping right turn onto the well-maintained, four-lane boulevard leading to the massive pyramid complex and pulls into the first of a long row of bus-sized parking spots. An EV transport carrying bribed security and a man in a white suit pulls aside the bus like pirates preparing to hijack a cargo ship. The bus driver flings the door open, allowing the Egyptian in the tailored white suit and thin black tie to hop aboard and move down the narrow aisle. An imposing guard ducks into the bus in his wake, blocking the exit.

Removal of his Panama hat reveals coarse, charcoal hair, while his deep-tan countenance, dominated by an impressive mustache, swivels left and right down the aisles. The second coming of Omar Sharif pauses at Owen's row, declaring in an authoritative English accent, "Today, we are not allowing purses, backpacks, or bags of any kind on the premises. Water is available throughout your tour, so there is no need to bring it with you. Pat-downs and inspections of cameras and electronic devices will be carried out by my colleagues as you exit the bus. If you have contraband, leave it behind or risk confiscation."

Earl's wife confronts the dark and handsome man in the sparkling white suit, expressing what everyone on the bus thinks: "We paid for our tickets, and nobody mentioned your so-called no-bag policy."

Returning to the front of the bus, he addresses the plucky lady from Plano, Texas, "Madame, I am just the messenger."

Everyone hears Earl attempting to defuse his wife's resistance, "Don't you worry, Mabel. We'll be fine and dandy as long as we can take our cameras. This feller in the fancy white suit is just doing his job."

The plucky Texan banter draws a scattering of nervous laughter from the disembarking bagless tourists as Owen looks from the invasive pat-downs administered by ham-fisted muscle to the mission-critical daypack on his lap, "Now what?"

Flynn leans across the aisle, "Owen, leave the bag; I'll take it from here." The foursome exits the bus, abandoning the golden ellipse in the daypack propped on Rachel's vacated window seat.

Exiting the air-conditioned bus into the heat, everyone traverses the vacant parking lot toward a rope-lined path where a raven-haired female tour guide waits.

From the tail-end of the group, a nervous Owen makes an over-the-shoulder check of their bus, "What happened to Flynn?"

Louie scans the sweltering environs, "He'll catch up."

Earl and Mabel allow the bulk of the tour group to move around them, snapping pictures of each other with the Great Pyramid of Giza piercing the cloudless azure morning sky behind their smiling faces.

Rachel pauses and turns on an impulse toward the cute older couple, "Would you like me to take a picture of both of you together?"

Mabel beams from ear to ear, "Why, that is so nice of you, dear. Isn't that nice, Earl? What a pretty young thing you are, too."

Rachel acquaints herself with the bulky antique digital camera's LED viewfinder. Composing the couple in strategic alignment with the pyramid, she snaps smiling portraits between sneezes, eye blinks, goofy grins, and one swat at a large fly atop Earl's bald head. Passing the heavy camera back to the Texan, "I think there are a few good ones to share with your family back home."

Earl shields the camera's LED with a pudgy hand and checks the previews on his camera's backside. Swiping his brow in the heat, "You did just fine, Miss Rachel." Gesturing at the massive Giza pyramid, "This is the bucket list trip of a lifetime for us, so thank you kindly."

"No problem. Can you believe I neglected to bring a camera?"

"Say it 'ain't so, little lady! Get your new husband over here! We'll take a nice picture and message it to you. Or put it on a drive at the hotel. Whichever is more convenient."

"Owen! Come over here."

Approaching the beaming, happy faces, Owen mutters, "Rachel, we are supposed to be saving the world."

Louie stays by the tour group, on the lookout for Flynn.

Earl motions for the couple to pose and smile for the camera, capturing 42 high-resolution images of the happy couple.

"Thank you, Mr. Warren. Have fun today. I know we will." Rachel and Owen retrace their steps along the pathway toward Louie, arms crossed with a bemused look on his face.

"Okay, we can work out how to get these your way later, I suppose." The burly Texan squints in the bright sun, checking previews of the smiling couple on the camera's two-inch LED screen.

Mabel smooths her copper-red hair in the stiff breeze, watching the handsome, athletic couple stride along the pathway toward the group. The young lovers elicit wistful recollections of life before artificial hips and knees became her reality. She breaks from the rumination to light a fire under her shutterbug of a husband, still fiddling around with his damn camera.

Earl's brow furrows, hunched over to shield his camera viewscreen from the brightness, "Damn! There it is again." He notices a dark cloud with bright specks of light hovering above the beaming newlywed couple, marring the last 20 photos. "What the tarnation is that?"

Blowing dust from the lens, he grumbles a phrase a man of the cloth should not say.

"Earl! I heard that. Stop fooling with your cameras. We're missing the tour guide's talk."

"For Pete's sake, Mabel, it's not as if the world will end if we miss something."

* * *

Ignoring the rehearsed spiel from Cassandra, the loquacious tour guide, Owen shifts from foot to foot at the rear of the gathered tour group, hoping to spot the missing Agent Flynn. Checking toward the lot, he watches a line of newly arrived buses angle into spots, obscuring their coach from view. "It is about to get much more crowded, which should help our situation. Right, Rachel?"

Rachel nods in the affirmative, but Owen perceives her mind is off in another world, "Do you want to make out right here in front of all of these people?"

"Sure, Owen, whatever you say."

"I thought so." Owen turns to advise Louie he was only making a point, but it proves unnecessary. The robot is too engrossed in the guide's lengthy introduction to hear Owen's small talk, engaged in his pre-planned role of inquisitive tourist. Standing betwixt his unresponsive wife and the distracted robot, the frustrated banker wipes his brow, cursing under his breath.

Louie abandons his cohorts without preamble, shouldering his way to the front of their group, feigning interest in the deluge of ancient Egyptian trivia as he pushes forward. The humorless bucket of bolts even manages a hearty chuckle at the guide's cornball King Tut joke.

"You know what, Rachel, I think our guy is enjoying this."

Rachel nods again, "Sure, Owen, whatever you say." With a mischievous smile, she turns to her partner in crime, "And this is no time for a snog."

"Snog?"

The sexy blond throws caution to the wind, leaning into Owen for a long, passionate kiss.

"Oh, yeah."

The public display of affection simultaneously quells Owen's apprehension and Rachel's distracted focus.

"Our guide has droned on for fifteen minutes now."

"I think she is filibustering to allow those arriving busloads time to get to their starting areas, so all the tour groups commence in unison. At the hotel, Reverend Earl told me the heightened security started in 2028 when a terrorist destroyed half the sphinx. It is a wonder they allow people up here at all."

"They have no choice. It is the only game in town. I understand the Egyptians' heightened security measures, but arbitrary rules like no backpack day would make the TSA blush." He scans the vista, noting an armed military presence bolsters the private security stationed across the ancient plateau. "We should have scouted the site before jumping in with both feet. I don't see how we can extricate ourselves from the rest of our group. And we left the ellipse on the bus. And armed security watches our every move. Otherwise, this is going swell."

"Have faith, my dear. Louie is doing his part. Once Flynn shows up with the ellipse, things will fall in place."

Owen smiles at his beautiful wife's optimism, casting her gaze up the pyramid with lovely hands cupped together, shielding her eyes from the intense sunshine. Contemplating her use of the word, dear, he wonders if that nickname will stick. Married life is indeed a mysterious journey.

The new husband drops his random musing, spying Flynn's form materializing out of the midday glare. "There he is. It's about damn time."

They watch the agent navigate a sea of pint-sized schoolchildren exiting buses in uniforms and marching across the blazing lot to the cadence of teachers and chaperones cajoling the pupils into some semblance of orderly lines. To Owen, the scene appeared as it usually did, like herding cats.

Rachel can't resist a smile, "Aww, look at the cute children! Can you imagine taking a field trip to a place like this when you were in grade school?"

"In third grade, my class visited a dairy farm. It's why I won't touch cottage cheese to this day."

Viewing the spectacle from afar, the linear columns proceeding uphill toward waiting tour guides resembles a Napoleonic reenactment of capturing the pyramids. Owen makes eye contact with their colleague, who gives a thumbs-up, quickening his pace after bisecting the last prepubescent queue.

Flynn joins his co-conspirators as the tour proceeds through a tall wire gate along a well-trod path rising above the sweltering parking lots toward the Great Pyramid of Giza, dominating the plateau.

Owen squints through his new shades, noting it is far more impressive than pictures could ever convey and much larger than the Khafre structure looming in the background to the west.

Flynn produces a discarded school permission form folded in half, containing the golden ellipse, and backhands it to Owen, "Zip this into your pickpocket-proof pants."

"My Mom already signed my permission slip."

"Bloody hell, Owen, just fucking do it."

"Should I even ask how you managed to get the ellipse past

Omar Sharif and his bodyguards on the bus?"

"That Egyptian bloke is not even part of the security here on the plateau. His name is Tarek Hamed. He is an adjunct professor of archeology at the Cairo Egyptian Museum." Flynn can't suppress a quick laugh, "He had ZERO authority to make everyone leave their bags on the bus. People never question authority figures in suits and ties, especially when traveling abroad. He was looking for something."

Owen's eyes widen, "Do you think he was after the ellipse?"

"The only thing I know for sure is the wanker, and his two mates will be a bit dizzy after coming a cropper in the back of the bus. Hopefully, this will all be over by then."

Rachel's ears perk up, listening to the conversation as they meander up the path toward the northwest corner of the pyramid, multiple paces behind their group, "What will the sky look like if we succeed?"

Her non-sequitur raises eyebrows in unison, but neither of her colleagues has a satisfactory answer or a witticism.

Flynn is the first to break the silence, "Are you all right, Rachel?"

Owen puts a sweaty hand on Flynn's shoulder, "You should know by now, 'Are you all right, Rachel?' is my line. When this is over, I'm having it screen-printed on a t-shirt."

"Sorry, man. No offense."

Owen gives Flynn his best "I was only joking." smile while admonishing Rachel with a gentle, "Let's try to keep this from becoming weirder than it already is, okay?"

* * *

A hot wind whips through the barren expanse between the Khufu and Khafre pyramids. Earl and Mabel, the boisterous Spanish clan, and the Korean contingent shuffle to the first point of interest at the Great Pyramid's northwest corner. The guide raises her voice over the gusts, answering questions, as everyone fans out in smaller groups to take pictures and selfies, mainly selfies.

Louie sticks to the guide like glue.

Scanning the marked pathway along the pyramid's westerly side, paralleling a narrow, paved access road, Owen hopes Rachel's imminent revelation—coming any minute now—is reachable from somewhere along their route. He frowns at the English translation on a directional sign pointing to something called the Western Cemetery. How fitting. Their whole plan hinges on an apparition's cryptic direction for his new wife to follow her instincts and trust no one. So far, she has come up empty, and they put their trust in a wonky robot and a snarky secret agent. Their group was still within easy eyeshot of the parking lots lined with tour buses. "Rachel, anything?"

Already sweating through her Nina-curated ensemble, Rachel wipes her brow, "You'll be the first to know." So much for fresh and clean. An open-air electric tram filled with schoolchildren bumps past their position down the access road. A young girl wearing a bright blue school uniform catches her gaze with a subtle wave.

* * *

Masking annoyance at his companions' cheeky repartee while his gut instinct compels him to do something—anything, Flynn regrets his acquiescence to their hasty plan, realizing the world's fate lies in the hands of this unlikely duo, flying by the seats of their well-defined pants. Louie plays his part, peppering the bookish tour guide with questions as she holds her own against the walking encyclopedia's limitless knowledge.

Their fellow tourists spread out, wielding cameras and smart devices with varying degrees of proficiency, recording ultra-high-definition images along the pyramid's northwest corner under Cassandra's watchful gaze, braced against the stiff breeze like a Bedouin herder.

Flynn nudges Owen, "Bloody hell. More armed guards." The

pair watch an electric cart pull to a stop, and two Egyptian soldiers hop out, slinging rifles over their shoulders, taking positions at the back end of the slow-moving group.

"Your people didn't warn us the security here is off the charts."

"It's not usually this intense. Maybe the Egyptians got a tip; something else is going down."

Owen realizes the senior guard's suspicious gaze is already firmly fixed on himself and his companions, visibly removed from the rest of their tour group.

"How are we going shake these guys? The older fellow is looking right at us."

Captain Mohammed Faisel | Great Pyramid, Giza Plateau
11:15 a.m. | August 22, 2044

Captain Mohammed Faisel's foul mood started well before hopping out of the electric cart at the Great Pyramid's northwest corner. The prospect of babysitting a bunch of gawking foreigners and schoolchildren darkens the grizzled military veteran's demeanor. Watching his wet-behind-the-ears deputy fumble his rifle while exiting the cart, the captain wonders who he pissed off to garner this disrespect. Rousting social media miscreants and terrorist wannabes hardly required his experience and stature. It had been years since the last serious incident, yet here he was, guarding the old pile of rocks against the whims of disrespectful tourists. What's next, crossing guard duty?

Right off the bat, the Egyptian Army captain zeroes in on the Western trio, lagging well behind their assigned group. His anti-terror training and body language expertise inform him they are trouble, so he points them out to his clueless partner. The gap widens between the trio and the bratty, unattended Spanish children bent on throwing rocks and horsing around.

The monotonous shift is off to a bad start. With an irritated sigh, Faisel places a dark brown hand atop his holstered sidearm while stepping toward the malingering Westerners, "Come on. Come on. You must keep up with your group, or I will escort you from the premises."

His command is interrupted by an ear-piercing scream echoing off the massive limestone blocks across the ancient plateau. He turns and sees the bloody aftermath—chaos reigns.

Flynn | Great Pyramid, Giza Plateau
11:15 a.m. | August 22, 2044

Covering her ears, "What is that horrible noise?" Rachel scans the tour group looking for the ear-splitting source.

Flynn produces a devilish grin, seeing one of the misbehaving boys from the large Spanish family hit his brother in the head with a rock. "Ever hear the story of Cain and Abel?"

The guards' attention veers toward the raucous domestic dispute. Owen nudges Rachel as the boy's father—a living manifestation of Pinocchio's Mangiafuoco—booms a Castilian tirade at his unruly progenies. The enraged man pushes aside gawking Korean shutterbugs snapping viral images of his screaming kid. Grabbing the injured boy—bleeding like a stuck pig—and giggling sibling by their skinny arms, he scowls at the looky-loos. Seconds later, the family matriarch arrives on the scene, pleading with her husband to show mercy.

Owen looks at the ridiculous drama before them, "Man, I wish this had subtitles."

Flynn smiles, "Sometimes it is better to be lucky than good."

* * *

Captain Faisel raises his voice to quell the wailing family chaos, subduing the father's tirade, the mother's operatic pleas, and the blood-smeared boy's pathetic whines. With order restored, he commands his deputy to round up the Spanish clan and escort them to the urgent care facility inside the main offices.

The younger soldier herds the yelling and cursing family toward the main lot and the administrative offices beyond. The veteran officer engages in a nose-to-nose argument with the livid father, like a baseball manager arguing balls and strikes with the home plate umpire.

In the escalating commotion, the trio escapes notice, backpedaling toward the northwest corner of the pyramid.

***

Louie, Cassandra, and the Koreans spectate toward the disturbance midway down the pyramid's western face with apathetic amusement.

Louie turns to Cassandra, "It is my experience some people are more accustomed to armed guards dictating their daily lives than others."

The tour guide peers over her tortoiseshell sunglasses, studying the strange man with an unlit cigarette held at a jaunty angle under a meticulously maintained mustache. "What are you doing later?"

Louie's left eyebrow raises, and a twitch of a smile cracks his inscrutable countenance.

***

Flynn monitors the distracted senior guard's heated conversation with the Spanish patriarch fifty paces down the western side as the deputy corrals the Spaniards into a manageable group. "Okay, I'm calling an audible. You lot need time alone without the pyramid cops watching your every move. When I give the signal, take off around the northern face and try not to get caught." Recognizing the fortuitous distraction could end at any moment, "Now! Run!"

After a quick fist bump, Owen and Rachel sprint along the

base level of limestone and disappear around the northern side as Flynn hoists his six-foot frame atop a block of stone and awaits the predictable attention.

* * *

Howls, cries, and laughter fade down the access road as the junior guard escorts the Spanish family toward the parking lot. Grumbling under his breath, Faisel resumes babysitting the remaining tour group, especially the three Westerners.

Previous interactions with Americans informed him their sole interest in the ancient structures was performing a hair-brained stunt and posting it on social media. Not on his watch. Peering down the path, he huffs, noting the tour leader had moved on without him. A breach in protocol he would address with her later. But where were the troublemakers? Looking up the western face, he spies one of the men, four layers up the pyramid's side, flaunting marked restrictions. The audacity of these damnable foreigners! Eyes bug out of Faisel's weathered face, and metaphorical steam shoots from his ears. "Come down at once! You are under arrest for trespassing!"

The strapping black fellow's shit-eating grin exacerbates the captain's rage, feigning ignorance with an infuriating, "Who? Me?"

Rachel | Great Pyramid, Giza Plateau
12:05 p.m. | August 22, 2044

Hunkering along the northern side, the couple watches the humorless guard frog-marching Flynn toward the sun-bleached ticket and administrative offices away from their precarious, exposed position.

"They arrested Agent Flynn."

Owen wipes his brow, "Between the Spaniards and Flynn, it will be a busy day at the Giza security office."

Rachel taps her husband's shoulder, "What now?"

"We can't stay here. We are just a wee bit conspicuous."

Owen turns and sees the look of fear and frustration on Rachel's face verging on tears. "Hey. Don't do that. We'll be fine."

"I'm sorry, Owen. I thought just being here would reveal the next step in my mind, but nothing is happening, and I am starting to lose faith." She removes stylish shades, courtesy of Nina, dabbing her eyes with her sleeve and heaving a huge sigh.

"Okay, let's not panic; we're so close. Let's go farther along the north side and see what happens. The more I think about it, we never had a plan. Things just fall in place." His pep talk is cut short, "Shit. Maybe we are screwed. Here comes another soldier."

Owen and Rachel freeze, watching the oblivious young man in an ill-fitting uniform amble toward them, rifle slung over his shoulder. "Did you bring your camera?"

"The one you made me promise to leave behind?"

"Yeah, Owen. That one. Take it out. It's time for a little photoshoot." Rachel scrambles atop the pyramid's base level, surprised by her agility, and assumes what she hopes is an eye-catching pose. Unbuttoning her blouse to reveal more skin, she flings her thick blond hair and lets out a playful, "I'm ready, Mr. DeMille." drawing the boy's lascivious stare. Predictable. Assuming the personae of a self-absorbed, attention-starved social media model, she beams toward her husband, ignoring the guard's approach.

"Just a second, Snookums." Owen winces at his ham-fisted, improvised reply. Swollen hands fumble past the generic family picture tucked in his new Velcro wallet to access his credit card hi-def camera.

Pressing the bottom right corner of the thin camera, Owen captures random images, not checking if Rachel is even within the frame while glancing up the northern side of the Great Pyramid. "Of course. That is our way inside." Targeting the robbers entrance six levels up the face, he turns to address the young guard with an innocent smile.

The guard's disheveled appearance invokes none of the stern authority directed their way by the earlier guard. The ill-fitting uniform hangs off his narrow frame, dragging in the sand and dirt. Nonetheless, the young lad overcomes his physical limitations with a loud and threatening, "What is going on here? Miss, you must come down at once. You are not allowed in this area. Where is your tour leader?"

In a wide stance atop the limestone block with her hands on her hips, Rachel felt more like a cosplay Wonder Woman than a viral supermodel looking down at the flummoxed young man with an effervescent pouty smile, mimicking sexualized poses littering the internet. "Oh, please, sir. I promised my followers I would post new pictures posing on this big pyramid."

Spectating on his wife's alluring performance, Owen suppresses a smile, wanting to tell the young guy, "Now you know what I have to deal with." Instead, he pats the guard on the back, "What do you say, pal?"

The guard glances left and right before offering a conspiratorial, "Five minutes. No longer. I am serious."

"Thanks, man. We owe you one." Thinking fast, he turns to the little fellow, "Hey, I know. Would you like a picture with my foxy friend up there?"

The guard's smooth, olive-skin face breaks into a sheepish, crooked-toothed smile. "Well, maybe just one."

Rachel chimes in, "Yeah! Come on up here, handsome!"

Unable to resist the flirtatious couple, the guard stands next to the vivacious American woman before he knows what hit him. Sensing the lady's long arm draped across his shoulder within reach of his rifle, he stares toward the annoying photographer snapping a series of compromising photos, a bewildered look on his peach fuzz face.

Positioned half a step behind the short kid, Rachel wonders where this is going. Pulling herself together, she gives Owen a quizzical look.

Gesturing toward the shaded opening, Owen proofers his wife a wink, as in follow my lead. "We need one more set of pictures. Hey, I know. How about higher up so we can get a better view. We'll make you famous, my friend!"

"I don't know …."

In the blink of the guard's beady eyes, the attractive couple bookends the kid, towering over his short frame.

Cluing into Owen's plan, Rachel nudges the kid's shoulder, jostling his rifle, "Hey, I know. Let's check out that opening up over there."

Owen heaves a relieved smile, "What a great idea! Come with us!"

The young man's naivete vanishes, pushing away from the couple and brandishing a Beretta M9 pistol aimed between Owen's eyes. Taking a cautious step backward, "No one is allowed to climb the pyramids, especially Westerners. Climb down. Now."

Owen raises his hands, like in the movies, "Easy there, young man. You do realize the fate of the world is at stake here."

"That's a new one. Move it, or I will blow your brains all over the side of this pyramid."

"We better do as he says, Owen."

"Yeah, I guess …." In a singular motion, Owen's left hand comes up, redirecting the pistol beyond his right side, and twisting up and around the guard's scrawny arm, he slides the heavy sidearm out of the boy's sweaty grasp.

"Krav Maga. Learn it. Live it. Love it. I don't want to hurt you, kid, but the missus and I don't have time to play army with you. We are heading to that hole in the wall, and you will stand guard right here and tell your boss you never saw us. If you don't, I will show him the pictures I took of you standing on top of this rock in full Egyptian army uniform next to my attractive wife."

"You are bluffing." He thinks for a moment, "and under arrest!"

Rachel sidles close to her husband, ignoring the obstinate little guy, peering through the midday glare, "Nothing about that hole in the rocks is calling out to me, but I'm getting desperate, so let's go."

"That's the spirit, Rachel. Plus, we are on borrowed time loitering out here in the open."

Watching the back and forth, the guard cups his right hand above his eyes and peers toward the point of interest, "That is the robbers entrance." With a reluctant sigh, "I will help you enter the pyramid."

Rachel turns toward the skinny kid, "What was that? You will?"

"Yes. But we must hurry."

The guard reacquires his sidearm from a dumbstruck Owen, scampering across the Great Pyramid's northern base. The surprised couple follows, perplexed and amused by the guard's shifting behavior: from wet-behind-the-ears recruit to gun-wielding soldier to whatever this is. The trio pauses below the robbers entrance, slightly askew from the pyramid's centerline. Without explanation, the agile Egyptian climbs six rows of limestone blocks with unsettling ease, standing athwart the shadowed orifice.

Owen turns to Rachel with a smile, "I know what you are thinking, but that was hardly the strangest thing we have witnessed in recent days."

Rachel fails to see the humor, "True, but I have never seen anyone who could climb like that." Shaking her head, acknowledging her optimistic husband, she glances up at the daunting levels of blocks. "Let's get up there before he changes his mind."

Climbing the layers of blocks, Owen holds out his hand and pulls his better half onto the carved limestone purchase fronting the jagged fissure bored out by eighth-century Arabs. Peering beyond the hunched kid, Owen is relieved to see a human-sized, easily navigable entrance; however, his eyes adjust to the dark shadows and make out a medieval-looking wrought iron gate recessed five feet into the blocks. Cursing to himself, Owen angles around the kid to inspect the rust-covered obstruction with chicken wiring snaking in and out of the slats holding a weathered multi-language sign: KEEP OUT.

Tugging the industrial-sized padlock, he slams it back against the chipped metal frame wedged in place and torqued into the rock with thick hexagonal bolts. "Shit! I knew it!"

"Knew what?"

"This damn thing is locked up tighter than Fort Knox."

The guard taps Owen on the shoulder with a surprised look distorting his odd features, "Entering the pyramids is against the law. Only official visits by academics and researchers are permitted. Even they have to apply months in advance. I thought that was common knowledge. Didn't you listen to your tour guide when you arrived?"

Owen cannot tear his gaze from the imposing lock. "What? No. Not really."

Rachel chimes in, "We were under the impression there might be another way inside, but it looks like my guide took the day off."

The kid scoots past Owen and grasps the heavy padlock from the latch, "It is not a problem; I have a key."

"Really? They hand out keys to low-level security guards?"

Rachel places her hand on Owen's shoulder and glances down from their position, ensuring they are still alone, "Owen, be nice, remember?"

"It's okay, Miss. To answer your question, Mr. Owen, I won it in a game of chance."

Despite the heat, a chill goes down Owen's spine. Baffled by the young man's unexpected reply, "Owen is fine, thanks."

"As you wish." Digging into a deep pocket in his oversized uniform shirt, the guard produces a metal key dangling from a gnarled ring with a devilish grin on his goofy face.

Owen | Robbers Entrance, Great Pyramid
12:55 p.m. | August 22, 2044

Opening the padlock proved only half the battle. The bent gate's bottom edge ground into the limestone a few inches from the frame, allowing it to open just wide enough for the svelte couple, led by their skinny co-conspirator, to squeeze past into the jagged tunnel.

Owen is the last one inside the claustrophobic space, sucking in his gut while scraping past the rusty metal gate to avoid ripping his shirt. "Phew! I almost didn't fit; I need to cut back on dessert." Without checking on the others, he grinds the slatted obstruction closed with an abrasive clank.

Pausing for one last breath of fresh air, Owen admires the blue Egyptian sky beyond the craggy opening, "Tight spaces are not my strong suit, but here it goes." Ducking to avoid banging his head against the rough-cut interior passage, he is startled by the darkness before realizing he is still wearing his shades. Tamping down his anxiety, he tucks a post into his open collar and surveys the dusty passage, finding a battered old lantern dangling from a wooden support beam. Bent and rusted metal signage half-screwed into the limestone and busted fixtures lay scattered about the Seventh Wonder of the World that used to welcome tourists, signed waivers in hand.

Sliding past a chiseled outcropping, Owen peers into the inky blackness, expecting to see Rachel and their new friend. Neither is within sight of his hunched, wide-legged stance, setting off alarm bells in his head. Venturing into the darkness, his head bumps against the low ceiling. Rubbing the knot on his scalp, his voice echoes off the narrow walls, "Rachel? Hold up, dammit! Let's stick together."

No reply.

Stumbling through the bored-out passage, Owen probes forward with his outstretched hands expecting to goose his beautiful wife, or the guard, at any moment while lamenting that they never bothered to read a detailed description of the Great Pyramid. Why bother? Rachel was supposed to have her Giza Plateau epiphany and lead the way. "Man, that was stupid."

Perceiving a leftward turn after too many paces through the tunnel to count, his hand brushes against a smooth cylindrical metal railing. Grasping the solid shape in the dark, he inches forward and hears shuffling noises mere feet ahead of his position.

"Owen."

"There you are! Jesus, Rachel. Don't scare me like that. Why did you ...."

"Owen, please."

"Rachel, I'm such an idiot! The flashlight from the Jeep was in my pocket this whole time!" With distractions at every turn, he forgot he had it until now. "Hang on, just a second. Boy, you had me worried."

Extricating the light from his pants, he fumbles for the switch and flips it on. The tight beam darts around the expanse before illuminating Rachel, splayed on her back, her arms and legs pinned out from her torso against a chiseled staircase.

Above and behind her battered head is the roughened aperture where Arabs broke through and discovered the Ascending Passage hundreds of years before.

Startled by the love of his life's vulnerable position, Owen widens the beam onto a shrouded entity, teeming with familiar-looking specks, restraining her immobilized form. A horrifying bony hand reaches down, grasping Rachel's neck with a palpable lasciviousness. Owen hears the being's evil whiny chortling mix with her terrified sobs.

Rachel struggles to free her left leg for a fleeting moment before a heavy boot crushes her thigh into the limestone step.

Stunned beyond measure, caught completely flat-footed by the paranormal spectacle, Owen swallows hard to calm himself and modulates his voice to an even tone. "Rachel, how bad are you hurt?"

"Owen, the security guard, had one more surprise for us, after all."

"So, I see." Masking his dreaded fear, Owen summons as much authority as he can project, "Let her go, and then we can talk."

For a brief moment, a hideous human face appears from under a shrouded hood, rasping a screechy reply, "Owen, I'm hurt that you don't know who I am?"

Rachel lets out a defeated sob.

"You are Harry Stark."

"Bingo. Give this man a cigar."

"No, thanks, just Rachel will be fine."

Harry's triumphant cackle pierces the stifling air over Rachel's blond head to Owen's flat-footed, off-kilter stance inside the suffocating passage. "I suppose you are both owed my eternal gratitude for transporting the golden ellipse to its place of origin at the end of days. Hand it to me, and you and Miss Alexander can leave in peace to fend for yourselves from the shitstorm heading toward Earth as we speak."

"I cannot do that, and you know it."

"Time is of the essence. Give me the ellipse. I refuse to argue with you."

* * *

Rachel endures the tense stand-off, rendered mute by the strange force who went from the hapless recruit to a terrifying monster in the blink of an eye. The temperature inside the pitch-black tunnel exceeds triple digits, yet the captive woman shivers under Harry's terrible dead weight, making every gasp for air a struggle. The cold-hearted apparition presses down on her like a ragdoll, and sweaty, filthy hair clings over her face. Unable to peer downward, she hears the argument elevate in pitch. On the verge of passing out, she senses the ghoulish hand release from her neck, leaving behind a stinking ooze smeared across her chest. The unexpected reprieve allows a gasping inhalation of stale thin air before a smothering black mist permeates the space around her, paralyzing the

24-year-old, staring upward into the blackness.

Frozen inside the alien miasma, Rachel hears the brutal struggle on the hard limestone where visitors gathered before mounting the staircase and crawling through the rough-cut opening into the Ascending Passage.

The guttural wail of Owen's voice cuts through the violent cacophony, "No! No! You can't take it!"

Belligerent laughter screeches in reply.

Rachel tries to follow the raging hand-to-hand combat, hoping Owen has one more Krav Maga move up his sleeve to foil the hideous monster. Pelting rocks and dirt ricocheting off the limestone walls around her body make her fear the worst. The melee crashes to a halt in a crescendo of shattered glass from an old lantern, followed by an anguished outcry.

Before Rachel can mourn Owen's defeat at the hands of Harry Stark, swarms of stinging lights materialize inside the murkiness surrounding her body like angry bees. Shock turns to agony, wincing in dire pain as the energized specks pierce her arms and legs like Swiss cheese, devouring inward clothes and all, erasing the 24-year-old daughter and heir to the Alexander family fortune from the physical world. Gripped like a steel trap in a paralytic state, a disorienting sensation of transitioning through solid matter marks her final lucid thought before lights out.

Owen | Banishment
02:46 p.m. | August 22, 2044

"It's gone. Damn it all to hell!"

The lamentation from a familiar male voice awakens Rachel from a deep hypnotic trance. The young bride's emerald eyes widen onto utter blackness, standing on a smooth surface in an expanse devoid of light.

"He took the ellipse! What am I going to do?"

The unfortunate events flood Rachel's memory like a rogue wave crashing over logic and reason and pulling her far out to sea. Smoothing a sweaty hand down her left side, the tactility of cotton cloth elicits a relieved sigh. Removing a wadded-up tissue from a side pocket in her travel pants, she dabs her chest, attempting to rid herself of the stinking ooze left behind by the thing called Harry. The stench lingers, and she casts the crumpled wad into the darkness, disgusted. Clearing her dry throat, she rasps a tentative, "Owen?"

A dead silence hangs in the darkness, awaiting a reply.

"Rachel? Is that you? Where are you?"

"I'd ask you the same, but my gut tells me we are in the same place."

"Stay put. But keep talking. I will come to you."

With her mind a sieve, she sings the first words that enter her mind: "Here I am sitting in a tin can. Planet Earth is blue, and there is nothing I can …."

"There you are!"

Rachel feels Owen's firm grasp. The relief between them is palpable as Owen pulls her close and hugs her tight.

"Ow! Careful, Owen, my back can't take much more pressure."

"Sorry. How bad are you hurt?"

"I had the wind knocked out of me, but I'll live." Filling her lungs with the stifling hot air, "There is not much air here, but at least we are alive, I think."

"Way to put a positive spin on things; your therapist would be proud."

Still clinging to Owen, Rachel stretches out her free right hand, groping for anybody or anything else. "The floor feels slippery, like walking on ice. I wish it weren't so dark. Where is the flashlight? Did Harry take that, too?"

Owen senses her movement, "Don't let go." Taking his first cautious step, left hand outstretched, his shoe kicks something, sending it skidding across the smooth floor. "Rachel, that might be our flashlight."

Feeling herself tugged in the opposite direction, "Owen! Wait a minute. You almost pulled me over."

His gentle nudge orients her in the right direction. Hand-in-hand, they smooth their feet across the floor, like Astaire and Rogers dancing in the dark, hoping to stumble across the Jeep's souvenir flashlight.

Rachel's lucky Chelsea boot taps against something. Reaching forward, bending at the waist, she probes her right hand across the floor while holding onto Owen with her left, "Whatever it is, I hope it doesn't bite."

Owen clasps her hand tight, afraid to let go, "Great, that possibility didn't even occur to me."

The flashlight beam penetrates the darkness causing Owen to wheel toward Rachel's uplit face, looking a little worse for wear.

"Ahh! Bad lighting!"

"Hilarious, Owen. I found our flashlight."

"I can see that; you are freaking me out."

"You should talk; Harry did a number on you, too."

Projecting the widened beam around them illuminates their off-center position inside a low-ceiling hexagonal chamber.

"Owen, what do you think these weird-looking symbols covering the walls represent?"

"Well, they look like hieroglyphics, Rachel." Owen ventures to the nearest wall using the ambiance from the widened beam. While standing too close to the etched symbols, his puffy-eyed vision blurs them into a single helical design. Stepping backward, he blinks and rubs his swollen eyes, and the familiar shape reverts to a disparate grouping of glyphs, "You know, Rachel. I might need to get my eyes checked."

"I'll put you down for next Tuesday."

"No. Very funny. I mean, I am starting to see patterns in these symbols. Squint your eyes. Can you see it?"

Rachel trains the flashlight on the wall and stares. "Oh, yeah. DNA. Oh, wait. Those look like cells. That's a virus. Weird. These optical illusions remind me of a book I had in my younger days. It contained patterned images called stereograms. You stare at them long enough, and a 3D image appears. My Dad bought it for me."

"Keep staring, Rachel. As you were reminiscing, a human figure came into focus. Wait, make that two humans—a man and a woman—inside a circle … or maybe a droplet. Like liquid. Water? Who the hell knows?"

Rachel hesitates to interrupt his breathless epiphany but freaks out at lights emerging from the blackness under their feet. "Owen, look down."

Reluctant to pull his swollen gaze from the wall's hidden pictograms, Owen kneels and raps his bloody knuckles on the velvet-smooth floor, "There is something strange going on."

Rachel angles the light across the slippery surface, "I think it's translucent, like stained glass."

"Yeah, it sure looks that way."

The pair watch the lights swirl into a familiar mass of sparkles rising under their boots.

"No way. Can it be?"

Rachel huffs an exhausted sigh and shines the flashlight on Owen's battered face, "What? I hate it when you leave me in suspense."

"I'm not an astronomer, but the lights are spiraling into a dead ringer for the Milky Way galaxy."

"My husband, ladies, and gentlemen, never at a loss for worthless trivia in times of crisis."

"Not so fast, Rachel; maybe it's the key to our escape." His mind racing, "It can't be a coincidence …."

"What can't be a coincidence?"

"Things happen for a reason. Nothing is accidental." Turning back to the wall, his eyes recapture the human representations inside a drop. "Not water, Rachel. It's human blood. DNA from our blood identifies our place in the universe. It must be how the beacon operates."

"Owen. Do you think we are inside the beacon?"

Trying to coalesce the disjointed parts into a coherent theory they can use, he shakes his head, "I don't know. Maybe it is a coincidence."

Shining the light around the space, large enough to park a decent size SUV but not much more, she searches one more time for an exit but comes up empty. Directing the light back on Owen, she sees him again on his knees, smoothing his hands across the black glass.

Resting beside her husband, Rachel holds the light above the floor, where Owen examines the galactic spiral. Noticing the pinkie digit next to his ring finger is jutting sideways at an unnatural angle makes her wince with an empathic sense of pain. She also notes cuts and bruises on his hands and arms for the first time, exacerbated by scorched skin in the shape of the horrible monster's skeletal handprints. Tugging at his singed shirt sleeve hanging tattered from his right elbow, "Were you always so rough on your clothes, Owen? You must have given your poor mother fits."

Failing to lighten the mood, the levity in her voice turns to worry, "Seriously, how bad are you hurt?"

Collapsing on the glassy floor in an exhausted heap, Owen faces Rachel, tears of frustration welling in his bloodshot hazel eyes. "I let us down. We worked so damn hard to find the ellipse, and I let that thing take it from me. I never stood a chance."

Rachel sees a young boy accustomed to winning still living rent-free inside the man she married. Losing was not a part of his vocabulary. It pained her to witness his attempt to reconcile defeat in his stubborn head. She sits back and points the cheap flashlight straight up, pushing back the darkness between them. "Owen, we'll be fine. But you have to hold it together. You came into my life and saved me when I needed someone the most. Don't leave me now."

Emanating serenity from somewhere deep inside, Rachel becomes the caregiver. Faced with impending disaster, she needs the cocksure resourceful man she married back online. "Did I ever tell you, Owen, when I was a kid, I wanted to be a doctor?"

With a tearful laugh at the reminiscence from her youth, "People told me I would be good at it because I made them feel better with just my smile. That is pretty stupid, right? But up until the night of my sexual assault, I believed it was true."

Wiping tears from her bruised and cut cheeks, she pulls a matted lock of hair behind her ear and gives Owen the bravest smile she can muster through the darkness, "Now, give me your hand and hold still." With a firm yet gentle grasp on Owen's bloody left hand, she pulls his dislocated pinkie finger back in place with an audible snap.

Owen's eyes squeeze shut while muffling a painful cry, "Ow! Ow! Ow! Dammit, that hurts, Rachel." After rocking back and forth for close to a minute, he opens his eyes, clenching and unclenching a fist. "Thanks. I think. It hurts like hell, but I didn't want to say anything."

Tearing a swath of fabric from Owen's sleeve, Rachel ties the repositioned pinkie to his swollen ring finger. "Okay. That's a start. Let's see what else needs attention …."

Remaining calm in the dark expanse, an improvising Doctor Rachel examines Owen's burned forearms. Ripping the remainder of his shirt sleeves at the elbows, she wraps both arms, covering the scorched skin. Next, she scoots her bottom onto the shiny floor, crisscrossing long legs while removing her blouse, "You are bleeding pretty bad from your head."

Owen swallows back a light-headed feeling, "I was hoping that was sweat."

"Nope. Blood. Bear with me; I'll make sure you are all right."

"Okay."

"Hold still, Owen. I hope you don't mind a little spit."

Moistening a semi-clean section of her blouse with a bit of well-placed saliva, she leans in and dabs the cuts and scrapes on his chest and face, "I don't know, Owen; it looks like you put up a pretty good fight from what I can see under the light."

Rising onto her knees, Rachel hovers close to Owen, her smooth skin glistening with sweat, saturating her pale pink sports bra pressed against his cheek.

Aware of the fire she is lighting, she moves closer to examine his matted scalp, finding a glass shard stabbed into his noggin, seeping blood through his thick auburn hair. Extracting the glass with a quick pull, she presses her shirt into the open wound to staunch the bleeding. "Ugh. I need to keep pressure until the bleeding stops or starts slowing down. You may have a concussion."

Face to face with Rachel's small perky breasts corralled under the thin sports bra, unsure of what, if any, signal he is getting, while she keeps him from bleeding out on the slick flooring, "You'll get no complaints from me. Your shirt, Rachel. You didn't have to do that."

"Yeah. I guess I could let you bleed to death. I might think about it if you don't stop staring at my chest."

"Oh, was I staring? In my defense, you do make for one heck of a sexy nurse."

"Doctor."

"Right. Doctor."

Scooting onto her feet, she ties the blood-stained shirt around her waist. "Wait until you get my bill." Unsure of what to do next, she redirects the flashlight onto the mystery spiral inching closer by the minute through the dark glass while Owen watches the beam's progression.

"Hey! Stop right there!"

"What did you see?" Rachel redirects the light where Owen's bandaged fingers are pointing.

"Maybe nothing," he lowers his square chin just above the floor and taps a spot with his damaged hand, "Shine it here, please." The tight beam reverses over a verdant jewel shimmering halfway down the inner part of a spiraling arm of the scaled Milky Way. "There it is again!"

"There, what is again?"

"Earth, my dear. Home to you and me."

Contemplating the planetary representation standing out amidst the galactic scale model, the gash on Owen's head drips blood onto the black glass. "Huh. What the hell?" Instead of leaving small splats across the smooth surface, he watches the droplets pass through the glass, forming glowing red dots hurtling comet-like into the shimmering galaxy. An epiphany reverberates inside Owen's rattled head like a choir of angels, "Rachel, I have an idea. Hold the light steady while I give something a try."

"Give what a try?"

"You'll see."

Wetting his index finger from the cut on his head, Owen eyeballs the bloody digit—like a bombardier over a target—waiting for a large droplet to release from his fingertip and continue on a downward trajectory to the luminous green dot. "Knock-knock. We're here."

Flynn | Giza Pyramids security office
03:25 p.m. | August 22, 2044

"My name is Flynn." The PTB agent produces his signature defiant grin that helped him endure interrogations making the current predicament seem mellow by comparison. "One name. You know, like a pop star."

The attempt to lighten the mood fails to break Captain Mohammed Faisel's stone-faced countenance propping onto the front of his desk, arms crossed, heaving a weary sigh, "You have no ID of any kind?"

"I told you already; everyone left their belongings on the bus as instructed."

"That is nonsense. Under what authority?"

"You tell me. Some white-suited piece of shit and his hired goons."

Handcuffed to the metal chair, the agent watches a deputy peek inside the office, motioning for Captain Mohammed Faisel's immediate attention.

The Egyptian rises and exits with an exasperated huff, "Now what?"

Flynn calls behind the humorless man stomping out of the room, "I'll wait here."

Alone in the cramped office space, unsure what jurisdiction keeps him chained to a chair for hours without even his phone call, he wonders if Owen and Rachel ever made it into the pyramid. And whatever happened to Louie?

Flynn's ruminating is interrupted as none other than the idiot in the white suit, himself, Professor Tarek Hamed, pushes the door open with a menacing smile flashing from under the brim of his Panama hat, "Here you are."

Lifting his handcuffed right wrist, Flynn proffers an amiable grin, "Yep. Here I am. I'd shake your hand, but well …."

Although the Egyptian's dapper appearance remains intact after hours spent crumpled in the tour bus heaped atop his knuckle-dragging lackeys, he also sports a fresh purplish shiner encircling his left eye, "Who gave you the black eye? Was it a jealous husband?"

"No. You are responsible, but I will let that slide for now." The erudite reincarnation of Omar Sharif fingers the end of his thick mustache, oblivious to any villainous archetype it mimics, "It appears you have pulled the proverbial wool over the eyes of the local constabulary. Well done. I understand Giza security contacted the private aviation company at the Cairo airport, who indeed vouched for your employment."

Unable to suppress a too-clever smile, Flynn asks, "Did they talk to Nina?" his wary gaze watches the evil man remove his Panama hat while angling around Faisel's desk to check outside through the filthy window. Talking to the back of Hamed's white suit jacket, "Nina is a real looker, Hamed."

Hamed ignores Flynn's attempt to throw him off his game, slanting apart the dusty blinds to scan the blue sky above the parking lots and the trio of pyramids silhouetted in the mid-afternoon sunshine.

Undeterred, Flynn presses further, "And, better yet, she is single. Just saying." Flynn frowns, failing to raise the man's hackles while curious about what the natty dresser looks for in the sky.

Immune to Flynn's attempt to get under his skin, "The Chrysalis Air representative indeed confirmed your identity. However, they were less forthcoming about why you are on the Plateau. And they professed no knowledge of your missing colleagues." Releasing the cheap metal blinds with a clatter, he turns to face Flynn, pulling a pilfered tour manifest from his pocket. With an officious tone, he reads two circled names, "Owen Haig and Rachel Haig. Americans." Wheeling Faisel's chair before Flynn's seated position, the professor straddles the seat, leans forward on the backrest, and focuses his most threatening, gap-toothed grin at the detainee. "Before we continue, you caught me at a disadvantage on the bus."

Flynn's stubbled jawline hardens into a scowl, scooting nose-to-nose with the Egyptian, "You were too busy rifling through folks' private property to notice my approach. Tough guys like yourself always take the least amount of sleep dust before lights out. It's not my fault your face smacked into the bus floor before I could catch you."

Hamed's malicious stare-down meets the agent's unrepentant forward-leaning posture. "I will cut to the chase, my friend. Where is the golden ellipse?"

Hearing the magic words spoken aloud in a refined, English-accented query sends a shiver down the agent's spine, "I have no idea what in the hell you are talking about."

"You, sir, are a terrible liar."

The door opens, and Captain Faisel reenters, interrupting the antagonistic tête-à-tête. Flynn emits a subtle sigh of relief as the no-nonsense captain dresses down the white-suited intruder. "How did you get in here? Get out, or I will toss you in a cell for trespassing on government property!"

Grabbing his Panama hat off the desk and brushing off a speck of lint, Tarek pauses before Flynn, prolonging his dramatized exit. "I wish you were more forthcoming. The fate of our world is at stake."

Faisel has suffered enough fools and heard enough crap for one day. Grappling the white-suited interloper by the collar, the army officer hustles the man from his office into the hallway and barks an order at a deputy, "Escort this man off the plateau. If he gives you any trouble, shoot him."

Watching the no-nonsense man confer in a lowered voice with another security officer, Flynn overhears, "Yes. Escort them into my office on the double."

With a troubled expression creasing his deep-tan face, Faisel turns to Flynn and forces an apologetic tone, "Not sure how that guy got in here. He works for the museum. Very strange. This place has gone to the dogs." Unlocking the agent's handcuffed wrist, he continues, "I just reviewed a surveillance feed showing the north face of the Great Pyramid. It appears a security staff member escorted your colleagues inside the pyramid through the robbers entrance."

Flynn's reply is cut short by Faisel. "Enough lies! What is your business here?"

A sharp double knock breaks the tension. "Yes! Come in."

The door flings open, and Flynn beams at the sight of Louie, accompanied by the tour guide, escorted into the office by a uniformed deputy.

"Sir, here are the others from the tour group."

Louie meets Agent Flynn's puzzled gaze, "I see we are well into our plan. Excellent!"

Rolling his chair back behind his desk, Faisel collapses in his seat and accesses an aspirin bottle from a side drawer. After swallowing a handful of uncoated pills, he reacquires his train of thought, "I watched the high-definition feed from the north face and identified your friends, Owen and Rachel Haig. But the weird part is what I saw next." Clasping his hands together atop his blotter, he exhales a weary sigh, "We identified the security officer assisting their entry as a young recruit who was murdered three days ago."

Agent Flynn arches his right eyebrow, heartened by the Egyptian's candor, "That is weird."

The Egyptian rocks backward on the swivel chair's squeaking springs, heaving a demonstrative sigh, "On second thought, I am beyond caring why you are here. However, I would be remiss in my duties if I did not assume the worst and assemble a rescue team. Mr. Flynn, would you care to join me?"

Reeling from the news, afraid their attempt to return the golden ellipse may have already failed, Agent Flynn's affirmative reply is cut short by a low rumble. The experienced agent's eyes widen, realizing a catastrophic event is imminent, "Everybody, get down!"

Diving to the floor, hands cupped over his head, he sees Faisel dive under his desk. Louie tackles Cassandra to his left as an ear-splitting force of energy crashes inward, sending jagged broken glass projectiles hurtling over the shocked group. Battered metal blinds clatter against the busted-out window frames as the thunderous shockwave continues its devastating path across the North African topography. Sirens, car alarms, and exploding transformers peppered with the shrieks, screams, and cries of a terrified Egyptian citizenry churn into a cacophonous pandemonium outside Faisel's shattered office window.

"What in the world was that!?" Crunching across broken glass,

Faisel rips the ruined mass of thin metal slats from the battered frame and casts it into a corner. Jutting his head outside, he sees chaos in every direction. His day just got demonstrably worse. The only positive he can pull from this shitstorm is the day's tours had already vacated the plateau before the blast. "Thank God for small favors."

Flynn, Louie, and Cassandra peer over Faisel's broad shoulders witnessing a fiery gash spreading across the late afternoon blue sky. A massive fleet of enormous, silhouetted shapes is visible inside the smoke and flames. Resembling dystopian nightmares depicted in countless sci-fi movies, watching an actual fleet of alien invaders breaching Earth's atmosphere conjures a sense of disbelief. Like it is all happening on a screen.

Cassandra yells over the din, "Are those meteors?"

Louie observes the controlled descent while brushing glass from his shirt and reaching for a new cigarette from his pocket. "We may have to delay our dinner date, my dear."

Flynn turns to Faisel with eyes widened in terror. "Okay. I'm ready to talk. We have to get into the pyramid. Now! We are out of time!"

Artemus Pennywell | PTB HQ, Scotland
04:00 p.m. | August 22, 2044

An unhinged chorus of bleats from an agitated and unruly flock of sheep punctuates thunder reverberating across Lowland pastures. Arcs of green lightning illuminate the terrified animals hunkering under a stand of dripping wet alders in a protective hollow as a pelting downpour drenches their thick wool coats, hooves kicking and sliding in the slippery mud and trampled grass.

Ruins of an erstwhile Scottish castle tower into the foreboding sky from its elevated vantage atop a sloped rise overlooking the jittery livestock, the River Tyne beyond, and Edinburgh farther north and west. Unbeknownst to the local Scottish population and all elected pols, minus a select few in key positions paid to look the other way, the unheralded and crumbling stone edifice sits atop a labyrinthine underground complex branching outward in multi-level radii beneath the surrounding pastures. Bore out of solid rock in sections following a master plan approved in the 1950s, the hidden complex comprises the clandestine headquarters for The Powers That Be.

Within a subterranean Level B suite, Artemus Pennywell, the storied organization's CEO for over half a century, reclines slumped into a fully extended Scandinavian leather recliner in his well-appointed wood-paneled study, snoring into the filtered air.

A shrill *buuuuuurrrrr-buuuuuurrrrr-buuuuuurrrrr* ratchets on an irritating loop, jolting the CEO from his daily power nap. Grasping for the noisy earphone device, vibrating next to an empty tumbler on a side table, he focuses bleary eyes beyond his socked feet on vestigial embers still aglow in a virtual floor-to-ceiling fireplace, "Goddammit! How long was I asleep?"

Fumbling the annoying comm device into his ear, he returns his seat to its upright position and snarls an irritated, "I'm awake. What is it?"

Andrew, Pennywell's replicant valet, replies in his typical calm, soothing voice, "Sir, the Advisor, Ping, is on the line."

After the connection syncs to Pennywell's ear device, the CEO leans forward, struggling to comprehend the Gray alien's computerized translation. "What the hell?" A grating static interference punctuated by eerie and threatening screeches ratchets in his ear, "Ping, I can't hear you. We have a bad connection. Maybe it's a solar flare."

Pennywell stands out of his chair and stretches his tall, spry frame with a loud yawn. "I still can't hear you, Ping. This bloody satellite communications system is for the fucking birds!"

Cursing his earphone—the bane of his existence—he strides

across the study toward his fully stocked wet bar for a calming refill.

Pennywell's blood runs cold as ice with the aromatic cork from a half-empty bottle of 16-year-old Lagavulin clenched in his right hand. The words he has dreaded for over half a century break through the crackling clutter in a crystal-clear robotic voice: *"Artemus, they are here. It is time to go."*

**Most men are within a finger's breadth
of being mad.**

– Diogenes Laërtius

Chapter Nine:
The Horseman

**Lieutenant Harry Stark | Aix-en-Provence, France
03:30 a.m. | August 17, 1944 (Flashback)**

Harry swooped behind his wingman's killing machine, silhouetted against a fiery maelstrom skimming the far side of the targeted area after obliterating the Nazi locomotive in a hail of blistering-hot Browning .50 caliber wing-mounted gunfire. "Nice shooting, Captain!"

The spine-tingling ecstasy of another dance with death coursed Lieutenant Harry Stark's veins, honing his aviator prowess to a razor's edge. Flying even lower than Neil, Harry's P-47 buzzed quaint tile rooftops, almost decapitating a church spire, while sighting the line of train cars lit up like a Christmas tree in the railyard cauldron. Gloved hand covering the firing button, he clamped down hard, blasting the evil-filled line of Pullmans. Fires ignited ordnance exploding in reverberating shockwaves throughout Aix-en-Provence and the surrounding countryside. Glowing plumes of smoke and debris blossomed into the night, and suffocating fumes choked terrified people trying to escape the carnage. "So much for minimizing damage to the rest of the yard; war is a messy business."

Completing his run, Harry heard Neil's decision to maneuver around for a second go at the locomotive. Before he could respond, his olive-green fighter bomber absorbed a barrage from vengeful antiaircraft gunners. Cursing a blue streak into his mask, Harry yanked back hard on the stick into a tight starboard turn, putting tremendous strain on his jug's lumbering aeronautics to evade the German gunners. Specks of light peppered his vision as he struggled to maintain consciousness enduring the high g-force maneuver.

A fire emerged from the bullet-riddled plane's engine cowling and grew into an inferno in the blink of an eye. Licking flames engulfed the cockpit, setting Harry's arms and legs ablaze. The brash pilot's lucky streak ended with screamed epithets as his chaotic trajectory rocketed skyward in a ball of flame.

Harry grasped a new reality through his excruciating pain; something else controlled his fate as he tied to quantify the distorted, horrifying sight of his scorched body through his melted goggles. The P-47's shattered canopy tore from the bullet-riddled fuselage into the slipstream. Freezing air buffeted the lapping blaze away from the cockpit, allowing glimpses through the acrid smoke while the plane shot higher into the night on a near-vertical ascent.

The P-47 reached the apex like a Roman candle, thrusting Harry from the open cockpit into thin air. His frail body separated from the flaming Thunderbolt, and time slowed to a stop. An amorphous cloud formed from the clear night sky, engulfing his wild-eyed midair frozen position. Spectral orbs inside the miasma combined into a sphere of pure energy, exploding outward with a resounding crack like a thunderbolt. The chaotic nightmare at 10,000 feet resumed with a vengeance, buffeting Stark's twisting, plummeting form in panicked darkness. His last lucidity was an overwhelming desire to possess his golden ellipse one more time. The deployed chute decelerated his freefall with a violent jerk. Harry's burnt head slumped forward, dangling puppet-like in the tangled mess of lines below the billowing canopy.

The flaming missile that was Harry's P-47 nosedived toward the railyard and contacted the Nazi escape train with meteoric force. The only thing left was the familiar shape of the tail section jutting from the wreckage.

Burned over three-quarters of his stocky frame, Harry swung in a helpless elliptical arc below his chute, drifting over dense forest east of town.

* * *

In the predawn hours outside Aix-en-Provence, Harry lay shrouded in dark shadows, flat on his back, spread-eagle in a pasture of tall grass. Thin gray smoke trailed from his tattered flight suit and charred skin into the dewy air.

Regaining consciousness, gasping for air, he saw nothing and feared he had lost his sight. Feeling around his face with his mangled left hand, he pushed against the melted goggles still pulled over his eyes. Using his forearm, he nudged the protective eyewear off his still-smoldering head. An unnerving sensation of loose skin sliding across his scalp sickened him, prompting his stomach to churn up thick greenish bile puked from his mouth. The noxious ooze mixed with chunks of grapes and pastries spread across his chest, covering the sizzled Black Scorpion squadron patch on his zipped flight jacket. He regretted eating all of that crap hours before the mission.

The mission! What in the hell happened? Was Neil alive? How did he survive? Where was he? "Oh yeah, Nazi-occupied France. Great. Just great."

The direness of his predicament flooded his racing mind. The inevitable outcome of capture would involve Nazi goons discovering his connection to the ellipse. And then what? He could not let that happen. His only option was to make it to the tree line and wait out the war until the Allies captured this parcel of France. Of course, dealing with those assholes would not be a picnic, either. Everyone wanted his ellipse. That was just not an option.

Footsteps rustling across the grass froze Harry in place. Somebody was approaching his position. Goddammit! Goddammit!

He closed his eyes and awaited the butt of a German rifle upside his fried noggin.

A low guttural mooing and air huffing from large snot-filled nostrils drew near. A wet lolling tongue licked Harry's bloody face, forcing swollen, crusted eyes to open.

Golf ball-sized black orbs recessed into the bony skull of an emaciated black and white cow widened in comical reaction to Harry's feeble movement. A rusted bell hanging from its neck bellowed as the bovine head swung from side to side, pantomiming the word, "No."

"No? Now what? And don't lick my blood. That can't be healthy for either of us!"

The cow reacted genuinely surprised, disappointed Harry was alive, and scuttled off, clanking its stupid bell. The pilot sat up and winced from the searing pain tearing every fiber of his body. Eyeballing over the tall grass, he noted the foreboding wall of forest encircling the pasture. The orange glow from the railyard inferno colored the sky to the west above the high treetops. "I hope you motherfuckers burn as good as I did."

Shifting to face eastward, he caught the sheen of his white nylon chute, hanging limp, tangled in branches. "How did I end up over here? Maybe I am dead."

A whistling sound emanated from the woods behind his back, breaking the silence. Risking capture, he reciprocated in a low, raspy note approximating a whistle. It was all he could muster from his burned and bloodied.

Harry heard a high-pitch chirped reply but could do no more. Blood loss and the severity of his burns left him unable to answer. The crunch of leaves and grass grew louder from behind his seated position. He wished he had his sidearm. God only knew where it ended up.

A gangly scarecrow entered the periphery of Harry's blurred vision from his left side. Adjusting a rifle slung over his bony shoulder, the stranger struck a wooden match, revealing Harry's blackened face and dead eyes staring back in defeat.

"Monsieur Harry Stark?"

Harry's head did not move, but dead-to-the-world eyes turned toward the silhouetted figure. He could see the trees right through the man's tall transparent frame, filled with specks of light, like fireflies.

The man pulled Harry bodily onto his feet without a hint of exertion. "The Germans will return within the hour. They come here often. It is time to go."

Harry's charred flight suit hung in blood-smeared shreds exposing his blackened, stocky legs. The puke from earlier slid down his flight jacket, dripping onto the scuffed leather uppers of his relatively unscathed boots. He spits and sputters: "Everyone wants to die with their boots on."

Realizing the full extent of Stark's injuries, Dreyfus took a long step backward, upwind of the smell of fresh vomit mixed with burnt flesh. The Frenchman hoped the wavering American pilot could walk; otherwise, he would have to bite the bullet and carry him. Not ideal. A curiosity crossed Dreyfus's mind: This man should be dead by all rights. Is Harry's imperviousness to what appears to be agonizing, torturous wounds covering his body integral to the Dark Specters' plan for the disfigured pilot? Perhaps, he is in shock, nothing more.

The whites of his eyes rotated upward on his blackened face, and Harry focused the tattered remnants of his wits on the tall, lanky stranger, "Who the hell are you supposed to be?"

Ignoring the query, the man took stock of the fighter pilot's condition, "It appears you can walk. Let's go." The man pivoted and took long strides toward the relative safety of the old-growth woods.

As Harry watched the gangly man's retreating form, he recalled a character in a book lifted from the New York Public Library during his troublemaking street urchin youth. The book was The Legend of Sleepy Hollow. The character was Ichabod Crane. With his first tentative step, he surmised his tall, gawky rescuer could pass for the French version.

Entering the line of trees, Harry struggled to catch up with the man's steady pace. While ducking under branches, pulling over moss-covered logs, and forging through the dense musky undergrowth, a loud buzz caught his attention. He saw a clearing gouged out of the forest through the trees to his right. Harry deviated from the man's path, oblivious to flying pests attracted to the smell of fresh blood and festering wounds. Breaking free from a tangle of leafy vines, he halted at the muddy ledge of a fetid pit under a thick cloud of flies. At first, he could not discern what he saw through the shadows, but as his vision adjusted, unmistakable shapes of human bodies resolved before his stunned eyes. Harry realized it was a mass grave of people twisted into a nightmarish stew. The decaying visage of a child in a pink dress returned his gaze, cast atop other bodies. Incapable of despair, the terrible reality of innocent life snuffed out by human wickedness consumed him with rage for his fellow man.

A firm hand on Harry's shoulder startled him back to the present. The man scolded Harry in an unsympathetic tone, "We need to go. My friend, there is more misery and death beyond this shallow grave."

Dreyfus | Farmhouse outside Aix-en-Provence, France
05:42 p.m. | September 1, 1944

Harry Stark awoke to something burning; however, this time,

it had the sweet aroma of pipe tobacco. Sprawled atop a narrow cot, he turned his bandaged head sideways into the semi-darkness. A single candle flickered, illuminating the left side of the man's gaunt face.

A long skinny leg crossed over the other, reclined in a simple wooden chair beside a small table, the man noted the stricken aviator had regained consciousness. He took a long pull from the curved pipe nestled in the crook of his gnarled hand and shifted in his chair.

Harry studied the Frenchman's weathered features through a cloud of pipe smoke hanging in the stillness. The man no longer appeared transparent, and the dancing specks of light were gone. Under the dim lighting, he also realized the man was much older. However, the guy remained a walking, talking embodiment of Ichabod Crane.

Shifting beneath a scratchy wool blanket, the pilot started to speak but crusted skin pulled and ripped across his swollen cheeks, mouth, and chin, freeing oozing wetness from scabbed blisters, rolling down his neck onto the mattress. The soaked cot stunk from his sweat and filth. Disgusted yet determined to speak aloud, he mustered a laryngitic-voiced observation, "You remind me of a character from my favorite book."

"Monsieur, my name is Armand Dreyfus."

"Are you with the resistance?"

"In a way, I guess you could say that."

"Where am I?"

"You are in a cellar hidden underneath my farmhouse outside Aix-en-Provence." The man scooped a lukewarm cloth from a bucket and dabbed it across Harry's face. "Our mutual benefactor instructed me to sit on my front porch the night of your raid and wait for a signal. I sat for hours; nothing happened. Eventually, I fell asleep. It was not until early the next morning when explosions from town woke me with a start; I knew my time had finally arrived."

The gangly man stood, his balding head close to scraping a rusted nail jutting halfway from the splintery ceiling. Shuffling to a far corner of the room, he grabbed a roll of gauze and scissors from a middle drawer in a paint-chipped French Provincial sideboard.

Returning to his chair, he looked at Harry with a bemused look, creasing his angular features, "You have drifted in and out of consciousness since I carried you down here over two weeks ago." Relighting his pipe, "Allow me to bring you up-to-date, Monsieur. The Germans retreated, and the Americans marched through town on the twenty-second of August. The Seventh Army moved on since then, but black-suited investigators remained behind, searching for you and your missing wingman. They have darkened my cabin door twice. Each time I was able to convince them, I knew nothing of your whereabouts."

Unable to move, Harry contemplated the new information while losing himself in the wood grain patterns swirling into complicated knots in the weathered planks above his head. "Neil did not make it. I did not know that." He tried to feel something other than a morbid curiosity but failed to conjure a human emotion after learning his only friend in the world had perished.

Clenching the stem of his pipe in his mouth to free his cold arthritic hands, the man who called himself Armand Dreyfus lifted Harry's head and shoulders from the cot.

The sensation of singed skin on his neck and back peeling from the course cotton bedding sent an unpleasant chill along Harry's spine. Propped on a rolled cloth wedged behind him, stinging prickles from Dreyfus' indelicate unwrapping of caked gauze from seared scalp made the tough-as-nails Army Air Corps officer wince in pain, "How does it look, Dreyfus? Am I ready for my close-up?"

Armand smiled at the grasp for levity, caustic though it may be. In a previous reality, this man entertained compatriots with a rapier wit. A trait the straight-shooting former scientist never mastered. While it no longer mattered, it troubled him.

Inspecting a patchwork of blackened scalp mixed with sad remnants of flaming-red hair, he shrugged at the progress and added more detail from the night of the raid. "After locating your position, I had to act fast. Your chute snagged a high tree branch leaving you swinging in midair, twenty-five feet off the ground." Armand snipped a length of clean gauze, "I cut you from your straps, but you fell to the ground before I could grab you." Rewrapping Harry's gruesome noggin, "You were fortunate, Monsieur, not to break any bones." Armand removed the roll, replacing it with a clean folded towel, and lowered Harry's fresh-bandaged head.

"You should have let me die."

"I could not let that happen, my friend. I was in the process of dragging you across the pasture when the Germans arrived. I abandoned you in the tall grass and took cover. The soldiers assumed you cut yourself free and escaped the area on your own accord. You were lucky they did not see you.

"So that is why I woke up in the pasture. Mystery solved."

"Oui. The pasture is not a pleasant place to linger. Fortunately, I arrived before they did. You killed a lot of Nazis, my friend."

"Don't you think those bastards deserved it? I saw children in that stinking pit." The circumstances surrounding the raid and its bizarre aftermath crept into his frontal lobe, "And who allowed a cow to wander near a mass grave?"

"You can rest assured, Monsieur Stark, that all of the livestock in this region was slaughtered long ago to feed starving troops or relocated to greener pastures by the Nazis. Perhaps you dreamt it."

Harry's reply was cut short. His body went rigid, bandaged head thrust backward at a severe angle, eyeballs rolling into his skull.

Dreyfus sat back, relighting his pipe, waiting for the out-of-control convulsions to abate. No sense wiping the thick spittle foaming at the poor man's mouth until the sickening gurgle from his smoke-damaged lungs ebbed and teeth unclenched, relaxing the grimace on his oozing face.

Dreyfus lifted the wool blanket to check the leather restraints holding the unconscious man's grotesque arms and legs to the cot's metal frame. He adjusted the tension on the right strap, ensuring the pilot could not move it more than a few inches. Satisfied, he reached into his vest and removed a morphine syrette.

Pinching the ampoule end of the syrette between his thumb and index finger, Dreyfus broke the seal at the tip of the needle, hunched forward, and jabbed it into the meaty part of Harry's right shoulder in a lightning-quick motion.

Harry's rigid body relaxed into a blissful opioid-induced sleep. The scientist checked Harry's pulse, determining the patient remained stable. With the disfigured pilot back in dreamland, Dreyfus grabbed his pipe, blew out the candle, and placed his last syrette atop the table beside the roll of gauze.

A quick scamper up the ladder through the camouflaged hatch above the sideboard, and Dreyfus was back on the cabin's main floor. Sliding the unwieldy bureau back atop the secret hatch, the man scuffed his boots across the dirty floor to obscure the telltale tracks. Noting the vivid Mediterranean sunset outside the cabin's western-facing window on the world meant it was dinner time. While his body's need for nourishment ended over 150 years ago, he enjoyed cooking. It helped kill time.

* * *

With the Dark Specters' brash human recruit beginning his dark and painful odyssey, Armand Dreyfus' extended retirement ended abruptly.

The archeologist stepped into the cramped kitchen, striking a match against the rough stone outer wall to light his stove, reigniting a memory of Napoleon's lit torch 150 years earlier.

In a dreaded final heartbeat, Dreyfus's loose bond with the physical world incinerated in mid-rumination as intense heat radiated inside his lanky frame. The matchbox dropped from his crumbling charcoal hand, and his eyeballs widened in surprise before he collapsed into an ashen pile on the kitchen floor amongst the spilled box of wooden matchsticks.

Light specks vacated his smoldering remains before an animated swirl whisked Armand Dreyfus out the open bay window above the sink and scattered him into the Provence countryside.

* * *

With their devilish bargain with Dreyfus finished, the Dark Specters formed into a blacker-than-black cloud teeming with malevolent lights. Passing through the uneven floorboards, they frowned with utter contempt upon the disfigured human bound atop a filthy bent-metal cot in the cellar's darkness. This uncouth wretch paled compared to the Nazi spy Hans Gruber, who foiled the Machine and detached the golden ellipse after eons of failed attempts.

However, in an unpredicted twist to their final solution for all humankind, the spy made the grievous error of sharing the golden ellipse with his Nazi superior, who shot him between the eyes and claimed the relic before the Dark Specters could intervene.

Gruber's miscalculation triggered a series of events, culminating with the golden ellipse falling into Allied hands. If the Americans discovered the Egyptian artifact's energizing purpose, they could have returned it to the beacon, thwarting the extraterrestrial invaders while still light-years away from Earth.

Determined not to let success slip from their ethereal grasp, but with no time to seek out another Hans Gruber among the Allied ranks, the Dark Specters manipulated a pliable Army quartermaster named Hodges to rig a late-night poker game in favor of Harry Stark—the American fighter languishing in Dreyfus' cellar at death's door. Possessing none of the German spy's debonair charm, the ham-fisted fighter pilot with a checkered past would have to do.

Harry Stark | Captured airbase outside Tripoli, Libya

0230 Hours | August 12, 1943 (One year earlier)

"Captain! Wake up! I won something in a poker game that will change our lives, but we have to hide it! Get up!"

Harry pulled his only friend in this man's army, Captain Neil Alexander, from his Army cot and lifted the taller man onto his bare feet.

Half asleep, Neil shook the cobwebs from his head and tried to fathom his wingman's maniacal expression, "Harry, what the hell did you do this time?"

"We have to leave! Now! There is no time to explain." Harry pushed his somnambulant friend into a stolen Jeep and motored into the godforsaken Libyan desert in the dead of night.

With a dark presence entering his sleepy head, Neil lulled from side to side, dazed and confused. Forcing his eyes open, the handsome pilot turned toward his copilot and saw him hunched over the wheel, peering through the windscreen into the darkness with the headlights off, "Where are we going? Are we still behind our lines?"

Without averting his eyes while hitting every bump along a rutted dirt road, "I won something in a poker game put on by that asshole, Hodges. Captain, we will be rich beyond our wildest dreams when this war is over, but for now, we have to hide it."

"Hide what? You are making less sense than usual."

Veering into a hairpin turn, Harry reached from behind the wheel and grabbed Neil by the jacket to keep him from falling out while zig-zagging up a series of switchbacks to a barren ridgeline. At the top, Harry floored it, bounding at breakneck speed to the base of a sheer limestone formation jutting out of the hardscrabble like an ancient sentinel. "We're here."

Rubbing his eyes, Neil mumbled in his anesthetized slumber, "Where is here?"

As Harry vaulted out of the Jeep, Neil caught a blurred glimpse of an oval object reflecting the first rays of sunrise in his wingman's chubby hands. "Harry, what is that? Did you steal it? Is that why you drove us out here?" Neil failed to comprehend Harry's blithe retort before the Dark Specters slipped him from the Libyan desert to a silvery representation of his wife in a vivid dream.

Harry looked from his snoring friend to the golden ellipse in his sweaty grasp, mesmerized by its unspeakable perfection. Unsure what came next, Harry's boots left solid ground, causing a brief panic before an overwhelming sense of peace drowned his apprehension. The invisible hands dropped him on a dizzying precipice near the top of the sentinel high above the Jeep and a sleeping Neil.

Harry gazed beyond the pictographs covering the wall and saw an opening in the rock. Following a psychic command, he wriggled through the narrow slot with the golden ellipse held outstretched in his hands like an ancient sacrificial offering before suspending it above a deep echoing shaft and letting it go. Instead of dropping like a rock, the golden ellipse defied gravity, floating and shimmering in midair before shooting upward and embedding into a domed apex high above the pitch-black emptiness.

Assured by the Dark Specters that his prize was secure, Harry scooched his stocky frame backward and caught a glimpse of metal jutting from solid rock. Wriggling sideways, he smoothed his hand over a cleat hammered into the stone with a knotted rope hanging into the abyss.

"What is this for?"

"A diversion. Nothing more. Here is all you need to know: 32 degrees, 33 minutes, 48.1 seconds north, and 13 degrees, 31 minutes, 18.1 seconds east. Keep the coordinates safe from prying eyes. Trust nobody. The golden ellipse is in your hands, Harry, and you can keep it after everything is finished."

"After what is finished?"

"Humanity."

Still slumped in the Jeep, Neil's gritty eyes reawakened in the remote desert at the base of a sheer rock wall. He turned and saw Harry sweating profusely, his beet-red face fixated on transcribing a series of numbers on the back of a bent photograph. "Harry? That better not be my photo of Carol." Sitting up, he grabs Harry by the arm to stop his scribbling, "Why did you drag me out here? Are you trying to get us court-martialed?"

Wiping his brow, Harry pulled from Neil's weak hold and finished writing the coordinates on the back of Neil's prized possession: a sexy black and white photo of his wife, Carol. Holding the picture up for his friend, he smiles, "This is for you, Captain. I wrote the coordinates to our treasure on the backside of the one thing I know you will never lose or share with anyone. Pretty clever, don't you think?"

Trying to quantify the awkward compromised position caused by Harry's insubordinate actions, Neil accepts the photo and calms his temper, "Lieutenant Stark, you have thirty seconds to explain yourself, or so help me God, I will beat the shit out of you and drag your sorry ass in front of the military police, myself."

Harry's round face widens into a mischievous smile. "I explained everything on the way out here, Captain. Don't you remember?"

Harry started the Jeep, emitting a raspy chuckle, "You are right about one thing, Captain. If we are not back soon, we will both be in a shitload of trouble." Turning to his only friend in the world, he smiled, "Both of us."

Realizing he was implicated no matter what he said or did from this point, Neil flipped the photo to read the scrawled numbers, "Well, Harry, I hope you can read your chicken scratch because I sure as hell can't."

"Don't worry, Captain. I have everything under control."

**Harry | Farmhouse cellar, Aix-en-Provence, France
1944 to 2043**

Harry's wounds healed with the extreme passage of time, leaving him scarred and disfigured—a graphic reminder of humankind's corruptible nature, lest anyone forget. With the pilot in a century-long comatose state, the Dark Specters preserved his physical form atop the cot in Dreyfus' cellar, assaulting the pilot's neural pathways with relentless brainwashing to poison the young man against his species.

* * *

Fighting through the undergrowth toward the pit of death, tears stream from Harry's swollen eyes, "I'm coming, little girl! Hang on!" Without hesitation, he wades into the gore-filled mass grave, gasping for air, crawling over mangled bodies toward the small blond creature in the pink dress. Reaching her back-turned petite form lying on her side atop a decaying corpse, he props himself on the intertwining mass of arms and legs and calls to her, "I'm here. What am I supposed to do?"

The child bolts upright at her tiny waist and pivots toward the disfigured pilot; dirty strands of golden hair obscure her return gaze. Raising her delicate index finger to rose-colored lips curling into a mischievous smile, she signals for quiet.

His heart pounding with morbid curiosity, Harry reaches forward and smooths the hair from her porcelain face with the side of his skeletal hand, revealing purplish eyelids sewn shut with red sutured X's. Recoiling in surprise and horror, he retreats while a growing chorus of laughter echoes inside Harry's mangled head. A loud, incoherent exhortation shrieks from her tiny mouth, commanding a twisted knot of reanimated hands to grasp and pull on the tatters of his filthy uniform, holding him in a vicelike grip. The blind girl blows him a goodbye kiss seconds before another hand juts upward from the wretched pile and grabs him by the neck.

The maddening laughter muffles to a suffocating silence as Harry is pulled face down through the charnel pit, like Alice through the looking glass.

****

Harry walks down the middle of a rutted country lane under dark clouds obscuring a half-moon rising in the inky vastness. A blue-hued ambiance penetrates the old-growth forest encroaching on both sides of the road, transfiguring dappled patterns of light and shadow into sinister wraithlike figures. The crack of a branch, followed by rustling leaves, propels the pilot into a panicked jog. His scorched throat swallows back a temptation to break into a sprint—a tacit acknowledgment that it would only make things worse.

Stumbling to a stop, Harry avoids bowling over the blind girl in the pink dress, reappearing out of the ether athwart his harried footsteps. Flashing her mischievous smile, she reaches out to hold his hand, pulling him toward a covered bridge coming into view around a crooked bend.

Childhood fear and fascination from the only book he ever felt compelled to steal manifests in vivid detail around Harry and his sightless guide. Somehow, he is inside Sleepy Hollow. He whirled on his feet with a flash of clarity, searching through the darkness for the phantasmagorical antagonist and a flaming pumpkin hurtling toward his head.

Harry pleads with his muse, fighting back a terrified, sobbing panic, "I want to go back."

The girl squeezes tight on his mangled hand with monstrous strength, "Monsieur, do not fear the horseman."

Taken aback by her frank reply, he yanks his hand from her pincer-like grasp, "Why the hell not?"

"Because you are the horseman."

The last hundred steps to the covered bridge entrance pass

without a flaming pumpkin or blazing gourds. Harry's heaving breaths following his fast-paced trek through Sleepy Hollow conjure an image of his chain-smoking commander's wheezy disposition. By contrast, Harry never smoked, yet his chronic shortness of breath prompted interminable suggestions for him to quit cold turkey. His ultimate pet peeve is do-gooders; he knew they did not give a damn.

Another raspy inhalation prompts a query for his prescient muse, "How the hell did I pass the Army physical?"

She wipes her wet button nose on the pink puffed sleeve of her dirty dress and shrugs, "I dunno."

Venturing from the girl's side, Harry steps to the covered bridge's carriage-sized maw calculating the perilous distance to a dim square of light at the far end. Dark Specters floating in the middle space between the spidery cross beams greet their recruit. With his tentative first steps onto the rickety structure, the rotted planks bend and creak under his filthy boots. The light specks dance around him, floating into the bat-infested rafters supporting the pitched, leaky roof. Halfway across, he pauses at a gaping hole in the floor. Looking down from the dizzying height, he studies the moonlit blanket of ferns and saplings covering the deep gorge down to a shimmering mountain stream snaking along the bottom, cutting deep into the Earth.

He turns to advise his young companion to watch her step but finds her small form still silhouetted at the entrance.

"Goodbye, Harry." Her pink dress makes a playful twirl as she turns and skips down the shadowy lane.

"Goodbye."

The egress from the covered bridge transforms into a Roman amphitheater vomitorium. Unfazed by the shift in scenery, Harry enters the empty arena to a deafening silence heralding his arrival under a moonless infinitude of stars filling the circular void above his head, bathing the ancient structure in an ethereal glow. Harry ascends a steep staircase to a platform with a commanding view. A trio of tiered sections leads on a steep angle toward the nosebleeds curving along the top, representing a hierarchical order. A memory of sneaking into the upper reaches of Yankee Stadium as an orphaned youth elicits a quick smile. He could care less about baseball; it was his retreat from the mean streets of the Bronx.

Reflecting on his wretched childhood, he reclines on an ornate red velvet chair and leans forward, waiting for the show to start. Glancing at the gilded table beside his exalted seat, he envisions thick juicy grapes in overflowing bunches on an extravagant silver platter. To his disappointment, none materialized. Oh well. A lavish array of comestibles conjures a hazed memory from his previous life, where a single stolen grape from a sidewalk produce cart was breakfast. Sustenance was no longer an issue. His active mind viewed a lack of grapes as a missed opportunity to lend authenticity to his hallucination. Now, if they were peeled and fed to him by slaves, no, that would be overkill.

* * *

Most men are within a finger's breadth of being mad. Watching Harry Stark lose his grip on reality and accept his transformation, the Dark Specters add to Diogenes' astute observation, *"some are already mad and don't realize it."*

* * *

Opposite his elevated position, a draped white canopy larger than a parachute stretches between massive Doric columns.

The stars fade to an empty expanse, and the bluish ambiance dissipates to total darkness. Harry could not see his disfigured hand in front of his ghastly face as light projected out of nothingness onto the cloth.

"The show is about to begin."

Producing an irony-laced smirk, Harry predicts cartoonish

dancing popcorn and soda pop ads followed by the ubiquitous coming attractions will not precede this feature. "It is just a thought. Lighten up."

Harry settles back onto the soft velvet as the show starts, like most things—in the beginning. The screen widens onto an aerial view of prehistoric human ancestors in mortal combat with a hapless tribe of victims. Judging by the lopsided barbarism that ensued, the mercy rule will not be used.

The melee in the tamped-down grassy area transforms into a barren desert, and a pyramid-shaped beacon animates from the sand and rocks.

Harry sees the golden ellipse at the northern facade's apex in all its glory. A heartbeat after viewing the beacon's out-of-this-world complexities powered by the golden ellipse, the screen goes dark.

A voice resonates in the arena: *"Harry Stark, it is up to you to ensure the golden ellipse is never returned to the beacon. In the cosmic silence following its deactivation, forces are en route to end the human experiment once and for all."*

"But what about me?"

"You have no significance beyond your purpose."

"What is that again?"

Exerting patience beyond reasonable tolerance, the Dark Specters ignore the man's impudence, *"Ensure the golden ellipse remains hidden at the remote location."*

"I can keep the ellipse?"

"Yes. Now relax and watch the presentation. We put some time into its preparation."

Harry proffers a rueful smile, anticipating his elliptical reunion.

"Harry Stark, if the ellipse finds its way back to the beacon, it is your task to misalign its energized reinstallation atop the beacon."

"What will that do?"

"Destroy everything."

"Will I die?"

"You are already dead."

The gut-churning show resumes before Harry can pry further about the nature of his demise or the Machine. Depictions of violence and mayhem reflect in his transfixed eyeballs. The mind-altering propaganda flips forward at a furious rate through corrupted leaders from every race, ethnicity, and creed, reenacting epic misdeeds in vivid detail.

Strangers from strange lands meet in pitched battles in the gore-filled chaos of nameless fields, glens, deserts, and forests where anonymous losers breathe their last and victors live to see another day.

Mechanized warfare bursts from hedgerows, driving across expansive plains, leveling villages and towns, gobbling vast territories only to get bogged down by nature's wrath and vengeful counterattacks.

Bombardiers endure sub-zero temperatures and enemy shells, targeting mission objectives from impersonal heights, reducing cultures built over centuries to wastelands of death and rubble in minutes.

Sailors dive from sinking ships into the oil-slicked waves while their burns and gaping wounds chum the shark-infested waters for days, watching comrades succumb to briny graves.

Families ripped apart by the promise of lives stolen without recompense, never healing, never forgiving, harboring resentments for those whose shell-shocked sons and daughters returned from war. Meanwhile, survivor's guilt and night terrors plague the stoic veterans to their dying days.

Harry leans forward, watching an unlucky bomber crew leaping from a B-17 Flying Fortress engulfed in flames. His rapt attention focuses on an airman's panicked flailing before his chute finally opens, only to get raked by enemy fighters on the way down. An unchivalrous deed Harry acknowledges committing in the heat of battle. "War is hell. He'd damn well do the same to me."

Emaciated prisoners languish amongst skeletal bodies stacked like cords of wood, confirming rumored death camps in Axis-controlled territories throughout Europe and the Soviet Union. Meanwhile, the Imperial Japanese commit inhuman atrocities on helpless POWs across southern China.

Barbwire-fenced encampments crammed with Japanese-Americans morph across the screen in a morose black-and-white newsreel montage.

The conquest of vast territories and the brutal tactics deployed to impose Western civilization across the hard-won badlands and flowing prairies play out like a John Ford film. The trail of tears fails to raise an eyebrow, "Man, this jumps around. I never cared for westerns; I can't relate."

Genocide, famine, and disease, the three-headed monster of every global conflict, flash before Harry's vision in rapid succession. Murder, rape, slavery, and a host of vileness intertwine with the subjugation of entire civilizations, culminating with the current world war. Harry reaches a point of saturation, his brain a sieve of horrible images.

The final section, a peek into the future—courtesy of Dark Spectral prognosticators—piques his curiosity beyond an imminent Cold War and an unending War on Terror that follows without a hair's breadth in between.

The attention-grabber for a misanthrope like Harry is the apocalyptic finale. A futuristic vision of wholesale destruction on an extinction-level scale. Marauding alien ships, more massive than aircraft carriers, crowding the sky in every direction, rampage over Planet Earth until nothing is left. Nothing.

Harry envisions a future version of himself, clutching the golden ellipse on the dark dead planet under a leaden, ash-filled sky. His unbreakable bond with the infinite power source proves his ticket to a new existence far from the place he used to call home.

The projection stops.

"Okay. I'll do it. All you had to do was ask."

Harry | Farmhouse cellar, Aix-en-Provence, France
06:30 p.m. | August 1, 2043 (One year before present time)

Happy people laughing and conversing in French break the monastic silence inside the dark cellar. Harry's brainwaves reactivate, nudging him from a decade's-long nap, like Rip Van Winkle, onto the modern-day world in the year of our Lord 2043. Flat on his back atop the cot, he listens to the conversation passing through the thin walls into his concealed space and realizes he comprehends their small talk. Prying open eyelids glued shut over time, he blinks to clear a thick layer of dried gunk and attempts to raise his hand to his face, but he remains belted at each wrist and across his ankles in leather restraints.

Wriggling and wrestling free from under the moth-eaten wool blanket, he flings it sideways, sending it halfway off the cot onto the cellar floor. Pressing his splotchy bearded chin to his chest, Harry looks down the length of his wrinkled nakedness and discovers his arms and legs strapped down where Dreyfus left him so long ago. "I look like a fucking raisin." Propping onto his elbows, he utilizes a century-worth of pent-up energy, pulling back on the dried-out leather cuffed around his right wrist, breaking free with a loud snap and a cloud of dust.

Harry startles, lifting his freed hand to his face in the dimness, gasping for air. It looks like a freakish Halloween skeleton hand. With crusted eyes widened in terror, he turns palm out, palm in, before squeezing a tight fist and flexing every strand of muscle. Relaxing his grip, he touches a bony index finger to what's left of his nose. Next, he counts to five, bending and flexing each digit. Growing more intrigued and less concerned, he makes a thumbs-up signal and then forms a hand pistol aimed toward the cheerful male and female voices outside.

His unstrapped left arm has the same freakish appearance.

Bending forward at his emaciated waist, he frees his stiff legs and swings them onto the floor. Looking down at his feet, he heaves a relieved sigh at their unburnt stub-toed appearance, remembering his boots remained intact after his fiery bail-out.

Standing off the cot, Harry considers his next move, unsure who or what he has become. Lifting a skeleton hand to his head, he feels leathery skin amassed in clumps all over his scalp and face. Scrunching his nose, opening and closing his mouth, and raising his hairless brows up and down, he can tell the burnt skin is healed, but he must be a scary-looking son-of-a-bitch.

First things first, his clothes. Moving to the sideboard, as quiet as the dead mouse lying in the corner, he pulls open the drawers and finds crumbled rolls of gauze, empty rubbing alcohol bottles, a tobacco tin, and a box of wooden matches. Bending low to check inside the cabinet, he finds his leather jacket and boots. "Where the hell is my flight suit? Dreyfus must have burned it to hide the evidence."

Struggling to unroll his jacket, hardened into a thick dried-out roll, rat droppings mixed with urine-stained fur tufts and bits of gnawed debris tumble to the floor. "So much for my jacket." To his delight, he inspects his boots and finds them free of infestation for some unknowable reason. Sliding his ruined Black Scorpions jacket back onto the dirty shelf, he closes cabinet doors, symbolizing the end of his previous life.

The tactile yet foreign sensation of pushing desiccated feet into his boots for the first time in 100 years courses a swooning vigor through his transformed body. Despite his grotesque appearance, he never felt better. Moving to the side table, he examines Dreyfus's old pipe, rusted shears, more decayed gauze, and one unused morphine syrette. He picks up the scissors and the syrette, blowing a thick layering of dust and cobwebs off with a single puff of air.

Glimmering specks materialize inside his semitransparent form. Harry disappears from the cellar.

* * *

Young fit hikers, three women, and two lucky men set up camp in an overgrown pasture downhill from an uninhabited, vine-covered farmhouse tucked away on a forested slope with a spanking-good view of their destination, Montagne Sainte-Victoire. The picturesque location is a popular spot for backpackers to work out the kinks in their pricey gear before trekking into the wilderness. Aix-en-Provence bars and nightlife are also close enough for one final blow-out before abandoning civilization.

Waving au revoir to his friends, Jean-Claude watched them disappear through the trees toward the country lane to hitch a ride into town for a final binge. The young man hated being the fifth wheel, but someone had to stay behind and keep an eye on their stuff. He volunteered. Despite a solemn promise to return around midnight, he knew he would not see their hungover faces until sunrise.

With a vacant-eyed stare into the glowing embers of his well-maintained campfire, the young man's idle thoughts linger on his best friend's new girlfriend, Henrietta. Although a newcomer to their tight-knit clique, she fit right in with her vivacious personality and flirtatious charm. He had to admit, he found her quite captivating from the word go.

Swigging a cabernet purchased at a winery earlier in the day, he smiles, musing on Henrietta's gift for gab. On the bus ride from town through the hike to their campsite, she regaled the group with viral ghost stories about the ancient stone structure hunkered in a stand of conifers behind Jean-Claude. He swivels from the fire, studying the asymmetrical stacking of limestone blocks held together with a crumbled mortar and thick vines, weighted under a pitched, dilapidated terracotta roof. Vestigial remnants of a porch jut from tall grasses and wildflowers lead to the rotted wood door to the right of an empty front window frame. "It's not haunted; it's collapsing."

After another swig, he pokes at the fire with a stick, causing embers to rise into the balmy late-summer evening air before extinguishing into the ether. To his surprise, a single fiery orb remains suspended before his tipsy-eyed stare.

Planting the bottle in the grass, the rattled young man scrambles onto his feet, watching the orb expand in size to a soccer ball and zoom uphill.

Another Henrietta story involved strange balls of light appearing out of thin air. Well, here's one, right in front of his eyes, "What is in this wine?"

Jean-Claude feels a presence behind him and whirls toward the farmhouse, catching a shadow move past the west-facing window. The sound of footsteps across creaking floorboards invades his ears. Freaking out just a little, he remembers the last part of the sexy brunette's tale: the original owner from the 1700s never left, still haunting his house and the surrounding forest. "You will know he is nearby when a sweet smell of pipe tobacco wafts up to your nose."

"It's probably hippie stoners coming up here to smoke a bowl of weed." Out of extreme caution, he sniffs the air, "Nothing sweet. That's good, I guess."

Looking at the half-assembled gear strewn about the grasses, he shakes his head in disgust, "Damn, my stupid friends! They should have stayed and worked on their gear. Why do I always have to be the responsible one?"

Despite severe reservations and the promised safety of his fully-assembled nylon single-sleeper fortress of solitude, he trudges uphill, bottle in hand, through the grass toward the farmhouse.

Parting waist-deep overgrowth obscuring the rotted front porch remnants, he sidles to the elevated threshold of the front door and pushes it wide, eliciting a squeaky groan. "How else would it sound?"

After another swig of liquid courage, he flips on his flashlight and shines it into the musty space. "Nobody but us ghosts."

Hefting his athletic frame inside, he springs onto his hiking boots and scoops his bottle by the neck. With its wooden drawers long gone, an old bureau sits askew in the far-left corner near an open hatch in the floor. Skeletal remains of dead birds and vermin lay amid various scat across the urine-stained floorboards, along with fur chunks stuck on rusted nails here and there. The place was a popular hangout for the locals but no sign of human habitation. "Of course, no one in their right mind would enter a haunted cabin." Light-headed from the alcohol on an empty stomach, he turns to leave. A packet of dehydrated beef stew awaits his culinary review.

Rationalizing the mystery light ball, "The orb was the setting sun playing tricks on my eyes. Nothing more."

On the verge of vacating the premises, he ponders a shut door on the far wall. What will he find on the other side? Swallowing back lingering fear, he steps across the dirty floor and turns the handle. Unlike the front door, this one opens without a sound like someone oiled the hinges. He leans into the shadowed space, training his light around what used to be a kitchen. A potbelly stove squats inside a boarded-up back door, and an empty rack hangs in the stillness from cobwebbed rafters above a salvageable porcelain basin.

A bony hand clamps down hard on Jean-Claude's right shoulder, immobilizing him. Surprised beyond measure, the flashlight fumbles from his loosened grip, clattering to the floor. Struggling to free himself from his assailant's heavy hand, he panics and flings the wine bottle backward at his assailant.

The feeble defense proves too little, too late: a painful prick in the jugular from a World War Two-era morphine syrette and its lights out for the young man from Montpelier.

* * *

Looking upon the young man lying crumpled in a facedown heap atop the floorboards in a pool of red wine seeping through the slats, a triumphant smile contorts Harry's gruesome countenance. "I am the Headless Horseman."

Harry held no antipathy toward his first victim. However, like the backpackers checking new equipment in the grassy pasture, he needed to test his new powers, and the youthful outdoor enthusiast proved all-too-accommodating for his task. "The stupid kid never saw me, yet I was right there the whole time."

Standing over his first victim in the darkness, Harry morphs from his transparent state, picks up the kid's flashlight in his skeleton hand, and aims it around the empty room. The former AAF fighter pilot muses on the ironic twist underlying his uncanny new ability to disappear like a ghost. Throughout his pathetic life, people looked right through him, like he was never really there. Now he could return the favor.

A disembodied voice interrupts Harry's altered state.

"Reach down and touch the deceased young man's face."

"Why would I want to do that?"

"You can assume your victims' physical forms and mannerisms. We have deployed shapeshifters throughout human history to infiltrate and corrupt humankind. You will now use the tall and handsome likeness of this poor young fellow who went by Jean-Claude to initiate the fulfillment of our plan."

"I am not your fucking pawn. I want the golden ellipse. A deal is a deal."

"We already accepted your terms. Now proceed."

Harry lowers onto his knees and pushes sweaty bangs from the fellow's forehead with his skeletonized index finger. Caressing the kid's exposed forehead with the back of his hand produces a shimmering and ecstatic electrical charge coursing every fiber of Harry Stark's burnt and disfigured body.

Harry rises and transforms into the strapping young man's athletic stark naked form. He picks up the torch and shines it down his new body, noting his vigorous and healthy arousal. The nascent shapeshifter sucks in the air while his heart beats out of his strapping chest. Rushing to the farmhouse's broken front window, he smiles at kaleidoscopic reflections of Jean Claude's handsome face returning his bright white grin.

"Harry, is that you?"

A Dark Spectral orb emerges from the ether, swirling with malicious lights. *"Your disguise will fade at an indeterminate moment, returning you to your macabre visage and skeletal hands. This shortcoming results from your reanimated frailty. Still, your facade should last weeks before you must replace it with a new victim."*

Harry acknowledges the wrinkle in his paranormal reality with a logical reply, "I'll time my transformations and get a handle on how long they will last."

Exiting Dreyfus' decayed farmhouse into the French evening air, Harry bounds down the hill toward the expensive camping gear scattered about the tall grass. Locating his victim's tent, Harry rifles through the kid's bag and selects a t-shirt and blue jeans. After dressing in the unfamiliar garb, he inventories the backpack and pulls out a strange timepiece. A voice in his head calls it an Apple Watch. The home screen alights with August 1, 2043. "No wonder I feel so good; my final sortie was almost 99 years ago. I wonder how the Yankees are doing?"

Giddy with his stolen youth, Harry laces up Jean Claude's Timberland hikers and pulls on a jet-black hoodie. Admiring the menacing skull design, he brushes back his thick mop of light-brown hair and smiles, "The skull looks about right."

Thrust into the modern-day world of 2043, Harry slings the backpack across his shoulder, kicks out the fire, and treks along the darkened path toward Aix-en-Provence.

Strolling down the rutted trail, a crash course on the Dark Specters' evil endgame resonates in his head: *"Time is of the essence. You have one year before the Gorkian invasion fleets breach the sky."*

"Gorkian invasion fleets? What kind of fubar mission is this?"

"The vile creatures are not your concern, Stark. Suffice it to say; their monstrous reputation is well-deserved. Refocus on your task: travel to the British Museum and assume the form of a research assistant named Yasmine Sardouk. In her guise, you can access a mummified cat sarcophagus concealing a pyramid-shaped crystal amulet."

"Shapeshifting into a woman will be interesting. Is she a looker? What will I do with this crystal thing?"

"Consummate Sardouk's transfer to a new position at the Cairo Museum and seek out an archeology professor named Tarek Hamed. You must give him the amulet."

"Why do we need this Hamed character?"

"In case you fail us."

* * *

Jean-Claude's hungover friends discover his body in a sticky pool of red wine on the farmhouse kitchen floor. The death is ruled a drug overdose by the incurious coroner whose weary eyes witnessed the sad demise of too many young people throughout his professional career. This tragic scene was no different.

The distraught friends press the insolent investigator about Jean-Claude's missing backpack.

"It was stolen. Case closed."

The bulk of the world's knowledge is an imaginary construction.

– *Helen Keller*

Chapter Ten:

The Invasion

Owen | Banishment
05:15 p.m. | August 22, 2044

Propping herself on skinned-up elbows while her sweaty midriff presses atop the slick surface, Rachel steadies the dimming flashlight onto a perfect droplet releasing from her battered husband's bloody fingertip elevated inches above the dark glass floor. Their spirits soar, watching it pass through and accelerate into the burgeoning galaxy below their swollen-eyed gaze.

"Rachel, it's working."

In rapt silence, they see a glowing red tail extending behind the blood drop on its eyeballed trajectory with the brilliant green pinpoint at a celestial spot along the Milky Way's spiraling outer arm.

Rachel taps her husband on the back to pull him from his

trance-like stare, "I would never have connected the depiction of human blood on the wall so literally. Any idea what is going to happen?"

Afraid to tear his eyes from the blood drop's extraordinary course, "No. Not really. But sometimes, it pays to be a boring left-brainer. I'm hoping the blood drop's impact into the green spot triggers a pathway out of here." Turning to his scared wife's uplit face, "That is if it does anything. I know it is a stretch, but we can't give up. I want to get out of here, kick that monster's ass, and take back my ellipse."

Rachel frowns at Owen's beaten profile, returning his laser-like focus onto the glowing red trail arcing into the stars. Alarm bells peel inside her pounding head at his use of a singular possessive pronoun. Hoping he just misspoke in his distracted state of mind, she follows his gaze onto the streaking red comet moments before it impacts with the bright green speck. Thunderstruck, the outlandish plan seemed to work; she forced a nervous smile while anticipating a just-in-the-nick-of-time turn of luck with bated breath. However, the promise of a post-collision miracle transforms into an anticlimactic dud as Owen's blood droplet vanishes into the ether, and nothing happens. They monitored the viridescence for signs of change for minutes before conceding it remained unaffected by the direct hit.

With a defeated sigh, Rachel turns to Owen, "One-in-a-million shot."

"It didn't make a difference where I dripped the blood." Looking through the darkness closing in on their prone positions, Owen peers at the hieroglyphic patterns covering the hexagonal chamber, "Nothing has changed. I thought a wall would open or something. Damn!"

On the brink of consoling the apparent failure of Owen's left-brained inspiration, a thunderous crack reverberates inside the six-walled cell. Rachel cups her hands over her ears on reflex, muffling her terrified scream in the chaotic din. Milliseconds after the initial bang, the mysterious glass surface evaporates, sending her on a stomach-churning head-over-heels descent into the reverberating pitch-blackness. Unable to see anything while flailing her arms and legs in a panicked freefall toward the Milky Way, she yells at the top of her lungs, "Owen! What the fuck did you do to us?" Failing to hear a response, "Are you still there?"

The tumultuous vortex subsides, and the six-sided cell transmogrifies before her startled eyes. A lightning storm spectrum flashes across her weightless body from a radiant nebula billowing out of nothingness, strobing off the walls within the electrified space. The disorienting aftermath of Owen's plasmatic experiment leaves the former trust fund murderess gasping for air. Rachel's enthralled emerald gaze reflects the wondrous spectacle of the scale version Milky Way spiraling around her sideways, levitating form.

She heaves a relieved sigh, relocating Owen floating upside down, looking ten ways at once, absorbed in the sheer grandeur of their home galaxy engulfing him in a shimmering sea of stars.

Without looking her way, he calls out in his annoying sing-song, "I told you something was going to happen!"

Their eyes meet through the shimmering swirl, like ancient gods on a midnight stroll through the cosmos.

"It is beautiful, but why is it here?" Rachel ventures an outstretched hand smoothing through sparkling clusters, leaving a stellar ripple in the wake of her flowing motion. Pushing blond locks from her face, she notices something new: the green light is blinking. Rolling sideways through the expanse, she curls herself to face Owen, "Look at the green star. Did we cause that?"

Facing her from his upside-down vantage, Owen cannot refrain from commenting on her graceful movements in the low gravity, "You are a natural! I knew you should have gone with me to the bumper room on the spaceship." Angling around to locate the green pinpoint amid the Milky Way's spiral arms, he observes the green blink. "It was not doing that before. Maybe we broke the galaxy."

Noting the reemergence of Owen's cavalier humor, Rachel

glides through the stars, "I'm starting to freak out in here."

"Okay, let's keep it together," Owen observes more green lights popping into view across the spinning mass, possibly in answer to the green blinker. "Huh, it looks like the galaxy is talking to itself."

"Maybe those spots all contain life."

"Now, who has seen too many movies?"

The pair are lost in the twinkling spectacle spiraling upward above their float.

"Rachel, we're still falling."

Like a slow-motion skydiver, Rachel angles herself into a hover above Owen, "Or, everything around us is rising."

Owen's startled yelp preempts his reply, dropping from a six-sided aperture onto a solid rocky surface in a cloud of dust. A sliver of time after contacting terra firma, his aching athletic frame breaks Rachel's fall, landing atop him in a twisted heap.

The familiar feel of Earth's gravitational pull in the uncomfortable form of loose gravel and rocks pressing into his back is a welcome respite from their prolonged detention in the cell, "I think we reached rock bottom."

Rachel rolls off her husband and arches her back to move a jagged rock, "I'm fine, by the way."

Resting their aching bodies in a side-by-side repose after their soul-crushing encounter with Harry, the couple stares into the hexagonal void twelve feet overhead at green lights sparkling to life across the Milky Way, backlit by the colorful blooming nebula.

Flynn | Robbers Entrance, Great Pyramid
05:25 p.m. | August 22, 2044

Liberated from the Light Specters' beacon warning that held them at bay for eons, the first race of marauding aliens to breach Earth's atmosphere neutralizes the fragile human world just by showing up.

Biding their time, expecting the Gorks' ultimate failure, malevolent time-traveling Grays monitor the invasion from the relative closeness of Jupiter's moons while dodging a flotilla of cube-shaped enigmas whose silence is deafening. Indeed, space seems more crowded as time expands inexorably outward.

***

On the devastated third rock from the sun, armadas of irregular-shaped gravity-defying Gork battle cruisers disengage cloaks, thundering from the heavens in chaotic formations encircling the blue marble, ripe for the picking.

The sky above the Mediterranean Sea blackens as hundreds of war machines assemble in low-altitude formations churning the pristine aquamarine waters into dark-gray, white-capped swells rising tens of stories into the sky before cresting into deep troughs. The fleets split and peel onto their devastating paths, half bearing down on Europe's soft underbelly and half over North Africa, vectoring east toward Egypt and the Sinai Peninsula.

The terrifying formations rumble over the arid North African topography, spawning seismic tremors and electrified biblical storms blasting everything with abrasive sands and a thick layering of powdery red dust.

Wailing police and ambulance sirens combined with blaring home and car alarms amplify into a frenzied ear-splitting din throughout Cairo's over-populated urban sprawl before ebbing to an ominous silence.

Electromagnetic pulsations generated by the anti-gravitational dreadnoughts blow the obsolete grid to smithereens while frying billions of microprocessor-enabled devices into worthless techno-junk. In a devastating worldwide domino effect, humanity plunges headfirst into a new dark age thirty minutes into the invasion.

* * *

Late afternoon sunlight filtering through a ruddy haze cast everything in an eerie blood-red glow. Protected from the worst of the hellacious winds on the Great Pyramid's leeward side outside the robbers entrance, Flynn, Louie, and Cassandra look like bandits. Souvenir bandanas tied behind their heads mask their faces below goggles thrown at them by a rattled deputy before the guy fled in terror.

Flynn fusses with the knot on his doubled bandana from his elevated vantage atop the plateau while focusing on the closest ship wobbling into a hover above the tenement rooftops. The Powers That Be agent studies the alien vessel with dreaded alarm. In his unusual occupation, he has seen various UAPs—from the infamous Tic Tacs to cigar shapes and the ubiquitous saucer and triangular designs—but nothing approaching the scale of these ugly ass ships. Each craft measures the length of five supertankers set end-to-end with spoked wheels at regular intervals rotating around an elongated central core that looks to Flynn like a gigantic, melted Snickers bar.

"Man, when did I last eat something?"

The back end of the amorphous fuselage radiates a deep cerulean blue, and a rainbow of glimmering lights flash across the entire length. Menacing cylindrical elements spike from numerous positions around the hull, resembling enormous cannons, "Don't shoot that green shit. Don't do it, goddamit."

Taking measured breaths through his army-provided desert camo mask, Captain Faisel casts a backward glance, overhearing the green shit remark, and notes the ship's threatening course, raising dark eyebrows underneath streaky goggles. The abridged version of why Flynn and his mates infiltrated the plateau rattled in his frontal cortex. Against his better judgment, he made the pragmatic command decision to take the agent's incredible tale at face value and assist in finding the missing American couple and their golden ellipse. It didn't take a military genius to see the fleet of alien warships mean they were outgunned, outmaneuvered, and out of time. Initial attempts to contact his superiors produced nothing but static in reply. For all he knows, his command structure is already dead or incommunicado within a secure bunker. Either way, he is in charge.

His perceived demotion to an over-qualified security guard at the world-renowned tourist trap looks more providential by the moment. He barks a command through his mask to "hurry the hell up" at his two remaining uniformed deputies. Everyone else fled following the initial sonic blast and the terrifying sight of the first spaceship.

The stalwart duo plods through stinging sands, hefting a heavy battering ram up the limestone blocks to the robbers entrance. Flynn, Louie, and Cassandra edge sideways on the gusty landing affording the young men room to pass. Gripping the unwieldy metal shaft by handles at each end, they take a position in front of the locked gate. Swinging it back and forth to gain momentum, they slam it through the overwrought metal barrier, separating the slatted obstruction from its rusted hinges on the third violent swing. Faisel grabs the battered KEEP OUT sign lying in the sand and flings it into the slipstream toward the ships.

Deciding the claustrophobic tunnels inside the pyramid will be crowded enough, Faisel commands the frightened young men, "Return to your barracks and seek out whoever is in charge. I will take it from here."

The flummoxed pair drop the ram with a metallic clank, salute the stern officer, and scamper off the pyramid. Sliding goggles onto his forehead, Faisel watches them run like hell. Turning to the masked threesome waiting on the windswept perch, "Okay, Agent Flynn. You are up!"

Springing past Captain Faisel, Flynn pulls the bandana around his neck and enters the tunnel past the ruined gate. His torch pierces darkness ahead of his quickened steps revealing a crumpled form splayed on its side ten feet inside the rutted passage. Hunching over the naked male, he flips the dead body face-up into his light and calls to the approaching Faisel, "I think this is your deceased security guard." Peering farther down the robbers tunnel, "Owen and Rachel Haig, where are you?"

With Flynn on point, Faisel, Louie, and Cassandra infiltrate the pyramid following the eighth-century tunnel. A bone-rattling shudder permeates the limestone blocks, ratcheting fear of being buried alive to an unspoken yet demonstrable level. The clattering sound of falling rocks exacerbates the tense situation. Their flashlights arc through dust clouds hanging in the stifling air as the group reaches a widened-out area at the base of a short flight of steps.

Cassandra offers her technical expertise, "Those steps lead up into the Ascending Passage. However, it is a long climb to the Grand Gallery and the King's Chamber. There is nothing of value up there."

Faisel crunches broken glass under his boots and crouches to examine a smashed lantern lying on the floor.

Flynn's light catches the glint of bloody handprints smeared across the limestone walls and the piped safety rail leading up the steps, "It does not take Sherlock Holmes to see a struggle took place right here."

Louie breaks from the group, vaults to the top step, and bends to pluck something off the limestone.

"What did you find, Louie?"

"I believe this came from Miss Rachel." The eagle-eyed robot dangles a wavy golden lock still attached to a bloody chunk of scalp before his light.

Crestfallen by the discovery, Flynn moves to get a closer look and collapses on the top step. "Fuck me. That is not good." Propping his left hand on the leading edge of the chiseled stair, he pulls it back on reflex. "What the hell?" Lifting his hand in front of his face, he smells more than sees a wet snotty ooze smeared on his palm. Swiping it off across the rough surface, "Whatever they battled in here left a stinky trail."

Faisel scoops up the busted lantern and recoils from the smell of more ooze dripping off its dented base, "It smells like death."

Cassandra remains motionless at the back of the group, wondering if her secret benefactor is still alive.

Captain Faisel tries to light a fire under his dejected troops, "Which way do we go from here, Flynn? Explain this scheme you were here to carry out one more time."

Louie answers for the distraught agent, "Sir, our mission here is to restart a warning beacon buried deep underneath this structure by returning a small gold ellipse atop its north face. The invaders arrived this afternoon due to its prolonged silence for over a century. Our job was to foil your security so Owen and Rachel could find the secret passage to the chamber where the beacon sits inoperable. Apparently, someone assumed the form of your dead guard and is more than likely now in possession of the ellipse."

Ignoring the paranormal aspect of Louie's synopsis, Faisel turns to his pyramid expert, "Cassandra, are you aware of any such chamber?"

The windblown woman pulls her long, straight jet-black hair from the bandana around her neck, reassuming her tour guide role: "I am aware of the conspiracy theories, but that's all. If a secret chamber exists, it is above my pay grade."

Faisel's attention is distracted, looking past the dark-haired tour guide onto a figure emerging from the shadows.

"Did I hear someone say, secret chamber?" Professor Tarek Hamed performs a surreptitious handoff of an object to Cassandra as he sidles past with an over-animated, "Pardon me, dear."

With all eyes focused on Hamed's sudden reappearance, she uses the dark shadows to slide the graphite pistol into the front waistband under her loose blouse.

Hamed takes center stage in the open space, removes his Panama hat, and brushes red dust from his white suit jacket. "Phew! It is hell out there. Quite unpleasant if I say so myself."

Harry Stark | Beacon chamber
05:25 p.m. | August 22, 2044

Harry Stark caresses the golden ellipse in his hideous clutches inside the beacon chamber's pitch-black confines far beneath the ravaged plateau. "I missed you, my friend. Our reunion was a long time coming."

Another sonorous rumble disrupts his reverie, "Now we wait for the demons to finish the job."

Contemplating the young couple's demise, "Even if they survived the Dark Specters' molecular transference, they must have suffocated deep inside the beacon." Rasping a sarcastic chuckle, "Neither possessed the mental acuity to break the code and escape into the catacombs underneath the beacon."

An uneasiness creeps into Harry's disfigured skull, "On second thought, they were resourceful enough to recover the ellipse." Angered by the recalcitrant thought, "No! They are as good as dead."

More tremors resound through solid rock, quaking the prehistoric chamber where Harry hunkers down in the shadow of the darkened beacon. Loosened black granite chunks from widening cracks in the chamber's glyph-covered ceiling plummet twenty feet, shattering into razor-sharp bits and pieces.

Harry's misanthropic glowering stare pierces the darkness, unalarmed by the seismic activity. He admires the upper nineteen feet of the inert proto-pyramidic structure, marveling at its intricate carved surfaces and musing how it must have radiated from the unknowable power within his golden ellipse.

A violent shudder knocks him onto his bony backside, causing him to shield from more loosened chunks of dome ricocheting off the beacon's sloped sides across the seamless black granite floor in a billowing dust cloud.

Harry coughs and sputters from blackened lungs, rasping into the abyss, "I did what you asked!" Yellow eyes aglow under his hood, he calls out to his dark spectral benefactors, squeezing hard on the golden ellipse, "I expect my reward."

* * *

The Machine initiates a surreptitious communication with the golden ellipse alerting that two organisms are trapped beneath the beacon.

A cryptic oval pattern morphs across the ellipse's lustrous surface, cautioning restraint.

Artemus Pennywell | PTB HQ, Scotland
05:32 p.m. | August 22, 2044

Fifteen miles southeast of Edinburgh, the spectacular thunder and lightning storm ebbs to a steady drizzle soaking the Midlothian countryside under a steely overcast. A quiet country lane winds past a crumbling church and cemetery, bisecting grazing pastures and a jittery, bleating flock of sheep huddled under trees before ending at a gravel lot. A short distance up a muddy path, the thick stone walls of the late 14th century Crichton Castle rise into the murky sky from its strategic spot overlooking the River Tyne. The storied venue witnessed political intrigue, marriages, sieges, betrayal, murders, ownership disputes, and even accusations of witchcraft, presaging its abandonment to ruins by the mid-17th century. Languishing as just another crumbling ward of the state in 1932, a mystery heir with ancestral ties to the original Crichton family came forward with an unusual—and lucrative—proposition the depression-ravaged Scottish government could not turn down.

Drawing modest yearly patronage interested in its well-preserved, architecturally significant design—and the solitude of its surroundings—it remains overshadowed by more famous and livable Scottish castles attracting hordes of tourists.

Crichton Castle's relative anonymity, hiding in plain sight, mimics its clandestine caretakers, The Power That Be.

* * *

Rainwater soaks Number 12's petite synthetic frame, unloading biohazardous specimen crates from a glistening wet autonomous drone hovering 3 feet off the puddled gravel lot adjacent to the castle's eastern facade.

Part of a test fleet owned and operated by Thundercorp—an aeronautics company founded by a wunderkind named Julius Hart—the gravity-defying craft resembles a giant silver-metallic toaster plastered with lightning bolt logos on its fuselage, stubby wings, and protruding nosecone.

With her task complete, the feminine robot verges on double-tapping a wet hand atop the drone, sending it on its way, when she hears a stern voice issuing a commanding: "Stop that drone, Number 12!"

Exuding athletic grace and aplomb with an authoritative gravitas, the rugged and handsome replicant bounds from a side entrance camouflaged in the castle wall wearing an army-green windbreaker zipped halfway over a black mock turtleneck and jeans. Splashing down the muddy path in his signature custom-made Western boots, he approaches the obedient cloned robot holding the drone at bay. Grabbing a line attached to a metal cleat protruding from the lot, he hooks it to the floating drone like a giant helium balloon at a children's birthday party.

After attaching a second carabiner to the opposite side, he casts a wary eye toward an ominous and freakish—even for Scotland—storm front pushing in from the north, "Store the delivery in refrigerated containment on Level C. After it is secure, power down and wait out this storm." Mulling multiple scenarios in his chiseled cybernetic skull, "Inform your sisters to do the same. Except for Number 4. Have her prep a hibernation chamber."

"Andrew, are we in danger?"

"With any luck, Number 12, they will never lift the castle and discover our facility hidden underneath."

* * *

Reflective of a nebulous centuries-old charter, The Powers That Be does not consider the underground facility carved through hundreds of millions of years of glacial and volcanic upheavals beneath the Crichton Castle ruins as a headquarters per se. With branch offices of shell companies spread across every continent, operating under common household names, the underground complex is more of a tri-level nerve center.

Level A encompasses everything above ground, including the castle, surrounding pasturelands, and camouflaged security apparatus. Occasional tourists get what they expect from their brochures and travel guides—an ancient Scottish ruin with zero access beyond its formidable walls.

Level B terraces below the grassy hillsides in a massive circular grid linked by corridors connecting well-appointed suites, storage, an armory, a broadcast studio, a health and wellness center, a gymnasium, meeting facilities, and a shielded communications hub. A garage packed with historic to exotic vehicles connects to a helipad via a two-mile tram tunnel snaking under the countryside to a remote glen framed by an old Roman wall jutting from the Lowland heath.

Level B is also the location of Pennywell's apartment home for the last few years. He likens his digs to Walt Disney's Main Street domicile at the original Anaheim, California, theme park.

Still reeling from the Advisor's urgent message, Artemus enters his study, "Fireplace—off. Table lamp—off." Picking up his tumbler, he polishes off the last swig, standing in his darkened apartment ostensibly for the last time. His thin gray hair combed back, a crisp white shirt buttoned to his neck with his signature bolo, black wool pants, polished black shoes, London Fog raincoat draped over his arm, cane in hand, he heaves a saddened sigh and scoops the strap on the go-bag Andrew packed for him. Proceeding into the grand foyer, he taps the button for his private lift, pausing to admire the priceless Cezanne landscape of Montagne Sainte-Victoire centered on the opposite wall over a French Provincial console brimming with photos and small mementos.

Tapping the button again, he mumbles to himself, "Toulouse. How in the hell am I supposed to get there now? I knew this was going to happen. I am screwed. Where the fuck is Andrew?"

The swift and dramatic worldwide destruction of human infrastructure left no means and zero time to reach his evacuation spaceship parked and waiting at the neo-Gothic facility outside Toulouse, France. No more than a two-hour milk run on an average day, like yesterday, between the Chrysalis Airdrome outside Edinburgh to the IOSC Spaceport in France, was obliterated in the blink of an eye. From what the Advisor said, fried microchips, lost data, destroyed property, and dead operators have rendered every semblance of civilization on Earth into useless techno-junk, as he predicted it would.

On a hunch, Pennywell takes the elevator down through the solid rock to Level C to ensure he is the last human motherfucker under this godforsaken castle.

The doors glide apart onto Professor Richard King's gleaming white laboratory, outfitted with every piece of equipment the eclectic man's scientific mind could want or need, maintained by sixteen identical laboratory assistants—built by Professor Mitsuo Kobayashi to accommodate the scientist's ideal lab technician: dexterous, intelligent, and multi-lingual, never squeamish, and impervious to a spectrum of hazardous substances.

Kobayashi replicated an athletic 5′ 6″ female prototype with shoulder-length brunette hair framing fair-skinned youthful features and a piercing and intelligent blue-eyed gaze from an anonymous human original whose tragic demise was sealed and labeled ultra-top secret.

Fifteen sequentially numbered replicant sisters joined Number 1. Their lovely appearance, friendly attitudes, and inhuman work ethic brightened Richard King's laboratory, generating well-earned respect and a few proposals from unsuspecting humans.

Terrible at remembering names, Richard numbered the girls based on their replication order, freeing the absent-minded professor to interact while keeping them straight in his all-too-human skull.

* * *

Pennywell strides down the central aisle, bisecting rows of lab benches brimming with chemistry paraphernalia, test tubes, glassware, monitors, and tabletop instrumentation left in complete disarray after the girls powered down as a precaution though, like Andrew, their shielded organic make-up would withstand an electromagnetic energized blast.

Peering across the bright-lit space toward the under-utilized high-output robotics and centrifuge equipment sitting idle inside a glassed-off clean room, the cost-conscious CEO mutters, "Those damn things burn through money, just looking at them. Oh well. I guess that doesn't matter anymore."

Midway along the adjoining wall, Pennywell notes red doors leading into a cavernous space known as the Think Tank, outfitted with multilevel ergonomic pods designed for meetings and brainstorming sessions, languishing dark and vacant. A fatalistic smirk breaks his sad countenance, "Not knowing if my people are dead or alive around the planet is bad enough; at least this place was empty today."

Pennywell walks through the lab, tapping his cane across the slick white linoleum before pausing at a murky green floor-standing aquarium. Venturing his roman nose to the glass, he peers through aquatic plants, snails, and minnows in search of his little friend. Furrowing his brow, he knocks on the glass with his cane handle and smiles at a gilled, monkey-like creature swimming up to the glass, "There you are, my little Amazon friend."

Turning from the juvenile sea monkey, Pennywell continues to an office tucked in the far corner and peeks inside at Professor King, copying files to a disk. With an unmasked annoyance tinging his words, "It does not matter anymore, Richard. Just get the hell out of here."

Hunched before a virtual screen, still wearing his lab coat over a wool argyle sweater and his signature tweed cap pulled atop his unruly knot of charcoal curls, he growls at the intrusion, "I'll be fine, Artemus. The last I heard, Stevens and his crew are still in South America, so I am the only human down here." He glances up, a sad and hesitant smile crossing his expressive face, "Present company excluded, of course."

"Go home, Richard. That is an order. I'm the captain of this fucking ship, and I will be the last one to leave."

Richard stands and stretches his stocky frame. Walking around his desk, he bearhugs a surprised Pennywell and starts to weep. "Artemus, my whole life is down here. I can't leave now. Can I stay in a hibernation chamber? Number 4 can wake me after the coast is clear. I have nowhere else to go."

An exaggerated throat-clearing breaks the ice, and both men, in a full hug, turn in tandem toward Pennywell's visibly amused valet.

"If I may, gentlemen, I must interrupt your farewell embrace. Professor King, I have a hibernation chamber ready for you."

Pennywell gives the professor a hearty shoulder pat, denying Andrew the pleasure of seeing him blush, before pushing himself an arm's length from the distraught scientist's face, "Sure, Richard. You stay and keep an eye on things while I am gone. Can you do that for me?"

Right on cue, Number 4 glides from behind Andrew, taking poor Richard by the hand. After a few tentative steps, the brilliant-minded professor turns and proffers a sheepish goodbye wave. Pennywell reciprocates, watching his friend led across the lab, like a small boy in a department store, and disappear through a garage-sized exit.

The latest Level C expansion carved out of the sedimentary rock houses six pill-shaped human-sized hibernation chambers resting atop metallic carts in a precise row. The second unit sits prepped and waiting for Richard while the first unit hums to its occupant's sleep-induced repose.

* * *

Hurtling upward through eons of Scotland's stratified geologic record, the elevator doors slide apart at Level A.

Andrew hefts the go-bag strap while assisting his boss down a narrow stairwell and through an archway into the open-air central courtyard with its signature diamond-rusticated façade. Sporadic raindrops splat across the uneven pavers, puddling in low spots around the voluminous space walled-in on all sides by three-story ramparts with dull light bleeding through arrow slits with various strategic sightlines.

Like the rest of the so-called Chosen Few scattered around the planet, Artemus Pennywell is deemed essential to humanity's future. The 134-year-old found his status ludicrous by definition but knew, deep down, he had too much intel buried between his ears to leave behind. It was tempting to send Andrew in his place and climb into the hibernation chamber next to Richard's pillbox and hope for the best. But here he is with his expressive, gray-eyed gaze turned toward the rough-hewn square of roiling sky above their heads, "Okay, Andrew. The world is dead. How the hell are we getting to France? Unless you have an EMP-shielded helicopter parked out front, we are grade-A fucked."

"As usual, sir, your colloquialisms could charm the stinger off a bee's behind."

"That's a new one. Did you just make that up?"

"Maybe." Stepping across the courtyard, "Follow me, sir. We are heading to the delivery lot."

"Why? Will we walk to the bus stop with thumbs up our collective ass?"

Andrew turns and smiles, "Not quite."

The secret side entrance leading onto the gravel lot swings open, revealing the dripping wet delivery drone, idling at the bottom of the muddy path, attached to cleats like a lead balloon.

"You have got to be shitting me, Andrew. I'm an old man. I can't fit in there!"

"Please, Artemus, this is serious. The cargo capacity on the drone will accommodate two adults—albeit a little cramped. We will fly at treetop level to offset the lack of pressurization and steer clear of the alien ships."

"Your sales pitch sucks, Andrew." Spiking his cane into the wet granite for emphasis, "I am not getting into that thing. Forget it. You go ahead. I will have Number 4 put me to bed to die in peace, like Richard."

"Sir, you are getting in that drone."

"No. I am not!"

"You can and you will, sir!"

The motivation behind Andrew's harsh rebuke uncloaks into an ominous black mass and trumpets its harrowing presence from a spectacular firestorm igniting the already threatening skies over Edinburgh. The destructive shockwave generated underneath the alien dreadnought shatters the Scottish Lowlands for miles in every direction.

Andrew takes Pennywell by the arm and moves him to the drone. With a voiced binary-encoded command, the fuselage loading hatch springs open while lowering its underside to the gravel lot. "Get in!"

Pennywell vaults onto the narrow metal bench meant to hold boxed deliveries and stares at a monolithic superstructure ripping the sky apart somewhere over Edinburgh.

"Holy Mother of Jesus, who are these blokes?"

After assisting his boss inside the wobbling drone, Andrew jumps to the front of the craft. Putting his multitasking processors into overdrive, he presses a synthetic right hand atop the lightning bolt icon on the drone's rounded nosecone. Resisting a peek over his shoulder at the alien ship, he waits for the touch-activated connection from his GPS-chipped right hand to the flight computer to finish uploading. The drone's onboard avionics will handle the rest.

Pressing inside the cargo hold next to his pill-popping boss, Andrew turns with a confident head nod.

Pennywell admonishes his valet, relishing every word, "Didn't you forget something, Andrew? We won't get very far, tied to the damn parking lot!"

Andrew's eyes widen in surprise at his uncharacteristic oversight, "My apologies, sir."

Soaking wet in his green nylon Patagonia windbreaker, Andrew jumps back inside and pulls the door closed. Without warning, the craft screams across the Scottish countryside at a terrifying velocity.

Pennywell feels his face pulling behind his ears, enduring the high-g escape. Swiveling his eyeballs, he watches Andrew reach forward and touch the metal frame inside the cramped compartment. Almost immediately, the drone reduces to a speed more conducive to human travel, "I failed to indicate fragile cargo. That is twice in five minutes, sir; I committed an error. Now. Aren't you glad you decided to come along?"

Pennywell does not answer. He is the last in a 300-year leadership succession charged with, among other things, safeguarding Earth from the omnipresent threat of alien apocalypse. Pressed against a rain-spattered 10-inch portal, he stares outside at the world's ignominious end whizzing past his sad face.

Flying onward, well under its advertised hypersonic speed, the Thundercorp autonomous flying toaster hugs the rugged topography, zigging east around a flotilla of invaders amassing over London before splashing above the chop, crossing the English Channel near Brighton. Dodging lightning bolts over Normandy, a murmuration of terrified starlings almost does them in east of Tours save for AI-controlled avionics precise predictions of the amorphous flock's chaotic path.

Pennywell mutters his first word since leaving the castle, "Impressive."

Rachel | Under the Beacon
06:00 p.m. | August 22, 2044

"You know I love you, but you knocked the wind out of me. You are heavier than you look."

Rachel produces a wan smile, turns on her side, and taps her beat-up husband in the chest, "I'm going to let that slide since you broke my fall." Standing and stretching their aching muscles, she grabs fistfuls of hot air. Kicking at graveled limestone under her boots, "Honestly, I cannot believe your blood drop theory worked; too weird for words."

Wincing from newfound pains while standing hip-to-hip aside his svelte and sweaty better half, Owen scans the encroaching darkness beyond the weakening glimmer above their stance, "We are not out of the woods yet." Arching backward with a grunt of pain, he ponders the receding galaxy from their new vantage underneath the open hexagon, "We fell through the stars from somewhere up there and landed here."

"Way to state the obvious."

"I am trying to establish a sense of place. It is my first time directing a sci-fi flick."

Rachel laughs despite herself, "I did refer to you as Mr. DeMille, didn't I?"

"Yes, you did." Venturing into the blackness from under the dimming ambiance emanating from their cell, "Rachel! There are more openings across the ceiling."

Rachel angles the flashlight upward, illuminating a configuration of hexagonal shapes trailing into the far reaches beyond the light's reach.

Owen's bloodshot eyes track the dim flashlight beam, checking the closest cells, "This one appears empty; no stars." Moving under an adjacent hexagon, "So is this one." Reaching both hands high over his head, he jumps, landing with a loud grunt, "Without a ladder, I don't see how we can climb up there, anyway."

Suppressing a smile at Owen's awkward white man jump, she flips the light off, conserving battery life. "It's okay, Owen; we are on solid ground and breathing air; that's a start." Brushing sand from her blood-smeared pants, she finds her last tissue and uses it to wipe off the foul ooze still smeared across her chest, "I'm never going to get that stink off of my skin." Tossing the crumpled paper into the dark, she ties her button-down shirt around her waist and tugs her dirty mane back into a ponytail. She discovers the missing chunk of the scalp on the back of her head and bites her lip to keep from crying out loud in the dark.

"Yes, you will, Rachel. Have faith. I love you, no matter how stinky you are. We are still here. Harry—or whoever that was—meant for us to die in that six-sided jail cell. He may let his guard down if he thinks we are out of the picture."

"Why, Owen Haig, that makes sense."

Owen smiles at the sarcasm directed at his leap of logic, not wanting to admit its movie trope origin. Squinting into the darkness around their exposed position, "We need to find a way out of here, and I am fresh out of crazy ideas. Hand me the light and stay put. I will scout in that direction and see what is out there."

"Why do you want to go that way?"

"I always lean right. I'm a greedy banker, remember?"

As the darkness swallows his receding form, she hears his caveat, "I would like to return to that job someday."

Absently rubbing her scar while watching the disembodied

beam's progression, tremors permeate the ground beneath her Chelsea boots. "Owen! Did you feel that?"

"Yes, I did. Not good, Rachel. Not good."

The unnerving quaking sensations compound her anxieties in the blackness. Unsure what else she can do besides standing there like a helpless waif, she yells into the abyss, "Hello! Is anybody out there? We need help!" The mocking repetition of her appeal resonates through the underground expanse before fading to nothingness.

In the distance, she hears a faint reply, "Nice try, Rachel."

Shifting the dimming beam from the inky honeycomb pattern overhead to the rutted uneven ground, Owen runs headfirst into solid rock in the pitch blackness. "I found a wall!"

Ratcheting down exuberance from his discovery, he drags his throbbing hand over vertical serrations, possibly gouged by industrial-sized earthmovers long ago. Looking back toward Rachel while moving leftward along the wall, he comments, "I think we are in a foundation excavated out of solid rock." Failing to monitor his forward progression in the dark, he stumbles over into a solid object with multiple sharpened edges jutting out of the limestone in front of him, "Ow! My knee! Dammit! What the hell is this?"

Rachel hears familiar curses from her put-upon husband. "Are you okay?"

"Rachel, come here!"

"Turn the light toward me so I can see what I am stepping over." Peering through the dark, Rachel stumbles toward the flashlight's dying beam.

After a few tenuous steps, circumnavigating a hulking mass, a blinding radiance alights the expanse.

Shielding her eyes, she hears her husband yell a triumphant, "Let there be light!"

Rubbing watery green eyes to clear the spots obscuring her vision, Rachel surveys the space, noting her off-centered position before gazing back at his grinning face, lit up behind a magnificent light-blue crystallized formation protruding out of the ground. His extended shadow animates behind him across a 12-foot wall of rough-hewn limestone streaked with ruddy brown and yellow-ochre striations.

"What the hell did you find?"

Wide eyes ablaze with brilliant white light, he looks down at the other-worldly mass of vibrant crystals, "I haven't got a goddamned clue."

Fearful the mysterious light source will time out, Rachel surveys the enormous square space, searching for a door. Instead, she spies weird, rounded shapes scattered on the hardscrabble, like boulders. Rachel heaves a frightened and frustrated sigh, "Aw, man. What are those things?"

Approaching the nearest lumpy shape, midway between herself and Owen, she makes out large eyes, returning her gape from under a reflective purplish-blue cloak. Dread creeps up her spine, realizing the covering conceals a small odd-proportioned body. A glint of gold braiding above the orbital sockets draws her closer, "Do I dare repeat the same mistake the dumb-ass chick makes in every horror movie?" Poised and ready to run, she grips the covering and pulls it aside. "What was this thing?"

An elongated skull attached to diminutive skeletal remains manifests in light and shadow below her frightened gaze, "Owen, we have to get out of here!"

Aching back and throbbing knees forgotten in a panicked beat of her heart, she freaks out and sprints across the dirt and sand. Pushing behind Owen and the brilliant blue and white crystal formation, her screams echoed off the ancient hewn walls across the underground space.

Holding her close in the luminescence behind the crystallized formation, Owen can't help but smile, seeing the fullness of his beautiful bride for the first time since entering the pyramid, "I was afraid I would never see you again. The flashlight batteries are dying."

Regaining her composure, "Apparently, we brought them to the right place for things to die."

"Gallows humor, that's the spirit."

Clearing her raspy throat, Rachel realizes how thirsty she is but refrains from saying anything to Owen. There is nothing he can do. With a deep, calming exhale, she focuses her attention on the glowing crystals. Not finding any discernible controls or buttons, she posits the obvious question in a throaty voice, "Okay, Owen. What did you press to turn on the lights?"

"Nothing! I just placed my hand atop this section, and the thing lit up like a Times Square." Owen slaps his right hand atop another crystalline shape, and the miraculous light source fades to black.

Rachel's exasperated sigh penetrates the silence standing aside Owen in the inky blackness, "Well, this is just great. Now we don't even have the flashlight anymore."

"Do you hear that?"

"Hear what? I don't … "A staticky noise buzzes in their ears. Rachel feels Owen's hand pulling her closer. "Don't let go, whatever you do."

"I won't."

The buzz rises in pitch, amplifying off the 12-foot rock walls and filling the 5,300-square-foot expanse with an eerie din. Covering her ears from the ear-splitting noise, Rachel sees the shiny royal-blue fabric covering her alien encounter shimmering to life like a beacon in the dark. Light radiating from the draped cloth intensifies from royal blue tones to a vivid cyan. "Owen, check it out!"

Holding tight to his scared wife, "I see it. Let's stay calm and see what happens."

One of the dead aliens reanimates in cerulean luminescence, rising Lazarus-like onto short spindly legs from the bony pile Rachel uncovered. Its oversized head rotates around the space, waving long, skinny arms through the stifling air. "Is it doing calisthenics?"

"Don't look now, but its friends are waking up, too."

Owen and Rachel spot six more holographic extraterrestrials standing from decayed husks draped under purple cloaks, joining the alien Rachel discovered. 4.5 millennia after the Machine struck them down in defense of the beacon, the recorded version of their final nefarious act commences. A cherry picker-style lift appears around the first alien's translucent blue form and elevates it through a shiny black membrane from the waist up. A blue-green hexagonal pattern illuminates the ceiling in response. Another miner slices into limestone with a raygun-like tool to Owen's left, followed by two more aliens depositing crystals into the narrow slot.

"Don't quote me, but the little bastards are planting explosive charges."

Exasperated, Rachel inhales a deep calming breath of the hot, dry air into her lungs, "Yep. Agreed. But is this happening now or some kind of recording?"

"I am certain this is a recorded event. I still see the shapes of their alien bodies under the blankets, and they don't seem to notice us at all."

"Let's keep it that way. Owen, it is getting harder to breathe down here. We need to find a way out."

"I'm aware, Rachel. I'm aware."

Peering past the cherry picker alien, still half inside the hexagon, she spies another lustrous-blue ET ambling along the far wall. It disappears behind an offset vertical slab before reemerging from the opposite side, causing Rachel to tug on Owen's tattered shirt sleeve. "That one over there! I saw it go behind some kind of offset wall. It has to be the way out of here. It's worth a try. We can't stay here forever. Let's go!"

Owen squints through the darkness, "It's a deal, but hold my hand and don't let go, no matter what. Okay?"

"No argument from me."

Leading the way around the crystallized formation into the darkness on a beeline to Rachel's discovery, Owen pauses near the cherry-picker alien, causing Rachel to bump into him in the dark.

"Warn me when you are about to put on the brakes."

"Sorry. I want to see what the alien is doing inside that cell."

"So do I."

Creeping underneath the first alien's elevated position, they peer upward.

"Oh, well, that's not good."

The bisected top half of the alien floats in a dim blue abyss—luminescent globules bubble from tubular entrails snaking from its pale torso in the hexagonal cell. The body turns face down, returning a glassy, vacant gaze upon the surprised couple.

"Wait until his union rep hears about this."

"Funny, Owen. I think we can assume they are dead."

"Yep. Let's not tempt fate. Keep moving."

The Haigs traverse the dark subterranean depths beneath the ancient proto-pyramid beacon, kicking outward with each precarious step across the rough surface.

On the cusp of exclaiming, they should have reached the other side already; Owen's injured pinkie finger jams into a rough-hewn vertical surface, "That hurt like hell. We're here."

Still clinging to his back in the dark, Rachel asks, "What?"

"The wall. We're here."

"Well, great, Owen. Let's find out what is behind door number one."

Smiling through the dark despite feeling like he was hit by a truck, "Door number one? Okay, that's pretty good." Owen feels along the surface and reaches a discernible edge but is hesitant to proceed around the corner. "Rachel, we have no idea what is back there. Are you sure you want to do this?"

Rachel pushes past Owen, "Screw it," venturing behind the

wall, "we're dead anyway if this does not lead out of here."

Against his better judgment, Owen lets their hands slip apart, muttering, "Be careful."

Seconds pass, and Owen is about to freak out when a blinding white light fills the space around him. Lifting his hand to shield his eyes from the glare, he hears his wife's beautiful and brave voice ring out.

"I found another crystal!" Rachel mounts the second crystallized formation illuminating the offset area behind the wall, and the four-foot tunnel lit up in stark relief above Rachel's perch.

"Rachel, you found the way out of here!"

Lifting her lean frame onto the leading edge, she peers down the passage, "Oh, man. It is tight."

Owen jumps atop the crystal and edges past her, "Let me go first, Rachel. If it is wide enough for me, it will be safe for you to follow."

"Makes sense." Meeting eye-to-eye before wriggling to the point position, he surprises Rachel with a white-hot passionate kiss. "I am so proud of you, Rachel. We will find our way out of here."

Pulling back from her husband, she studies his beaten face and wipes blood trickles off his forehead, "You pick the weirdest moments to get all romantic, you know that?"

"Near-death experiences bring out my emotional side, I guess."

"Man, I hate tight spaces." Crawling on all fours, he makes his way ten feet along the smoothed horizontal surface in the confining tunnel before coming to a sharp incline. "I guess it is good this thing angles upward at some point. You okay back there?"

"Just peachy."

The crystal's ambiance diminishes at the tunnel incline, and they crawl upward into the darkness beyond. Struggling for air, breathing hard, Owen fights back the tears, second-guessing whether this was a good idea. After fifty painful feet, hands, and knees throbbing with pain, Owen reaches a short landing.

"Hey. There is something through here."

Alarmed by her husband's vague remark, "Animal, vegetable, or mineral?"

"None of the above. We reached a vertical fork in the road."

Crawling forward in the dark, Owen sticks his right arm down into a shaft. Angling onto his side, he reaches up and feels inside the upward portion.

On her hands and knees in the dark tunnel, Rachel tugs on Owen's boot. "What? Are we screwed?"

"No. But you are going to have to do a little free climbing."

"Owen. I'm so tired. I don't think I can go any further. I keep feeling tremors in here. I have a terrible feeling shit is already going on, and we just don't know it.

A low rumble underscores her words, permeating the narrow walls with the gut-wrenching sound of falling rocks.

"Rachel Haig! Knock it off! You can and will climb! The new shaft is narrower than where we are now. It also appears near vertical, so use your body like a caterpillar. Can you do that for me?"

"Sure, Owen. Caterpillar. Got it."

Hearing her weak voice, he knows they are both oxygen-deprived and running out of time. "Okay. Listen to me. I am going first. Same drill. If I can fit, you will, too."

Squeezing himself up into the shaft, he struggles to get out his last words of advice. "If I get stuck, retreat to the foundation level, and wait for help. I love you."

It is indeed a tight fit. Owen utilizes his sore leg muscles and his last ounce of core strength to push his upper body higher, bracing against the shaft. Confident his braced position can support his weight; he pulls both legs upward before pressing his Timberlands against the smooth limestone and vaulting his body upward from his burning thighs. Repeating the process, he grunts, "Keep it going, Owen. This ordeal will soon be over, one way or another."

Alone in the darkness, Rachel muses on Owen's caterpillar

advice. "I get it. I would have said inchworm, but that seems a little nitpicky, considering I'm about to die down here in this stupid shaft."

Twisting onto her back, she scooches her upper body into the vertical shaft, resting her bottom at the precipice. Small, chipped pieces of limestone cascade down from Owen's position somewhere above her blond head, "Hey. I'm climbing here!"

Owen's muffled apology echoes through the shaft.

Leaning her back against the vertical shaft, she wriggles herself to a standing position inside the 30-inch space with the soles of her lucky Chelsea boots propped at the tunnel's sharp edge. "Now what. How does a caterpillar help me do this?"

Hearing loud grunting noises echoing from above, she refrains from bothering Owen.

"Well, I can't stay like this forever and end up like those ETs." Pressing her back hard into the wall, she lifts her left boot into the shaft and wedges it into the corner. Trusting her braced position, she lifts her long right leg, bringing her knee to her chest before pressing the right boot into the corner. Vaulting herself upward on her right leg as high as she can reach, she pauses to suck in a thin gulp of air. Wedged inside the shaft, she wriggles herself upward and tries not to panic, scraping her back into the rough limestone, and cries, "This is impossible."

On-again, off-again yoga eclipses the hungry-hungry caterpillar in a heartbeat as she inches higher, wondering how far they have to climb like this.

Owen hears Rachel making progress, but he cannot speak. His right calf cramps. Wracked in pain, he bites his lip bloody, waiting it out and praying not to fall.

Rachel wriggles higher, establishing a steady rhythm. Another tremor sends small rocks pelting down on her body before tumbling into the abyss. The distraction causes her to lose focus for a split second. Her left boot slips, and she slides a harrowing distance down the smooth wall before putting on the brakes. Anger overwhelms her exhausted mind, swallowing back terrified sobs in the dark.

Victimized by a rapist who stole the promise of her youth, she now battles evilness trying to destroy the whole world. With a hallucinatory vision of her skin radiating in response to her near-death experience, she summons strength she did not know she possessed and climbs.

Owen's cramp subsides enough to resume the nightmarish endurance test—even for an experienced climber such as himself as his memory wanders onto a similar climb in Southern Utah he took a pass on when he was ten years younger and in much better condition.

The tedious process pushes his heavy frame a couple of feet higher at a time. Angling backward for another push-off, he falls backward onto a level surface. Lying flat on his back and overcome with relief, he pulls his lower half up and out of the shaft and scrambles his head and shoulders back into the emptiness. "Rachel, I made it to the top! You can breathe easier up here, too!"

Relieved beyond measure to once again be on a solid surface, he peers into the blackness and listens for signs of life, "Rachel?"

Agent Flynn | Inside the Great Pyramid
06:00 p.m. | August 22, 2044

Flynn restrains himself from vaulting off the step and beating the pulp out of the implacable Tarek Hamed. Instead, desperate for a solid lead, he bites his tongue as the professor elbows center stage in the bored-out space deep inside the Great Pyramid.

Reveling in the spotlight, the dapper man tips his Panama hat toward Louie, who proffers a perfunctory return nod.

Flynn reprimands his friend, "Louie, this guy is nothing but trouble. Don't let him fool you into thinking otherwise."

Hamed winks at the raven-haired Cassandra standing behind

him, "I don't know, Agent Flynn. Perhaps Louie is a better judge of character than yourself."

Annoyed beyond measure, Captain Faisel speaks his mind, "We do not have time for your bullshit, Hamed. Tell us what you know or get out."

Hamed wheels to address the Egyptian officer's open antipathy, "Captain, a word of advice. Focus on recruiting soldiers who will not run for the hills at the first sign of alien invasion."

Hamed revels in the peanut gallery's hatred, "I tried to warn you all before the good captain threw me off the plateau." Hearing more chunks of limestone cascading back down the tunnel, "And now humanity hangs in the balance. Tsk-tsk—what a shame."

His patience gone, Flynn jumps up and challenges the professor nose-to-nose, "If you had not cocked up our plans on the coach, we might have had time enough to return the ellipse to the beacon before the bloody alien invasion."

Hamed stands his ground, "If you and your friends had a plan beyond coming here and waiting for some miracle to occur, let's hear it, mate. I had a plan. Do you think I wanted to spend my last day on Earth with the likes of you?"

Captain Mohammed Faisel separates the enraged men in the confining space. "Enough! I hate both of you, but you are all I got. Professor, enlighten us on your plan."

Flynn steps back in disgust, "Blimey! You are going to trust this tosser?"

Faisel turns to the distraught Powers That Be agent, "Unless you have a better idea, Agent Flynn."

Louie interjects, "Monsieur, let's hear him out."

Hamed produces the crystal pyramid from his white suit jacket in the palm of his hand before his captive audience, like a magician, before pricking his index finger on the sharp tip. "It is a little tight in here but watch what happens."

The one-inch shape glows to life, projecting a scaled pyramid before their stunned faces.

Faisel's gaze follows a tunnel system underneath leading to a smaller pyramid inside a domed chamber, "What is that?"

"That is our destination, Captain."

* * *

Hacking past the warning signs, police tape, and a rusted metal grate obstructing access to the Descending Passage, Faisel rips off the last tarp hammered around the square-cut limestone shaft. His torch's powerful beam is swallowed in absolute darkness while peering down the 26-degree sloped tunnel. Scrunched on his aching haunches in the ridiculous space, he ducks as another tremor agitates more fine choking dust into the air.

Hamed cuts in front of the hesitant Faisel and proceeds down the 345-foot tunnel with an air of confident familiarity.

Faisel growls while climbing inside, "By all means, after you, professor."

Before angling his heavy manmade frame into the four-foot shaft, the chivalrous Louie gestures for Cassandra to proceed. Turning to address the reticent and claustrophobic Agent Flynn, loitering at the back of the line, "I know what you are thinking, Agent; where are Owen and Rachel?"

"Louie, you read my mind."

Hunkering low, trying to avoid scraping his head in the narrow space, Flynn feels the burn in his thigh and calf muscles. Pulling his bandana back onto his face, he sees the beams from his cohorts' lights piercing the dusty stillness, illuminating the chiseled limestone passage.

After a grueling descent, Flynn exits the Descending Passage and tries to catch his breath inside the rough-hewn Subterranean Chamber. Casting his light off the haphazard, hollowed-out cavern walls, he can't help but notice its stark contrast to the Great Pyramid's geometric precision. Shining his beam onto the south wall behind Faisel, Flynn catches the white cuffs of Hamed's pants leg squirming into another, even smaller shaft, "Bloody fucking hell, where is he going? I don't know if I can fit in that tunnel."

Cassandra turns to Louie, tears welling in her eyes, "I enjoyed spending the morning with you. That much is true. Please don't hate me."

Before Louie can reply, she turns on her heels and dives through the opening after Hamed.

Flynn shines his light on Louie, "What the hell was that all about?"

A new sparkle of light radiates from Louie's eyes. "Believe it or not, we are proceeding as planned."

Faisel and Flynn peer inside and back at each other. "Okay, who wants to volunteer to go first this time?"

Louie steps forward, "Gentleman, allow me to take point."

The tired duo watches the large android hunch his frame before the two-foot opening. Louie turns toward Flynn, his backlit eyes aglow, "I'll see you on the other side."

The phrase resonates in Flynn's head, watching his friend wriggle inside and disappear.

"Agent Flynn?"

Still distracted, he turns to Faisel, "What?"

"Snap out of it. Do you have a weapon?"

Flynn shrugs and reaches down to access a stubby pistol concealed in a holster in his right boot. "Just this. Your deputy missed it when he frisked me earlier at your office."

Displaying his armchair knowledge of weaponry, Faisel comments on the miniature weapon, "It looks like the Derringer that took down Lincoln."

"Not quite." The PTB agent proffers an impressed smile at Faisel's reference to the 16th president, "If we live through this, remind me to enlighten you about Lincoln. As a PTB insider, I know stuff that would blow your mind."

Faisel nods, "Perhaps, I will."

The security officer turns to the tunnel, but Flynn grabs him by the arm, "Captain, we should not trust Tarek Hamed. He only showed us to this point on his 3D map. We have no idea what is down this bloody tunnel. Also, there is no evidence Owen and Rachel Haig ever passed this way."

Faisel places a hand on the agent's shoulder, "Agent Flynn, I will let you in on a secret. I was ready to submit my retirement paperwork from the Egyptian army today. I was through babysitting these bloody pyramids. However, sometimes you have to be a good soldier and follow where the path leads."

Flynn shakes his head and chuckles, "Mate, you and I are about the same age, yeah? And yet, you come off far more mature."

* * *

After a 30-foot belly crawl, Professor Tarek Hamed reaches the Southern Tunnel's chiseled endpoint. Calm and focused after months of mental rehearsals imagining this moment, he pulls the crystal pyramid from his suit in total darkness, flips it pointy-side down, and inserts it into a grooved cut-out in the smooth limestone. A blue glow illuminates his gap-toothed maniacal smile as he gives it a quarter turn. Solid rock moves aside on an invisible rail, exposing the passage's continuation and his long-awaited destiny.

Cassandra squirms behind Hamed with her dimmed flashlight, "It worked, Tarek! You did it."

"Quiet, my dear. The others will hear you."

Hamed tucks the crystal inside his jacket, and the conniving pair slink forward.

* * *

Crawling through the shoulder-width horizontal tunnel to where it should end, Louie pauses, noting the turned keyhole camouflaged in the rock with his night vision. Glancing over his shoulder, he checks to ensure the others have yet to enter before proceeding through the opened extension. An illogical sadness swells within his breast as a strange thought pierces his acute psyche: *"Does a synthetic afterlife await?"*

* * *

The Egyptian and the Englishman curse a blue-streaked chorus, struggling to catch up to Louie, unaware they crawled beyond the tunnel's previous known endpoint before blundering to a steep ledge at the terminus. Both men scramble onto their feet atop the narrow purchase positioned midway inside a rounded-out 20-foot diameter highpoint of a dark vertical shaft.

Flynn's torch alights Hamed and Cassandra standing atop a platform suspended out of reach inside the shaft.

Hamed's voice echoes upward, "Sorry, boys. The train has left the station."

Confident in his ability, Flynn assesses the situation, knowing he has bettered worse actors than these two idiots. All he has to do is leap the 20-foot distance down onto the platform and beat the truth out of Hamed. But what about his less-than-agile colleague? The hesitation costs him the split second between a slight chance of success and a plummet to certain death somewhere far below.

Standing to Flynn's right on the ledge, Faisel trains his light from thick ropes feeding through an elaborate pulley mechanism bolted into the chiseled ceiling and down onto the smiling couple on the descending platform. He cannot mask the confusion behind his resonant voice inside the cavernous space, "Where is Louie?"

"The poor fellow stumbled off the ledge. I am a little disappointed you two did not suffer the same fate. Oh well. I am sure he is down there somewhere, in pieces, anyway. Perhaps he is still under warranty."

Reeling from the news of Louie's demise, Flynn is distracted by a red laser dot on Faisel's chest. Looking down, he sees a smiling Cassandra aiming a mean-looking 9 mm sidearm, catching him flat-footed. "Bloody hell, you two tosspots want to go there, eh?"

"Toss your weapons into the tunnel. I won't ask again."

Hamed addresses his gun-wielding co-conspirator, "If the agent does not comply in five seconds, kill the Captain."

"You win, asshole!" Flynn holds up the tiny pistol eliciting a hearty laugh from Hamed.

"Weapon size correlates to its owner. Very telling for you, Agent Flynn."

Resisting an urge to engage in a useless exchange of insults, Flynn tosses the small but powerful gun into the darkness, listening for it to hit bottom, but hears nothing.

"By the way, gentleman, the tunnel behind you will seal shut, leaving you stranded in this inhospitable place. If you hurry, you can escape in time and continue searching for the Haigs."

Devastated by the turn of events, the pair watch the evil duo's accelerated descent, disappearing into the darkness.

Flynn shakes his head, "I hate being right all the time."

Faisel turns to Flynn. "I doubt what they are looking for is at the bottom of this dark hole. Once the rope stops, we can recall it and follow."

"And help Louie! I refuse to believe he blundered off this ledge on accident. I watched him locate a strand of Rachel's hair from ten feet away in the dark."

Rachel | Beacon tunnel complex
07:25 p.m. | August 22, 2044

"Owen, I can't make it."

Thinking all was lost after agonizing minutes without any sign of life from his better half, the muffled sound of Rachel's weak voice carrying up the narrow shaft causes Owen's heart to beat out of his chest. He hurries onto his hands and knees and wedges headfirst back inside the squared void, stretching bloody fingertips beyond his reach, "Feel for my hands, honey! You can do it! You have made it so far!" Feeling nothing but air, he panics and pulls himself lower, stretching and probing into the dark. With an overwhelming sense of relief, his hand brushes against what feels like soft hair. Desperate not to lose touch, he angles his right side farther down and feels smooth skin dripping with sweat.

"Owen, that's my face. You almost poked me in the eye."

"Sorry, Rachel. Grab my arm and push through your legs. Come on; you can do it!"

Rachel's ragged and spent form rises precious inches, allowing Owen's hand to grasp under her left armpit. "Okay, I got you. I am not letting go. Push again, Rachel! You are almost there!"

Rachel yells inside the claustrophobic nightmare, exerting upward pressure through her screaming leg muscles.

Teeth clenched into a pained grimace, struggling to maintain a tenuous hold on the love of his life, Rachel's pitched shriek rings in Owen's ears while the sharp-edged shaft opening digs into his torso. Grunting and tugging, wriggling backward in hard-fought increments to accommodate her tantalizing slow rise, he reemerges from the shaft. Without letting go, he scuttles onto his knees, grabs under both arms, and pulls his wife's heaving form free of the confining space.

In a spasmodic freak-out, she wrestles from his grasp and flings herself backward onto the hard limestone, knocking Owen backward with a sharp and bloody elbow to his cheek in the pitch-blackness.

The heaving pair lie flat on their backs, Rachel's left leg still dangling into the shaft, and stare face-up into the blackness, gasping for air.

"Owen, I almost gave up down there. Once again, you saved my life."

"I could not go on without you."

"Sorry for clocking you in the side of the face, too."

"What's another blow to the cheek?" A seismic vibration sends rocks and dirt tumbling around them, drowning out the rest of Owen's heartfelt reply. He hears something metallic clanking across the chiseled surface, triggering an idea in his recovering wits, "Rachel, stay here and rest. I'll be right back."

Before she can protest a need to stay close in the utter blackness, he is gone. Unable to see a thing, she makes out the sound of Owen's nervous whistle, followed by the grating noise of a heavy object sliding across the grit and sand-covered floor.

"Man, this thing weighs a ton!"

"What weighs a ton?" After the arduous climb, Rachel's rubbery leg muscles slowly recover as she stands and hears the muffled sounds of a large pile of objects collapsing in a heap.

"Shit! Sorry, everybody. My bad."

"Owen, who are you talking to?"

Next comes a series of ripping noises, "Almost there, Rachel. Hang tight!"

The clinking of sharpened metal struck against solid limestone sends sparks flying out of the blackness, followed by a flame flickering to life. Seeing Owen's smiling face in the warm glow, she watches it blaze to life, pushing back the darkness.

The fiery illumination paints the hollowed-out grotto in a flickering orange glow as Owen sidesteps around the shaft of death, proffering a proud smile toward his breathless, beat-up bride.

"Way to go, honey! How did you know to do that?"

Owen can't resist a dimpled smile across his bruised and bloodied face while holding the improvised torch in his injured left hand. "I heard a metallic noise and perceived something big and heavy had fallen over there." He directs the torch to illuminate the frightening profile of a fifteen-foot basalt statue of Anubis standing athwart an alcove stacked with a dried-out pile of mummified remains.

"Sure enough, I found the metal tip from his staff and used it to create enough friction to ignite a swath of decayed fabric from one of those mummies. I can't believe it worked. I have trouble lighting a charcoal grill."

"Owen, I'm almost afraid to ask, but your torch isn't a human appendage, is it?"

"Hell no, Rachel, we are in enough trouble without pissing off some ancient Egyptian god. I did rip off a dried-out wad of old cloth to make my torch." Casting the firelight onto the collapsed stack of mummified remains, "I can make you one if you want."

"That's okay. I'll let your torch light the way."

The couple revels in the warmth dancing in light and shadow across the spacious chiseled corridor, moving on from the Anubis-guarded catacomb and the hellacious shaft experience.

On the lookout for booby traps or tripwires, Rachel feels her rubbery leg muscles recovering while taking careful steps across the rutted surface, "Owen, I am surprised you have not made any references to your favorite movie hero."

"Real life is proving far more interesting."

"And a lot more dangerous."

Exploring hand-in-hand through the long dark passage, Rachel and Owen stumble up to their ragged reflections flickering in a smooth black garage door-sized barrier blocking the way forward.

"Great. Another dead-end. Hold the light steady, please." Rachel checks her mirrored image, adjusting her ragged clothing and smoothing dirt-streaked hair off her sad face.

"Rachel, can you hold the torch for a second?"

With a huff, Rachel accepts Owen's makeshift light, noting with trepidation the ball of cloth wound around the business end, burning through to the old chunk of wood, "I wish we had the magic fire pellets from Flynn's jacket."

A tinkling sound from the shadows interrupts her wishful thinking, "Owen, what are you doing?"

"Three guesses, Rachel."

"I asked you if you had to go before leaving reality."

Stepping back to his still-fetching bride, he retakes the glowing stick. "Hilarious, Rachel. Oh, boy, our light is burning out fast."

"Did you hear something?"

Owen's puffy eyes widen, "Like what?"

"I swear to God, Owen. I heard someone say my name." Looping dirty blond strands behind her right ear, Rachel presses her head against the smooth black wall, "I think it came from the other side of this wall."

"Maybe they brought some D-cells for our flashlight." The last flickering embers on the torch burn out, immersing the couple in inky blackness.

Louie | Beacon tunnel complex
07:45 p.m. | August 22, 2044

Louie's Kobayashi-built humanoid form lay at an unnatural angle, curved on his back over a limestone boulder in pitch-blackness. The deadweight of his smashed head lolls sideways, pulling a tangled mass of oily wiring out of his broken neck. With a dead-eyed vacancy, he stares toward an elevated square base far beneath a rope and pulley platform lowering Hamed and Cassandra from high above.

Light orbs emanate from Louie's lifeless face and form a luminous sphere. The pure energy sentience rotates on its axis and proceeds into a steep-angled side passage oriented due north. Reaching a dead-end, it removes a heavy granite plug before dropping into the antechamber outside the southernmost point of the black granite dome where the

Light Specters' beacon languishes in total darkness.

Transmogrifying into the radiant form of Neil Alexander, it checks the circular hatch centered on the black granite dome section left exposed within the precision-cut limestone space. Sensing the dark spectral presence waiting for the world to end on the opposite side of the hatch inside the dome elicits abject pity for whatever remains of his former friend.

Turning from the dome, he moves to a smooth flat wall on the far side of the antechamber, whispering, "Rachel. I am here."

The muffled sounds of excited voices are audible through the thick stone. Smiling despite the grave circumstances, Neil passes through the wall to greet the bedraggled couple.

Julius Hart | IOSC Spaceport, Toulouse, France
07:54 p.m. | August 22, 2044

Corkscrewing to a jarring stop, a foot off the wet macadam in the neo-gothic IOSC complex's employee lot, Pennywell's Cathedral to the Stars, attendants whisk their disheveled CEO and his valet through the deserted Toulouse terminal and down the path to the waiting monorail.

A smattering of movers and shakers with names checked against a top-secret list proffer sullen nods aboard the blacked-out luxury monorail as Artemus Pennywell and Andrew move down the aisle like a defeated general and his aide-de-camp. The pair slump into thick leather seats in a row toward the back, relieved to have made it this far. No warm towels or water bottles await their use.

A fit young man across their aisle smiles while offering a metal flask in his outstretched hand, "Mister, you look like you could use a drink."

Pennywell notes the engraved J and H while accepting the flask with a perfunctory nod, ignoring the "Tsk, tsk," coming from his valet.

"Are you old enough to drink this rotgut?"

"Well, it's the Hart family brand of Kentucky bourbon, and I built the drone in which you just landed. So, I will say, yes, sir, I'm old enough."

"Age isn't everything. It's the only thing." Pennywell follows his non-sequitur with a long pull, "Damn, I needed that."

"No, you didn't."

"Shut up, Andrew."

Handing the flask back across the aisle to none other than Julius Hart himself, Pennywell offers, "I'm glad you made it. Not too many did."

"As luck would have it, I was already on the grounds working with my engineers on a new idea: Satellite warehouses in stationary orbits around Earth."

"Sounds like a pipe dream, son."

Hart stares outside at the gathering storm, "We'll see." Turning back toward Pennywell, "I guess thanks are in order. I did not know I was among the chosen few until an hour ago. You should have seen the look on my girlfriend's face."

"Why would they not let you bring her? Procreation will be an important activity in our new normal."

Wearing a t-shirt, jeans, and broken-in western boots, the rakish entrepreneur scratches messy brown hair, grinning, "Oh, she's on board. I sent her in search of snacks."

Pennywell replies, "Look, kid, I had nothing to do with the list of essential humans, but if we survive, I want to hear more about your satellites."

"It's a deal."

Thirty seconds later, a feisty French beauty in a denim vest over a low-cut floral-patterned romper and red sneakers plops into the seat across from Julius Hart. The ginger-haired, fair-skinned woman throws a bag of chips in his face while crisscrossing her long thin legs, "La prochaine fois, trouvez vos propres collations."

Pennywell proffers a weak smile, "I see humanity is in good shape."

Tarek Hamed | Beacon tunnel complex
07:54 p.m. | August 22, 2044

Professor Tarek Hamed languished outside the unmovable curve of settled science, a fact he learned to embrace. From the Egyptian's first pyramid visit on a third-grade field trip, he knew humans had nothing to do with their construction. The question of who did build them fired his youthful imagination, setting him on his quest. However, that day, his idiot teacher's dogmatized drone regarding ramps, pulleys, and thousands of slaves also marked the beginning of the pablum he butted against throughout his archeology career.

Enduring scorn and ridicule from all corners of academia, he adhered to his unconventional pyramid theories. Less than a year after his breakthrough discovery, no small thanks to the departed Yasmine Sardouk, the zenith of his life's work was at hand.

He did not need any more help from Cassandra, the annoying, know-it-all woman standing at his side on the rickety platform.

His deal with the indebted woman ends as the remorseless Hamed plunges a thin titanium blade deep into her chest. The raven-haired academic looks at him with dark, pleading eyes, but he has seen and heard enough from the lot he employed to get to this point, "I apologize, Cassandra, but as it turns out, I prefer to work alone."

Cassandra's surprised expression looks down at the dark stain spreading across her chest. She struggles to utter a sound as Hamed slides out the blade and swipes it on her sleeve. She coughs a fine spray of blood, and spittle gurgles from her lips across the breast of his jacket as he lays her onto the platform. Scrunching his wet nose and mustache, he notes the graphite handle of the small laser-guided pistol tucked in her front waistband, "I don't think you will need this; one can never be too careful."

Avoiding the expanding pool of blood at his feet, Hamed dabs his face but refrains from smearing the splatter pattern marring his white suit jacket. He refuses to open the floodgates of his repressed psychotic rage and allow a few blood spots to mar what will become his crowning achievement. And yet, dammit all, he knows that dam will break at some point.

He is content to continue down a narrow side passage to the beacon's antechamber for now.

Rachel | Beacon antechamber
07:59 p.m. | August 22, 2044

Rachel strains to hear the voice, leaning on her right side into the smooth wall with a hand cupped around her ear pressed into the surface.

Over her shoulder, a shocked Owen booms out of the stillness, "Neil Alexander! Where the hell have you been? We are getting our ass handed to us down here!"

Rachel spins on her worn and scuffed heels, and her eyes meet the smiling countenance of her great-great-grandpa, brighter and more translucent than he first appeared back in the French cavern.

"You came back!" Suppressing a desire to jump into his arms, she straightens, reeling in the tattered remnants of her composure. "Owen is right. We screwed this up pretty bad. Where the hell have you been?"

Even in his luminous, semi-transparent state, Neil exudes the same effortless aplomb that eased anxiety among jittery squadron mates back in his human life. "Rachel, my dear, all is not lost. Do you remember what I told you back in France?"

"Let the Machine do the work?"

"Bingo." Another violent quake permeates the solid stone creating eerie-sounding cracking noises through solid limestone. "As I am sure you are both aware, Earth is under siege, and time is running out. I am forbidden to fight your battle, but nothing stops me from opening a door."

Neil gives his granddaughter a reassuring wink while waving his hand over the smooth surface, sliding the megalithic obstruction sideways into the strata. His glowing human form illuminates the antechamber and the exposed portion of the black granite dome.

Owen leads Rachel across the threshold, the smoldering makeshift torch still held in his bloody grasp.

A whoosh of dust-filled air puffs into the grotto as the wall slides shut behind the couple.

Owen whispers to his bride, glued to his left shoulder, "I wish Neil would stick around a little longer."

Rachel's whispered reply, "It does not matter. We are here."

Neil's swift departure threw the antechamber back into utter darkness except for the faint orange glow from Owen's torch. "Man, the next time, I am bringing an extra torch whether you want to hold one or not."

Rachel peers forward at a faint phosphorescent circular outline, ignoring her husband's complaint. Approaching the black granite dome, careful not to trip in the dark, she makes out stress fractures spidering outward from the glowing two-foot circumference.

Bursting with excitement, Rachel pats her hands atop the polished granite dome ensconced in subterranean strata deep beneath the Giza Plateau almost 5,000 years earlier, "This circle outlines the hatch leading inside the beacon chamber."

"Are you sure?" Owen feels around the edge, searching for a grip or a handle. His gnarled fingertips probe into a weird four-hole configuration, like an extra hole in a bowling ball. He tugs the handle with a loud grunt, but it does not budge. "It does not matter, Rachel."

"What are you saying, Owen?"

"We don't have the golden ellipse."

Placing a hand over Owen's shoulder, Rachel pulls him close and whispers in his ear, "Harry has it. He is waiting for us inside."

An intense light pierces the antechamber behind Owen and Rachel to their left. Distracted by the hatch discovery, neither noticed the unplugged access out of the antechamber.

Jolted by the abrupt presence of another human this far underground, Rachel and Owen shield their eyes from the disorienting flashlight beamed in their faces. After hours of darkness, the brightness blinds their vision, compounding the couple's dazed confusion.

A familiar English-accented baritone voice echoes inside the antechamber, "Owen and Rachel Haig, I presume?"

Someday, after mastering the winds, the waves, the tides and gravity, we shall harness for God the energies of love, and then, for a second time in the history of the world, man will have discovered fire.

– Pierre Teilhard de Chardin

Chapter Eleven:

The Metamorphosis

Tarek Hamed | Beacon antechamber
08:15 p.m. | August 22, 2044

Hamed lowers into the antechamber behind his flashlight's blinding glare, "Fancy running into the two of you way down here!" flicking the red laser sight on Cassandra's blood-smeared pistol between the stricken couple. "You slipped past a small army of security outside on the plateau and managed to navigate a maze of passages to reach the finish line. Impressive. However, I am sad to report; you are too late. The alien invasion has already begun." Gesturing with the gun barrel for the American couple to step back from the hatch, the archeologist continues, "If you two behave and refrain from ill-advised shenanigans, I will allow you to accompany me inside the beacon chamber. It is, after all, why we are all down here inside such an inhospitable place."

Rachel shields her eyes from the bright flashlight beam, "Who the hell are you?"

Owen pulls her close, "She means aside from the asshole on the bus."

Rachel elbows Owen, "Ixnay on calling him Omar Shariff."

Hamed moves to the hatch before answering the American couple and acknowledging the tour bus clusterfuck. "Yes, the bus. Hard to believe our first encounter was only a few hours ago." He laments with a world-weary sigh, "It was a good plan, poorly executed. I will concede the point." After a pregnant pause, a thought pops into his amphetamine-fueled frontal lobe, "Are either of you in possession of the golden ellipse?"

Watching their puzzled expressions nodding "No." in unison, Hamed smiles and shrugs, "No matter. It is around here somewhere." Reaching under the lapel of his blood-spattered suit jacket, he produces the prized crystal pyramid, "When opening a door onto a new reality, it helps to have the key."

Rachel and Owen watch their captor insert the pyramid-shaped amulet's point into the uppermost hole in the hatch door. Nothing happens. Owen can't resist a verbal jab, "Maybe someone changed the lock."

Ignoring the peanut gallery, a hint of agitation crosses Hamed's face, "Huh. That should have worked."

Peering across the dark antechamber, Rachel sees the focused man remove a spec from the pyramid's tip, like lint from a record needle.

Muttering to himself, "Let's try that again, shall we?" he reinserts his key into the hole, and the crystal lights up in shades of blue. With a well-timed step backward, Hamed avoids the heavy two-foot diameter granite hatch swinging open.

Rachel and Owen feel the rush of hot air sucking through the orifice into the pitch-black vacuum of the unsealed beacon chamber.

Hamed straightens his blood-flecked jacket and trains the laser square into Owen's chest, "Mr. Haig, how about you enter first."

Stalling for time, the bedraggled couple falls into each other's arms.

"Okay, let's break it up; no time to waste, what with the end of the world and all." Hamed separates the couple with the pistol and pulls Owen to the opened hatch.

Seated on the curved hatch rim, legs dangling into the unknown, Owen winks toward Rachel and lets his weight pull him through. Distributing the impact through his two-point landing, he rolls on the hard granite, wincing with new pain glommed atop previous aches, "I'm okay! Rachel, it's about a ten-foot drop, be careful."

"Indeed, you are next, Mrs. Haig."

Rachel emulates Owen, passing feet-first through the hatch, lowering her long body as much as possible before letting go. Her jarring landing onto the hard floor still comes with a bone-rattling swiftness.

The pair step backward into the pitch-blackness on the smooth surface, crunching broken bits of rock under their boots. Hamed drops with alacrity, maintaining a steady aim with his flashlight and gun.

Owen poises to rush the Egyptian, but Rachel raises her hand, "Don't do it, Owen."

Overhearing her admonition, Hamed's derisive laugh cuts across the darkness, "Yes, Owen. Only fools rush in." Kicking aside fallen debris littering the polished black granite rotunda, his narrowed torch beam searches across the hieroglyphic-covered dome interior. Locating an inconspicuous symbol lost in the dense hodge-podge of glyphs, he fingers a hidden indentation and inserts the skeleton key. Within seconds, a twilight blue ambiance fills the 71-foot diameter space. "Excellent! Let there be light."

Rachel's head angles backward, following the dome's elegant symmetry to its 22-foot highpoint.

Hamed's expressive Egyptian features contort into a feigned look of concern upon seeing the hapless couple, "Well, well, aren't the both of you a sight for sore eyes. Although I must say, Mrs. Haig, the blue lighting suits you! Your skin is downright radiant. Owen, my friend, you are punching way above your weight class."

Fists clenched, Owen is about to parry the remark, but Rachel physically steers him by the shoulders toward the center of the alien-built expanse, indeed noticing her skin aglow in the weird lighting. Biting her lower lip, she decides to keep it to herself.

Their banter cuts to silent awestruck stares dwarfed through the dim blue light before the looming silhouette of the proto-pyramidic beacon's southwest elevation jutting from the rotunda. Large fallen chunks and gritty debris from the damaged granite dome holding back hundreds of feet of limestone strata mar the pristine alien-engineered space.

Another seismic reminder of the shitstorm on the surface world loosens a jagged hunk of the dome from the main crack spidering across the upper reaches of hieroglyphics-covered granite. The fist-sized chunk ricochets off the beacon before bouncing into the shadows.

Concerned the structure might collapse, ending their quest under untold tons of rock, Rachel squints through the dimness toward White Suit, swaying on his feet in a deep trance, the mustachioed schemer's gun held in a loose grip at his side. Watching him stumble forward zombie-like around the beacon's western face, she grabs Owen's sleeve, "Hey Owen, check it out. Something hypnotized Hamed."

Failing to register Owen's mumbled reply, Rachel realizes her husband also staring at the ancient structure with a slackened vacancy. Before she can shake some sense back into her man, he staggers toward the beacon.

Caught off guard by Owen's hypnotized state, Rachel winces,

watching his face plant onto the beacon's intricate grooved surface with a discernible smack and a weird grunt.

Poised in a wide-legged stance for whatever happens next, Rachel watches as her husband fumbles his bent and bloodied fingertips into the beacon's carved matrix. Whispering like she is in her mother's church, "What the hell are you trying to do?" No reply. Contemplating throwing caution to the wind and yelling for him to wake up and help, an almost imperceptible background hum rises in pitch to an electrified buzz.

Resonating in her ears from something—or somebody—inside the domed expanse, a tingling dread creeps up Rachel's spine, "Oh, man, what is that noise? Owen, damn you, wake up!"

The ear-piercing sound rises in frequency, like amplifying the steady pitch of a tuning fork. Rachel sees Owen's bruised head lift, stretching long strands of drool between his bloodied mouth and the beacon, "Owen, snap the fuck out of it. Naptime is over!"

* * *

The Machine identifies the organism on its southern face as a DNA match for the human who broke the code inside the galactic map room. Modulating security protocols to less-than-lethal, like a phaser set to stun, the beacon's defense jolts the slobbering individual from its side with a not-so-gentle "Get off."

* * *

Rachel's undeniable glow brightens, and a latent mental fortitude underpinning her psyche prevents the Machine's repeated attempts to breach her neural pathways while zapping White Suit and Owen into submission with a frequency higher than a dog whistle.

"You can knock, but you can't come in."

Feet planted in the same spot as when Owen pushed from her side, Rachel scans around her into the shadows. A prickly sensation raises goosebumps on her luminous arms and legs, sensing another presence lurking within the domed chamber.

A foul mixture of ozone, smoke, and stinking decay wafts past her runny nose. Rachel cannot see Harry but smells the bastard, watching and waiting.

Rachel drops onto her knees and clears shards of rock and dirt, revealing the polished black surface Owen's lifeless body lay upon in her terrible dream. Inside her living nightmare, foreshadowing Owen's violent death and the end of the world, she hurls a chunk of limestone off the glyph-covered wall. "No! It does not have to be this way!" Grasping at her scar through her ripped, half-unbuttoned linen shirt, she vomits before wiping tears from her luminous green eyes. Sucking the foulness into her lungs, she studies her glowing hands and fingers, "Why is this happening to me?"

Sensing the tangible threat inside the chamber, Rachel grabs a sharp rock for self-defense—or to throw at Owen—scrambling onto her feet as a triumphant burst of corrosive laughter resonates through the expanse. Recognizing White Suit's echoing baritone, she swallows back a second heaving urge and wipes her mouth on her bloody sleeve, "Fuck! Get ahold of yourself."

Rachel freezes in place, hearing the Egyptian's triumphant exclamation from the opposite side of the beacon: "The golden ellipse was right here the whole time!"

* * *

Hamed's jubilant outburst snaps Owen from his Machine-induced trance. With a cobweb-clearing headshake, his throbbing head turns toward Rachel's glowing face. Struggling to comprehend her ethereal appearance, his bleary eyes fixate on his wife's luminous hands, motioning him to act. "What?" Dumbstruck by her wild gesticulations through the low-blue lighting, "Rachel, why are you glowing?"

Absorbing her pantomime act, tracking her out turned

illuminated palms, Owen grabs a clue. With a comical self-awareness, he points at himself, "Oh. You want me to stand still! I get it. Why do I need to do that?"

Alarm bells peal through the pea soup fog inside Owen's pounding head as a wraithlike presence bisects the 10-foot gap separating the pair's game of charades.

* * *

Harry proceeds around the beacon's southeast corner, trailing a faint whiff of death in his invisible wake. Ignoring the resilient American couple, for now, his first priority is the white-suited usurper coveting his golden ellipse.

Flynn | Beacon tunnel complex
08:45 p.m. | August 22, 2044

Furious at themselves for allowing the archeologist, Hamed, to get the drop on them, Agent Flynn and Captain Faisel are left stranded atop the narrow precipice. Contemplating their predicament, they watch as the taught platform cable lowers the conniving bastard and his accomplice, Cassandra, into the deep black shaft. Watching the line slacken, still well beyond their reach, they hear voices punctuated by an anguished cry echo from far below.

"They must have hit rock bottom."

"Well put, mate, in more ways than one."

Faisel shines his light on the cable leading up from the dark abyss above their position. His right elbow smacks into a protrusion from the wall in the dark. "I bet this was the platform return switch." Studying the busted mechanism, "They sabotaged it."

"Bloody hell, they really don't want us to follow, do they?"

"Apparently not, Agent."

Peering into the unknowable depths, "Bollocks, my RAF basic training was a long time ago, but it looks like a long rappel is our only option."

Faisel trains his dark-eyed scowl on Flynn, "I once served as a drill instructor in the Egyptian army. The rope climb took out more than a few conscripts, but as you can see, my friend, the platform cabling is beyond our reach."

Accessing a small case from under his belt, the agent aims it at the rope and fires a barbed metal spear attached to a thin filament. The razor-sharp arrow misses wide left, arching into the blackness. "Blast! A bit rusty, I suppose. Let's have another go, shall we?" Recoiling the line with the press of a button, Flynn corrects his aim and punctures the cable with the barbed metal tip. Reeling the thick braided line within their reach, he hides a genuine surprise, muttering, "One in a million shot."

"What was that?"

"Nothing. Grab the cable, yeah. I don't want to do that again."

Faisel loops the slackened length of cabling over the ruined return switch baseplate bolted into the solid rock. "That should hold the line against the side of the shaft so we can rappel down. Much better than shimmying in midair."

"No argument from me."

Rappelling downward into the dark shaft, Flynn's hands are already rope burned. "What the hell happened to my gloves? Oh yeah, I offered them to Owen back in Libya." The PTB agent checks above him and finds the heavier Faisel coming on fast. "Shit, Captain! Give me a chance!"

"I'm fighting a little thing called gravity here, my friend."

"Next time, let's do this one at a time!"

"If there is a next time doing this, I will shoot myself."

"Before or after you shoot me and everyone else?"

"After."

With his flashlight hooked to a belt loop in his khakis, courtesy of Nina, Flynn sees rock bottom below his boots. "Blimey, just about there."

Releasing the last five feet from the cable, Flynn's boots splat atop wet sand. Directing his light toward the platform, he discovers Cassandra's prone form. Realizing he is standing in the woman's blood pooling off the elevated eight-foot platform, he rushes to her side, "What the fuck happened here?"

Faisel drops in a heap and rushes to join Flynn, standing over Cassandra, "She is dead, Flynn."

"Really, mate? It is a good thing I brought you along."

Widening his torch beam into the shadows, the agent finds Louie's broken form splayed across a limestone cube. "Good Christ, what a mess. Even though Louie was not human, I feel terrible for him, and yet, I don't give a bloody rip for that fucking traitorous tour guide. What does that say about me?"

Faisel consoles his new friend with a firm pat on the shoulder, "I think it makes you a good judge of character."

"Thanks, mate." Beyond Louie's broken body, Flynn gestures toward the opening of another steep passage. "This way, I suppose." Near the entrance, he stumbles on his pistol lying atop a piling of loose sand, "Hey, look what I found."

"Good. Now we are both armed." Captain Faisel raises the cuff on his right pants leg, exposing a small sidearm holstered on his inner calf. He removes it and checks the clip.

"Why didn't they make you toss your weapon?"

"In our haste to come out here, I left my sidearm in my office. Hamed never asked if I was carrying anything else."

Squatting low, they enter the steep downhill passage as more rumblings permeate the chiseled limestone, "Bollocks! This could all be for naught."

Tarek Hamed | Beacon chamber
09:15 p.m. | August 22, 2044

Tipping back his hat brim with the muzzle from the forgotten pistol clutched in his right hand, Professor Tarek Hamed hunches before the elusive golden ellipse. Gobsmacked by its perfection gleaming through the darkness, he suppresses a nagging thought, *"Nothing is this easy."*

Pondering the relic's centered placement at the base of the proto-pyramid's northern façade, the archeologist turns his maleficent gaze twenty feet upward to the mirrored elliptical-shaped keep at the beacon's apex. A gauzy memory from Hamed's brutal youth conjures in his fevered mind: A single foil-wrapped present, wool socks, tucked under the family Christmas tree. A gap-toothed grin widens under the archeologist's salt-and-pepper mustache as he mutters aloud, "I hated my parents."

"At least you had parents."

Hamed straightens and wheels toward the disembodied voice, aiming the gun's laser through a phantasmic presence resolving out of the ether. His mouth agape, he sees the red beam passing through a translucent vision of the alluring Yasmine Sardouk.

"Tarek, pick up the golden ellipse. I dare you."

"Yasmine is dead. Who might you be?"

The professor's deadpan query prompts the deceased young researcher's visage to falter and transmogrify from the youthful beauty into a hooded monster, wreaking decay and emanating wispy fumes of burnt flesh. A deep-throated rasp oozes from under the hood, "Very well. It requires an immense output of energy to maintain her facade."

Regretting his impertinence, Hamed realizes the being's sallow glowering stare pierces his psyche from the shadowed hood while its vaporous stench assaults his bulbous nose. The sickening smell pickles his brain with an intoxicating cocktail of hatred, fear, greed, and a wanton desire to kill the wretched shapeshifting monster.

Tarek Hamed believed a higher purpose justified the antisocial behavior and murderous deeds veiled behind his collegial manner and dapper appearance throughout his life and archeology career. His self-delusion reaches its ignominious conclusion at the end of days. Conniving an ad hoc plan to snatch the golden ellipse from this hideous creature—his apparent benefactor the entire time—he drops the facade and lets the evilness flow. Screw humanity. He was never going to play the hero. He is the villain. Ask Cassandra.

Warding off lightheadedness from the ridiculous smell, Hamed buys time, pleading his case before the malodorous entity, "I am not here to save the world. I am here to end it, once and for all!"

Harry's hatred and frustration toward the misanthrope swell to gargantuan proportions. Flinging off his black hood in an overt, hostile sweep with his skeletonized hand, he scowls at Hamed's intemperate self-defense, "That is not for you to decide, you worthless piece of shit."

Unfazed by the exposed head of Harry Stark, Hamed nonetheless feigns folding like a cheap suit before the repulsive entity. Crumpling into his most obsequious posture, he falls onto his knees, pleading for mercy. In the process, shifting the pistol to his left hand while extending his right hand toward the golden ellipse. Poised to grab it and run, the tell-tale amulet glows bright blue under his bloodied suit jacket.

Throughout Harry Stark's short, tragic existence—from his brutal Bronx orphanage youth through his army life, he recognized and dealt with a host of jerks and phonies who put Hamed's act to shame. Realizing that the misanthropic bastard has so little regard for his danger triggers his mercurial, psychotic rage.

Oozing rivulets break free from boils clustering on the scarred and tattered remnants of Harry's deformed head. After reigning a hellfire of death upon the conniving weasel, he will torch the young couple— enough playing around.

Venturing a quick glimpse at the hideous face glowering at

him like a decomposing candlelit pumpkin, Hamed concludes that the odiferous freak of nature is not buying his act. Recoiling from putrid bursts of noxious ooze flecking his face and chest, the Egyptian sees pinpricks of light flickering inside the semitransparent monster. The specks stir into violent light streaks generating a blood-boiling cauldron inside the deformed creature.

Scared stiff and melting under the intense radiating heat, Hamed nonetheless produces a confused frown, hearing the excoriating words spitting from its skeletonized mouth.

"The Horseman decides the fate of humanity! This beacon chamber will crumble after human extermination, and the golden ellipse will belong to me. Not you! The Dark Specters wanted you as a fail-safe. That was your sole purpose. Nothing more! At least the cowering humans—who refuse to die—on the other side of the beacon understand why they are here. Tarek Hamed, your services are no longer required!"

Eyes shut tight and fists clenched around the gun and the ellipse, Hamed waits at death's door and the eternal damnation that follows.

Nothing happens.

With morbid curiosity, Hamed peeks at charred ligaments and dripping masses of putrefied flesh covering his executioner's beaten and exposed skull, furrowing into a scowl while eyeballing a disembodied presence whispering in its smoky earhole. Sensing a last-second reprieve, Hamed prepares to bolt as the enigmatic hothead roars a furious reply toward his invisible puppeteers.

"We had a deal! We do not need this fool! What have I done wrong? Why don't you trust me? No one ever trusted me!"

"I did, Harry."

Hamed peers beyond the monster toward a glowing profile approaching from the shadows in a dashing flight suit and jacket adorned with a black scorpion patch. Not giving a flying fuck who the new guy is, Hamed attempts his getaway, but the weight of the golden ellipse holds him to the granite floor. He is not going anywhere.

* * *

"Harry, you look like shit. What did they do to you?"

Reeling from the interruption, Harry Stark's sallow eyeballs turn and absorb the handsome countenance of Neil Alexander, smiling his shit-eating grin. Forgetting the human excrement cowering at his boots, Stark redirects his white-hot ire on his debonair former friend and confidante, materializing out of the blue-tinged shadows.

"Goddamn you, Captain, you should have stayed away."

"You don't have to do this, Harry."

"Yes, I do. But now you have ruined things for the last time."

For a nanosecond, everything goes still as the night before the putrid embodiment of Harry Stark explodes in a raging supernova of destructive dark energy. His plan to take down himself and Neil in a final blow to humanity ends with a cosmic explosion incinerating the decaying vestiges of the pugnacious former army pilot to base elements swirled into a violent whirlwind inside the compromised dome.

Unharmed because he was never really there, Neil recedes into the shadows. Meanwhile, like a blender set to liquefy, razor-edged jags of granite and limestone whip into a maelstrom of flying debris inside the circular expanse.

Inconsolable after Harry Stark's suicidal detonation to sub-atomic particles, the Dark Specters focus their wrath on the luminous manifestation of Neil Alexander, who triggered Harry's demise. Freed from sustaining the walking corpse, the evil lights focus their cosmic energies into an undulating leviathan with lit tentacles grappling the Light Specters' meddlesome human asset above the black granite rotunda before twisting and squeezing him in a furious rage. While he cannot die, they can prevent him from further meddling as their vile plans shift onto the Americans.

Flynn | Beacon tunnel complex
10:05 p.m. | August 22, 2044

The middle-aged pair descends to the cramped tunnel's endpoint and wriggles through a carved hole into an antechamber. Drawn to the strange blue glow emanating from an opened hatch, the men sneak over, peer inside, and startle in unison as a thunderous angry voice resonates from somewhere down below.

"Who the devil is that?"

"More like, what the devil was that?"

The echoing tirade fades, and Faisel indicates he will drop through first into the blue-cast expanse.

"Okay, mate. It looks like a pretty good drop. Try not to break anything."

Situating his large frame on the curved hatch rim, Faisel gives a thumbs-up and disappears through the orifice. Before Flynn can follow suit, an explosive blast of energy fills the void sending a suffocating cloud of dust and debris billowing through the two-foot opening, blowing the agent off his feet.

Ears ringing inside his pounding head, Flynn struggles back to the hatch. Shielding his face from pelting debris whipped into a frenzy from the raging vortex churning down below, he spies Faisel writhing in pain on the smooth black chamber floor, "Fuck me! I knew I should have gone first. Hang on, mate, I'm coming down!"

* * *

At ground zero for the explosive demise of Harry Stark, the concussive blast of energy vaults Hamed's gore-drenched body into the dome's granite wall like a ragdoll. Knocked unconscious, he maintains a solid grip on the golden ellipse and his pistol.

Neil Alexander | Beacon chamber
10:05 p.m. | August 22, 2044

Gritting perfect teeth into a determined scowl, the embodiment of Neil Alexander spreads his arms wide and flings a twisted mass of lights into the ether, only to watch them reappear on his opposite side, snaking around him, squeezing tighter and tighter. Neil's distracted focus turns to his brave granddaughter, huddled with her new husband on the opposite side of the chamber. "Anytime now, Rachel. I am getting my ass kicked."

Rachel | Beacon chamber
10:15 p.m. | August 22, 2044

Rachel dives through the pandemonium to Owen's position midway along the base of the beacon's south-facing side to shelter from the thunderous explosion of energy generated by Harry's self-inflicted detonation. Wrapped up in each other's embrace, the pair weather the storm, huddling as low and small as possible.

Pelted by flying debris, Rachel hears Neil Alexander's pleading voice resonating over the cacophony inside her reeling head. Her reedy voice yells into Owen's ear over the bedlam, "Owen, I need to end this."

Owen risks separating from Rachel an arm's length to look upon her transformed radiance, "You are burning hot, Rachel. Literally. What is happening to you?"

"I don't know, Owen."

"All right, here's the plan. I'll follow the Egyptian's path and draw him and anything else in my direction." Ducking to avoid a flying rock, he continues, "Give me a few minutes before sneaking around from the eastern side. I don't think they will expect us to split up, just a hunch."

Rachel stifles tears, nose-to-nose with Owen's beaten face, searching his bloodshot eyes for signs of doubt, "Are you sure?"

Another flying shard strikes Owen in the back of the head, "Ow! Shit that hurts! No. I'm not sure of anything. But I can make enough of a distraction to allow you to fulfill your destiny or whatever they think you can do. And remember, whatever happens, I love the hell out of you, Rachel."

Before turning to hustle off in the opposite direction, Owen holds Rachel tight, not wanting to let go. His eyes stinging and his face, hands, and arms a blood-covered mess, Owen looks into his bride's stunning radiance and offers a confident smile, "I will see you on the other side."

Reaching what appears to be the penultimate moment of their heartrending honeymoon experience, Rachel digs deep for the perfect words to express her love but gets lost in Owen's battered face. With a radiant irony-laced smile, she realizes their connection defies a schmaltzy reply.

Surrendering to the moment, Rachel closes her eyes, feeling the soft caress of Owen's hand against her cheek. Blinking them open, she watches him hunkering along the base of the darkened beacon through the debris-filled turbulence, disappearing around the southwest corner. Uncurling from her huddled position against the beacon's southern side, she smooths a trembling hand over her tingling three-inch scar. Gasping the thin hot air into her burning lungs, familiar energy courses through every fiber of her luminous body, "I know what this is."

Owen | Beacon chamber

10:30 p.m. | August 22, 2044

Owen's raised arms shield against a cascade of flying rocks ricocheting off the beacon's western face, crashing around his sprinting form. Skidding to a stop at the northwest corner, he heaves and gasps for air. Squinting through the supernatural pandemonium and ignoring the stinging sands, he sees none other than Neil Alexander waging mortal combat against a monstrous cephalopod teeming with lights through its snaking limbs. "What fresh hell is this?"

Rachel's ancestor rips writhing arms off the hulking body and flings them into a netherworld abyss, only to endure multiple grappling tentacles sprouting out of nowhere, twisting him inside a hopeless knot of vengeful lights.

Owen endures a sharp thwack of granite to the side of his head, venturing along the northern face. Smearing blood and dirt across his brow, he continues through the bedlam, "This might be harder than I thought." Coughing up something gross and sticky, he spits and clears his throat, "Hey, assholes! Down here! Come and get me, you evil pricks!"

Distracted by the shitstorm, Owen fails to see a crazed Hamed vault from the shadows on a bone-crunching beeline from his six.

The wild-eyed Egyptian body slams him into the unforgiving granite rotunda. Owen rolls, looking into his attacker's snarling gore-covered face, twisting sideways as the maniac smashes a hunk of granite where his head was a heartbeat earlier.

Scrambling onto his feet, Owen circles White Suit, struggling to recall anything from years of Krav Maga training. Shaking his head and wiping blood from his nose, he realizes someone or something is pulling his levers. In mid-rumination, backed against the beacon, Owen fails to thwart Hamed's tight-fisted uppercut to the jaw. Like an over-the-hill prizefighter, Owen crumbles against the sloped side, down for the count. 10, 9, 8, 7 … Bouncing onto his feet, Owen's fists raise to parry the next pummeling attack. Instead, his puffy eyes see his pugilistic adversary seizing the opportunity to advance down the north side.

Rubbing his sore jaw, Owen glances at the nightmarish battle raging above him. Neither the leviathan nor Neil seemed to notice his beat-down at the hands of the older man. So far, his diversionary tactics are falling on deaf ears inside the domed beacon chamber.

A hand on Owen's shoulder twists his wide-eyed, swollen countenance onto a familiar smiling face.

"Where the fuck have you been?"

Rachel | Beacon chamber
10:55 p.m. | August 22, 2044

A nerve-wracking 30-count after Owen vanishes into the swirling storm, Rachel ducks along the beacon to outmaneuver White Suit and the Dark Specters from the eastern side. Shielding her cut up face in the dim blue light, she bears down, cursing the debris-carrying gale coming from all directions at once. *How is that even possible?*

Ten steps into her solo trek, a granite projectile hits Rachel between the shoulder blades, sending her reeling onto the hard surface. Gasping for dirty air after having the wind knocked from her lungs for the second time, the pain radiating down her spine extinguishes her last flickering resolve. Curling into a fetal repose against the beacon's sloped southeastern corner, her emotional dam breaks, swamping her battered psyche. "I cannot do this! Oh, my God, it hurts to move!"

Shielding her bleeding face against another stinging barrage, she screams into the vortex, "I quit! Do you hear me now? I don't care what happens anymore—screw everybody!"

Rachel's resignation echoes across the domed chamber like the mournful cry of a wounded animal abandoned and left to die on an African savannah. A teeming miasma of Dark Specters mimics a kettle of vultures encircling a helpless victim before swallowing her under a veil of evil lights.

Surrendering to a persuasive admonition to lie still and take it, Rachel withdraws into the darkened recesses of her mind. Desperate for a hiding place, she jiggles door handles to rooms locked away in her subconscious. Reaching the last door, she turns the knob and pushes it open, stumbling into the dark shadows of a dingy back alley. Through a noxious early-morning haze, a threatening presence crouches atop a startled young woman. Rachel steps closer, focusing on the sad, pale complexion of the confused and lonely younger version of herself, pinned underneath a hulking presence amid a widening pool of blood.

Watching her rape scene play out, she shields her eyes, anticipating a flash of energy turning night into day. The lecherous attacker recoils, coughing bloody spittle all over his victim as the glinted reflection from a long hunting knife exits the flabby back of his gaudy silk shirt.

Ignoring the dead assailant, Rachel kneels and catches the incriminating aroma of alcohol and cigarettes she always tried to eliminate before returning home. Swallowing back bitter regret, she smooths a fingertip through tears mixed with mascara dripping down the smooth cheeks of her former self, out cold on the pavement. Brushing aside a long golden strand speckled with blood, the last glimmer of energy fades from her 18-year-old face, along with the hollow promise of a miraculous sequel.

Back inside the red-carpeted hallway, Rachel laments her hubris, conned into believing she could transcend human physiology and save the world. She was never the one. Biting her lower lip bloody, she locks the door and throws away the key.

Retracing her path down the door-lined corridor, the prickly sensation of malicious lights erasing her from the physical world returns with a vengeance.

"Don't fight back. It will all be over soon enough."

"Okay."

Strong hands grapple around Rachel's beaten form from out of the blueness and lift her limp form off the rotunda. Forcing her swollen eyes open while cradled in the muscular-armed embrace, she stares into the strong paternal countenance of none other than the Egyptian army officer from back on the plateau. "How did you get here? Am I dead?"

The man's face tightens into a grimace, shifting to avoid putting weight on his broken left leg, "No, Miss, but you need to stand on your own two feet and get your ass in gear!"

Extricating from his faltering grasp, Rachel plants her feet in the raucous chamber. Touching her hands against his stubbled face, she absorbs the brusque officer's agonizing pain and soul-crushing fears.

Captain Mohammed Faisel winces in obvious pain, pushing her away, "For the love of God, finish this, Mrs. Haig."

Unfazed by the ill-timed arrival of the stoic Captain Faisel, the Dark Specters morph into a serpentine phantasm. Coiling tight, the vicious snake strikes the Egyptian, casting his limp form into the shadows. With the broken man out of commission, the evil orbs' attention turns to the American woman.

Liberated from the Dark Specters' oppressive mind control, anxious thoughts for Earl, his lovely wife, and the rest of the tour group glom atop Rachel's vexing concern for the injured security guard. How did he make it down here? Was the rest of her tour group dead or alive?

Another rocky fusillade whips past Rachel Alexander Haig, but she is through playing the victim. Unlocking the door to her inner trust fund murderess releases a spark of energy preserved deep within her lithe frame. Wheeling toward the snake-shaped mass of malicious lights, her subtle glow brightens to a white-hot intensity radiating from her defiant "You're fucking with the wrong girl" stance.

Pulling dirty, sweaty blond strands into a loose knot over the black and purple welt spread across most of her back, she alights with a cocksure warrior smile, ready for battle. Concentrating glowing green eyes on the threatening phantasm's battle line reassembling in a wall of lights athwart the beacon's eastern side, her luminous resolve hits a snag, "Now what?"

Taking the measure of her malicious adversaries across the dim-blue expanse, every single Dark Specter is delineated in hi-definition, amassing next to the beacon's intricate surface, which she now sees in stark relief. Coursing with extreme power through every fiber of her being, she remains unsure how to proceed. Nattering voices inside her head snipe back and forth, debating the next step: *What will happen? What if I do it wrong? Do what wrong?* Exactly.

Deciding enough talk, the young woman positions herself before the regrouped enemy line. Emulating a medieval commander, Rachel taunts the enemy, attempting to disrupt their defenses, "Leave now! Or I am going to fuck you up!" Thick, reverberating laughter swells inside her mind, drowning out natterers still jabbering away, "Oh really? Do you find that amusing? Well, how about this!" Long arms covered in cuts and bruises stretch straight out from her sure-footed stance, flexing muscles to her thin outstretched fingertips aimed at the writhing evilness blocking her path. Muttering to herself, she clenches her teeth, "Here we go!"

Yelling a full-throated scream at the top of her lungs, initial shock flips to jubilation as fiery energy streams burst from her hands. Thunderstruck by her rekindled supernatural powers, Rachel glides her left Chelsea boot in front of the right and presses her attack with a wild yell, "I can keep this up all day long, motherfuckers!"

Absorbing the exhilarating release of energy inside every pore in her body, Rachel shoves the vile lights backward. The wondrous woman she has become advances down the beacon's eastern side and smiles as the amorphous mass thins and separates, billowing backward, retreating from her formidable advance. "If my mother could see me now! This is working! I'm doing it!"

A less-than-impressed voice counters her elation, "It's about goddamn time."

Glancing around the northern side, hoping to find Owen, Rachel's euphoria screeches to a horrifying halt. Straining to see upward through swirling dust and debris, she spies her husband holding on at the beacon's apex for dear life. Clutched firm in his grasp, she sees a glimmer of gold mocking her hollow victory.

Dropping her arms, the energized stream abates. Screaming through the pandemonium, she attempts to yank Owen's attention in her direction, but he seems not to notice her or care, "Owen! Stop!"

Owen | Beacon chamber
11:00 p.m. | August 22, 2044

"It's just me, Owen. Calm down. What in the bloody hell is going on down here?"

"Agent Flynn! Nice of you to join us." Straightening from his defensive crouch, like a field general amid a raging battle, Owen gestures at the extraterrestrial spectacle, "That is Light and Dark Specters battling each other. At least for now. The white suit guy from the bus is down here, too."

"So is the Egyptian guard we ran across this morning." Flynn gestures over his shoulder, "He busted his leg jumping into this shitstorm. I gave the poor bloke a painkiller and told him to stay low."

"Still carrying your pharmacy, I see."

"Yeah, still got it. Where is Rachel?"

"I sent Rachel around the other side. I planned to draw the evil bastards my way so she could do her thing." Spitting a clot of blood, "Whatever the fuck that is."

Both men spy Hamed climbing the beacon with the golden ellipse tucked under his right arm. "Ah shit, mate! There goes your plan."

Owen cannot believe his eyes, "Jesus, what is that jackass doing?"

Flynn raises his handgun, "Not to worry, Owen, I can take that tosspot out from right here."

Realizing humanity is under scrutiny, even at this late hour, Owen redirects the gun away from Hamed, "Let's try to save the world without killing each other if possible. It's important."

Tarek Hamed | Beacon chamber

11:10 p.m. | August 22, 2044

Monitoring the slow-developing, uncoordinated Gork invasion while simultaneously battling the Light Specters' emissaries to a draw, the Dark Specters reconsider entrusting human destruction to the bumbling Gorks. After all, reducing Earth, and its satellite, to sub-atomic particles through a direct human action would be a sublime climax after eons of cold and conniving calculation and end the Light Specters' misguided faith in humankind once and for all.

Contrary to Harry Stark's explosive tirade, Tarek Hamed remains the Dark Specters' fail-safe. And better yet, the crazed individual is already two-thirds up the beacon with the most destructive power in the cosmos grasped in his grubby hands. If planet Earth, and the entire solar system, for that matter, become collateral damage, so be it.

* * *

Grasping for handholds in the sloped beacon's north face, Hamed deflects a hurtling granite shard, sending his Panama hat into the furious swirl within the chamber. Watching it take flight, he spies Owen Haig and the indefatigable Agent Flynn coming on fast. Despite his seething antipathy, he had to give it to these people; they were not going down without a fight. "So be it."

Jamming his blood-stained boots into the carved matrix, Hamed squeezes off a few rounds at his pursuers. Unsure if he hit either man, he resumes his destiny-fueled climb through the pelting rocks whipping around the upper reaches of the domed expanse.

Peering toward the apex, Tarek Hamed sees the beguiling form of Yasmine Sardouk reappear before his bloodshot eyeballs, arms outstretched, and an apocalyptic siren song on her lips, "Tarek, bring me the ellipse."

Owen | Beacon chamber
11:20 p.m. | August 22, 2044

Dodging left and right to avoid a hail of ricocheting bullets through a frenzied cascade of flying projectiles of all shapes and sizes, Owen and Flynn race to stop the Egyptian before he blows everything to kingdom come. A stray hollow-point 9mm round drops the agent, sending him toppling to the ground and grabbing the gut wound.

The sickening thud of hot metal hitting his friend causes Owen to snap. Primal bloodlust hijacks his brain, thrusting him on a vengeful trajectory to kill the man in the white suit and take back his golden ellipse.

Flynn applies pressure to his lower abdomen and tries to control his breathing as a bright red circle spreads across his multi-pocketed shirt. Reaching for the same healing powder he gave Owen on the flight into Cairo, a stinging gust causes the vial to fumble from his rope-burned hands.

The last thing the PTB agent sees before losing consciousness is Owen Haig cutting up the beacon on a collision course toward Hamed. "Get him, mate."

* * *

While battling the embodiment of Neil Alexander to a stalemate, the Dark Specters keep an evil eye trained on the drama unfolding inside the chamber, now featuring a craven human competitor to their fail-safe, Hamed. Fantastic. Jettisoning luminous spheres from their phantasmal leviathan, they penetrate the auburn-headed fellow's frontal cortex like a hot knife through butter, unleashing kill-or-be-killed lower brain instincts buried deep within his primitive brain core. The deathmatch between Hamed and this new recruit will decide which one earns the ignominious title: *Destroyer of Worlds*.

* * *

The Dark Specters erase the last shred of civility inside Owen's brain. Propelling him nineteen feet up the beacon's sloped northern side on a homicidal tear, they launch him through the shitstorm. Like he was shot from a cannon, upward momentum sends Owen into Hamed's knees, steroid-enraged linebacker style.

Stunned by the speed and ferocity of Owen's attack, Hamed fumbles the pistol, firing a wild shot into the crumbling dome before flailing backward. Arms and legs locked together in a mortal struggle, both men tumble down the side and crash to the hard rotunda in a heap of animalistic grunts, curses, and snarls. The brutal hand-to-hand combat morphs into a teeth-gritting rictus of straining muscles exerting equal forces until Hamed breaks the stalemate by chomping into Owen's bandaged forearm, drawing copious blood loss and an agonized scream.

Owen pummels his freed left fist into Hamed's bloodied face in retaliation. Out of his swollen-eyed periphery, he diverts Hamed's rising gun muzzle from the side of his head before the ear-splitting blast reverberates through his throbbing skull like Big Ben on New Year's Eve.

Out of his mind with a vengeful bloodlust, Owen Haig, investment banker, financier, and all-around American boy, squeezes the archeologist's windpipe in his misshapen bloody fingers until his foe stops breathing and goes limp.

Basking in vanquishing his foe like a prize fighter, Owen scoops up a soccer ball-size hunk of granite and is on the brink of crashing it into the Egyptian's skull before realizing the man in the white suit no longer poses a threat. Owen's rage transforms into elation, straddling his defeated enemy, writhing on his back, and gasping for air with the pistol clutched at his neck.

Owen kicks the weapon from Hamed's grasp, catching the man's scrabbled chin with the corner of his Timberland boot and knocking him unconscious. Through the chaos churning around him, he stares at a hairy morsel of flesh clinging to the jagged hunk of granite gripped in his hand. Emulating a victorious gladiator, Owen Haig lifts the rock above his head and awaits the Dark Specters' verdict.

The spectacular knot of evil twisting lights offers a virtualized downturned thumb.

While positioning the jagged rock over Hamed, a random memory of the stone-throwing Spanish brothers on the plateau stymies Owen's murderous intention. Glancing through the chaos toward Flynn elicits ironic full-throated laughter, "Cain and Abel." Flinging the rock aside, he mutters, "Do it yourselves."

Owen's foggy-eyed gape latches onto the golden ellipse—shimmering in the pale blue light, lying in the same position where Hamed first discovered it. Scooping it up in his ruined hands, Owen kicks the inert man in the white suit one more time and climbs the northern face with a myopic verve to prevail at any and all cost.

Hell-bent on his dark undertaking, violent bolts of lightning illuminate Owen's beaten profile from the eastern side of the beacon. Two-thirds of the way to the apex, where he tackled Hamed, he ignores a strident voice from below. "Sorry, honey, Owen has left the building."

Pennywell | Evacuation
11:30 p.m. | August 22, 2044

While the unremarkable human manifest, peppered with a few progenies like Hart, sniped over accommodations aboard the anti-gravitational spacecraft, Artemus Pennywell parted from the well-heeled refugees after a briefing on the liftoff procedures and a dire update on the alien invasion. With a litany of questions, complaints, and protestations from the peanut gallery ringing in his ears, the spry CEO retreats to his private quarters in the corporate flagship's secured grid of offices and conference rooms. Once there, he watches the end of the world in solitude. He now understands why the captain of the Titanic never left his place on the bridge.

Entering the posh suite of offices on the ship for the first time, Pennywell nods a tacit approval. Perusing the empty built-in shelves behind the large mahogany desk bolted to the hi-tech hardwood decking, he laments abandoning mementos from his early days in the clandestine services to his current lofty post. Soon, it will all be gone, leaving nothing but fading memories.

"Sir, we lost another one."

Andrew's clipped report breaks his boss' selfish reverie, swamping the CEO's razor-sharp mind with an overwhelming sense of survivor's guilt.

Artemus Pennywell's bony fingers clench into white-knuckled fists absorbing the nightmarish news. His angular, scruffy countenance distorts into an all-too-familiar scowl, internalizing anger and grief at the grim reality of another downed IOSC ship filled with unlucky space tourists. Heaving a weary sigh, the PTB CEO loosens the trademark silver cactus bolo at the collar of his wrinkled button-down shirt, slumping into his plush desk chair, "Show me. I need to know what is happening out there."

His sad gray eyes reflect the bright holographic screen materializing before his grizzled and worried face with new footage recorded within the last twenty minutes. A chase drone's high-definition video captures an International Outer Space Consortium ship initiating an emergency reentry toward the nearest IOSC Space Port in Sapporo, Japan. All appears normal, but the hundreds of terrified space tourists must wonder what the hell is happening. Seconds into the hasty descent, a massive alien ship uncloaks its marauding path on a collision course with the triangular ship's downward trajectory. Pennywell leans close, watching the anti-gravity engines on the dwarfed IOSC ship swivel in a gut-wrenching attempt to avoid impact, but it is too late. The engine cowling at one of the vertices contacts the misshapen alien superstructure, sending the passenger-carrying craft into an end-over-end death spiral. The chase drone angles into a steep dive, following the stricken ship full of souls and recording its impact at well over a thousand miles per hour into the white-capped Sea of Japan, disintegrating into millions of pieces.

"That's enough." The screen vanishes. Shaking his head, he compartmentalizes the horrific scene, "Can I talk to anybody out there? The president, perhaps?"

Pennywell's valet—Louie's Kobayashi-built cousin—offers a reply to the semi-rhetorical question, "Sir, EMP retrofits are failing around the world. The only functioning lines of communication are through the Advisors' shielding technology. However, we are the only global entity that has it enabled across all of our systems."

"Right. Thanks, Andrew. Of course, I knew that." Having just boarded a ship almost identical in design to the one from the drone's video feed, Pennywell leans back in sheer frustration behind his desk. "You know what, Andrew? I warned them. But every country on Earth was too busy navel-gazing over feel-good technologies with no purpose beyond political correctness."

"Sir?"

"I wanted them to install the fucking nanotech shielding we fucking offered to them free of fucking charge, so I could call the fucking president when the shit hit the fan!"

Pennywell's tantrum pierces the eerie silence aboard the ship, bouncing off the calming blue-green lit surfaces and reverberating through the anti-gravitational IOSC flagship's unoccupied suites and conference facilities.

In reaction to the outburst, Andrew slips out the door and beats a path down the darkened corridor to retrieve another dose of happy pills and perhaps cobble together some comestibles. Humans love to eat.

* * *

With mixed emotions of grief and anger swirling in his head, Pennywell snatches his cane and stands before the floor-to-ceiling windowpanes and sees his reflection in the rain-spattered one-way glass. Peering southwest from the teetering spaceship, he feels the floor shift beneath his leather shoes, like standing on the deck of a boat tied to a dock or an early twentieth-century steamship in the North Atlantic. Unable to erase the terrible maritime disaster from his mind, "Maybe I should lay off the pills for a while."

Under strict blackout orders akin to the Blitz during World War Two, the ship teeters sixteen stories atop one of the Toulouse Spaceport launch pads. Pennywell watches brilliant lightning bolts spidering across the French nighttime skies, illuminating the menacing undersides of thunderheads burgeoning out of the electrified atmosphere. Hurricane-force winds whip large raindrops across the glass mixed with a swirl of papers and debris. Pennywell muses, "Some of that paperwork was no doubt important to someone."

Andrew reenters, pushing a draped cart holding a dinner plate under a silver-domed lid with a linen-rolled set of flatware angled on top. The impromptu food service is complete with a coffee-filled carafe, a souvenir IOSC logo mug, a glass of water, and a capped bottle of anxiety pills.

Pennywell smirks at the unsolicited food offering. "Andrew, I wish you would have asked first. I'm not hungry."

"Sir, please try to eat something. We are waiting on the Spanish PM, who is still twenty minutes out, and then we will leave." His humor protocol kicks in, "Every meal will come from a tube after takeoff. I know how much you despise that."

"I don't give a rat's ass about tubes, Andrew." Ruminating on the late arrival, Pennywell adds, "I see the pols are well-represented amongst the so-called Chosen Few. What a joke."

Andrew locks the cart in place, offering, "Sir, the rulers make the rules," and exits the office before Pennywell can spit out a sarcastic reply.

Turning from the window, a morose Pennywell steps toward the food offering on the locked cart. Removing the magnetized lid, he sees triangles of grilled sourdough oozing with expensive French cheese from the thick crust, a side of plump purple grapes, and a bag of chips. With a grinning recollection of the coquettish French girl from back on the monorail, he notes it is the same brand.

The ominous trumpeting noise grows louder and louder, reverberating through the ship's thick windows. Pennywell's smile fades. Wiping away tears, he curses himself, "I should never have entrusted humanity's fate to Owen and Rachel Haig. What the hell did I think they were going to do? They never stood a chance. Meanwhile, I had every resource in the world, plus an advanced race of alien advisors, for over half a century and still couldn't solve the riddle in time."

Glancing at the uncloaked alien warship looming toward the platform through the shitstorm outside the window, just a few miles distant through the darkness, he straightens, jamming his cane into the floor in frustration, "Damn! We are not going to make it!"

Looking down at the plate of food, he exclaims with mocked incredulity, "It's the apocalypse, and I'm supposed to choke down a grilled cheese?"

Scooping half the sandwich off the filigreed bone china plate, Pennywell contemplates its simplicity, yet its components stem from the dawn of human civilization: Agriculture. Animal husbandry. Harnessed energy. "It will all be gone. All of it. Goddammit all to hell."

Wheeling on his cane, he hurls the gooey mass of bread and cheese at the ship, coming on fast outside the window. The two halves separate, sticking to the glass like glue.

Pennywell watches as one side drops to the floor with a splat.

He waits for the other half to follow suit, but it holds firm to the glass. With a loud huff of frustration, he stomps across the office, flings open the door, and bellows loud enough for everyone to hear, "We are leaving! Now! That's an order! Get this ship off the deck, or we will all die!"

Owen | Beacon chamber
11:48 p.m. | August 22, 2044

A woman's crying voice echoes through the swirling bedlam to Owen's battered ears, begging for him to stop and come down. Tuning out the hysterical pleas, Owen's dead-eyed gaze fixates on an ethereal presence coaxing him upward, jamming swollen fingers into the grooved matrix and climbing toward his destiny. Out of his mind, he pulls himself the last few feet to the apex, where the mirrored elliptical keep awaits the return of the golden ellipse.

With the ellipse held in his bloody right hand, Owen hugs his burnt left forearm around the beacon's tip and curls into a fetal position on his left side, shielding the concavity pressed against his heaving chest. Obeying the voices in his head, he positions the golden ellipse inches above its perfect-matched ovular depression at the confluence of the beacon's complicated matrix.

* * *

Over 90,000 years ago, utilizing the golden ellipse' unquantifiable dark energy was an acknowledged gamble for the Light Specters. The extremity of time and infinite energy required to maintain the beacon's signal without pause, for even an instant, left the quintessential beings with no other option. Inside the beacon chamber, their hubris reflects the apocalyptic repercussion of an imminent misaligned reconnection.

The Light Specters understand that dark energy will reign supreme regardless of what the human manages to do or not do, as it had since before time.

The Light Specters also monitor a previous human civilization that reached a similar inflection point, persevered, evolved, and vanished without a trace. Their mysterious cubed flotilla spread throughout the cosmos awaits this version of the species' outcome, anticipating a return to the planet they once called home.

* * *

Gritting his teeth into a maniacal snarl, Owen's beaten face furrows a brutalized patchwork of blacks and purples as he clings atop the beacon's steep northern side as the Dark Specters push the golden ellipse between his bent and swollen fingertips into a catastrophic misalignment.

Sensing imminent disaster, the golden ellipse signals the Machine with an infinite pattern of swirling ovals across its smooth surface. Only centimeters from contact, the beacon's guardian reacts to the malevolence influencing the carbon-based lifeform's involuntary actions by applying an equivalent outward force to Owen's bloody hand.

Its function is to protect the beacon.

The opposing forces teeter within tantalizing proximity of annihilation. With the brinksmanship tearing at the human's capacity to hang on, the Machine secretes an anesthetizing drug through the human's skin, breaking the impasse. Owen's vision fades to black milliseconds before an electrified shock expels his limp form from the apex. Cartwheeling through the maelstrom, Owen crashes into the rotunda in a bloody broken heap, emulating Rachel's dream.

* * *

Neil Alexander watches Owen's downfall, ripping illuminated tentacles from his ghostly form. New writhing masses wriggle from the ether, replacing every vile appendage he tears off, "How long do you want to keep this up?"

"You are as dead as your former friend. Harry Stark is now a swirl of ashes. Tarek Hamed proved a psychopathic disappointment, but you, Neil Alexander, are no better. You led your beautiful relation to certain death."

The cutting remark chainsaws through Neil's resolve, amplified by the anguished cries of his beautiful granddaughter through the hellfire reigning down from the Dark Specters' furious rage. Sensing imminent defeat while entangled in the malicious orbs' mesh of writhing tentacles, the former fighter pilot abandons his physical embodiment and separates from the evil struggle.

Neil Alexander | Outside space and time

Parting from his ghostly doppelganger battling the dark enemy to a stalemate inside the chamber, Neil's quintessence streams through time and space to where stars do more than shine before a tribunal of Light Specters.

"What can we do for you, Neil Alexander?"

"What can you do? We need your help. Your refusal to permit direct intervention opened the floodgates leading to the full-scale invasion of my planet. Unless something changes, the end of my race is all but certain."

"We cannot intervene. Our interest lies in studying how the human race weathers adversities over time. One eventuality among many is sheltering the human world from alien interference to achieve cosmic relevancy.

Unfortunately, implementing the golden ellipse to power our warning beacon elicited a vituperative rage, cleaving us into diametrical factions. After millennia of failed attempts to extinguish our signal, a random quirk of fate proved successful. We were as astonished as our brethren Dark Specters and ill-prepared to react in time. We pulled you from your plane to restore a level playing field and counter the corruption of your friend, Harry

Stark."

"So, to you, I am nothing but a pawn on an intergalactic chessboard? I thought my purpose was to guide my granddaughter to the golden ellipse in time to save the world?"

"Your strategic moves far exceed those of a pawn, Neil Alexander. You fail to notice everything you have done to this point is self-directed. We played no role. We only observed. Your interactions throughout Rachel's short lifespan resulted in a startling new wrinkle in human evolution and activated her blue spark. However, while her energy manipulation is formidable against another human, it cannot withstand the Dark Specters."

"Are you joking? Don't you see what I did? I sent my beautiful granddaughter and her new husband into an unwinnable battle against a horrible beast." Neil envisions Rachel struggling to fend against the maelstrom inside the chamber, "What have I done?"

"Neil Alexander, your misgivings are premature. Throughout world history, certain individuals have risen from obscurity in a crisis. Their focused energies rescued humanity from apocalyptic scenarios too numerous to count. You, yourself, averted a terrible outcome at the hands of the Nazis by assisting your former friend in hiding the golden ellipse in the desert."

"What is the golden ellipse?"

"It is the energy source for the beacon."

"I know what follows: Let the Machine do the work. How do we know the Machine won't decide to kill my granddaughter? It allowed the Nazis to remove the ellipse. Who knows which side it will take?"

"Neil, the Machine functions to protect the beacon, and the beacon functions to safeguard humanity. The Nazi, as you call him, manipulated the ellipse, so the Machine had no choice but to let it part, the lesser of two evils.

The golden ellipse contains dark energy that existed before us and will be around long after we are gone. When our kind transcended beyond a need for physical vessels, we discovered its infinite potential comes with risk. The chaotic dark power flowing in concert with the elliptical shape's golden symmetry is incomprehensible. To answer your question, Neil Alexander, attempting to understand the golden ellipse is a fool's errand."

"You are telling me the whole thing boils down to nothing more than a lucky guess?"

"Yes. We can make educated predictions, but no one knows the future. Randomness will also determine whether humanity or the Dark Specters prevail. Small details that appear inconsequential can have the greatest impact but prove impossible to forecast ahead of time. However, seeing how the golden ellipse reacts will be fascinating."

"I don't think fascinating is the word I would use! I no longer wish to be a party to your human experiment."

"Your resignation is based on a false construct. You were never here. Like a pharaoh millennia ago, we captured your life force and extended it beyond your final moments, enabling your transcendence. You are instrumental in Rachel's life, and she remains humanity's last and best hope for survival."

"What happened to Harry?"

"He perished on the same night as your demise. Our dark brethren seized Harry's soul and reanimated his ruined physical form. His morbid decayed appearance should have made that obvious by the time he reclaimed the golden ellipse inside the pyramid."

"So, this is it. You are not going to help. And all I can do is battle the Dark Specters to a stalemate and hope for the best?"

"Neil, your ability to stave off the Dark Specters is another remarkable occurrence. You have our blessing to redirect the beacon's power on the invasion force. However, Rachel must first prevail and restore the golden ellipse onto the beacon."

* * *

With the weight of a million suns crushing his soul, Neil streams past stars—separated by millions of light-years—in the blink of an eye, one final time. Incapable of tears, he slams back into his doppelganger and rips away at the Dark Specters.

"I am sorry, Rachel. I let you down."

Rachel | Beacon chamber
12:05 a.m. | August 23, 2044

With both hands tied, battling the evil lights, Rachel can only watch as the Machine cartwheels Owen's limp form through the chaos before smacking him onto the black granite in an all-too-familiar downward-facing position.

Dropping her attack, Rachel sprints through the madness to Owen's downturned body. Tugging him onto his back to break her nightmarish paradigm, she sobs at the lifeless stare from his blackened face. Her heart breaks into two hardened chunks of irreparable grief and a determined lust for revenge. Finding zero solace in either emotion, she swipes away her tears and grabs her best friend by the collar, "Don't you leave me, Owen Haig! Damn you! I can't do this by myself!"

Rachel's emotional outburst causes an electrified current to flow from her hands into Owen's chest like defibrillator paddles, reviving him with an electrifying jolt. Twisting sideways, he heaves bloody phlegm, sputters, and coughs, causing his cracked ribcage to scream in pain. Through his swollen-eyed trauma, he stares in awe at his wife's stellar appearance.

Reaching under his tattered shirt, Owen removes the golden ellipse. Freed from the Dark Specters' mind control seconds before expulsion from the beacon, he tucked it into his pants on reflex. In the pale blue light, he presents the glimmering relic to a mystified Rachel.

"Owen, how …."

"Stop." A pained smile dimples his battered features, rasping out words of encouragement for his life partner, "This is for you."

Rachel's wide green eyes gaze upon the golden ellipse for the first time through her evolutionary radiance. She never saw it from Libya through Cairo or on the ride to the Giza Plateau. It was always wrapped inside a duffel or a backpack. Feeling its burden, she reciprocates Owen's worried smile, "So, this is what all of the fuss is about." Peering closer, a frenetic network of crisscrossing lines morph and swirl into complicated designs across the smooth gold surface under her glowing fingertips, "I think it likes me."

"There you go again, Rach, always the star."

Another violent shudder cascades rocks, dirt, and graveled bits from the wrecked dome. Rachel cups the ellipse in one hand and smooths crumbled bits from her husband's matted hair with the other, "Try not to move. I'll be right back."

"Okay, Doctor Rachel. Remember, let the Machine do the work."

"Hey, big dummy, that's my line."

Owen's head slumps sideways. Rachel rises from his side, resilient to the debris pelting her body, "I am getting used to this."

Looking at the oval disk in her glorious hands, Rachel sees her glowing reflection, "What the hell are you looking at?" Impervious to its elliptical allure, she blocks an attempted mind control, "I think you just met your match." Not wanting to tempt her luck, she shoves the nine-inch oval into a pickpocket-proof enclosure positioned mid-right-thigh on her travel pants and smiles, thinking of Nina, "A perfect fit."

Ready to rock and roll, Rachel tucks her tattered blouse around Owen's head and shoulders, knowing deep inside that his injuries require more than a little well-placed spit and makeshift bandages. "Hang in there, Owen. I got this."

Turning her steely gaze to the beacon, Rachel loose braids her scraggly blond hair over a widening purple bruise silhouetted across her luminous back—her evolutionary physique radiating through the dirty pink sports bra and hip-hugging travel pants.

Smoothing a hand across the three-inch vertical scar contrasting on her glistening lower-left bare midriff, she confronts a phalanx of vengeful orbs blocking her path up the beacon. Summoning her powerful gift, she blasts the phantasmal blockade into a scattering of evil lights retreating to the undulating central mass of twisted tentacles battling Neil's diversionary attack.

Awestruck by the ferocity and sheer spectacle of Neil's glittering hand-to-hand combat with a leviathan straight out of one of her sci-fi pulp novels, Rachel's hoarse voice cries into the swirling chaos, "I got this, Grandpa!"

The Dark Specters | Beacon chamber
12:35 a.m. | August 23, 2044

Blasting her way through the Dark Specters' ineffective blockade, Rachel climbs through the swirling gale but is stopped by a fiery wall halfway up to the elliptical keep. Corkscrewing twisters of fire lap at her unyielding presence like standing before hell's gate. The old Rachel would have burned to a crisp, but the new Rachel aims elegant fingers onto the flaming barricade, extinguishing the impediment. The stench of brimstone layered atop ozone wafting across the electrified upper reaches makes her head swoon as she trudges upward. Or is it from something else?

* * *

Abandoning the blazing countermeasures, the Dark Specters are forced to acknowledge the female's level-up requires a shift in tactics. However, while she is a formidable adversary, each discharge causes irreparable physiological harm on a sub-cellular level in her fragile human body. Good-old Grandpa failed to warn the white-hot female that evolutionary pioneers suffer slow, painful deaths.

Anxious to terminate the resilient woman, the Dark Specters

play their ace in the hole: Rachel's apocalyptic nightmare, featuring a ghastly apparition of Harry Stark.

* * *

In a single beat of Rachel's racing heart, the blue-cast vortex flips to a pitch-black void punctuated by the crashing and clattering of the shitstorm of pelting debris falling back onto the rotunda. Afterward, the space turns silent and still.

Steeling herself in the darkness for the Dark Specters' next attack, a wide circle of flames ignites above Rachel's head, delineating the dome's crown. The licking and snapping ring of fire remind her of an old country tune from her father's record collection.

Rachel's Man in Black recollection fades as Harry Stark's grotesque larger-than-life projection fills the domed ceiling inferno. A cacophonous screeching from skeletal, scorched, and decayed facial muscles, stretching open and closed in a rictus of laughter, assaults her ears while gore-filled ooze bursts from his putrefied skin, like a cheesy 3D movie effect sans popcorn.

Climbing faster, Rachel picks her way around the sickening discharge ruining her hand and footholds, cognizant of the doorknobs rattling inside her head. The Dark Specters use Harry as a diversion to invade her thoughts and open rooms, storing a lifetime of soul-crushing anxieties. Venturing a quick peek at the horrible sight of Harry's bloodshot eyeballs lolling from blackened sockets wafting smoky gray wisps, she sees them darting about the expanse independent of each other. A retro comparison to a Marty Feldman-themed acid trip conjures a brave smile on her face.

The phantasmagorical projection demands her attention, *"Look at me, Rachel Haig! Look at me and be damned to the eternal hellfire, which is human destiny!"*

Rachel | Beacon chamber
01:05 a.m. | August 23, 2044

Rachel Haig's radiant form perseveres upward through the Dark Specters' psychological assault on her sanity. Swallowing back stomach-churning nausea from splattered volleys of acidic goo, a chorus of insults spew from Harry's ugly mouth at herself, her family, and Owen.

The repulsive ramblings rise to a fevered pitch as Rachel's glowing hands grab the beacon's sharp tip.

"The senator's son tells me you lured him into the back alley. What a naughty girl you are, Rachel Alexander."

"You just crossed the line, Harry!" Rachel extends her right palm toward the fire-engulfed image of Harry Stark and bursts a stream of energy right between his dangling eyeballs, feet above her head.

Harry's projection breaks into a wicked fit of laughter, unfazed by her close-range bolt of lightning, while a bone-jarring crack pierces the flickering chamber from the ancient dome, holding back tons of limestone strata.

Realizing her retaliatory blast did nothing but further compromise the crumbling dome, Rachel curses herself, falling for the Dark Specters' obvious ploy, "Okay, that was stupid."

With humanity's fate hinging upon her rendezvous with destiny, Rachel tunes out Harry's clamorous string of insults. Using light from the fire and the ambiance of her glowing skin, she studies the elliptical keep, matching the shimmering oval inside the pocket midway along her right thigh. With one final "Fuck you!" at the ugliness lurking overhead, she grabs the golden ellipse and thrusts it at Harry's droning face. Watching his flinching response, like a vampire before a cross, "What's the matter, Harry? Oh yeah, in my nightmare, you had the ellipse. Reality is a bitch!"

* * *

"This human's tenacity is incomparable and unexpected."

Watching the paranormal creep show devolve into a spectacular flop, the Dark Specters admit the psychodrama they embedded in Rachel's head failed. The quintessential evil in the cosmos kills the nightmarish projection and its gut-wrenching 3D shitshow.

With a phantasmagorical release of energy, the glittering leviathan explodes into a quantum void and vanishes along with Neil's glowing form.

The Dark Specters coalesce millennia of vitriolic rage on Rachel Haig in the blacker-than-black aftermath. Shapeshifting into fast-replicating organic particles, they reanimate cell-by-cell into an indestructible alien beast with a dreaded reputation throughout the universe.

* * *

The golden ellipse shines bright in Rachel's radiant grip under Harry's ugly visage. Positioning the ellipse before its ancient keep, she compares both shapes, "Nothing is this easy." Right on cue, Harry is gone, and her vulnerable glowing form is swallowed in suffocating darkness, "Goddamit! Don't you ever give up?"

Frozen in place for an unquantifiable amount of time, Rachel clings from her left-handed grip at the tip of the beacon, wondering if the sensory deprivation was a new mind game. "It won't work! I am afraid of almost everything! But I am not afraid of the dark."

"You should be afraid."

Startled by the menacing voice from below, "Who might you be? That better not be you down there, Owen."

Silence and a new pungent odor follow her last echoing words. Rachel's glow intensifies from the danger lurking below her feet as ravenous, snarling, hissing, and smacking noises rise to her exposed position. A glowing frown crosses her bloody, dirt-smeared face, "Oh, man. What the hell is down there?"

A shiny, scaly tendril slithers out of the darkness causing Rachel to freeze like a deer in the huntsman's scope. Suppressing a total freak out, she sees the wriggling appendage refracting her glowing skin and gasps as it slaps across her ankle, coiling up and around her right calf. More noodling limbs slink around her left calf, winding into a knot. Unable to move, the violating sensation of a wet alien tentacle snaking between her wide-legged stance up the curve of her back and wrapping around her hips causes her to bite her lower lip hard enough to draw blood.

Another alien arm smooths around her chest like a lecherous casting director. She rotates her green eyes downward and studies its glistening interlocking armor against her glowing midriff. Blinking to clear her tear-filled vision, she watches the scales flex apart, revealing an oily, semi-translucent tubular arm underneath, filled with a teeming mass of lights.

Surmising the monstrous alien is enjoying itself too much, she slides the ellipse back into her pocket. She would never get it back. In response to her movement, reflexive, rope-like tendrils whip out, almost dislocating her arm at the shoulder.

Losing feeling in her extremities from the constricting tendrils, Rachel refuses to accept defeat, even while verging on a horrible death—and the end of everything. Instead, she takes a deep breath and girds herself for a final superhero-sized explosion of energy.

Agonizing over her fatal plan, a chorus of fears and anxieties clamor for attention from locked rooms inside her head, *"One more expulsion of energy, and you will die! Do you want to die, Rachel?"*

"I am dead either way."

More glistening tentacles violate her luminous form, "Enjoy it while you can, buddy boy. Payback will be a bitch. Ask the last guy who tried to fuck with me."

Rachel makes one final gut-wrenching determination: she will get one shot at killing this creature; injuring it will only prolong her fate.

Immobilized under a monstrous knot from head to toe, Rachel sees a massive head looming upward out of the blackness. Compound eyeballs dominating the creature's oblong skull ringed with a wormy mane meet Rachel's determined stare. The old Rachel of five minutes ago would be screaming in terror right about now. Instead, a sad smile widens her cut-up, purplish cheeks, acknowledging her fate. The rattling doors inside her head go silent, and her fears dissolve into the ether like a bad dream.

Unfazed by its prey's fortified mental state, the alien beast contrasts before her radiance in light and shadow.

Contemplating multiple rows of long yellow fangs lining the creature's cartoonish oversized mouth, Rachel goads her assailant, "Come closer. I can't run away with your disgusting arms twisted all over me. If you keep this up, we will both need a smoke."

Greasy coiling tendrils squeeze tighter in response to her strained voice. Fighting to remain conscious as the blood flow to her brain constricts, tears well up in her eyes, "You are the Dark Specters, but I bet you don't know what they call me!"

Beachball-sized hideous insect eyes seethe with palpable fury while it ratchets muscular appendages tighter to quell the human's insolence.

With whiplike speed, the creature's bulging head swivels inches above Rachel's matted blond hair. Tilting her head back, she looks into the dank maw widening over her upper body. The restrictive tendrils uncoil and slither out of its mouth, allowing the monster to chomp its foot-long fangs into its prey without injuring itself.

Acidic saliva drops burn holes into her skin as light specks dance around her head, taunting her last moments of life while the monstrous fangs close on her stricken form.

"I never heard your answer. Do you know what I am called?"

Not waiting for the beast's reply to her semi-rhetorical query, she bears down with white-hot intensity, summoning the last sparks of her evolutionary manifestation into one final expulsion of energy. Razor-sharp teeth press into her glowing skin in tandem with her reverberating outburst into the alien's disgusting head, "They called me the trust fund murderess because I killed a man by doing this!"

* * *

The golden ellipse calculates the disastrous consequences of Rachel's imminent energy expulsion. Squeezed inside a deep pocket between her luminous right thigh and a monstrous alien tentacle, it animates a spiraling design of oval shapes to no avail. A fractional nanosecond before her energized escalation reaches its zenith, the golden ellipse absorbs her apocalyptic discharge, preserving her transformative body and the beacon from annihilation.

Next, the golden ellipse compresses Rachel's arrested energy to a scintilla of dark matter and blasts the reformed particle through a microscopic chasm of stretchy material in her pants pocket. The point-blank volley contacts an oily scale with the weight of a sun. A shockwave spreads at light speed throughout the hideous alien's body, disintegrating the Dark Specters' organic creation and freeing Rachel at death's door.

* * *

From Rachel's stunned perspective, the Dark Specters and their beastly incarnation vanished from the pitch-black expanse before she could finish her screamed counterattack.

"What just happened? Did I do that?"

Almost falling backward, she grabs ahold of the beacon in the dark. "Jesus, get a grip, for fuck's sake! I'm still at the top of the beacon."

Surprised to be alive, Rachel peers through the dark, waiting for the next evil iteration to appear. No smell, no snarl, only the pervasive blackness surrounding her body. Raising her fist out of reflex to cover wheezing coughs, she realizes her skin is no longer aglow. The evolutionary power coursing her body is gone. Welts from the monster's acidic saliva and teeth punctures across her abdomen are unwelcome additions to a litany of aches, pains, and injuries.

Processing her dance with death, Rachel feels the golden ellipse demanding attention from inside her pocket. Now. Cradling the Light Specters' perilous solution to infinite power in her non-glowing hand, Rachel squints through the dark and feels for the north-facing mirrored keep. "It figures; I am finally ready to do this, and I can't see a thing."

An intricate oval pattern morphs across the golden ellipse, communicating a simple message: *Let the Machine do the work.*

The Gorks | Above France
01:06 a.m. | August 23, 2044

Green shit blasting from cannons spiked from the marauding ships' asymmetrical superstructures carves vast swaths out of Mother Earth. Technologically superior in every conceivable way, the Gork arsenals decimate token resistance while obliterating centuries of infrastructure across every continent. Initiating coordinated attacks on densely populated metropolises, the fleets split into attack groups slamming preassigned strategic targets: military bases, transportation hubs, bridges, ports, dams, airports, factories, and power grids. Passing over small towns and rural communities, the destructive forces churned underneath terrifying anti-gravitational warships' propulsion drives wreak unfathomable collateral damage in the initial fog of war. The granular task of killing every member of the human species would commence with waves of ground forces after the first strikes laid waste on the planet.

The Gork fleet commanders planned their order of battle to commence by neutralizing weak human defenses. The sporadic and ineffective resistance comes as a pleasant surprise but leaves most fleets with nothing to do but bide their time until the commencement of ground invasions.

Standing before a green glowing console on the command deck inside the alien flagship parked above a gridded-off section of the European continent encompassing the French city of Toulouse, a reptilian spotter calls out a target hurtling skyward.

The Gork commander swivels in his seat, iridescent scales across his long toothy snout shift hues in anticipation of action. Any kind of action. "Finally! Something to shoot at!"

An unencrypted briefing through commandeered communication satellites warned of a few nimble alien-tech vessels darting through their thick armadas, attempting to evacuate toward the Moon. They are presumably ferrying humans off the planet. Zooming in on the craft centered on his screen, the Gork recognizes the triangular design with a subtle nod. The ship is the handiwork of a race of skinny gray human collaborators.

Slamming a scaly three-clawed fist down onto the thick arm of his throne, he directs cannon crews to blast the ship from the sky.

Andrew | IOSC flagship
01:12 a.m. | August 23, 2044

A glancing laser blast off an engine cowling sends the IOSC ship spinning like a top. Artemus Pennywell hangs on for dear life, strapped into the locked-down seat behind his desk. The unbolted door swings open, horrified passengers' screams reverberating from the nearest sections facing the ship's sealed-off rotunda. With a grim headshake, Pennywell surmises anyone not buckled in their seats probably incurred grave injuries. "This is intolerable!"

Andrew fixes the office door in an open position to keep it from swinging and meets his boss's distressed and angry glare.

Trying to maintain his composure and abstain from hurling up his guts from the centrifugal force inside the reeling ship, Pennywell blurts out, "I could go for a brandy with an Ativan chaser right about now, Andrew."

Calm as a cucumber, Andrew raises a hand to reassure his boss, "Remain seated, sir, and try to tough it out minus your liquid courage and your vitamins."

"Andrew, you are a piece of shit! Did I ever tell you that? Goddammit, the next time I say right now, I fucking mean it! It doesn't matter that the Spanish PM made it aboard if we go down in flames."

The ship's cybernetic pilots dodge the chartreuse laser blasts, looking for opportunities to gain altitude while gyrating left and right, up, and down, in wild evasive maneuvers buzzing traumatized French towns and villages at treetop level.

Andrew knows their ship's maneuverability—even with one engine out of commission—is sufficient to save them from certain destruction against their unwieldy pursuers. But he also knows they cannot keep this up for much longer. Immune to the sickening motion, he presses a button on Pennywell's desk, and a virtual screen appears before his intelligent eyes. More laser fire arcs past the autonomous ship's evasive port side roll. Sickening green flashes from the near-miss cast Pennywell's cringing face in sharp relief, bursting past too close outside the floor-to-ceiling windows.

Annoyed beyond measure by his valet's composed deportment in the face of annihilation, the CEO watches Andrew's handsome profile study a complex grouping of holographic diagrams and screens. Perusing the virtual instrumentation like swiping through old-timey Seinfeld reruns on a widescreen TV, his stance stiffens as nimble fingertips tap virtual buttons, selecting from a menu of on-screen commands.

Pennywell snarls, gripping tighter on his leather armrests, "Andrew, you bag of bolts, don't you think I would have enabled the cloaking if it worked?"

Andrew turns to his boss with a bemused grin on his chiseled face, "Bag of bolts? That one hurts, sir."

Billions of nano tiles covering the IOSC ship do more than shield it from the intense heat of reentry into Earth's normally-friendly atmosphere. They can also mirror their surroundings down to the pixel, fading the ship from view in a chameleon-like fashion. Not too dissimilar to the advanced cloaking technology used by the invaders. Just tweaked for human use and fully functional, much to Pennywell's surprise.

Always armed with one last dig at his irascible boss, "It pays to read your daily briefings, sir."

"Andrew, I swear to God, you had better not be enjoying this!"

The black triangular space tourism ship vanishes midair allowing the wild spin to ease into gentle clockwise motion, flying on two anti-gravity engines—the third out of commission—the evacuating human cargo vaults through the invading armada of ships undetected.

The death-defying escape rings hollow for Artemus Pennywell. Releasing from his crash cushion seat into the near zero-g, he pushes toward the window without his cane and catches his first glimpse of the receding blue planet. The sphere is pock-marked with widening charcoal plumes flecked with frightening bursts of lightning. Refocusing on his cragged reflection in the thick glass, he looks to his right at the remaining half of the grilled cheese still glued to the window as his eyes fill with tears.

Andrew stands beside his boss in magnetized shoes synched to the ship's decking and presents a tube filled with soothing amber liquid.

"Thank you, Andrew."

"Think nothing of it, sir."

Rachel | Beacon apex
01:36 a.m. | August 23, 2044

The Dark Specters' demise allows faint blue light to return inside the ravaged black granite dome. Clinging to the apex, Rachel surveys the damage down below: Owen's sideways form lies pushed against the curved wall, covered in debris, White Suit's battered repose is crumpled against the beacon, and another man's upper torso sticks out of a pile of rubble. "This is madness. I need to finish this one way or another."

Reminiscent of an alien engineer over 90,000 years earlier, Rachel cradles the ellipse, pulled into its perfection. Angling the artifact before her swollen eyes, she grimaces at her mirrored reflection, "Good Christ, I look worse than I feel." Wiping at the blood trickling down her cheek, she flips the ellipse and positions it close to her cheek but fails to see herself on the shiny golden surface.

Flipping the golden ellipse exasperates her fatigue, "Oh, come on! Should the reflective side face in or out? Shit! I hate stuff like this!"

"Dammit, I could use Owen's lefty brain to help me sort this out."

A broken record refrain inside Rachel's head for days on end repeats one final time: *Let the Machine do the work.*

"That is much easier said than done. I need to be sure."

Not expecting an answer, Neil Alexander's calming voice resonates in her head. *"My dear Rachel, you can never be sure. That is the point. No matter how long you agonize, your ultimate fate hinges on your next action. The golden ellipse epitomizes the razor's edge upon which existence rests. Good versus bad. Up versus down. Light versus dark. Gray areas and half measures are useless wastes of time and energy. The essence of the universe is binary; likewise, consequences follow actions."*

Flipping the ellipse in her hand like a frisbee, "Well then, I'll just give this a whirl and see what happens. Is that what I should do?"

"Damn your stubborn streak, Rachel Haig! You are just as bull-headed as your ancestors. So quick to anger."

Tears well in Rachel's eyes, gripping the golden ellipse by its smooth curved edge, "Anything else you want to throw at me before I seal the fate of the world?"

"*There is one more thing, Rachel.*"

"What? Please tell me. I need to know."

"*You need to believe in your choice. Faith elevates sentience beyond the randomness of the universe.*"

"What about the Machine?"

"*Have faith, Rachel.*"

Bracing her shaking legs against the carved surface, Rachel balances atop the beacon, holding the golden ellipse in her non-glowing fingertips before the mirrored keep at the northern apex. "Have faith, Rachel. You can do it. Trust your judgment." Biting her lip and sucking in stale air, she lets go of the ellipse in midair and watches it float below her mesmerized gaze. Lost in the moment, she almost falls backward before grabbing back ahold of the beacon.

The golden ellipse rotates a half-turn, adjusting its pitch, roll, and yaw in precise increments and pauses for an agonizing moment before reattaching to the beacon, just like that.

Back atop the beacon after its 100-year absence, spiraling ovals animate across the enigmatic golden ellipse's reflective surface, intensifying to a blur in a succession of rhythmic loops to the beat of a powerful resonant hum.

"What the hell does this mean? Is it working or not?"

Neil Alexander's voice returns inside her head, "*Rachel, the golden ellipse is executing its countdown mode. You need to climb down and don't look back!*"

Rachel flips onto her bruised backside and slides off the beacon. Hitting the slick black granite rotunda in her worn Chelsea boots, she stumbles through the debris, rushing to her unconscious husband's side. Shielding her eyes with one hand, she covers Owen's black and blue face with her other hand. The former trust fund murderess pushes her throbbing head into his chest, huddled as low and small as possible, and waits for something to happen.

Neil Alexander | Beacon chamber
01:58 a.m. | August 23, 2044

Rachel curls her legs up to her chin, her eyes closed tight as the domed beacon chamber floods with a brilliant white light. "Please don't blind me. I want to see it."

After what seemed like an eternity, but in actuality approximated sixty seconds, the explosion of light permeating her tight-closed eyelids ebbs to a calming blue ambiance. Like a baby inside its mother's womb, Rachel's ears are caressed by a soothing rhythmic hum, filling the expanse. Opening her swollen eyes, she sees glyphs covering the dome and coursing with a spectrum of colorful lights. Flipping onto her back, she props on scraped elbows and scans the ethereal light permeating cracks and fissures into the surrounding strata.

Without pulling her green eyes from the mesmerizing alien-engineered splendor, Rachel scoots onto her bottom and crosses her long legs beside Owen's repose. Awestruck by the majestic orchestra of lights, colors, and sounds, she muses, "Who would ever want to turn off something this beautiful?"

Hearing Rachel's voice, Owen regains consciousness, lifting his throbbing head to see the majestic show, "You did it, Rachel … I am so proud of you. Ow, ow, damn, it hurts. I don't think I am going to make it."

"Yes, you will. Lie still, Owen. Help is on the way."

Right on cue, Rachel spots a luminous manifestation of Neil Alexander in his Army Air Force uniform and Black Scorpions flight jacket striding through the rocks and debris from around the beacon's western side. Flashing his matinee idol smile with a confident thumbs up in her direction, he proceeds midway along the beacon's northern side to a subset of glyphs embedded within the overall carved matrix, like an alien control panel. Rachel watches him tap a sequence of symbols, eliciting a spectacular strobing response. A thunderous thrum rises in pitch before crashing into a crescendo of resounding booms, timed with energized blasts pulsating from the beacon's apex through the cracked dome.

After consummating his bargain with the Light Specters, Neil settles before the battered young couple, reading the confused expression on Rachel's face. "Good job, Rachel. The beacon is back online and fully operational."

Rachel feels the ground shake underneath her, "It's too late. The invasion has already begun. There is no use for the signal anymore. Come to think of it, why did we go through all of this?"

Hunched before his exhausted granddaughter, Neil nods, comprehending her question's logic, "I held the Light Specters to their promise. Those are energy pulses directed at every lead ship inside Earth's atmosphere." The World War Two fighter pilot shrugs a weary half-smile, "I am only targeting the locomotives. The rest will turn and run; I guarantee it."

Scanning Rachel's bloodied face, he winces, "You have been through a lot. Starting from your premature birth, I knew you were the one."

"You had faith in me."

With a hearty laugh, "Well, what do you know? You listened to my ridiculous ramblings, after all."

Rachel extends her hand, passing it through him, leaving a shimmering trail in its wake. "Sorry, I have wanted to do that since France." Scooting to check on Owen, "Did my friend on the other side of the beacon survive?"

"Yes, Mr. Faisel will be fine. He has a concussion and a broken leg." Gesturing toward Flynn's still form, lying adjacent to the northwest corner where Hamed's bullet stopped him in his tracks, "Agent Flynn's bullet wound just missed vital organs. I located his magic alien dust. It appears the agent has taken a few bullets in his day."

Gesturing at the man in the bloody white suit, "Your white-suited friend will also live. Your husband did a number on the man's face, but his injuries are superficial. Considering what he did, he may wish he was dead."

"That's true, but I'm glad Owen did not kill him."

"Me, too, Rachel."

A palpable sadness transforms Neil's translucent features, "I will be leaving you now." Redirecting her watery gaze onto Owen, "My dear, I regret to say Owen's internal injuries are severe; I am not sure he will survive, even with the magic alien dust."

Looking toward Owen's bruised and bloody face, Rachel sobs, "Yes, he will. He still owes me a damn honeymoon." Looking back toward Neil, she finds he is no longer there and Flynn's magic dust vial in her right hand.

The Gorks | Above France
02:02 a.m. | August 23, 2044

Inside the massive dreadnought looming above the decimated French countryside, the Gork commander eyeballs the blip on his display like a cat stalking a mouse. His slit pupils dilate as it vanishes without a trace. Swiping sideways in disgust, he calls for the functionary already at attention behind his musclebound girth. "What just happened here?"

"The humans enabled cloaking technology we did not know they possessed. However, that is their last ship. Only two others managed to escape. The rest were destroyed on the ground or in the air. They are en route toward a larger vessel stationed on the far side of their Moon. Should we pursue?"

"No. We know where the humans are heading. Let's finish ridding this planet of life first. Then we will pay the Grays a visit and exact revenge for assisting the vile creatures."

The boorish crewmember elicits guttural sounds akin to a

mean-spirited laugh, "Right! The Light Specters never warned against destroying that race of meddling do-gooders."

Before the guffawing commander can pile on his carefully crafted insult regarding the creepy little gray bastards, an energized blast contacts the superstructure and reduces the ship and everyone in it to base elements in the blink of a bulging yellow reptilian eye.

***

A French farmer watches from the middle of his field, pitchfork in hand, ready to take on the invaders. However, the man's lust for vengeance goes unrequited. He spits and curses, watching a ball of light blast up from the southeastern horizon on a beeline, impacting the massive ship with a shimmering soundless explosion. He shields his eyes from the brightness, watching it intensify before reducing to a tiny point and disappearing into the stormy late-night sky 300 feet above the French countryside.

Jamming the sharp fork into the fertile soil, "Sacré bleu. Maybe next time."

Neil Alexander | Aix-en-Provence, France
0425 Hours | August 17, 1944 (Flashback)

"Your injuries are too severe. You are dying."

"Who are you? Where are you taking me?"

Captain Neil Alexander's fighter bomber sputtered and quit, the propeller jerking to a stop. The P-47 Thunderbolt dipped sideways into a sickening nosedive.

Neil steeled himself for the end, his left side a bloody mess of ripped flesh and broken bones. Trapped inside the spiraling aircraft, he acknowledged his imminent demise with sadness for a life he would never know. Letting go of the stick, he grasped his wife's photo from its place of honor in his right hand, hugging it close to his chest. Pushed back in his seat by the incredible downward velocity, Neil squeezed his eyes shut, gasped for one last breath of air, and died.

Foo fighters swarmed the shot-up aircraft and carried it deep inside a hidden cavern before setting it down on the slick limestone bank of a fast-flowing subterranean stream.

Neil's final resting place.

Epilogue One

The sun indeed rose on The Day After. A sallow glowing orb permeates a clinging fog of suffocating dust and smoke in the eerie stillness of the invasion aftermath. Barking dogs and mournful wails echo across the decimated Cairo metropolis. Across every corner of the world, shell-shocked survivors, overwhelmed by the sheer numbers of dead and dying, realize help is not coming anytime soon.

With every modern conveyance rendered inoperable, the sound of chopper blades cutting through the ruddy haze turns a battered and confused populace looking skyward, following two shadowy forms flying toward the pyramid complex on the Giza Plateau.

By late afternoon, a diverse assemblage of Cairo denizens had picked through the smoldering rubble toward the pyramids seeking answers, retribution, or both. The locals had no clue the aliens laid waste to the planet, not just their small corner of the world. What lay over the horizon would remain a matter of speculation for weeks after the invasion came and went.

Meanwhile, six athletic teens, three boys, and three girls, tromp across a golf course in the pyramids' shadows. At the Main Gate leading onto the plateau, they join a curious crowd butting against a phalanx of stone-faced men wielding heavy machine guns blocking entry into the bus parking lot below the Great Pyramid's northern face.

Craning to see beyond the security, they spy two futuristic matte black helicopters in the littered lot spinning up composite blades mounted on coaxial rotors with pusher props at each long craft's forked tail section.

One of the eagle-eyed girls looks up at the pyramids, spying a flurry of activity at the robbers' entrance. She sees a group struggling to remove an individual strapped atop a stretcher off the narrow limestone level.

The chiseled commander of the shorthanded extraction unit pressed into securing a rancorous perimeter notes the fit young newcomers, "Let those kids pass through!"

The wide-eyed teens sidle through the agitated crowd and assemble before the grizzled British soldier.

"Follow me!"

Conscripted into the ranks of the PTB unbeknownst to them, the sextet breaks into a sprint, trailing the strapping mercenary to the pyramid's base layer.

Exuding a deft command of the situation, the camouflaged mercenary, sporting a butterfly patch on his vest, arranges the teens into a human chain straight up dust-covered blocks to the Robber's Entrance. Scampering to the uppermost level, the grimacing soldier tips the first stretcher downward, passing it through trembling, sweaty hands to the lot where two men shoulder their weapons and hustle an unconscious Egyptian man in a bloody and tattered white suit over to a waiting chopper.

The teens look upward in unison with a better grasp of what to expect as the next stretcher holding a mature Egyptian security officer, tips downward, followed by a well-built black man with a bleeding gunshot wound to the gut. Both men were unconscious or dead; it was hard to tell as they passed to stretcher-bearers poised to rush them to the idling choppers.

The kids take a breather stationed on the ancient limestone blocks. They look at each other and shrug, "Is that it?"

The gruff Brit barks at them, "Don't bloody move. There are more on the way!"

One of the girls winks at her friend a block down and gestures toward a well-dressed lady standing by herself in the middle of the lot in an anxious cross-armed pose, "I wonder who she is?"

"Maybe somebody's mother."

"Who knows? The poor woman looks upset."

The teenage recruits watch as a tall, lanky man wearing a cowboy hat escorts the distraught woman onto the first chopper. He helps her aboard and straps her into a jumpseat, where she attends to the injured black man. Loaded and ready to go, the first chopper revs its double set of blades and rises into the sky, whipping dirty air into a swirling vortex.

The Cowboy jogs back through the dusty cloud, swiping a dirty sleeve across his mustachioed face, and nods a broad smile at the chain gang below the entrance, "Okay, y'all—time's a-wastin' here. Let's get this show on the road. The locals are startin' to get a little ugly over at the gate."

Two more dust-covered men from the extraction detail emerge from the pyramid, struggling to hoist another stretcher toward the waiting hands. The teens see a half-undressed woman covered in cuts, scrapes, and bruises strapped tight to the board, passing through their strong-handed grips. A swollen hand drops from the woman's side, swinging in midair. The teenage girl at the lowest position notices a star-shaped burn mark centered on the dangling palm.

Cowboy turns to the stretcher-bearers, "Load this woman into my bird and return to your original security assignments. We'll take it from here. These young people can help load the last patient."

Echoing Cowboy's words, the gravel-voiced British soldier calls down from the robber's entrance, "Look alive, people! Here comes one more heading your way!"

Their arms and shoulders aching, the teens pass the last stretcher downward with care, his appearance causing the teens to stifle back tears. He looked like a plane crash survivor. Hustling back after helping secure the female patient inside the chopper, the Cowboy addresses the teens: "You two, carry this man to the chopper."

The boys hoist the stretcher and hustle to the waiting chopper; their friends and the man called Cowboy trailing close behind. Sliding the unconscious man inside the sleek black aircraft next to the woman, they snap the frame to cleats soldered to the deck and step back, mindful of the blades above their heads.

With both trauma patients fastened inside, Cowboy slides the door shut with a firm pull, double-tapping a hand-painted Chrysalis Air butterfly symbol for luck. Before angling his dusty, weary frame into the cockpit, he beckons the group with a short-armed wave and flips each teen a shiny gold coin, "Much obliged for your assistance. Now get your asses out of here. This place is about to be locked down tighter than Fort Knox."

After a cursory preflight check, he turns to the kids, "Y'all don't have to tell anyone about what you saw today. Just go home and try to help others the way you helped here. The coins are worth more than their weight in gold. They will also serve y'all as reminders that the future will be what you make of it. Now keep your heads down. I need to skedaddle before those two yokels in the back, up and die on me. Adios, amigos!"

The six teens smile and wave as the American tips the brim of his Stetson while piloting the airship into the mottled overcast.

The former Army Ranger pilot buzzes over a city in flames, trying to keep the cutting-edge helicopter from bucking like a bronco in the swirling, smoky air.

Part of the PTB extraction team prepositioned at the pyramids, Cowboy witnessed the aliens leaving Dodge with their tails between their legs. After a collective sigh of relief and a hearty round of celebratory chest bumps and back slaps, the battle-hardened special forces men followed a diminutive silver-suited Gray through hidden tunnels leading hundreds of feet below the Great Pyramid to the hidden chamber.

Squinting through mirrored shades out his windscreen at the carnage, Cowboy navigates on a beeline heading to the trauma unit helipad high atop Cleopatra Hospital's brand-new medical tower. Calling over his shoulder to the unconscious man and woman languishing in the back of the chopper, "I'm getting y'all there as fast as I can! Hang on and don't fuckin' die on me, ya hear?"

Approaching through columns of sooty black smoke, Cowboy sees every window in the 22-story building is blown out and the magnificent front entrance transformed into crumbled, twisted concrete and rebar. More concerning, he sees mobs of displaced Cairo denizens watching him maneuver the chopper above the rooftop. "So much for a stealthy fuckin' arrival."

Fighting a strong crosswind, Cowboy sets down dead center on a helipad designed for a much lighter airship.

Applying brakes and powering off the engines, the quick-witted Texan sees a man and a woman in bloody scrubs marching toward him. "Well, I'll be a son of a gun—those two don't look happy to see us at all."

With the world teetering on the edge of God knows what, Cowboy replays the firm directive passed down the ranks from The Powers That Be CEO: "Do not trust anyone and maintain the Haig couple's anonymity at all costs."

A Texas Longhorn quarterback in his salad years long before the Army and a love of flight took centerstage, Cowboy calls a last-second audible. "Listen up, back there. If you can hear me, listen up. Your new names are Barney and Betty Hill."

Epilogue Two

Ping | Beacon chamber
07:31 p.m. | August 23, 2044

The Light Specters' gamble paid off. The one called Rachel Alexander Haig had fulfilled the promise of her blue spark and preserved the human race to see another day. In the process, she danced on the razor's edge of human evolution. The eternal energy beings doubted her physiological makeup could withstand another energized outburst; however, someone had to be the first.

More pioneering souls will emerge in the coming years.

While Rachel's success vindicated the Light Specters' faith in the human race, it cast the protective beacon in a new light. The pyramidic structure's purpose had expired as assuredly as the Dark Specters' misanthropic ways.

It was time to turn it off for good.

* * *

Following the PTB extraction crew's hasty exit, hauling the injured parties out of the chamber, Ping remained behind.

During the Gray being's centuries-long collaboration with the Powers That Be, he rubbed elbows with many brilliant minds: Franklin, Tesla, Curie, Einstein, Oppenheimer, et al. A brief interaction with Abraham Lincoln always stood out as a watershed moment in his time on Earth.

Ping's friendship with Artemus Pennywell had also stood the testament of time, in no small measure due to the alien's gift of a longer-than-average lifespan for his gruff but brilliant friend. However, the alien acknowledged that neither Pennywell nor himself were long for this world—nor any other.

But not on this day of days. Ping stood before the beacon, taking in its magnificence a final time.

It pained the intellectually advanced alien to turn off the incredible machine, but the Light Specters had spoken. It was time for humanity to fend for itself. More tests loomed just beyond the horizon, Ping's violent Gray cousins, for one, but the humans would not be caught by surprise a second time. Their evolutionary foothold in the universe was secure.

Following a detailed set of instructions, Ping disconnects The Machine. With his risk of death minimized, the 325-year-old alien ascends to the apex of the pyramidic structure, takes a deep breath, and pulls the Golden Ellipse out of its cradle. Just like that, the ravaged domed chamber plunges back into absolute darkness.

Hefting the weight of the Golden Ellipse in his nimble grasp, Ping caresses its smooth elliptical edge, flush with a euphoric sense of its extreme power. A fantastical notion tempts his resolve, "I can keep it for myself." Still contemplating his first move, a bright orb burst from the ether, steals the Golden Ellipse from the alien's long-fingered hands without ceremony and vanishes into the blackness.

A loud warning crack resonating through the pitch-black chamber shakes the alien from his transfixed stare. Liberated from the elliptical shape's intoxicating allure, Ping exhibits nimble agility belying his advanced years, beating a speedy retreat from the beacon chamber. Seconds later, the domed walls give way, burying the beacon under tons of rock.

Epilogue Three

Artemus Pennywell | Toulouse Spaceport, France
12:30 p.m. | August 26, 2044

With one of its three anti-gravity engines out of commission, the triangular flagship touches down on the remaining structurally sound platform at the Toulouse IOSC Spaceport. The Chosen Few staggers toward the exits, leaving ten injured and two deceased passengers in the capable hands of a robotic medical staff unfazed by the gore and painful human wails.

Artemus Pennywell stares daggers into a virtual screen, watching the shaken passengers' ignominious departure from his ship, led by the Spanish asshole whose tardiness delayed their escape. "I'll tell you what, Andrew, good riddance to the thankless lot of them. Next time, I want to see that list of so-called important people beforehand."

Half-listening to his simmering boss, Andrew looks for the metallic toaster-shaped drone in the employee lot behind the neo-Gothic IOSC Main Terminal, "Sir, we need to return to Edinburgh, but our makeshift mode of transportation is nowhere in sight."

"Good! I was not about to cram back inside Hart's drone. Never again. I'd rather walk."

"Toulouse Airport is not far. Perhaps we can hop a ride across the Channel and spare you the indignity of attempting to walk across water."

"Are you afraid I'd sink like a stone?"

"I'm more concerned you would succeed."

* * *

Throwing his weight and a considerable amount of cash at a frantic, clipboard-carrying administrator inside the local airfield's chaotic office, Pennywell finagles two seats aboard a vintage C-47 pulled into service ferrying relief supplies between the British Isles and the European continent. Slumping into the cracked leather jump seat, Pennywell proffers a wicked smile toward his valet, "Not first-class, Andrew, but at least it is a fucking airplane designed with the human body in mind."

"Good show, sir. Jolly good show."

Flying low and slow out of Toulouse, their plane makes relief stops in Paris and Manchester. After witnessing widespread devastation over France and the UK, they fly over a downed Gork battlecruiser jutting from the ruins of St. Andrews before descending into the smoky chaos of Edinburgh. With his favorite golf destination obliterated, Pennywell's morale takes another dive seeing the Chrysalis Airdrome in a collapsed heap along with the Edinburgh Airport's main terminal, hangars, and outbuildings.

Poking through the PTB-owned hangar complex, Lady Luck smiles upon the pair; Andrew discovers an undamaged black chopper gassed-up and ready for flight, "Sir, I found us a ride."

"It looks like one of our people did not get here in time."

"That individual would be you, sir. Before the invasion, I asked Chrysalis Air to have it ready in case we needed to come this way before the invasion."

"Sometimes, I wonder why humans bother anymore. You lot take care of everything."

"At your service, sir."

On the short flight over the Scottish capital to the helipad a few klicks from Crichton Castle, Pennywell grimaces in disgust from his shotgun seat, looking down on mobs of crazed survivors burning and looting all that the aliens failed to destroy. Saddened but not surprised at the wanton destruction happening in population centers worldwide—he laments into his headset, "Mother of Christ, Andrew, is there no end to the madness?"

Sporting mirrored aviators, Andrew's dashing profile concentrates on the dense array of gauges and deft control of the stick, "Apparently not, sir."

By the sheer grace of God, the verdant rolling countryside within eyeshot of Crichton Castle appears as picturesque as it did before the worldwide alien assault. Post setting down at the helipad and a quick tunnel ride to the HQ subterranean complex, Pennywell enters his apartment, having not slept for more than thirty minutes at a time in over two days.

After a hot shower and change of clothes, the rejuvenated 134-year-old returns to his memento-filled office, musing on the fickleness of existence while downing the dregs from an IOSC mug kept as a souvenir of the harrowing ordeal walk."

* * *

The Powers That Be CEO focuses on a ridiculous pile of paper, Number 7 already stacked on his desk. Paper. Pulling a sheet from the top, he notes the Cyrillic typeset in dense, single-spaced paragraphs and huffs with exasperation. "It would help if I spoke Russian." Realizing half the stack will require a translator, Pennywell expresses an exasperated sigh, "What a pain in the ass this is going to be."

Andrew enters with a new carafe in hand. "You will be pleased to hear, sir, Numbers 4 and 8 are assisting Professor King in waking up from his prolonged nap."

"Great. Now Richard can get back to his laboratory and burn through money what's left of our coffers." With a defeated chuckle, "At least the crazy bastard got some sleep."

"More coffee, sir?"

Unable to focus on a thin sheet filled with words in his grasp, the miraculous whirlwind conclusion of the death-defying shitshow refloods his thoughts. Against all odds, the Haig couple and Agent Flynn came through. Pennywell recalls a favorite Churchill quote:

"Never in the field of human conflict was so much owed by so many to so few."

Now the fun begins.

Pennywell's brow furrows on the handwritten screed, "This one is from some worthless Canadian piece of manure. Jesus H. Christ, Andrew, does anyone not want to drag my ass behind the barn and beat the crap out of me? We did our level best! They all knew it was coming since Disclosure Day. Now, every politician on the planet needs to make The Powers That Be their fucking scapegoat. They can shove it up their politically correct behinds!"

Grabbing his cane and a silver flask from a desk drawer, Pennywell turns to his friend, "Screw it. Andrew, let's go for a walk."

* * *

Pennywell exits the ultra-modern steel elevator into the castle's former grandeur, turning his squinting eyes skyward beyond the Italianate courtyard facade to the deep blue sky above. In the CEO's mind, the word pleasant did not adequately describe the idyllic August afternoon, so he went with the obvious, "What a difference from two short days ago."

Andrew looks toward the heavens, "Indeed."

A youthful vigor washes over Pennywell, breathing the fresh

country air, boots crunching across the empty gravel lot outside the stony ramparts of Crichton Castle looming above their relaxed gait. Climbing steps built into a rugged granite escarpment pocked with bird nests rising behind the castle, they watch as puffy white clouds drift higher overhead, riding a frigid jet stream out of the North Atlantic. Far-off bleats break the quietude from grazing sheep dotting the bucolic Scottish Lowlands.

Peering at smoke plumes on the horizon from the riots rollicking Edinburgh—thrust backward to an analog era—in the chaotic wake of the invaders' abrupt retreat, "Andrew, the world is broken. I will not live long enough to see it put back together."

"Nonsense, sir." Watching a new charcoal plume billowing skyward far off in the distance, "the rioting will stop when civilization comes back online."

"Maybe now, the bastards will incorporate the Advisor's shielding tech."

"Without a doubt."

With a self-righteous harrumph, Pennywell sits on a weather-beaten wooden bench overlooking the world, such as it is. Propping his cane across a bony knee, the CEO slips the flask from his vest, "You know, Julius Hart was right, I'm not much for the taste of bourbon, but his brand is quite good."

"That is wonderful news, sir." Not waiting for Pennywell to address his facetiousness, "Mr. Hart and his date accepted your dinner invitation. However, they are unsure when they can safely get here."

"As soon as possible is what I would tell the young man. And bring more of the family bourbon. Whatever this world rebuilds into will be determined by people like Hart. Not a bunch of whiny bureaucrats crying over spilled milk." With a too-mean chuckle, "I heard the UN headquarters is a pile of rubble. Is that right?"

"The aliens did quite a number on Lower Manhattan."

Taking another swig, "Yes, so I heard. I better work on my cavalier attitude." Pressing Andrew for more intel, "I believe the Haigs lived in Manhattan. What is the latest on our heroes?"

"They are on a private floor of the Cleopatra Hospital in Cairo. Per our agreement with the new administrator, our engineers are making remarkable progress in restoring its much-needed health resources online. We have a security team protecting the couple from the press and a host of crazy idiots trying to get at them. Unfortunately, someone at the hospital leaked Mrs. Haig's former nickname. It is an ongoing situation, sir."

"Keep me posted. Did the red peonies arrangement and my proposal make it to the hospital?"

"Yes, sir. However, the Haigs are fighting to recover; I doubt they have had time to focus on anything but their health."

"Yes, of course. It can wait." Shifting subjects, he pokes for more news from his valet, "I hear we had a few bad apples among our ranks, too."

"A statistician named Greta Thornberry, to name one, working out of our Chrysalis offices in Cairo. She jumped off a ten-story apartment building before we could apprehend her."

"Or perhaps someone pushed her." Emptying the flask with a final pull, "What about Agent Flynn? Recovering from another bullet wound, I take it? Jesus, that man has nine lives."

"Nina is escorting Agent Flynn to our lunar medical facility. They should arrive within the next few hours."

Pennywell smiles at the thought of the lovely and sophisticated Miss Nina.

Sliding the spent flask back into his vest pocket, Pennywell turns to face his friend and confidante, "Andrew. I am very sorry for your loss, as well."

"Thank you, Artemus. Mr. Kobayashi was a great man. It is hard to believe he is gone. However, he left behind a little of himself in all of his creations." Before Pennywell can react to the cryptic notion, Andrew taps the bench, "We should head back."

Thank you for reading

THE GOLDEN ELLIPSE.

Look for the second thrilling

sci-fi adventure novel in

The Powers That Be trilogy

THE LOST SHIP

*The following is an excerpt from **THE LOST SHIP** ...*

Owen | Nile boardwalk café, Cairo
11:36 a.m. | September 12, 2044

After an eye-opening walk through burnt-out rubble and broken glass along the former upscale boulevard, the Haigs follow spray-painted arrows, entering the boarded-up Ritz Carlton. Owen provides a printed copy of their reservation and room number to an armed private security guard, who leads them into a massive ballroom filled with haphazard jumbled piles of luggage, bags, and personal items from hotel guests missing since invasion day. The ominous line of strollers hits Rachel hard.

A monotonal figure seated behind a makeshift table with a pen and ledger proffers a dead-eyed stare toward the new arrivals across the plush carpeted expanse.

The couple shrugs at each other and enters the darkened space, sifting through masses of expensive luggage. "Here, Owen, I found your old backpack."

Owen wades farther into the piles and pulls out Nina's heavy portmanteau filled with clothes, cash, and cards, like finding a 3-week-old time capsule from a former reality. Reaching into his pocket, he pulls out a key and opens the lid. "Bingo."

After stuffing filthy reclaimed daypacks with the portmanteau's contents, the Haigs sign legal waivers pushed forward by the dour hotel employee. Watching the survivors sign for their stuff, the man's mood brightens, and he mentions his aunt and uncle's café is open and serving coffee and food—a miracle amid shuttered eateries and shops along the palm-lined Nile River boardwalk.

Hefting the daypack over a shoulder, he turns to Rachel, "Why not? It sure beats sitting around here, waiting for Roy to find a pet store that still has cat food."

"Sure, Owen. Whatever you say."

"Okay. Yes. What I say."

* * * * *

Owen tips up the bill of a white ball cap with an embroidered butterfly logo protecting his stubbly head from the bright Egyptian sunshine and downs a second bittersweet Egyptian coffee. Raising his right arm wrapped in a bright-green 3D-printed cast, he hails the busy hostess.

"We'll take the check whenever you are ready."

The matronly Egyptian creases a wry smile across her distinguished, dark-complected face, refilling Owen's cup, "If you are who I think you are, it is on the house." Swiping another table on her way back to a long bar at the far end of the open-air café, she turns with a dismissive wave, "Besides, our payment processor is down, like everywhere else. My husband and I just have nothing better to do."

Taken aback at having a so-called veil of anonymity punctured by their first human interaction outside the hospital, Owen slides a generous wad of Egyptian pound notes under his plate. "Wow, that was weird, right, Rachel?"

Receiving a heaping dose of the silent treatment, he studies Rachel's silhouetted profile beneath the wide-brimmed straw sun hat with a colorful red bow tied at the back. Sipping the bitter coffee, he muses her bruises and cuts will heal with time, but the absurd notion of joining The Powers That Be could prove terminal. Shaking his head in disgust, he laments Pennywell's damn employment offer pushing them apart.

Swallowing back his pill regimen with a gulp of bottled water, he finishes with an exaggerated belch forcing Rachel to acknowledge his presence.

Without a flinch in his direction, "That's a nice touch, Owen. Doctor Said warned to ease off on the painkillers."

"I will if you will."

Rachel avoids Owen's probing hazel eyes, seated sideways with legs crossed in her sleeveless white linen dress buttoned to her knees, watching old gasoline-powered watercraft ferry relief supplies up and down the dirty brown river. Swatting at a fly with the audacity to land on her sandaled foot propped on a short brick wall, she shifts to the table and slides her untouched baklava off to the side, "I'm not hungry."

Acknowledging Rachel's sullenness and the rift between them since the offer from The Powers That Be CEO, Owen pulls the thin folded sheet at the root of their troubles from a shirt pocket, "Rachel, I am tired of fighting you on this ridiculous proposal. I care about you too much. We both almost died. What am I saying? For fuck's sake, the doctor said I was dead. I feel like we have a new lease on life and a helluva story for our children someday. And guess what? I remember what you did under the pyramids. Your hands, Rachel. Those scars are your badge of honor for saving this ungrateful world. You have nothing left to prove."

Angling his healing face to make eye contact with his wife's defiant stare hidden behind dark shades under the hat's broad brim, he projects his most disarming, persuasive smile, "Let's head back to France, hang out at the villa for as long as we like, and then get back home. Remember home, Rachel?"

Removing the designer tortoiseshell sunglasses she found inside Nina's portmanteau, Rachel squints through the hazy late-morning Cairo sunshine toward Owen, unmasked annoyance wrinkling her makeup-free face, "I don't understand you, Owen. Didn't your boss at Ford and Poole Capital, what's his name, Henry Tate, send a note saying the firm is dead in the water for the foreseeable future?

"It came with my letter from Mom and Dad, like the one you received. Who knows what is really going on back there?"

"Owen, you can't be serious? The invasion ruined my father's business. We are fortunate our families survived; millions did not. Who knows when people can attend a concert or sporting event again? There is nothing left for us back there."

Déjà vu of a similar contentious debate at the OASIS hotel bar in Tripoli only three weeks earlier—a lifetime ago—conjures in Owen's mind, "Rachel, your father is a survivor. That man can sell ice cubes to Eskimos."

An abrasive and loud staticky radio noise interrupts the conversation from devolving into another pointless argument. Thankful for the distraction, Owen swivels toward the crackling sounds, observing the bartender fiddling with a shortwave tuner on a vintage boombox while fussing with its extended antenna. The hostess hustles to the long teak bar and slides her tray of dirty cups and plates next to the old receiver. After scolding her clumsy husband, she slaps his thick fingers from the oversized round knob and makes a delicate adjustment. The noise fades, and the assertive voice of President Lena Jackson comes through loud and clear, broadcasting from atop the bar to a worldwide human populace desperate for news.

Sticking a pin in their disagreement, Owen and Rachel sidle to the bar, relieved to discover the leader of the free world is among the living and curious to hear what she has to report in the apocalypse's wake.

After serving as Christopher Pratt's vice president for his second term, Lena Jackson transcended the two-party divide and swept to an easy electoral college landslide in 2040. The attractive young politician proved an easy decision for Rachel's first presidential election and appeared primed for a repeat in 2044 until the Gorks changed everything.

By contrast, Owen despised politics: money talked, bullshit walked, and that was that.

The 56-year-old former Army lieutenant colonel's resolute delivery masks the unbearable weight of the direst moment in human history as the glitchy signal fades in and out: "… *my friends, the gloves are off. Our world is under a grave threat. For reasons I am not at liberty to discuss, the initial alien invaders reversed course and departed. However, their antigravity dreadnoughts and attack ships killed millions and left paths of indescribable destruction across urban centers on every continent.*

To our extraterrestrial allies, I request your sage guidance. And I warn humanity to take advantage of this reprieve because, as I speak, other forces lie in wait within our solar system. Whether their intent is hostile or not, we must remain vigilant and assume the worst. Every human on Earth is entitled to know what we are up against. No more secrets, lies, and obfuscations. May God instill courage, wisdom, maturity, and fortitude we will need to meet the threat head-on and defeat it.

Most countries declared martial law per their constitutions to safeguard citizens by maintaining order and the rule of law. Equitable distributions of food, water, and medical aid in coordination with a host of relief organizations and The Powers That Be proceed, albeit too slow, leading to riots and widespread looting.

Please, I beg you, do not compound the chaos caused by the alien invaders. Assist local law enforcement agencies in containing mayhem and disorder plaguing your cities and towns. We must unite and communicate that humankind's strength flows through our diverse and hard-won experiences. We will not surrender. We will not recede into the heavens! We are one human family! If we fail to come together in this hour of crisis, a crowded universe will attack again, leading to unconscionable consequences. Of that, you can be sure. We got lucky once; it will not happen again.

I will use this frequency to broadcast updates and information. In the meantime, stay safe, remain calm, and carry on. Maintain contact with your local authorities. If your situation is dire, please trust that assistance is on the way.

May God bless you and keep you in these trying times."

Rachel's eyes linger on the boombox, reminiscent of a beat-up old receiver her dad kept on a workshelf in the family estate's 10-car garage.

Owen places his cast arm around Rachel's shoulders, snapping her back to reality. Leaning close, he whispers in her ear, "Rachel, my love, I just changed my mind. Let's do it. If Mr. Pennywell thinks we are suited for The Powers That Be, that is where our path should lead."

Rachel tips up the brim of her sun hat, producing an effervescent smile, "Owen, are you sure? We can still take as much time as we need to heal before jumping in with both feet."

"I'm sure. Apparently, we are too well-known ever to lead normal lives."

Owen turns to their Egyptian hostess, fiddling with the radio in search of more news, "Excuse me, mam, would you mind explaining how you know our identities?

Flinging a dirty rag over her shoulder, "Dear boy, your pictures are plastered across local newsprints all over Cairo. It is the power of the press." Refocusing on the radio dial, she pauses and turns back toward the tall, handsome American couple with a skeptical look across her dark-brown visage, "By the way, can you two shoot lightning bolts from your hands? That is the report in the latest article I read."

Owen's eyes widen with surprise, "The latest what now?"

On reflex, Rachel clasps her hands behind her back as the woman reaches into her apron and produces a folded tabloid-size sheet, "Here you are; this one is in English; read it for yourselves." Noticing Rachel's unbandaged hands, the woman raises a dark eyebrow, "Huh, maybe the article is accurate after all."

Noting the server's prying gaze, Owen angles in front of his wife, "Look, lady, don't believe everything you read."

The woman shrugs, "Oh, don't worry about me. The lightning story is mild compared to other wild speculation and rumors."

Rachel's curiosity piques, "Like what?"

"Well, for one. There is a hidden golden chamber under the pyramids. That is a direct quote from an interview with an Egyptian army captain who claims he was inside the chamber when the invasion began."

Something snaps inside Rachel's head, emitting a spirited laugh at the mention of the nightmarish beacon chamber and the heroic Captain Faisel who pulled her from the abyss in the nick of time, "The chamber is a seamless hollowed block of polished black granite. No gold. Well, except for the ellipse. But that is gone."

The woman shoots Rachel a dumbfounded stare, "Uh-huh."

Rachel smiles at the lady, "Is there anything else you would like to know? What the hell? Check out my hands—forever scarred from those lightning bolts, as you call them. They burn, but I cannot make fire anymore. Now you know the truth. Like the president said, enough with all of the lies."

Owen grabs Rachel by the waist, checking his wristwatch, "Uh, we should head out; Roy is probably waiting for us."

Rachel extends her scarred hand, reaching for the paper, "Can I take this?"

"Go right ahead, dear; the city is littered with papers featuring your pretty face. I can grab another one anytime I want."

Rachel nods and pivots to follow Owen toward the hotel before seeing her halftoned image above the thin Cairo tattler's fold, "Aw, man! Owen, look at this picture. I look terrible!"

Owen leads Rachel toward the ruined street before making a final over-the-shoulder glance toward the café, "What else has Roy and the PTB kept from us over the last three weeks?"

Bibliography

Epigraphy

Chapter One:

Greenwald, Jeff. "I am Buzz Lightyear!" *Salon*, 20 Jul. 1999, https://www.salon.com/1999/07/20/aldrin/

Chapter Two:

Sagan, Carl. *Cosmos*. Illustrated Ed., p. 30, Ballantine Books, 2013.

Chapter Three:

Churchill, Winston. "Neville Chamberlain Speech to the House of Commons." *National Churchill Museum*, 12 Nov. 1940, https://www.nationalchurchillmuseum.org/neville-chamberlain-speech-1940.html

Chapter Four:

Verne, Jules. *Twenty Thousand Leagues Under the Sea.*, p. 14, Barnes & Noble Classics, 2005.

Chapter Five:

Dick, Philip K. "What Dead Men Say." *Worlds of Tomorrow Magazine*. Barmaray Co., 1964.

Chapter Six:

Nietzsche, Friedrich. *Beyond Good and Evil*. Corundum Classics, 2014.

Chapter Seven:

Earhart, Amelia. *The Family of Amelia Earhart*, https://www.ameliaearhart.com

Chapter Eight:

Rohm, Robert. *You've Got Style: Your Personal Guide for Relating to Others.*, Personality Insights Inc, 2001.

Chapter Nine:

Laërtius, Diogenes. *Lives and Opinions of Eminent Philosophers, Books 6-10.* Independent, 2020.

Chapter Ten:

Keller, Helen. *The World I Live In*. The Century Company, 1908.

Chapter Eleven:

Teilhard de Chardin, Pierre. *Toward the Future.*, pp. 86-87, Mariner Books, 2002.

Books

Anonymous. *Miscellaneous Works of Mr. John Greaves ...: The Life and Writings of Mr. John Greaves.- Pyramidographia. 1736.- a Discourse On the Roman Foot and ... &c. 1736.- a Description of the Grand Seig.* Andesite Press, 2017.

Atkinson, Rick. *An Army at Dawn. (The Liberation Trilogy, 1)*. Henry Holt and Co., 2002.

Atkinson, Rick. *The Day of Battle. (The Liberation Trilogy, 2)*. Henry Holt and Co., 2006.

Campobasso, Craig. *The Extraterrestrial Species Almanac: The Ultimate Guide to Greys, Reptilians, Hybrids, and Nordics*. MUFON, 2021.

Coventry, Martin. *The Castles of Scotland: A Comprehensive Guide to More Than 4100 Castles, Towers, Historic*. Goblinshead, 2015.

Elliot, Virgil. *Traditional Oil Painting: Advanced Techniques and Concepts from the Renaissance to the Present*. pp. 6-8. Watson-Guptill Publications, 2007.

Greer, Steven. *Unacknowledged: An Expose of the World's Greatest Secret*. Crossing Point Inc, 2017.

Hancock, Graham. *The Divine Spark: Psychedelics, Consciousness And The Birth Of Civilization*. Hay House, 2015.

Huntley, H.E. *The Divine Proportion*. Dover Publications, 2012.

Irving, Washington. *The Legend of Sleepy Hollow*. Illustrated by Rackham, Arthur, David McKay Company, 1928.

Meisner, Gary. *The Golden Ratio: The Divine Beauty of Mathematics*. Race Point Publishing, 2018.

Strabo. *The Geography of Strabo*. Cambridge University Press, 2014.

Teilhard de Chardin, Pierre. *The Phenomenon of Man*. Harper Collins, 2008.

Tesla, Nikola. *The Problem of Increasing Human Energy*. Cosimo Classics, 2008.

___, *Time Out France: Perfect Places to Stay, Eat and Explore*. p. 282. Time Out, 2009.

Visconti, Sofia. *Egyptian Mythology: Explore The Mysterious Ancient Civilisation of Egypt, The Myths, Legends, History, Gods, Goddesses & More That Have Fascinated Mankind For Centuries*. Independent, 2020.

Von-Bruening, RJ. *Unlocking the Dream Vision: The Secret History of Creation*. Independent, 2018.

Videos

"Atelier de Cézanne - Aix en Provence." *YouTube*, uploaded by Office de Tourisme, 1 Dec. 2015, https://www.youtube.com/watch?v=54DycDbiqv8&t=5s

"The Public Door to the Great Pyramid, Al Mamoun's Forced Passage." *YouTube*, uploaded by The Great Pyramid AIP, 14 Nov. 2018, https://www.youtube.com/watch?v=Q7eENl63ScI

"Great Pyramid- al Ma'Mun's Breach - Robber's Entrance. How did they know?" *YouTube*, uploaded by SGD SacredGeometry Decoded, 26 Aug. 2019, https://www.youtube.com/watch?v=vGoqsUJdZuk

"Interview With The Lifelike Hot Robot Named Sophia" *YouTube*, uploaded by CNBC, 25 Oct. 2017, https://www.youtube.com/watch?v=S5t6K9iwcdw

"Nazi UFO | Forbidden History | Yesterday." *YouTube*, uploaded by UKTV, 6 Nov. 2015, https://www.youtube.com/watch?v=gLKcJTI25Ts

"Uncovering the ancient secrets of the Great Pyramid." *YouTube*, uploaded by 60 Minutes Australia, 3 May 2019, https://www.youtube.com/watch?v=oomK6gzJfxA&t=336s

"What are "Foo Fighters"?" *YouTube*, uploaded by Simon & Schuster Books, 4 Sep. 2016, https://www.youtube.com/watch?v=sf_JNMtoAHo

Articles, Papers, and Websites

"57th Fighter Group." *American Air Museum*, Accessed 2019, http://www.americanairmuseum.com/unit/4092

"Aix-en-Provence, ville de Cezanne." *Cezanne en Provence*, Accessed 2016, https://www.cezanne-en-provence.com/en/

"Alto Airfield." *Forgotten Airfields in Europe*, Accessed 2016, https://www.forgottenairfields.com/airfield-alto-1279.html

"Alto Airfield." *American Air Museum*, Accessed 2019, http://www.americanairmuseum.com/place/169979

Archaeological Institute of America. "World War II Aircraft Crash Sites." *Archeology Magazine*, Vol. 64, No. 3, May/June 2011, https://archive.archaeology.org/1105/features/world_war_II_aircraft.html

Bayuk, Andrew. "The Great Pyramid of Khufu." *Guardian's Egypt,* 2005, https://guardians.net/egypt/pyramids/GreatPyramid.htm#p&c

Bockman, Chris. "Recovering a WWII bomber hidden in a French cave," *BBC*, Sep. 2013, https://www.bbc.com/news/magazine-24159975

Bostrom, Nick. "Transhumanism: The World's Most Dangerous Idea?" *Nick Bostrom*, Accessed 2019, https://www.nickbostrom.com/papers/dangerous.html

Castillo, M. "The Omega Point and Beyond: The Singularity Event." *American Journal of Neuroradiology*, Mar. 2012, https://doi.org/10.3174/ajnr.A2664

"Crichton Castle." *Wikipedia*, Accessed 2020, https://en.wikipedia.org/wiki/Crichton_Castle

Dang, Sanjit Singh. "Artificial Intelligence In Humanoid Robots." *Forbes*, Accessed 2019, https://www.forbes.com/sites/cognitiveworld/2019/02/25/artificial-intelligence-in-humanoid-robots/?sh=2d7eb54d24c7

Dash, Mike. "Inside the Great Pyramid." *Smithsonian Magazine*, 1 Sep. 2011, https://www.smithsonianmag.com/travel/inside-the-great-pyramid-75164298/

Dendrinos, Dimitrios. "Mathematics of a Golden Ratio Ellipse: the Minoan 5-priestess gold signet ring from the Griffin Warrior tomb at Pylos. Update 2" *Academia*, 13 Dec. 2017, https://www.academia.edu/35420252/The_Ellipse_and_Minoan_Miniature_Art_Analysis_of_the_5_priestess_signet_ring_from_the_Mycenaean_Griffin_Warriors_tomb_at_Pylos_Update_2

DeSalvo, John, et al. "Napoleon visits the King's Chamber." Accessed 2019, *Great Pyramid of Giza Research Association*, http://www.gizapyramid.com/Stories.htm

Doyle, Jack. "The Daredevil Pilots Who Barnstormed Their Way Into The History Books." *OZY Live Curiously*, Accessed 2019, https://www.ozy.com/true-and-stories/the-daredevil-pilots-who-barnstormed-their-way-into-the-history-books/72401/

"Egyptian sculpture about 2686 BC-AD 396" *The British Museum*, Accessed 2019, https://www.britishmuseum.org/collection/galleries/egyptian-sculpture

"Elements of a Dome." *Wikipedia*, Accessed 2019, https://en.wikipedia.org/w/index.php?title=Dome&action=history

Encyclopedia Britannica Editors, "Tripoli." *Brittanica*, Accessed 2019, https://www.britannica.com/place/Tripoli

Ferraro, Susan. "QuickGuide: What's in a Single Drop of Blood." *New York Daily News*, 6 Nov. 2000, https://www.nydailynews.com/quickguide-single-drop-blood-article-1.877871

"Fourth Dynasty of Egypt." *Wikipedia*, Accessed 2019, https://en.wikipedia.org/wiki/Fourth_Dynasty_of_Egypt

"French Civilians Celebrate Their Liberation, Aix-en-Provence, France, 1944." *The Digital Collections of the National WWII Museum*, Accessed 2019, https://www.ww2online.org/image/french-civilians-celebrate-their-liberation-aix-en-provence-france-1944

"Geology of Scotland." *Wikipedia*, Accessed 2019, https://en.wikipedia.org/wiki/Geology_of_Scotland

Gershon, Livia. "Missing Great Pyramid Artifact Found in Cigar Box in Scotland." *Smithsonian Magazine, Smart News*, 16 Dec. 2020, https://www.smithsonianmag.com/smart-news/lost-great-pyramid-artifact-found-misfiled-museum-cigar-box-180976564/

Green, Ronald M. "Challenging Transhumanism's Values." *The Hastings Center Report*, vol. 43, no. 4, [The Hastings Center, Wiley], 2013, pp. 45–47, http://www.jstor.org/stable/23480982.

"How High is Space?" *Space Today Online*, http://www.spacetoday.org/SolSys/Earth/AltitudesChart.html

Hudson, Jamie. "A Comparison of Revival to Medieval Gothic Architecture." *Atmostfear Entertainment*, Accessed 2019, https://www.atmostfear-entertainment.com/culture/architecture/a-comparison-of-revival-to-medieval-gothic-architecture/

Huntley, H.E. "The Golden Ellipse." *Fibonacci Quarterly*, Accessed 2019, https://www.fq.math.ca/Scanned/12-1/huntley1.pdf

"Hyperboloid." *Wikipedia*, Accessed 2016, https://en.wikipedia.org/wiki/Hyperboloid

"Jeep History." *Jeep*, Accessed 2019, https://www.jeep.com/history.html

Judson, Jen. "Lockheed's Raider X enters construction in advance of US Army's decision on way forward," *Defense News*, Feb. 2020, https://www.defensenews.com/land/2020/02/20/lockheeds-raider-x-already-under-construction/

Kelly, Jack. "Sophia–The Humanoid Robot–Will Be Rolled Out This Year Potentially Replacing Workers." *Forbes*, 30 Apr. 2021, https://www.forbes.com/sites/jackkelly/2021/01/26/sophia-the-humanoid-robot-will-be-rolled-out-this-year-potentially-replacing-workers/?sh=b5999d16df2d

"Khufu Statuette." *Wikipedia*, Accessed 2019, https://en.wikipedia.org/w/index.php?title=Khufu_Statuette

LaBonta, Lo'eau. "Human Energy Converted to Electricity." *Stanford University, Dept. of Physics*, 6 Dec. 2014, http://large.stanford.edu/courses/2014/ph240/labonta1/

Larson, Hilarie. "Your Guide to Provence Wine Region (maps)." *Wine Folly*, Aug. 26, 2013, Updated 2 Dec. 2020, https://winefolly.com/deep-dive/provence-wine-region-guide-with-maps/

"Le Tholonet." *Provence Web*, Accessed 2016, https://www.provenceweb.fr/e/bouches/tholonet/tholonet.htm

Lieven et al. "Airbus-flying-bagel." *Exopolitics*, 30 Oct. 2014, https://exopolitics.org/wp-content/uploads/2014/11/Airbus-flying-bagel.jpg

"Limestone block from the pyramid of Khufu." *The British Museum Images*, Accessed 2019, https://www.bmimages.com/preview.asp?image=00032824001

"Lowland Heath." *The Wildlife Trusts*, Accessed 2021, https://www.wildlifetrusts.org/habitats/heathland-and-moorland/lowland-heath

Maish, Jeffrey, et al., "The Odyssey of an Egyptian Cat Sculpture." *The Iris, Behind the Scenes at the Getty*, 24 Mar. 2020, http://blogs.getty.edu/iris/hello-kitty-the-odyssey-of-an-egyptian-cat-sculpture/

Meisner, Gary. "Phi, Pi and the Great Pyramid of Egypt at Giza." *The Golden Number*, 18 Aug. 2012, https://www.goldennumber.net/phi-pi-great-pyramid-egypt/

"Montagne Sainte-Victoire." *Wikipedia*, Accessed 2016, https://en.wikipedia.org/wiki/Montagne_Sainte-Victoire

Moore, Don. "Belgium Underground saves P-47 pilot shot down over Nazi territory." *War Tales*, Accessed 2019, https://donmooreswartales.com/2010/03/28/robert-grace//

"Morphine Syrette." *Museum of Drugs*, http://www.museumofdrugs.com/morphine.html

Nunn, Paul. "Visualising Giza." *Graham Hancock*, 12 May 2011, https://grahamhancock.com/nunnp1/

Nguyen, Tuan. "This Flashlight Is Powered by the Touch of Your Hand." *Smithsonian Magazine*, 24 Mar. 2014, https://www.smithsonianmag.com/innovation/this-flashlight-is-powered-by-the-touch-of-your-hand-180950226/

"Paul Cezanne." *Musée de l'Orangerie,* Accessed 2016, https://www.musee-orangerie.fr/en/artist/paul-cezanne

Peregrine, Anthony. "Provence Travel Guide." *The Telegraph*, 29 Sep. 2017, https://www.telegraph.co.uk/travel/destinations/europe/france/provence/articles/provence-travel-guide/.

"Pickpocket-proof Travelwear." *Clothing Arts*, Accessed 2019, https://www.clothingarts.com/collections/adventure_travel_pickpocket_proof_pants

"Pictures of 57th Fighter Group." *57th Fighter Group Official Website*, Accessed 2019, http://www.57thfightergroup.org/pictures.html

"Pierre Teilhard de Chardin." *Wikipedia*, Accessed 2019, https://en.wikipedia.org/wiki/Pierre_Teilhard_de_Chardin

Rich, Kiersten, "Egypt Travel Guide." *The Blonde Abroad*, Accessed 2019, https://www.theblondeabroad.com/ultimate-egypt-travel-guide/

Ro, Lauren. "What Are the Best Chelsea Boots for Women?" *The Strategist*, 23 Oct. 2019, https://nymag.com/strategist/article/best-chelsea-boots-women.html

Squillario, Massimo. "A P-47 in WWII Italy and the Pilot's Story Finally Told." *War History Online*, 6 Jul. 2018, https://www.warhistoryonline.com/guest-bloggers/p-47-italy-wwii-pilots-story.html

Tagliabue, John, "Corsicans remember Americans of World War II." *The New York Times*, 10 Jun. 2008, https://www.nytimes.com/2008/06/10/world/europe/10iht-journal.1.13597855.html?_r=0

"The Black Scorpions, 64th Fighter Group." *American Air Museum*, Accessed 2019, http://www.americanairmuseum.com/unit/4093

"The Egyptian Museum." Ministry of Tourism and Antiquities, Accessed 2019, https://egymonuments.gov.eg/en/museums/egyptian-museum

Walsh, Kevin, and Florence Mocci. "Fame and Marginality: The Archaeology of the Montagne Sainte Victoire (Provence, France)." *American Journal of Archaeology*, vol. 107, no. 1, Archaeological Institute of America, 2003, pp. 45–69, http://www.jstor.org/stable/40026566.

About the Author

Author and artist John Hopkins' curiosity for what lies beyond common knowledge shapes his imaginative, character-driven storytelling. Following his muse, John created *Lost Cactus*, a comic strip set on an off-the-grid top-secret research base—think Area 51. The strip's quick wit, fearless lampoonery, and supernatural mythology expanded into a shared universe of science fiction short stories and novels. Sequels and graphic novels featuring the expansive world-building of **Lost Cactus** and **The Powers That Be** shared universe are in the works.

Stay tuned and keep an eye on the sky.

johnhopkinsauthor.com

www.ingrampublishinui.com

www.ingramcontent.com/pod-product-compliance
Lightning Source LLC
Chambersburg PA
CBHW010508100726
47902CB00011B/2125

* 9 780996 506779 *